PRETTY GIRLS MAKE GRAVES

A SECRET SOCIETY ROMANTIC SUSPENSE

STEFFANIE HOLMES

Cover design: Seventhstar

ISBN: 978-1-99-115048-6

❀ Created with Vellum

PRETTY GIRLS MAKE GRAVES

Don't go outside on Devil's Night.

I'm always the good girl. I never stand out. I follow the rules.

At Blackfriars University, there's one whispered rule: Stay inside the night before Halloween. Hide under your blankets and hope the Orpheus Society isn't the monster outside your window.

If they get you, you won't just be humiliated. They'll put you six feet under.

But I've screwed up.

I found bones in a shallow grave. Another good girl, just like me.

Now I'll do whatever it takes to get to the truth.
I'll catch the eye of the cruel aristocrat with a haunted gaze.
I'll tempt the dark priest with forbidden tastes.
I'll be their shameful little secret. Their plaything. Their *sacrifice*.

Maybe I don't want to be a good girl anymore.

Maybe it's time to break *all* the rules.

Pretty Girls Make Graves is a dark romantic suspense and part one of the Dark Academia duet. If you enjoy tales of clever heroines, ancient rites, secret societies, cruel princes and wicked priests, dusty libraries and decadent parties, twisted relationships and buried secrets, then prepare to enter the halls of Blackfriars University. You may not return.

Want to read chapters from William and Sebastian's POV? Get them in your free copy of *Cabinet of Curiosities* – a Steffanie Holmes compendium of short stories and bonus scenes – when you sign up for updates with the Steffanie Holmes newsletter.

JOIN THE NEWSLETTER FOR UPDATES

Want to read chapters from William and Sebastian's POV? Get them in your free copy of *Cabinet of Curiosities* – a Steffanie Holmes compendium of short stories and bonus scenes – when you sign up for updates with the Steffanie Holmes newsletter.

www.steffanieholmes.com/newsletter

Every week in my newsletter I talk about the true-life hauntings, strange happenings, crumbling ruins, and creepy facts that inspire my stories. You'll also get newsletter-exclusive bonus scenes and updates. I love to talk to my readers, so come join us for some spooky fun :)

A NOTE ON DARK CONTENT

I'm writing this note because I want you a heads up about some of the content in this book. Reading should be fun, so I want to make sure you don't get any nasty surprises. If you're cool with anything and you don't want spoilers, then skip this note and dive in.

Keep reading if you like a bit of warning about what to expect in this series.

- There is some bullying in this first book, but our heroine holds her own. No heroes in this story threaten or are involved in physical or sexual assault of the heroine.

- George is a sexual abuse survivor and she references this past trauma in places.

- George has also been at the side of her BFF, Claws, as Claws reclaimed her criminal empire in the *Stonehurst Prep* series. This means she sometimes references violent acts from that series, and the Dark Academia books contain spoilers for *Stonehurst Prep*.

- This book contains an age-gap, taboo relationship between George and her teacher/priest, Sebastian Pearce. If hot priests and sacrilegious altar sex aren't you thing, this probably isn't the book for you.

- There is some murder, violence, claustrophobic situations, and body horror in this and subsequent books.

I wouldn't call this book dark, but it's definitely a smidge 'grey.' I promise there will be suspense, hot sex, gothic ambience, and a clever heroine searching for the truth and finding her heart along the way. If that's not your jam, that's totally cool. I suggest you pick up my Nevermore Bookshop Mysteries series – all of the mystery without the gore and creepiness.

Enjoy, you beautiful depraved human, you :) Steff

To all the essential workers
For your strength and bravery

"He is life's liberating force.
He is release of limbs and communion through dance.
He is laughter, and music in flutes.
He is repose from all cares -- he is sleep!
When his blood bursts from the grape
and flows across tables laid in his honor
to fuse with our blood,
he gently, gradually, wraps us in shadows
of ivy-cool sleep."

– *Euripides,* The Bacchae

1

Nothing shatters the magic of my first day at Blackfriars University quite like a naked priest swimming the backstroke in the water fountain.

Until the moment I come face-to-dong with Father Sebastian Pearce, I've been enraptured by this place. Blackfriars is everything my life in Emerald Beach, California was not – I love the gothic arches and ancient, cobbled pathways, the hidden nooks and lichen-covered stone fountains. I love the storybook British names and customs for everything. I love lining up with the other students in our black subfusc robes for the matriculation ceremony, and looking up at the blackened church spires piercing the grey sky.

And turrets. I *adore* the metric fuckton of turrets (a 'fuckton' is the only thing I can correctly measure using the metric system, but I'm learning) at my new university.

Blackfriars is all my Hogwarts dreams come true.

At least, that's how I felt this morning. But then I tripped on the uneven cobbles and tore my skirt, and *then* squirmed for two hours on a hard church pew while a dusky-haired priest performed the High Mass. In Latin. My initial enchantment gave way to boredom and a numb ass. I've never attended a High Mass before (or a Low Mass or even a Medium Mass). My sole exposure to the Catholic Church has been watching scenes from my father's horror movies, and they usually end in someone summoning a demon and getting their brains sucked out through their nostrils.

A little nostril-sucking might've livened up this ceremony.

Blackfriars University is very *into* religion. The campus used to be a Benedictine monastery before King Henry VIII went on a bit of a beheading spree. There's a whole story about the so-called 'Black Monk,' Benet of Blackfriars, who made a last stand against the king before the monastery was closed. Since it reopened as a school, Blackfriars has stubbornly held onto their Catholic heritage despite numerous attempts to convert it to Church of England. As far as I can tell, there's not much difference between the two churches except that a CofE matriculation ceremony would be five minutes long instead of three hours, and in English. And my father never made a movie about it – not demonic enough for his tastes.

Not that I spent my summer memorizing the school's history. Not at all.

Because that would be a dorky thing to do. The sort of thing the *old* George would do – the George who got straight A's and whose only friends were dead punk rock musicians. The George who ate her school lunches in a bathroom stall and never said two words to anyone in case they landed her with her head down a toilet.

And I'm not that George anymore.

New school, new country, new me.

I can be whoever I want to be. And if the students at Blackfriars – the most insane, over-the-top liberal arts school in the world – can't accept me, then I'll have a blast anyway.

That sounds depressing. I swear it's not. I'm so excited about this year.

All around me, students whisper to each other or stare at their phones as the priest drones on. I try to talk to the girl next to me, but she wrinkles her perfect nose as if I smell bad. I probably do smell bad. I arrived by train from London with only minutes to spare before the ceremony, so I haven't even been able to take my bag to my room before they called us to enter the church. So I stare straight ahead with my suitcase wedged awkwardly on my lap and think about all the classes I'm excited about this semester.

Not semester. *Term*. I'm learning the lingo.

We're finally dismissed, and I discreetly massage my numb ass as we shuffle outside. The main quad – Martyrs' Quad – fills with students, leaning against the historical fountain and snapping selfies with their friends. How do they have friends already? We only just got here. The porter barks at one group to get off the immaculate green lawn, but they ignore him.

"I don't know who he thinks he is, trying to tell Orpheans what to do," a girl scoffs to her friend as she walks past. They throw the lawn-ruining students an admiring look.

Now I'm curious. *Orpheans?*

There are ten of them – five guys, five girls – standing around on the grass and completely ignoring the porter as he hops about angrily and jabs his finger at the STAY OFF THE GRASS sign. I've never seen anything like them before, and I come from Emerald Beach, so I have seen a *lot*.

They look like characters from a story – some twisted gothic tale of crumbling estates and rich widows filled with longing. The girls wear floaty, calf-length dresses and blazers with the sleeves rolled up. The boys' trousers have pleats that could draw blood. Their tailored jackets and wing-tipped shoes drip with a certain kind of wealth and power. In Emerald Beach, if you're wealthy, you shove that wealth in everyone's face. But this lot look like they couldn't care less about fashion. They're pale with flushed cheeks, like they've just come from tending the horses or whipping a recalcitrant servant.

Two of the guys in particular stand out. One leans against the fountain, his arm slung casually around the waist of the prettiest girl. Angular and elegant, he has one of those petulant mouths with a full lower lip that my friend Claws would say is begging to be bitten, and eyes the deep blue of the ocean at midnight. The other, despite his starched shirt and black tie, has a kind of messy, sloppy look, with a mop of golden hair falling over one eye and a smile that might be called cheeky if not for the cruel twist at the edges. He takes a long drag from a cigarette and – with carbon grey eyes trained on the porter – grinds the butt into the grass with his heel.

The girl who called them Orpheans catches me staring, and breaks off into giggles.

I hurry away. The hope that's fluttered in my chest since graduation takes a beating. *It's going to be exactly the same as high school.* If people like that are the norm, I'm out of my league. Everyone here already knows each other. They met at their fancy boarding schools or yacht races or private clubs or wherever the fuck rich people make friends.

I'm on the outside.

Again.

But you know what? That's fine with me.

I squeeze the handle of my suitcase as I think about my best friend, Claws. I need to channel her attitude. She wouldn't give a fuck if no one liked her – but then, she runs a crime empire so she's probably not the best example.

It took me until senior year to make a single friend, and I left them all to come here. I left my mom, my house, the Brawley theatre – all the places in the city that remind me of Dad. And I deluded myself into believing things would be different. Despite its Catholic leanings, Blackfriars is supposed to be a bohemian, artsy-fartsy college. There's got to be at least a few kids here like me – the lonely, weird outsiders...

Yes, I know you want to hear about the naked priest. I promise I'm getting there. Existential crisis stuff first, okay?

I can't bear another minute in the quad, being the weird American who's laughed at by strangers. I know it's only in my imagination because I'm tired and raw, but it's ruining my new school buzz. So I do something I've never done in my life. I slip away into the shadows, and bunk off the orientation seminar.

Claws will be so proud.

As the students are being herded into the dining hall, I dart along a covered walkway, peering into the open doors of small lecture theatres and classrooms beneath gothic stone arches. Everything is so old and grand and *cool*. I wonder what kind of ghosts linger in these walls. My bright-red New Rocks make a clomping sound on the cobbles.

I pass under an archway and along a rose-lined walk into St. Benedict's Quad, thinking I'll head toward the college meadow for some fresh air, when I spy a narrow gap in the towering hedge. I step closer. An iron gate hangs open an inch, revealing a secret garden.

A covered walkway of gothic arches frames the hidden courtyard, which bursts with tall herb bushes and scraggly orange trees that obscure my view across to the other side. It's so different from the neat roses and manicured lawns of the rest of Blackfriars. There's something forbidden about it, something wild. Somewhere deeper in the garden, I hear water trickling and splashing.

I can't contain my curiosity. I push the gate open and step through.

The path steps down as I enter the courtyard. I breathe in

the fresh, herby air, and feel some of the tension slip from my shoulders as I push through the overgrown—

Oh.

Oh.

My hand flies to my mouth.

A man floats on his back in the central fountain, spinning in lazy circles as the spray from the tip of Orpheus' lyre cascades off his chiseled body. And what a man he is – probably in his early thirties, and built like a Greek god. Everything about him *glistens*, like his skin is dipped in gold. His smoky black eyes contemplate the heavens, and his strong jaw is relaxed, his lips falling open in silent reverie. A smattering of ink along his abdomen draws my eye down to that lickable V of muscle, and below that, to a package that any god would envy. Heat flares in my cheeks.

He's so perfect it makes my throat hurt.

Beside the pool is a pile of clothes – a black shirt folded neatly on top of what looks like designer jeans and some chunky boots, and a white collar nestled on top.

It doesn't take a true-crime podcaster to figure out this guy is a priest.

A very naked, *very hot*, priest.

Turn away. Just turn away and run back the way you came and he won't even see you—

Too late. The man lifts his head, and his anthracite eyes widen as they see me. I expect him to flail about for something to cover himself, but he seems to sense it's pointless. I've already got an eyeful of the goods.

Instead, the corner of his mouth quirks up into an amused smile.

"Hello, there," he says.

It's the most anyone has spoken to me all day. His voice is

rich and deep and friendly. It crackles at the edges, like a blazing, cozy fire. And that British accent...mmm...

Pity I'm about to be struck by a lightning bolt for having such thoughts about a priest.

I can't speak. My face burns with fifty shades of get-me-the-fuck out of here.

The priest flips over and dog-paddles to the side, resting his hands on the edge. "I don't suppose," his voice is so perfectly British, all clipped and fictive and wonderful, "you'd mind *terribly* passing me that towel."

I nod, still unable to form words. I pick up the towel from the corner and hold it in front of me like a medieval shield protecting me from the power of his peen. The priest pulls himself out of the water, swinging his legs as he dries his face. *Holy father.* Droplets roll down the Celtic cross tattoo over his heart, and my throat dries as I imagine licking them off.

Which is insane. That's not a George thought at all. That's something Claws with her three besotted boyfriends would say.

This must be what jet lag does to my brain.

"You came up today? You're supposed to be at the orientation," he says without shame as he rubs the towel in his hair. He has great hair, I notice. It's longer than I'd expect from a priest, down around his shoulders, with a little curl. It's dark like his eyes, and hopelessly disheveled. I'm a sucker for long hair.

And British accents. And sexy tattooed priests swimming in fountains.

I'm going to hell.

"I...I..."

He slides a pair of boxers over his hips. I'm transfixed by the material of his trousers as he pulls them on.

"The pool in the rec center is closed for renovations at the moment," he says, which I think is supposed to be an explanation.

I nod, as if it's totally normal to swim in a fountain instead of, say, going for a run instead. Maybe it is normal in England. I don't know.

"I'm Sebastian Pearce." He buttons his shirt, hiding away that beautiful ink. "I'm one of the dons here at Blackfriars. I believe you've had the pleasure of meeting my colleague, Father Duncan, at matriculation."

I manage to choke out some words. "Was he the old man chanting the lyrics to a Cradle of Filth song?"

He laughs at this, his whole face crumpling with joy. "We do love dead languages around here. And religion. There's a persistent rumor that a student will receive automatic graduation if they can recite the gospels from memory in their original Greek. And you are?"

"An atheist."

"Ah, excellent. I do love a challenge." He cracks his knuckles. "But I was actually asking about your name."

"Oh, it's Georgina. Georgina Fisher. But everyone calls me George."

"George. I love it. A nice British name. Well, George Fisher, if you ever need to talk about this harrowing experience, you know where to find me." He grins as he slides his feet into a pair of immaculately-shined dress shoes. "I mean, I'll be at the church, not usually in this fountain."

I swallow. "Right."

Silence stretches between us. He seems utterly comfortable with it, but I'm desperate to fill it so I don't keep picturing his body. "What do you teach?"

"History of Religion." He fixes the collar around his neck. With his sleeves rolled up to the elbows, I notice the tattoos on his arm depict figures from Greek mythology – Theseus slaying the minotaur, Cassandra witnessing the fall of Troy. He sees me staring at his ink. "Not just Catholicism. All the religions, new and old and everything in between. I'm only picky when it comes to the salvation of my own soul. Are you lost? Would you like me to walk you to the dining hall?"

I shake my head. "Not lost. I...I guess I was feeling a bit overwhelmed."

"It's hard being away from home, especially if your home is across the ocean." He makes it sound as though I've come on some epic quest, like Odysseus making his way over the seas from Troy, instead of drowning my nerves in daiquiris on the ten-hour flight. "I'll tell you what, I'll show you to your room and then you'll have a bit of time to get used to the campus at your own pace."

Sebastian walks me back through the secret garden to St. Benedict's Quad. It's no longer empty of people, and it takes us forever to navigate to the other side because he's stopped every few feet by senior students or fellow dons. Sebastian has a heart-melting smile and friendly words for every one of them.

We finally reach the opposite corner and head through another gothic archway into a quieter quad with another immaculate lawn and an ancient-looking stone well in the center. "This is Cavendish Quad. There are four staircases, and each one has its own scout, who cleans the rooms and looks after the students."

In the far corner of the quad, Sebastian introduces me to a stony-faced woman named Sally, who is my scout. "You're supposed to be at orientation," she snaps at me.

"George's train arrived late. She'll catch up on the details from the other students. You know what those lectures are like – most of it is self-explanatory. Dining hall hours, library usage, instructions for the laundry machines, how not to get recruited by a secret society with designs on taking over the world." Sebastian asks Sally about her new border collie puppy, and the woman's sour expression dissolves into smiles. Sebastian Pearce has that effect on people. I drag my suitcase up the wheelchair ramp, my cheeks flushing with heat. I can feel strands of hair whipping around my face and yup, my pits could knock out an elephant.

He's a priest. It doesn't matter what you look like or smell like because he's not interested in anything except your immortal soul.

"Goodbye, George Fisher." Sebastian's eyes twinkle as he takes my hand in his. My fingers tingle with the warmth of his touch. "I hope Blackfriars is everything you wished for."

Me too.

I stand awkwardly at the foot of the staircase, waiting for the scout to return from her office to give me the key to my room. As I watch Sebastian's perfect ass stroll back across the quad, I'm seized by an overwhelming and uncharacteristic urge to be reckless.

Before I have time to think about what I'm doing, I pull out my phone and navigate to the Blackfriars app, which lists my class schedule. I slide my finger across the screen, deleting 'Gender and Social History of Popular Music' from my schedule. I click another button to enroll in the 'History of Religion.'

Yup. Booked my one-way ticket to eternal damnation.

2

So, do you know what's not so excellent about turrets?

No elevators.

If I looked frazzled after my encounter with the naked swimming priest, by the time I huffed my suitcase four floors up the winding medieval staircase to my new room, I'm a disaster.

Sally leads me through a fire door and down a narrow corridor. It's littered with open suitcases, packing crates, clothing racks, and other bric-a-brac from students moving in. Everyone has so much *stuff*. My suitcase wheel catches on a pastel pink scarf.

"That's *Hermès*." A girl snatches the scarf from under my wheel. She's the only other person in the hallway. Everyone else is still at the orientation.

"I'm sorry. It was just lying there in the way—"

"Whatever, freak." She slams her door in my face. From the end of the hall, Sally motions for me to hurry up. I pick up my suitcase and hobble after her.

"Here's your room." Sally pushes open the door and shoves a keyring into my hands. It contains a swipecard and a stack of old-fashioned clunky keys. "As you'd know if you attended the orientation, we have formal hall every evening at 7PM, academic gowns required, but if you need to eat quickly you can grab something from the buffet from six. You've got keys to the art studios, but students aren't supposed to be there after hours without signing in, so make sure you sign in—"

I stumble in after her, taking in the room that will be my home for the year. Two walls slope under the eaves of the roof, creating some challenging angles within which some clever person has slotted two beds, two desks, a fireplace, and a bank of closets and bookshelves. Between the beds are a couple of threadbare armchairs beneath the dormer window.

I drop my suitcase and move to the window. I can see across Cavendish Quad and the athletic fields beyond to the edge of the wood that surrounds Blackfriars.

The bed nearest the door has already been claimed. It's covered in a pastel coverlet and a stack of matching pillows made from what looks suspiciously like real silk. Rows of shoes are stacked in the bookshelves, and the closet is stuffed with clothes, with several unopened cases littering the floor. I notice my bed has been shoved right up into the corner beneath the eaves, as far away from my roommate as possible without actually being outside on the roof.

"—gates and porter's lodge will be open from 7AM-10PM every day, and until midnight on weekends. If you need to leave the grounds after hours, use the large key to open the wicket—"

"Wait, what's a wicket?"

But Sally ignores me and keeps running off instructions without a breath. "—laundry facilities are in the basement, down the stairs from the junior common room. You'll need the square key to get in. Welcome to Blackfriars University. Don't make a nuisance of yourself and we'll get along fine."

She glares at me as if that ship has well and truly sailed, then flies out of the room, narrowly avoiding slamming into someone entering.

My visitor flops onto the bed. "Such a yawnfest. Laundry instructions? As if I'm a culchie who scrubs my own clothes."

She has a breathy, thick Irish accent and chestnut hair falling over her shoulders in luscious waves.

"Hello, I'm George." I extend a hand to her. It feels so weird and formal, but that's what everyone had been doing in the quad. "I guess we're roommates."

She stares at my hand like I'm an alien. "George is a boy's name. I ain't rooming with a boy."

"It's short for Georgina." I'm angry she's made me feel defensive of my name. My dad was the one who started calling me George.

"Well, *Georgina,*" she trills in her musical accent as she picks up a fashion magazine and starts flicking through the pages. "I'm Keely O'Sullivan, of the Dublin O'Sullivans, and I'm delira and excira to make your acquaintance. We best lay out how this is going to work. I've taken the liberty of drawing out a line on the rug. This line denotes our respective territories. If I find a single item belonging to you on my side of the room or even *touching* my things, I will burn it."

"That's—"

"If I'm in the room, you will not speak to me. You will not play music or watch telly without headphones in. You will take your phone calls out in the hallway. If I have friends in the room, which will be often, you are not to address them. I don't want anyone to think we *asked* to bunk together."

"But I—"

"I'm only here because my skint parents claim they can't afford a single room for me, which is bollocks considering Ma's showing off her brand new nose." Keely set down the magazine and kicked over one of her boxes. I leaped out of the way to avoid being taken down by an avalanche of makeup. "Stick to the rules and we'll get along grand. But know this – I am going to be an Orphean, and if you stand in my way, I will crush your little Yankee heart under my Louboutins, got it?"

That's the second time I've heard that word today. The question is out of my mouth before I have the chance to regret it. "What's an Orphean?"

Keely snorts as she reaches for one of her boxes. "Christ on the cross, they've roomed me with a right culchie."

I also don't know what culchie means, but I'm not about to ask. I sink into my bed, staring at a spot on the wall behind Keely's head, in case looking directly at her is a hanging offense. At the foot of Keely's bed is a stack of rectangular objects covered in brown packing paper. I pretend I'm not watching as she slides a frame from its paper wrapping and holds up a painting above her bed.

I gasp.

I don't mean to, but it's *beautiful*. It's one of the most arresting pieces of art I've ever seen.

It's a study of the surface of water – ripples reflecting and refracting the light like a prism. I can practically *feel* the coolness lapping against my legs. The paint is so thick it stands up in stiff peaks and ridges, bringing the piece into three dimensions. The artist has made the water look perfectly translucent, and yet beneath the surface I can see faint, vaguely threatening shapes mutilated by the disturbances on the surface. Objects hidden but in plain sight.

"Did you paint that?" I ask Keely. She shoots me a filthy look, like how dare I suggest she have such talent.

"You mean you don't recognize a Windsor-Forsyth?" She makes a face. "How did you even get into this school?"

Perfect. She has high-fallutin' art tastes. I have a roll of punk posters and two pairs of scuffed New Rock boots. We're going to get along *great*.

I start unpacking my clothes into the two tiny drawers Keely left for me, wishing I could put on some music to break the uncomfortable silence. Outside, I can hear other students shouting and laughing as they fix up their own rooms. I've just built up the courage to try to make conversation with Keely again when there's a sharp rap on our door.

I jump up, welcoming the distraction and half-hoping it'll be Sebastian Pearce on the other side. But Keely elbows me in the ribs and gets to the door first. She fluffs her hair in the mirror before she pulls the door open.

"William." Keely throws her arms around someone and drags them inside. "It's been a whole week since I saw you. I'm upset with the movers. They broke the frames on two of my paintings. It's atrocious—"

As Keely talks at him, I take the chance to surreptitiously scope out her friend. I'm surprised to see it's one of the guys from the fountain – the one with the pouty mouth and azure gaze. In the dim lighting of our dorm room, his eyes appear smooth, calm – but I know that in the sunlight they take on a dappled quality, like the water in Keely's painting. Those eyes roam the room, darting over Keely's boxes before resting on me for longer than is polite. I shift under his gaze, and I feel this weird urge to look at the floor. Instead, I meet his eyes and try for a friendly smile.

"That's..." Keely waves her hand at me. "I forgot her name. She won't bother us. She's *American*."

She draws out the word American in a faux-Southern accent, like just the name of my country is an insult.

William smirks. His eyes follow me as I move to my desk and start pulling out my podcast gear. I won my scholarship for Blackfriars based on the success of my podcast (and with a little bit of help from my friend, Gabe), and even though I've been too busy to make a second season, you never know when inspiration might strike.

"...I couldn't bear to leave it with my parents. They're such heathens when it comes to art. Besides, *you* painted it for me. I wanted to keep my William Windsor-Forsyth close by. Will you help me put it up? Where's the best place for it, do you think?"

I dare another look over my shoulder. Keely's holding up the water painting over her bed. She moves it along the wall so it's beside the window. William flips through one of her textbooks, looking bored. *He painted that?* I try to see that haughty expression and aristocratic nose in a different light. Somewhere behind those chilly eyes is the soul of an artist.

"I don't do manual labor." William leans out into the hall and snaps his fingers. "Sally, you're required."

Sally pokes her head into the room. A hint of nervousness creeps into her voice. "What do you need, William?"

"Hang this painting," William says.

She looks up at him and tries a feeble smile. "Um...see...I'm really not supposed to let students make permanent holes in the wall. You'll need to fetch the porter and—"

"If Keely wants to hang a painting in the room she pays good money for, then she can hang a painting. You have a toolkit in that little ground floor hovel you call a room, I presume? Run along and fetch it."

Sally fixes him with a withering stare. No more special treatment for him. "That's not my job, you little shit, and I don't appreciate being spoken to like that. You may think you run this school, but you're not on my staircase, so you don't control me. Hang your own damn painting, *your highness*."

With a toss of her brown hair, she flounces off.

Okay, I officially have mad respect for Sally.

Keely tries to kick William in the arm. "Why did you feck her off like that? Now how will we—"

"I'll do it," I offer.

Keely whirls around to glare at me. "I told you not to talk to us."

I shrug. "Fine. But it's just hammering a nail into the wall. I have the tools in my bag. It's easy."

Dad always carried around a little portable toolbox wherever he went, largely so he could make his production team's life a misery by knocking holes in the sets on a whim. After he died I started to carry it around, too. It's tucked in the bottom of my suitcase. I dump my clothes in a pile on my bed (Keely visibly shudders) and pull out a hammer, nail, and stud finder. I go to climb up on Keely's bed, but she plants a hand on my shoulder and throws me back. "Don't you dare stand on my sheets in those filthy boots."

William snickers. I kick off my New Rocks, my cheeks burning. I'm already regretting my offer to help. I'm wearing a pair of red socks with little cartoon ghost cats on them, but after ten hours on the plane and four on the train from London, they're sweaty and smelly and gross.

I don't want to be gross in front of William Windsor-Forsyth, and I don't know why.

I hold up the painting against the wall. It's so large that I can barely keep it steady with my short arms. "Is here okay?"

"Perfect." Keely peers at her nails.

I lean the painting against the wall and reach for the stud-finder, running it along the wall until it beeps. When I've centered the painting on the stud, I unwrap a package of picture hooks, cursing as they fall through my fingers and scatter over Keely's bed. William shakes with laughter as I bend over to pick up a hook.

"You'd better pick all those up," Keely frowns.

You're welcome.

I hammer in the hook and hang the painting. It looks pretty straight, but I step back to check. A screw jabs into my foot and I jerk away, throwing myself off-balance. I wobble, then fall, and I throw out my hands to the nearest object to save myself from dashing my brains open on the corner of the closet.

The nearest object turns out to be William, who curses as my full weight descends on him, sending us both crashing into the closet. His head bounces off the door with a *CRACK* and his elbow drives into my chest, knocking the wind out of me. I grasp at him as I struggle for breath. In my mortification, I discover my hand is resting on his crotch.

Wow. This guy could win a competition against the naked priest.

"Get off me. What the fuck?" William scrambles away, staring down at his crotch like it now has leprosy. Heat flares in my cheeks, and for the second time today I beg the earth to open up and swallow me.

"Are you okay?" Keely helps him to his feet, dusting invisible George germs off his blazer. "Americans are so crass, always throwing themselves at our royalty."

"She's practicing for her future job," William says in a bored voice, running his fingers through his hair. His hair is beautiful, too – a russet color with a hint of curl that looks impossibly soft to touch. Before my disastrous fall it had been immaculately parted on the side, but now it's all mussed up, so he looks like he just rolled out of bed. "Bowing and scraping."

My cheeks blaze with heat. *Is he implying I should be a servant? Gross.*

Keely links arms with William. "Is it time for a drink already? I'm parched."

"Don't you have to finish unpacking?" William's boredom has a hint of panic to it. "I'm supposed to meet Monty and Percy and the others, anyway—"

"I'll come with you. I can do this later." Keely nods to the frames stacked at the end of the bed. "Hang the rest of those while we're gone, there's a good girl."

William's laugh booms from the rafters long after they disappear down the staircase. I toss my hammer onto Keely's nightstand and slump on my bed, wringing my shaking hands.

What the hell just happened?

I desperately want to call Claws. I've been at Blackfriars for four hours and already I want to crawl under my bed and hide for the next three years. I long to hear her reassuring voice and the sound of Eli playing with their cats in the background. I want her to put Gabe on the phone so he can tell me about some obscure new German punk band he's discovered.

But it's mid-morning in Emerald Beach – when Claws is at work. And hers is not the kind of work that welcomes interruptions. What can Claws do from Emerald Beach, anyway? She'll rant and rave and threaten to have William and Keely murdered and I'll tell her not to worry and then I'll hang up and things will still be the same.

I still have to go out there and face this big, weird, scary school and its shitty peers and naked priests on my own.

3

Formal Hall is a new kind of hell.

When I read about the Blackfriars tradition of eating a three-course meal every night wearing academic dress with the college fellows sitting at the high table having lively academic discussions, I imagined it would be amazing.

And it's true that when I walk into the dining room I'm instantly transported to Hogwarts. This lofty medieval hall with its long banks of dark oak tables, ornate vaulted ceiling, and heavy gilded portraits adorning the walls perks me up a bit. There's a little magic in the air.

But the similarities stop there. For one thing, I see no floating candles or ghosts moving in the gilded portraits. For another, at Hogwarts even the dorky students had a place at the table, a house where they could sit and feel...if not accepted, then at least tolerated. But as I hover in the doorway, creating a traffic jam while I look for somewhere safe to sit, I realize I'm back in the school cafeteria and all its complex politics all over again. I don't have a table, and even though I know it's not true, it seems like everyone else does.

An elbow catches me in the side, and I stumble into the

room. The seats are filling up fast. *Just sit down somewhere, keep your chin high, look like you intended to sit there all along.* I perch on the end of one of the long tables near the back of the room, hoping people will fill in the spaces around me. What a joke. As the flood of students entering slows to a trickle, there are at least five seats on either side of my table. I'm not just alone – I'm *conspicuously* alone.

Fine. Whatever. I like being alone, anyway. More elbow room.

But then William and Keely sit down at the table directly behind me with those other students from the quad – the so-called Orpheans? – and some other friends. Their group is loud and lively. I hunch down low in my chair, hoping they won't notice me, but God must've been getting even with me for perving at his clergy, because I hear Keely mention my name.

"She's the freak roommate they stuck me with." Keely proceeds to describe me throwing myself at William to peals of laughter from their friends.

I stare at my plate throughout the meal, trying not to react as globs of food pelt the back of my robe. Keely again. I thought I left that shit behind in high school, but apparently she finds it hilarious to fire her peas at me. At least the food is delicious. Roast beef and potatoes and gravy and minted peas and a weird savory cupcake thing I hear someone call a 'Yorkshire pud.' The drinking age in England is eighteen, so open bottles of wine are passed down the tables, and I'm offered a small glass of sherry with my dessert.

As I punch a hole in the center of my chocolate fondant and watch the gooey center pool out, the Master of Blackfriars rises to speak. He welcomes us with a short quote in Latin and breaks into yet another speech about academic excellence and the illustrious history of the school. I get distracted checking out Sebastian as he chats with the history don sitting next to him until something in the master's speech catches my attention.

"—new students need to be aware that October 30th, the night before Halloween, is Devil's Night. The university gates will be locked at 7PM. Students are to remain in their rooms throughout the night, unless they are off-campus, in which case they're not able to return until sunrise the following day. Staircases will be locked and the junior and senior common rooms, library, pub, and other amenities will be closed. For this night only, the wickets will also be locked and your after-hours keys will not work—"

His ominous words are drowned out by a quiet chant from the table behind me that grows louder and louder until every head in the room is turned to them. I dare to twist my head to the side, straining out of the corner of my eye as William and his friends beat the table with their forks and yell a word that sounds like 'Cake-o-daimon-istee,' which has to be Greek or Latin or Orcish or something.

Beside William, the big guy with carbon-grey eyes and messy blond hair beats his fork on the table with such wild glee he gorges divots in the surface. A waiter hovers behind him with six dessert plates perched precariously in a silver tray, but doesn't dare make a move to finish his duties.

I expect the master to tell them to shut up, or the proctor to break up the group and administer fines for the disturbance. Surely in a school like this, with all its weird rituals, they don't allow interruptions during Formal Hall?

"Cake-o-daimon-istee!"

"Cake-o-daimon-istee!"

Maybe they just really like cake?

It goes on and on until the Master gets flustered and sits down. A cheer goes up from William's table, and then the entire room resumes their conversations as if the weird chanting never happened.

What the fuck was that?

After dessert, students trickle out of the room in groups. I gulp down the last mouthful of chocolate fondant and scramble for the door. The snickers rise from the table behind me, and I know they're laughing at the peas and gravy splattered down the back of my gown.

That settles that. I'm never going to Formal Hall again.

As I hurry across Martyrs' Quad, I type 'Cake-o-daimon-istee' into Google. It corrects to *Kakodaimonistai*, an ancient Greek word that literally translates into 'worshippers of the evil deamon.' Apparently, it was the name of a supper club in ancient Athens where members met to discuss politics. They chose the name specifically to mock the gods and the customs of Athens.

I know schools like this have elite societies, and the term 'supper club' is so beautifully British that I assume all they do is sit around talking about literature and eating pudding. Which sounds like the perfect Saturday night to me.

But that creepy chanting? And the whole school going into lockdown on *Devil's Night*, of all nights? What's that about?

I peer up at the looming hulk of Blackfriars cathedral. The bells strike ten o'clock – their tone a melancholy menace dragged up from the throat of the dark and brooding spire. A chill rolls down my spine that has nothing to do with the crisp night air.

What the hell happens on Devil's Night?

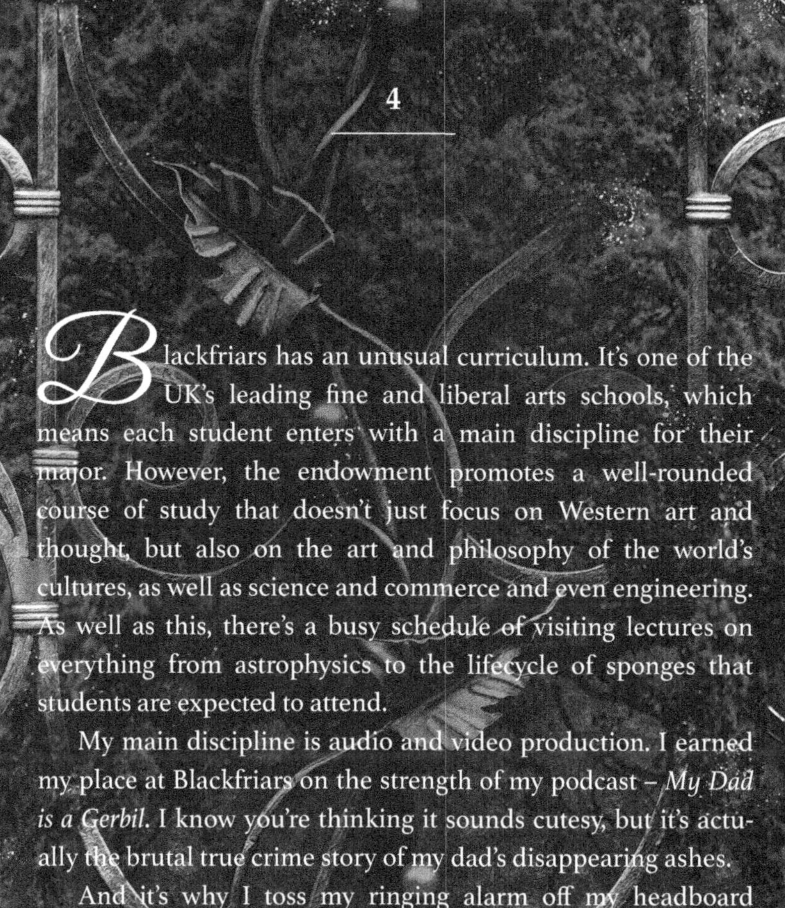

4

Blackfriars has an unusual curriculum. It's one of the UK's leading fine and liberal arts schools, which means each student enters with a main discipline for their major. However, the endowment promotes a well-rounded course of study that doesn't just focus on Western art and thought, but also on the art and philosophy of the world's cultures, as well as science and commerce and even engineering. As well as this, there's a busy schedule of visiting lectures on everything from astrophysics to the lifecycle of sponges that students are expected to attend.

My main discipline is audio and video production. I earned my place at Blackfriars on the strength of my podcast – *My Dad is a Gerbil*. I know you're thinking it sounds cutesy, but it's actually the brutal true crime story of my dad's disappearing ashes.

And it's why I toss my ringing alarm off my headboard before the sun has even risen and leap out of bed.

My audiovisual class doesn't start until 8AM, but I want to have breakfast and find the classroom, and if I stay in bed another minute I'll combust with excitement. I didn't have a chance to check out my classrooms yesterday because I was too busy perving at naked priests and freaking the fuck out.

"I hate you," Keely grunts as she tosses a shoe at me from the depths of her silken cocoon. I turn on the light, but she flicks it back off, so I grab clothes at random and stumble down the corridor to the bathroom. The staircase is dark and I can't hear anyone else stirring. I flick on the bathroom light, but the old bulb bursts and dies, so I shower and dress by the light of my mobile, and head downstairs and across to Martyrs' Quad for breakfast.

I'm surprised to discover I'm not the first one at breakfast. A dark-haired girl wearing a Buzzcocks hoodie sits hunched over a book in the darkest corner, spooning baked beans into her mouth with unerring precision. She might be a fellow nerd, and she has excellent taste in music. I debate sitting down across from her and striking up a conversation, but then I remember yesterday and my mouth goes dry.

Tomorrow, I tell myself. *Tomorrow I will be brave.*

I fill my plate at the buffet and sit in the opposite corner, beneath a large portrait of a monk wearing a terrifying black helmet and waving his sword at some heathens. In the background, orange flames leap from a crumbling stone building. I devour a huge stack of hashbrowns, sausages, bacon, eggs, tomatoes, beans, and something unknown and delicious called 'black pudding,' and wash it down with two cups of coffee. My mother would not approve but, praise the gods, there aren't any kale and hemp smoothies offered.

I scroll through my phone while I eat. For a blissful half hour, no one throws anything at me or whispers about me behind my back. I read over my textbook list, check the news on the Blackfriars app, and text Claws to tell her about my first day.

I emerge from the dining hall feeling much more human.

The university is starting to wake up. Bleary-eyed students with early classes emerge from their staircases. A pair of ravens hobble across the lawn in blatant disregard for the law, and the church bells toll the hour. I locate my classroom (it took five minutes – Blackfriars isn't big) and kill time by taking a walk around the campus.

The audiovisual labs are located in St. Benedict's Quad, right beside this weird burned-out section of the wall. There clearly used to be a building there, but instead it's just some charred walls forming a long room with what had once been a vaulted ceiling. The walls are relatively intact – apart from the charring around the narrow windows – but the entire roof has been blown away. On the end wall, a painted fresco is preserved behind glass – Jesus and the disciples at the last supper. It's no Leonardo de Vinci – Jesus' head is out of proportion and the apostles have overbites.

I look it up on the Blackfriars app and discover the structure is 'The Old Refectory,' where the monks used to have their meals. Apparently, the monks were caught inside when the king's soldiers attacked the monastery, and they were all slaughtered.

That's a cheery story for first thing in the morning.

As I lean against the charred wall and take in the monks' sacrifice, I hear voices on the other side. One belongs to William, and another is a husky, breathy female.

"—Monty says he has something positively *wicked* planned for Devil's Night," the girl says. "He's been yammering on about it all summer, about the god as a transgressor of borders, of society. He's been quoting that passage from Livy about the decay of the rites into sacred murders and obscene dancing—"

"Is it any wonder who put those ideas in his head?" William murmurs back. "I adore Monty, we all do, but he does have a tendency to get too intense about these things. And now he's been goaded...*Kakoû kórakos kakòn ōón.* From a bad crow, a bad egg."

What language is that? I guess more ancient Greek.

Who just tosses Ancient Greek randomly into conversation?

I press my back against the stones, straining to hear more of the conversation. I have to know more about this Devil's Night. But the bells chime, and the pair move on. I scoop up my bookbag and head to my class.

I hurry inside and take a seat around a circular table, squished into one corner of a vast, high-tech AV suite with recording studios, a soundstage, racks of equipment, and posters of student projects covering every inch of wall space. There are about twenty students in total – I recognize William's blond-haired, messy-faced friend, and two of the girls who'd been standing around the fountain looking bleak and beautiful in perfectly-tailored vintage suits. The three of them lean in close and whisper amongst themselves, while the rest of the students talk around them like they don't exist. At my old school, Stonehurst Prep, the popular kids had this constant retinue of admirers. The Orpheans clearly exert immense power at Blackfriars, but people give them a wide berth. It's almost as though they are...feared.

I pull out my laptop and shove my bookbag under my seat. A little shiver of excitement runs down my spine. I have no idea what to expect, but I've been dreaming about escaping Emerald Beach and going to a school like this for years, and I'm really, truly here. Dad used to tell wild stories about his days at film school in Berlin – him and his horror buddies pranking the arthouse kids. I feel the weight of his hand on my shoulder like he's standing behind me, and I'm instantly brightened.

Dad's with me. He'd love this.

Our professor steps out from an office and approaches the

table. He looks exactly how I expect an AV-academic to look– immaculately-groomed 'wild' beard, eyes rimmed in red from lack of sleep, a few cookie crumbs (I mean biscuit crumbs – I have to remember that in England cookies are called biscuits) stuck on his sweater. He yanks down a screen and starts fiddling with a projector.

"Welcome to the audiovisual stream." He pushes his glasses up his nose as the machine starts with a whir. "I'm Professor Morris Fletcher, and I'll be your tutor for the duration of your degree. We're going to be covering a variety of film theory and close readings across a range of genres, as well as working on a portfolio of practical work, both in groups and individually. At the end of your second year, you'll present your completed projects to a panel of industry professionals. If you do not pass the panel's scrutiny, you will not progress to your third year. There's also an element of collaboration to this discipline, as there is in reality. We expect students to work together to share their skills."

Pfft – that's the sound of my excited bubble popping.

I don't really like talking in front of people. Or working with other people. Okay, that's not strong enough. I hate it, more than I hate the dentist, people who talk through movies and pistachios that won't open *combined*. This might seem weird, because I have a podcast that literally *millions* of people listened to. But it's different. When I speak into the microphone, I can't see their faces. It's like talking to myself, which is a talent I've perfected over eighteen years of being a complete loner. Put me in front of other people and I babble and go off on weird tangents and... urgh, it's just not great.

I suck in a deep breath. *It's okay, you can do this.*

Morris makes us go around the room and introduce ourselves. I'm surprised to discover we're a mix of levels – five of the students, including the Orpheans, are in their third year.

The blond-haired boy stands and introduces himself as Monty Cavendish. It must be the same Monty that William was speaking about in the quad. There can't be that many guys named 'Monty' around.

Monty doesn't ask if he should go first. He just assumes that's the way of things. He plugs his laptop into an adaptor and a video flashes on screen. It's a short clip from a multimedia art installation on the commodification of food – humans stored in animal pens and fed through tubes while a woman (the blonde next to Monty) dressed as Anne Boleyn stuffs cake into her face to weird dubstep music. It's visceral and disgusting and *amazing*.

It's a masterpiece. And Monty knows it. He talks us through each stage of the project, from conception to its month-long exhibition in Berlin, with the kind of easy confidence of someone used to enchanting an entire room. When he sits down, everyone applauds.

As the other students take turns to deliver their project statements, I sink further down into my chair. These guys have made award-winning films, showcased at festivals, exhibited sound art at the Tate Modern. One of them – a spotty first-year named Damon – spent the summer filming meerkats in Botswana for a BBC nature documentary.

I made a podcast about my dead father.

From my bedroom.

Using equipment I bought secondhand off eBay.

I am *so* doomed.

I'm debating if I can claim a sudden onset of bubonic plague and run for the door when Morris calls on me. I stand up, gripping the edge of the table to keep my hands from shaking. Twenty faces peer up at me like the jury at a witch trial. Monty grins, but it's not an encouraging smile – it's a smile of someone who wants to slather me in butter and eat me, and not in a fun way.

"Hi, hello, um, so my name is George. Well, it's Georgina, but everyone calls me George. My dad died five years ago, which totally sucks and I don't recommend it." I laugh nervously. No one else does. "So, anyway...Dad wanted to be cremated, so we sent off his body and assumed we'd get an urn of ashes back to do whatever with. Only months go by and no ashes show up.

"So one day I go to the funeral home to try and sort it out. They hand me around to various staff members before someone finally goes out the back and returns with this tiny container filled with ashes. If you've met my roommate, Keely O'Sullivan, it's about the size of one of her jars of shea butter. That girl has so much shea butter she could open a massage parlor...yes, right, sorry. I go off on tangents sometimes... So yeah, I have Dad's ashes and I get this feeling, you know...it's not right. Something's not right."

I've told this story a hundred times in interviews on other true crime podcasts, and I know I tell it well. But in front of their judging faces, I wilt. I forget important bits and drop details. Instead of feeling empowered by Dad's story, I feel as though I'm throwing his memory to a pack of wolves.

"...I decide to test the ashes. I put together samples in my school lab and send them off for testing. And I find out we weren't given my dad's ashes at all, but the ashes of some small animal, probably a gerbil."

Monty snorts. The blonde on his left titters, a streak of meanness in her mirth. I suck in an unsteady breath and keep going.

"I tell my mom what I found, but she just wants to forget the whole thing. She won't even go to the police. I can't forget it. This is my *dad*. So I do the most George thing ever and make a podcast about following the clues to figure out what happened to his remains. Doing the podcast took my mind off missing Dad and hating school, and it turns out I'm quite good at investigating. I uncovered a body brokerage conspiracy. My podcast got insanely popular, and it was even used as evidence when the FBI took the funeral home to court. So I guess this year I want to make the second season. I'll find a different story to investigate, maybe some local unsolved mystery, and I'll follow the trail. That's all—"

"...is this thing on?"

My cheeks fire with heat as my voice is blasted through the room at top volume. Monty grins wide as he sets his iPhone on the table. From the speaker, my voice sounds tiny and uncertain.

Monty's gone and looked up my podcast. But he's not playing the first episode or even one of the slick final episodes I did where I covered the court case. Oh no. He's playing an outtake/blooper reel I did for fun – it features ten-and-a-half minutes of me tripping over my words, saying inadvertently sexual innuendo to interviewee subjects, and making fart noises with my lips.

The class erupts in laughter as the first of an entire medley of fart noises vibrates from the speakers. I can't do a thing. I just stand there with my hands balled in fists, wishing the floor will swallow me up.

Monty leans back in his chair, his hands folded behind his head and a look of casual glee playing across his wide mouth. He watches me carefully, drawing strength from every moment of my humiliation.

The Orpheans have painted a target on my back, and I don't even know why.

Fucking *great*.

THERE'S a cute little pub beside the library called The Bad Habit. Instead of going to the dining hall for lunch, I find a table in a dark, deserted corner and order a slice of pie. I need something sweet to get through the rest of this nightmare of a day. The bartender looks at me weird when I ask for whipped cream on the side.

When my plate arrives, I stare in horror. Instead of a sugary treat, I'm served a giant, steaming pastry filled with meat and gravy, with a pile of fries and what look like peas that someone else has already eaten and thrown up again. A dollop of whipped cream sits on top of the fries.

I scrape the whipped cream off into a napkin and devour the pie. It's amazing. Warm meat wrapped in pastry is my new favorite thing. There's even a layer of sharp cheddar cheese melted on top. I crunch my way through the french fries ('chips' according to the menu) and slide the pile of mushy peas onto the napkin to join the whipped cream.

Then I text Claws about my pie faux-pas, because I know it'll crack her up. I think about telling her what Monty did in class, but I don't want her to think I can't cope without her. The last thing I need is my best friend showing up with her knives.

It's just one class. No way can Monty ruin all of Blackfriars for me.

Famous last words.

After lunch, I have the first of my electives. I've chosen Criminology, History of Religion with Father Pearce, and Ancient Greek. I've never learned a language before, and Claws has found a cache of ancient texts her father had stashed away. She's pretty fluent in Latin, so I thought if I knew a bit of Greek maybe I could help her translate them. It'd be a fun summer project – much more fun than last summer, where I performed a backyard autopsy and watched a man being torn apart by a lion.

I told you – last year was a whole thing.

Ancient Greek is held in room 5C of the Martyrs' Tower – this was a tall, square Saxon tower overlooking the entrance to the school, where the monks could have seen pilgrims or enemy soldiers walking up the hill. I hump my way up the winding staircase and locate door 5C. The heavy wooden door is closed, and when I try the handle, it won't open. I assume I have the wrong place, so I double-check my schedule. Ancient Greek with Father Duncan – 5C, Martyrs' Tower. That's right.

I press my ear to the door. I can hear voices inside. Class isn't due to begin for another five minutes – maybe the door blew shut by accident? I knock gently.

When nothing happens, I knock again, louder this time.

The door flies open, and I find myself face-to-chest with Father Duncan. Up close, he's even more imposing than when he stands at the front of church, arms raised to the heavens, vestments flapping around his sculpted body. He towers over me – most people do, because I'm a shortstuff, but he really towers – and peers down his nose at me in a way that manages to look both amused and faintly annoyed. I thought he was old, because I have this stereotype in my mind of priests being grumpy old men (Father Pearce excepted) and because his voice booms through the lofty cathedral with such authority, but up close I can see he's probably in his early forties, with sun-kissed hair and a deep, aristocratic forehead.

Behind him, I see ten students sitting around a wooden table, upon which sits several bottles of wine, a selection of incredible-looking finger sandwiches and cakes, and stacks of books. I start as I recognize every face. William, Monty, and those other students they hang out with. The Orpheans. They look so *perfect* sitting around the picturesque table in their old-fashioned clothes with the sunlight hitting them just right.

William raises his eyes and glares at me, and there's such a cold hatred in that glare I feel ice slide through my veins.

Father Duncan peers down at me through a pair of unfashionable glasses that gave him an air of Socratic indifference. "Did you want something?"

"H-h-hi," I stammer out. "Is this Ancient Greek?"

It's a stupid question, because of course this is Ancient Greek. Father Duncan obviously thinks it's a stupid question, too, because he doesn't answer me. The line between his eyes deepens.

"Look, everyone, it's little Georgie Porgie, pudding and pie," says Monty with his mouth full of cake. "She kissed the girls and made them cry."

"Really, Monty, you don't have to be so cruel." A girl reaches across the table and whips the cake from his hand, bringing it to her own mouth. She has the kind of beauty that sinks ships. Her auburn hair streams in a silken waterfall over the back of her chair and her lips look like crushed berries.

Her voice is deep and husky like a '20s movie starlet. I'm certain she's the girl talking to William in the quad this morning.

"Yeah, Monty," William pipes up. "Don't be a barbarian. I thought you were a lover of all things Sapphic. *Kai potheo kai maomai.*"

They laugh. I don't understand the joke, but I get the context – they're calling me the snobby British Greek Scholar's version of a lesbian, because of my boy's name and flat chest and short hair. And it's so laughably stupid and homophobic and gross that I hate that it gets to me.

But it does.

Father Duncan doesn't laugh, which I appreciate. He even manages to twist his face into something like an apology. "I'm sorry that you've come here for nothing," he says. "I hate to be the bearer of disappointing news, but you're not in this class."

"That's not possible. I signed up months ago. I've got my books right here. The Liddell and Scott lexicon and—"

He tsks. “The office should know better by now. They mix this up every year, and disappointed students camp on my doorstep, wearing the same long face you make at me now. But I speak the truth. This class is full.”

He slams the door in my face.

5

I want to lock myself in a closet and punch a hole in the wall, but Keely's filled all the available closet space with her preppy designer clothes, so that plan is out. Instead, I stand out in the sunshine and take a few deep breaths.

It's fine. It's probably just a scheduling mixup. I'll go to the office and sort it out.

The front gates of the college are these huge wooden medieval things that pass beneath another tower to enter Martyrs' Quad. The porter's lodge is tucked in on the left – and it's where students can collect their mail and make inquiries. I step inside and peer over the desk at a stern-faced woman typing away at the computer. She doesn't acknowledge me in any way.

"Hi," I say. She finally looks up, her face collapsing in displeasure. "I just went to my lecture for Ancient Greek and I was told the class was full."

"It is full." Her head snaps back toward the screen.

"But it wasn't full when I signed up. It's been approved on my course list for months. I'll show you." I dig out my phone and flip to the app. "See? It's right there."

She peers at the list. “No, it’s not.”

I turn my phone around and look. Sure enough, the Ancient Greek class has disappeared. I refresh the screen. Still gone, with no indication it was ever there at all.

“But it was there twenty minutes ago, I swear. I used the map to navigate to the Martyrs’ Tower...” I tap on my search history, but that’s gone, too.

She sighs. “Look, can I give you one piece of advice? You don’t want to be in that course. Father Duncan is notoriously picky about the students he accepts, and his teaching style is rather...eccentric. It’s not as if you’re going to need a dead language in the real world.”

“But how can he be picky? He’s never even met me.”

She shrugs. “Sorry. Normally, we don’t allow fellows this level of interference with enrollments, but the father has a unique relationship with the university. Trust me, you dodged a bullet. Just pick another course and get out of my hair.”

I leave the office with a lump in my throat.

This is fine. Fine. It’s been a rough day, but nothing I can’t handle. I guess I’ll just go back to my room and look over the course catalog again. There were lots of interesting courses. Maybe I’ll take Figurative Painting, or Advertising in Modern Media or Urban Planning—

But I don’t go back to my room. My feet carry me across St. Benedict’s Quad and through the wooden doors of Blackfriars Cathedral.

Empty of people, the church seems even larger than I remember – the columns rising gracefully to spread out their branches across the vaulted ceiling, creating a stone forest through which the dappled light of the stained glass dances. I linger in the entrance, peering at the list of Mass and confessional times and the colorful holy cards on the rack.

Am I even allowed in here?

Do churches have, like, office hours?

Lonely people in movies are always going to churches to think, but maybe that's a movie thing and it's not true in real life—

"George? It's a pleasure to see you again."

I jump, knocking into the stand holding the holy cards and sending it crashing to the ground. Father Sebastian glides forward and picks it up again, bending to collect the scattered faces of the saints I toppled from their perches. He searches my face, his kind mouth turning down at the edges. I'm on the verge of tears and I know he can see it, and I *hate* that he can see it, but I'm also desperate for a friendly face.

And the fact my heart races a bit to see him again, all buttoned-up and priestly in his black shirt and slacks and white collar, with his long hair curling around his ears?

Yeah, I try not to think about that.

"Would you like to sit with me?" He offers a hand. "I was just about to perform None, but God isn't strict on timekeeping if you want to talk instead."

The air around his hand is charged with electricity. I don't take it. "What's None?"

"It's one of the Liturgy of the Hours." He rests his hand on my shoulder instead, sending a shudder of sparks down my spine. He nudges me gently into the nearest pew. "They are an official set of prayers marking the hours of each day. The monks who used to live at Blackfriars would pray the hours eight times a day. In modern times, priests are busy doing priestly things, so they aren't expected to pray all of the hours. None is not usually performed any longer. But here at Blackfriars, we like to keep the traditions of the original monastic order alive. Father Duncan has his Greek class this afternoon, so the duty of None falls to me."

"I'm supposed to be in his class," I say.

And I start crying.

I can't stop the tears once they spill over. They roll down my cheeks in defiance of my orders to stay back inside my skull. I can't even cry daintily, like a woman in a movie. I cry with snot pouring from my nose and loud sobs rising from my chest.

I'm not even that upset about the Greek class. It's just...everything.

Father Pearce takes my hand and squeezes it. It's so warm and sure and kind, and the heat that rockets up my arm feels so wrong that I cry harder. He pulls me against him, stroking my hair and back while I sob into his shoulder, getting snot all over his silk shirt.

"I can tell you from experience that Father Duncan's class is not worth shedding a single tear over," he says gently.

"I'm so sorry," I sniff. "I didn't mean to come here and—"

He pulls back so I'm staring into his face, my lips an inch from his, the tip of his nose whispering against mine. He waits a breath too long – a breath where a whole litany of forbidden hopes dance like fire across my skin – before he says, "This is what I'm here for, George. My job is to comfort, to guide. You're not the first student Duncan has sent into my arms to snot all over my shirt."

"It's so stupid," I turn away, rubbing my eyes with my fists in a vain attempt to stop the tears. Sebastian draws a box of tissues from the shelf on the back of the pew and drops them into my lap. "I chose Greek months ago when I first enrolled, but the way he stood there today and said I wasn't welcome, and all his students staring at me like I'm an alien, I just—"

"You don't have to explain if you don't want to. Father Duncan handpicks his Greek students, and he has very *specific* tastes. He wants minds that can be trained to think the way he does, to be cunning, fervent, of singular focus, and above all, righteous. You don't strike me as someone easily melded. The Greeks have a saying for his little clique, *Aeì koloiòs parà koloiôi hizánei.* A jackdaw is always found near a jackdaw."

"You know Ancient Greek?"

He nods. "I learned in seminary. I have an affinity for ancient languages. I know Greek, Latin, Coptic, Aramaic, a smattering of Hebrew… I have an interest in the ancient world, especially the time when Jesus was preaching. In another life, I might have been an archaeologist. So you haven't studied Greek before?"

"Weirdly, it was never on the curriculum at my Californian private school." I roll my eyes. "And I guess it's not available for me at Blackfriars, either."

"The course isn't all that's bothering you, is it?"

He leans back and tucks me into his shoulder again, so his arm is around me, his hand dangling close to my breast. I have the wicked thought that all I have to do is lean forward and his fingers will brush my nipple. *What kind of horrible person am I? Am I that desperate for attention that I'll trick a priest into breaking his vows?*

Why why why does Father Sebastian Pearce have to look so damn good? Why does he have to smell so delicious? Like frankincense and cinnamon, like anointing oils and black narcissus, like sin and salvation all rolled into one.

"George?" He prods me with that gentle voice. "I'm guessing you're feeling homesick."

"There's probably a little bit of that," I admit. "I've spent so many years being excited about escaping Emerald Beach and starting over that I never stopped to think about what I was leaving behind. At the end of senior year I had friends for the first time, and now I'm the weird loser loner freak all over again. I miss my mom. I worry about her. And all the memories of my dad are back there – they cling to the furniture in our house, they saturate the streets and buildings. Here, he's silent, and I think I miss him most of all. And I thought last year gave me the thick skin to cope with anything, but it's as if William and Keely and their gang work poison darts through the cracks in my armor, so I'm dying from the inside."

"William?" His tone takes a sharp edge. "William Windsor-Forsyth?"

Fresh tears spill as I recount the whole pathetic story of falling on William in my dorm room, and the run-ins I've had with them since.

"Ah," Sebastian says with resignation. "You ran afoul of the Orpheans."

"I keep hearing that word everywhere. Who are the Orpheans? Let me guess, it's a secret society where rich snobs host elaborate orgies, discuss Proust over decadent desserts, and dance around waving their underwear on sticks."

Sebastian laughs. "You're right about the puddings. And probably the orgies. The Orpheus Society is a student supper club here on campus. You have some famous collegiate secret societies in your country, like Skull and Bones at Yale. The Orpheans are similar, although their origins go back much further, to Benet of Blackfriars himself."

Sebastian helps me to rise and guides me into a small chapel off the south transept. A few ornate wooden chairs are arranged in front of a small altar. Set into the floor in front of the altar is a small stone bearing some words and dates in Latin. On the wall beside the altar is a large painting of a severe-looking monk holding open a book. The artist is different, but it's the same black-clad figure I sat beneath in the dining hall.

Sebastian nods to the picture. "When Henry VIII established the Church of England, he disbanded the monasteries and outlawed Catholicism. Most of the monasteries became schools or family seats for Henry's supporters, but some, like Blackfriars, held out against the king's orders. The head monk at the time was Benet of Blackfriars, who armed his fellow monks and some of the village people and met Henry's men in battle on Blackfriars' hill. It was a slaughter, and the monks were overrun. They retreated into the monastery, into the refectory where they took their meals and where they had stored huge barrels of gunpowder for the battle. As the king's men broke down the monastery doors, the monks set fire to the gunpowder, blowing up the refractory and becoming martyrs rather than be forced to convert to Protestantism."

I remember the burned-out ruins I explored that morning. Those charred stones told a sinister story.

Sebastian holds a taper and lights the candles on the altar. "When the soldiers combed the rubble, they found no trace of the infamous Black Monk of Blackfriars. It was believed he perished in the explosion until he showed up in Europe some years later, recruiting young and brilliant men and women to join his secret order. He called this order The Orpheus Society, after the Greek poet Orpheus who descended to the underworld to rescue his love, and combined the study of Catholicism with more ancient rites."

"That sounds blasphemous."

"The Church at the time agreed." Sebastian hands me the taper so I can light the candles on my side. It feels oddly calming, this action of lighting candles for a long-dead monk. "Benet was burned at the stake for the crime of heresy. The Church tried to stamp out every trace of the Orpheans, but the network endured underground. Centuries later, when Blackfriars converted back to Catholicism, the descendants of those Orpheans returned and started the club here in his honor." He winks at me. "Or so the story goes."

"And are they the same as *Kakodaimonistai*?"

He snorts, and the sound is so unexpected and joyful I can't help but smile. "That's a modern addition. The Orpheans are supposed to be a society for friendship and scholarship and a safe place for intellectual dialogue, but I'm afraid the years have corrupted that noble cause into something more destructive and hedonistic. They adopted *Kakodaimonistai* as their motto a few years ago. I think Montague Cavendish is behind that one."

The same Monty who took pleasure in humiliating me in front of our tutorial – I believed it. My mind whirs around this new information, and I sense the familiar flutter of a secret crawling up my spine. I am, after all, the girl behind *My Dad is a Gerbil*, and I need a new mystery to unravel. "Let me guess – you have to be a member of this illustrious society to be admitted to Father Duncan's class?"

"I don't know if it's as simple as that, but the Orpheans are the most powerful organization on campus. Montague is their president, and he's from the same Cavendish family who named your quad. Nowadays you have to be rich and connected and clever to be tapped, and Father Duncan is attracted to those qualities like a moth to a flame. Never underestimate a priest, especially one who combines zeal with ambition." Sebastian's mouth quirks up at the corner, reminding me of the moment he saw me watching him in the fountain, the moment when he could have done many things but chose to be friendly and kind. "I'd like to suggest something. I can't confess to being an expert and I couldn't offer you course credit, but if you really want to learn Greek for your own enjoyment, I'll teach you. We can have a little club of our own. Say, every Thursday night, 8PM, after Compline – that's the night prayer. Would you be interested?"

I should say no. He has a busy job and courses to teach and I shouldn't expect him to give up his time to teach me a completely useless dead language, and yet I hear myself say, "Yes. That would be amazing."

Yup, definitely going to hell.

6

Thursday takes forever to arrive. It doesn't help that time stretches on into infinity in this strange, storybook place without friends to fill it. I get up at the crack of dawn to eat alone in the dining hall (well, alone save my dark-haired companion on the other side of the room who I still haven't worked up the courage to speak to), stammer my way through my audiovisual classes (sorry, 'tutorials,' as they say over here) while Monty and his two Orphean muses (their names are Tabitha and Abigail, because of course they are) make snide comments, and spend every moment I'm not in class holed up in the library or stuffing meat pies at The Bad Habit.

At night I stare at William's painting while Keely snores beneath it, and wish for wild, impossible things. Our curtains don't quite close all the way, and a beam of moonlight slashes across the canvas, revealing a hidden detail I've never seen before – there's a woman beneath the water. She's rendered in the rainbow hues of the rippling water, her hands splayed wide, her eyes watery with fear. She's trapped and drowning, just like me.

Mostly, I don't mind being alone, but being lonely sucks balls.

It *also* doesn't help that I'm having a moral dilemma about Father Pearce, that my reasons for accepting his private Greek lessons have a lot to do with his naked form splashing around in the Cloister Garden fountain. I replay that moment in the pew over and over again, wondering if I imagined that sizzle of attraction between us – the skipping of my heart and the way he swallowed hard as he stared deep into my eyes...

He's a priest. And a teacher. He's at least a decade older than me. He's completely out of bounds. Nothing can ever happen between us, and every minute I'm with him I increase the risk I'll make a complete fool of myself.

So I shouldn't go.

It's a bad idea.

The worst idea since the CIA decided to implant listening devices in cats.

But Father Pearce is the one person at Blackfriars who hasn't treated me like...well, like me. Like the old me. His face lights up when he sees me, and maybe that's the way he is with all his students, but I can't throw away that brightness.

And then there was the way his voice stuck when he mentioned William's name, as if they knew each other. As if there was some history between them. And dammit if my Scooby-Doo senses aren't tingling at that.

I think Sebastian Pearce knows more about the Orphean Society than he's letting on. And I want to find a way to make him open up.

Just not with my lips. Or my non-existent tits.

Because he's a priest. He's untouchable.

Sigh.

I debate right up until the very last minute, leaning against the gate of the Cloister Garden and glancing across St. Benedict's Quad to the cathedral spires, then back at the narrow entrance to Cavendish Quad where my dorm was located, then back again. Keely had informed me earlier she was having William over for a late-night study session and I was to make myself scarce, and ultimately my desire not to walk in on them fucking or return to the drafty library with its hard plastic chairs makes the decision for me.

I hurry across St. Benedict's Quad toward the cathedral, my brand new Greek textbook and lexicon banging against my hip, just as the bells toll the hour. 8PM. *I wonder if I'll catch Sebastian at his prayers—*

"Hey, Georgie Porgie Pie, where are you going?"

William falls into step beside me. *What's he doing here? Isn't he supposed to be with Keely?* I don't look up at him, don't slow my pace as I head toward the sanctuary of the church.

"Hey, I'm talking to you." His voice sounds sharp, as if he somehow has the right to be annoyed with *me*. "Are you deaf as well as dumb?"

I stop.

Something hard snaps inside me.

I turn around. Slowly, like I have all the time in the world.

William stands behind me, haughty chin held high, aristocratic nose sniffing the fading light of the sun. One hand rests in the pocket of his slacks, and he has his tie a little loose and only one button done up on his blazer. He looks every bit like he owns the ground I walk on. He probably does.

He makes me think of another boy who thought he owned the world.

I *hate* him.

"It wouldn't matter if I were deaf," I say. "I still deserve to be at this school, same as you. And I'm *not* deaf. I'm choosing to ignore you."

That smirk again. It's so soft at the edges, you can almost

believe it's friendly. But the coldness in his eyes betrays his true purpose. "You're going to see Father Pearce, aren't you? It's awfully late for confession. Or is there another reason he's got you on your knees?"

I snort and turn away, but he grabs my wrist, his fingers digging into my flesh.

No.

Blood rushes to my ears.

The taunts and insults I can handle. The little humiliations that wear away at my soul are nothing new.

But this arrogant fucktard will *not* touch me without my permission.

I will not lose another night of sleep over men who think they own me.

I use the move Claws taught me to break his grip. William yelps in surprise as I twist his wrist so far he can feel it's on the edge of snapping. Above my head, the bell tolls with violent urgency.

I'm dimly aware that somewhere behind me, voices are gathering, watching, clamoring for blood. But I'm past caring what they think.

I lift my knee and smash it as hard as I can into William Windsor-Forsyth's crotch.

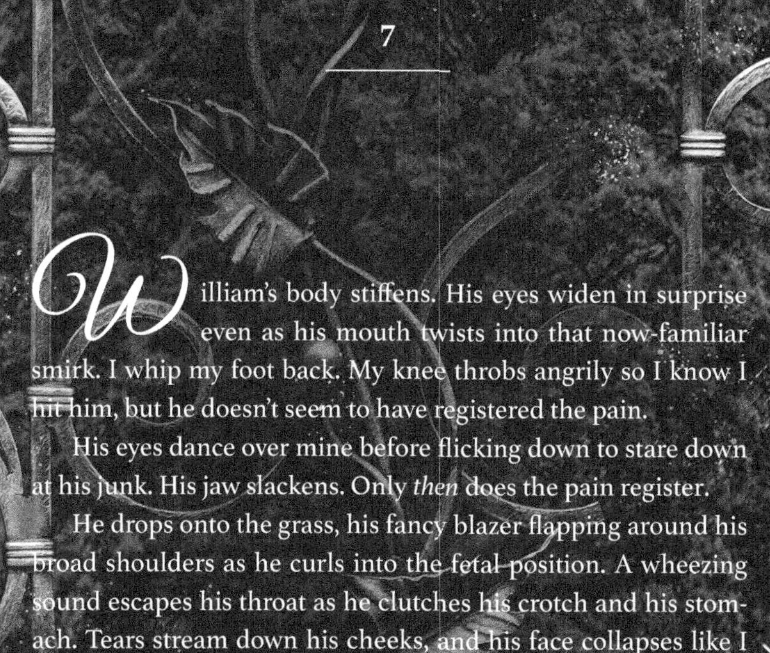

7

William's body stiffens. His eyes widen in surprise even as his mouth twists into that now-familiar smirk. I whip my foot back. My knee throbs angrily so I know I hit him, but he doesn't seem to have registered the pain.

His eyes dance over mine before flicking down to stare down at his junk. His jaw slackens. Only *then* does the pain register.

He drops onto the grass, his fancy blazer flapping around his broad shoulders as he curls into the fetal position. A wheezing sound escapes his throat as he clutches his crotch and his stomach. Tears stream down his cheeks, and his face collapses like I sucked out all the happiness from the universe while forcing him to insert a black mamba up his rectum.

It's fucking beautiful.

Above my head, the bells toll one final time, and as the rush of blood cools, as I look down at the writhing body of a felled king and realize what I've done, I hear them.

The voices.

Freak. Crazy bitch. Psycho stalker. She's even dressed like a serial killer. Words and phrases I don't even recognize but can't be anything good sail through the air and pierce my flesh.

In pummeling Willam's scrotum, I've also pummeled any hope of ever making a friend at Blackfriars.

Whatever. Fuck them all. I don't care what they think.

The voices wash over me, a choir of vitriol that sings to me of the hell I've brought down on my own head. Behind me, a lone person whistles with approval. I glance over and see my dark-haired comrade from breakfast lurking in the shadows. She sees me looking and scurries away.

And because I know I'm fucked, and I'll never have the chance again, I lean over William, taking a twisted enjoyment in his wild eyes swimming with agony, and the frantic swallowing as he fights not to vomit. "Don't touch me again. You might think you own this school, but you don't own me. And my business with Sebast—with Father Pearce is my own."

William's eyes squeeze shut. "He's not what he seems," he chokes out. "He lures you in with smiles and prayers until you feel safe in his arms. But he's no godly man. He's a monster. If you trust him, you're even more stupid than I thought."

I spin on my heel and stalk toward the church, William's chilling words echoing inside my head. No one stands in my way, but the whispers rise to a crescendo, a wave of ill-intent that threatens to drown me. I catch snatches of what I think might be Greek. My hand closes over the door handle, and it takes me three tries to turn it because I'm shaking so bad. As I slip inside, I dare a look back at the quad.

The auburn-haired girl leans over William. Today, she's wearing a dark velvet suit that disappears into the blooming night.

"There, there, William, it's not so bad. We'll get you a drink and you'll feel better in no time." She laughs as she lifts him to his feet, his arm slung over her shoulder. Her laugh is as pretty as springtime, and it draws the blood from the air. "While I've got you, I desperately need to copy your Greek composition. I had so much dandelion wine I'm afraid I'm utterly useless."

William wheezes. She laughs again. "Yes, yes, thank you, my darling. I knew you'd agree. Monty, dear, a little help?"

I see Monty rushing across the quad toward them, and I slip into the church and close the door with a *click*. I know William's wrath will come down on me, but I'd like to save it for another night.

Sebastian's voice fills the church, and as the words wash over me I release the adrenaline and panic that took over in the quad. He speaks in Latin – his last liturgy of the day – and the sound of it sends a chill down my spine.

What is it about Latin that makes it sound so *sexy?*

I walk as silently as I can through the nave and crossing. There's an iron gate separating the choir from the congregation, and another between the choir and the altar where Sebastian kneels. I'm not sure if I'm allowed to cross, so I lean against the gate and watch.

"...Ad te suspiramus, gementes et flentes..." Sebastian's voice sounds so strong, so certain, so faithful. He knows exactly who he is, what his purpose is in life. I think about William's whispered warnings, but when I search for any sign of truth in his words, I can find none. A man who kneels with such earnest devotion cannot be what William says he is.

He's a monster.

"...in hac lacrimarum valle."

Sebastian makes the sign of the cross and stands. There's a stillness in the air that feels charged with meaning as he turns and sees me and smiles. There's nothing monstrous about that smile. It makes my stomach drop into my feet.

"Hello. You're just in time." The gate squeaks as he stalks toward me. I notice he wears his vestments – a green poncho-kind-of thing over a white ankle-length gown, belted at his waist with a long, silver cord. He pauses on the other side of the gate and reaches up a hand as if he wants to touch my cheek, but he doesn't do it. "You look flushed."

I *am* flushed. My cheeks pulse with heat, and I can feel his hand an inch from my skin, begging for me to press my face against it.

I wish he hadn't noticed.

Why has he noticed?

"I ran into William Windsor-Forsyth," I say, by way of explanation.

"Oh, yes." I watch Sebastian's face for a reaction. Did his eye twitch a little bit? "Did something happen?"

"I kneeed him in the nuts."

Sebastian throws back his head and laughs. I can't help but smile, too. It is pretty funny.

"You really are something else, George Fisher." He pushes open the gate and offers his arm to me. I loop my arm through his, trying to ignore the racing in my veins at his touch. "Only you would groin-kick the future king of England."

"Wait, he's royalty?" I blurb out. "Monty called him Your Highness, but I thought it was a joke."

"It is a joke, because the royal family is a joke. But yes, William is distantly related to the royal bloodline. He's seventeenth in line for the throne, which means he's exceptionally unlikely to ever become king, especially given the status of his family. Would you like to see the sacristy?"

"Sure." I marvel at the nugget of information about William's family he dangled in front of me before smoothly changing the subject. And I feel certain something has gone down between the two of them – something more than the clash of religion and royalty, of rich entitlement and vows of poverty and chastity.

Sebastian leads me through a little iron gate and around the back of the altar. It feels strange to be back here, a little sacrilegious. There's an enormous carved crucifix hanging from the wall, and a towering edifice that Sebastian explains is a monstrance. "It's used to display the consecrated Eucharistic host during ceremonies. I wasn't even allowed to touch it until I was a deacon."

We duck through an arched doorway into a small room, where Sebastian shrugs off his vestments and hangs them neatly in a wooden cupboard while I examine glass cases filled with a variety of items.

"This is the sacristy," he said. "It's basically a walk-in closet for priests. It's where we dress before services, and it holds blessed items like our anointing oils and censers. We also keep some of the items of historical importance to the Church in here."

"What's that?" I point to a weird lump of itchy-looking fabric hanging on the wall.

"That is a *cilice*. It's a hairshirt made of coarse animal hair. A priest or ascetic might wear it against their skin. The discomfort is a form of penance or atonement – mortification of the flesh." He smiles. "It itches like you wouldn't believe."

I stare up at the cilice, thinking about what sins Sebastian had committed that he thought worthy of such a punishment. For some reason, this vision of him sliding into that rough fabric, feeling it scratch on his skin, makes a dark and extremely sacrilegious ache pool between my legs.

Then I imagine Father Duncan wearing it, and the feeling dissolves into disgust.

Catholics are weird.

I keep walking. Behind a second display case of jeweled communion chalices is a wooden door, barely wide enough for my small ass to fit through.

"What's this?" I ask.

"Oh, that?" Sebastian brightens. "It's actually quite interesting. I'll show you, but we'll need a light."

I whip out my mobile phone and flick on the flashlight app. He laughs. "I was going to go for a candle, but this is even better."

Sebastian fumbles in his pocket and withdraws a heavy set of old-fashioned keys. He inserts one into the lock and pushes the door open. "After you. It's perfectly safe."

I step inside, shining the phone at the floor in case there's a step, but all I see is rough-hewn stone cobbles – not the fine marble of the rest of the church. The walls are bare too, and the small room is empty of furniture save for a low stone bench along one wall and a pair of wooden shutters above. Sebastian slides a bolt across and pulls open the shutters, indicating I should look inside.

I kneel on the stone and shine my light around. I'm looking into a room about the same size as the one we're in now – roughly ten by twelve feet. On the left wall, facing the church, is a tiny window, barely large enough for a hand to fit through and blocked on the church side. On the right wall – the outer stone wall of the church – was a larger window, also shuttered from the outside, through which a frigid breeze and a thin beam of moonlight escaped.

"This is where the anchoress lived," Sebastian says. "An anchoress is a type of hermit – instead of living in a cave, she is anchored to a church. She chose to retreat from the secular world to live a life of solitude, prayer, and asceticism – the belief that physical hardship brings her closer to God. She would be shut inside this cell for her whole life. The small window into the church allowed her to receive the Eucharist. A servant would have attended her in the room we stand in now, offering her food through this window and removing her waste. Only women who could afford the upkeep of their servants were allowed to become anchoresses. That third window looks outside. Visitors to the church would often gather beneath that window and the anchoress would give spiritual guidance."

"That's incredible." I stare into the dark room, trying to imagine a woman who would choose such a life. What did she think about for all those endless dark hours walled up in solitude?

"When the anchoress was first walled inside, the priests would recite the office of the dead, to symbolize that she was now dead to the world." Sebastian's warm voice makes my toes curl against the cool stone. "Luckily, I've never had to perform such a task. Come. We should begin our lesson."

He leads me back through the church, stopping briefly to show me the small wooden hatch beside the pulpit where the priests could offer communion to the anchoress. We cross behind the altar and through another gothic doorway, up a set of stairs, and down a narrow passage into another medieval section of the cathedral, which Sebastian explained was where the monks conducted official business and received important visitors.

Five doorways branch off a central corridor. Cool air blasts from beneath the second one, raising goosebumps on my arms. Sebastian leads me to the furthest one and unlocks it with another of his clunky old keys. I gasp as I step inside one of the most beautiful rooms I've ever seen.

The room is vast, at least two stories high with central stone columns supporting the vaulted ceiling, which draws my gaze upward with rich paintings of biblical scenes. Apart from two narrow windows looking out into a small garden, every inch of wall space is covered with bookshelves. A spiral staircase leads to the second floor of books, and beneath it is a desk piled high with more books and loose papers. Two battered leather chairs and a coffee table covered with dirty teacups face a roaring fire, and a queen-sized bed is pushed into the corner, almost like an afterthought. Two doors lead off to a modern-looking kitchen and bathroom.

Sebastian runs a hand through his hair. "Welcome to my humble apartment. I hope it's okay if we work in here? I figure it's more comfortable than the church meeting room. Plus, it gets cold in this building at night, so I stoked the fire."

"It's perfect," I breathe. There's no other word to describe it. It even smells like Sebastian – frankincense and cinnamon, myrrh and black narcissus, earthly and holy and bewitching. I'd consider the life of an anchoress if it meant I can be walled up inside *this* room.

With him.

Argh, no. Bad George. That's the kind of thought that'll get you struck by lightning.

"Have a seat. Let me clear some of this away."

I perch in one of the armchairs and try to pretend I'm not watching him as he slides ungraded papers under the table and stacks the cups away. My lips dry. I stretch my feet toward the fire. He bends over, his black jeans clinging to his firm ass, and I remember droplets of water rolling over taut, naked skin, and just how very much of a man Father Pearce is under his vestments.

Stop being ridiculous. He's a priest. And a teacher. He's untouchable. He's literally the most impossible person for you to fall for. You like him because he's the only person at this stupid school who's been nice to you...

...and because he's clever and interesting and kind and he makes you laugh...

...and because William hates him...

...and because he swims naked in fountains.

Sebastian puts the kettle on. He lifts the cover on a turntable and selects a record, carefully setting the needle. I notice boxes of record sleeves shoved under the table, and my fingers itch to flip through them. I want to know what he listens to late at night in this comfortable room.

As Nina Simone coos through the speakers about sin and redemption, Sebastian brings over a tray holding a chipped blue teapot and saucers, a stack of books, and a plate of chocolate chip cookies. "I stole these from the college buttery," he grins, picking up a cookie and taking a big bite. "The chef, Mrs. Birtwhistle, has a soft spot for me."

I accept my hot cup of tea with hesitation, still not a hundred percent certain I actually like tea not sweetened with syrup and served with ice. Sebastian wipes crumbs off his black shirt and opens the textbook. I watch his fluid movements, the joy sparkling in his eyes as he mouths ancient words.

William was trying to mess with me. There's no monster in this room.

We get to work. I'm captivated by Sebastian's rich, deep voice as we go through the Greek alphabet, verb stems and endings, articles, and noun cases, with a couple of fascinating asides to discuss slavery in Greek society and the movie *300*. Sebastian gets up twice to change records and brew more tea. We listen to Budgie's *Never Turn Your Back on a Friend*, and he follows the old-school punk with something ethereal and soothing with lots of panflutes.

Too soon, he frowns at the clock above the door. "I've kept you too long."

Above our heads, the church bells toll midnight. I can't believe it – it feels like I only just arrived, but when I stand, I realize my legs are cramped from sitting down so long. My head feels heavy, filled with strange Greek words and Sebastian's divine scent.

"It's my fault. I wasn't watching the clock." I hurry to collect my books and notes, accidentally upsetting my saucer and spilling tea across the coffee table. I right the cup and saucer, but it's too late – tea dribbles over the side of the table and blurs the ink on his notes. "Oh, no. Let me get that—"

"—no, I'll do it—"

He whips a cloth from the kitchen and dabs at the spill as I shuffle books and papers out of the path of damage. *I should come with a tornado warning.*

Our fingers brush.

Sparks fly up my arm. Sebastian's head whips up, his obsidian eyes meeting mine, dark and curious and hard with something I can't define. His lips soften, parting a little, but he's not soft. His whole body has gone rigid, his nostrils flaring, his cheekbone chiseled in stone.

He doesn't move his hand away.

His fingers on mine are shooting stars.

We hover there, our lips an inch apart. This...*whatever* it is... sparks and fizzes between us, a fireworks display exploding with forbidden desires. For a minute I think he's going to kiss me. My heart skips, and I am suddenly aware of how dry my mouth is, how desperately I want to wet my lips, or lean forward slightly, or do *something,* anything to—

Sebastian steps away, his shoulders slanting. He turns his head, dropping the tea-stained cloth to the floor. "Goodnight, George."

"I'm sorry. I—"

"It's nothing, really." He holds the door open without looking at me. "It's very late, is all. Same time next week?"

As I sprint back across the deserted quad, the final bell tolls its ghoulish clang. The pale-faced moon watches me from behind the steeple, casting a long shadow of a stone cross over the cobbles.

The air crackles with righteous anger. The trees rustle with bilious demands. *Confess your sins.*

Okay. Okay.

The truth?

The fucking truth is...

I *wanted* Sebastian to kiss me.

There. Happy?

Despite everything I tell myself about needing a kind face, about learning Ancient Greek, about sticking it to William and his stupid friends, I went there tonight because every time I see Father Sebastian Pearce, I fall a tiny bit more in love with him.

It's so stupid and selfish and pointless, for a million reasons I already know. He's too old for me. He's a teacher. He doesn't feel the same way. He's a *priest.*

But that moment when his fingers touched mine...his eyes...I thought...

But even if there was a chance, I can't be the reason he breaks his vow. I can't be the woman who leads a good man into sin.

He already loves with his whole heart. He's pledged his soul to divine orders.

How the fuck can I compete with that?

8

My audiovisual tutorials are a special kind of torture. Mostly, the others ignore me unless we're working on an assignment together, but Monty takes every opportunity to make me look small and silly and incompetent in front of the class. Neither my classmates nor Professor Fletcher calls him out on it or asks him to stop.

And it doesn't help that I still haven't found a new case to investigate for my project. I'm trawling through old editions of the *Blackfriars Gazette*, looking for unsolved murders, but so far the most interesting thing that happened around here was a hijacked cider truck careening through the fence of a pig farm and making all the animals drunk.

Part of the problem *might* be that I spent my last library session googling articles about Monty Cavendish and William Windsor-Forsyth. Sun Tzu says to know thy enemy, and luckily for me, Britain's tabloids love to spill the tea on the Cavendish and Windsor-Forsyth clans. Sebastian is right – William is distantly related to the royal family, but he'll never get a shot at the crown. Despite William's insane upbringing – the castle in the south, the London residence, the Eton education, and a private island off Majorca – his arm of the family are considered black sheep. William's father married a common Irish barmaid and converted to Catholicism. Apparently, being Catholic in the peerage is basically treason, which might explain why the papers take great delight in splashing sordid details of satanic orgies, wife-swapping, and hallucinogenic drugs consumed at William's family seat. Every article about William's achievements – his Olympic gold in fencing, his summer tour with the London Philharmonic, his art exhibition in Berlin – is overshadowed by stories of his father's shenanigans and his mother's drug-fueled death on their estate.

And Monty… in most articles and pictures, Monty's been at William's side, often finding ways to make the story about himself or his father, the current Earl of Cavendish, a popular patron of the arts. The Cavendish and Windsor-Forsyth clans spend their holidays together and support their respective children into fancy schools, internships, and lucrative jobs. While William racks up achievements like Claws stacks up dead bodies, Monty's claims to fame are more salacious – school expulsions, police warnings, vulgar art shows arousing public protests, and getting kicked out of exclusive London clubs.

I store up this knowledge to use later. I know I'll need every weapon I can find. I haven't yet received any retaliation for kneeing William in the balls. But I know the dark prince is biding his time. Tension pulls the air taut whenever we pass each other, and I have a feeling I haven't escaped unscathed.

William Windsor-Forsyth won't allow such a slight to go unavenged.

So I wait. I go to classes. I brace myself for his attack.

Each afternoon I attend a different elective tutorial. It's these electives that make Blackfriars amazing. Since I'm not taking Greek, I make a list of ten other classes and decide to trial one each day until I decide what I want to add to my schedule. I've already been to Antarctic Exploration, Women in the Early Americas, and The Art of the Novel in the 21st Century.

Today, I have Figurative Drawing. I like drawing – some of my tattoos I drew myself – but I can only really draw cartoonish objects and animals, cutesy food and skeletons with bows, that kind of thing. So this should be fun. I head toward class from the university bookshop, with my new sketchpad and pencils tucked under my arm. My stomach rumbles, reminding me that I haven't eaten since my very early breakfast. The drawing tutorial is two hours, so I decide to make a quick stop at The Bad Habit.

There's an extra-long line, so I'm running late by the time I have a warm paper bag with a takeaway beef and Guinness pie. I scarf down the pie as I make my way into the studio, where I expect to see long communal tables filled with art supplies like my old school art department. Instead, I stagger into a marble-floored ballroom with easels arranged in a circle around a dais. Atop the dais William's friend Diana lies across a chaise lounge, luxuriating on a silk sheet.

She's completely naked.

Well, then.

I *cannot* sit through a class drawing a naked girl from the secret society that's out to get me. I whirl around to leave and smash straight into a wall.

Not just any wall.

A royal wall.

William flashes me a dirty look as he bends to retrieve the brushes I knocked from his hands. Fuck. *Obviously* he's in this class. He's an artist. He'll be taking as many fine art tutorials as he can.

I'm not safe.

I have to get out of here.

"Sorry." I try to shove my shitty cheap pencils into my bookbag as I sneak past him. He reaches up and grabs my ankle.

"You're not going anywhere," he hisses, his words laced with venom. "Class is about to begin. You wouldn't want to be *rude.*"

I jerk my leg, trying to break his grip, but I'm at the wrong angle. If I lift my foot off the ground, all he'll have to do is twist my leg a certain way and I'll crash down beside him. Judging by the way his mouth quirks up into the half-smirk, he knows it.

"Stay," he purrs. "I do so enjoy *outsider art.*"

"Georgie Porgie." One of William's friends, a floppy-haired blond named Reginald, waves from across the room. From a distance, he might appear friendly, but I hear the smirk in his voice. "So pleased you could make it. We're studying the female form – your favorite."

I can't take it any longer. "You guys know being a lesbian isn't an insult, right? Considering you hang out with the Prince of Debauchery over there, I'd have thought you would be a little sensitive to—"

"What did you just call me?" William jerks to his feet, catching my ankle and nearly sending me toppling backward. I manage to right myself, but not before I crash into Madame Ulrich, the lecturer.

She glares at me as she dabs at the coffee I've splashed on her red silk shirt. "Miss Fisher, are you in this class or out? Because I don't tolerate horseplay."

"Georgie Porgie loves horseplay," Reginald pipes up. "Strapping a bridle on and having someone ride her with a dildo—"

"I'm just leaving." I dart for the exit, but William grabs my wrist.

"Miss Fisher is next to me." He drags me across the room.

"Let go of me!"

"Miss Fisher, if you hold the class up one moment longer, I'll have you written up." Madame Ulrich beams at William. "Thank you for taking our new student under your wing,

William. It seems she needs a lesson in how things work at a *proper* university. Let us begin."

Twenty pairs of eyes follow me as William drags me across the room and deposits me in front of an empty easel where I have the perfect view of Diana in all her glory. All around me, students get to work. Madame circles the room, lecturing on form and technique as her stiletto heels clop on the marble. The only other sounds are the scratch of pencils and slip of paints. I glare at William, but he's no longer looking at me. He works in watercolors, dabbing paint on his paper and using washes to spread and dilute the colors to create form and shadow.

Remember what I said about my 'cartoonish' style? Yeah, it doesn't gel with drawing hot, naked girls with sad grey eyes that never stop staring at me. My painting looks like Homer Simpson's sister-in-law posing for *Playboy*. It doesn't help that William's beside me, creating perfection. I sneak a look over at him, at the frown of concentration on his face, the speckles of paint dotting his toned forearms, the wrinkle in his perfectly ironed shirt he doesn't attempt to smooth.

Then I sneak another look, and another.

He's fascinating to watch. He's always so aloof that it's impossible to imagine he has feelings. But as he dabs a blue wash on his canvas, making Diana appear to be reclining underwater, his face softens. Someone has removed the stick wedged up his butt. His eyes cloud over with intensity. Emotion swirls from every brushstroke.

He stands back, frowning at the piece, twisting his head to look at it from different angles. He stares at Diana with an artist's eye, breaking her body into shapes and contours. I thought this class would be filled with lewd banter from the Orpheans, but William doesn't see Diana as a woman. He sees only beauty.

And there's so much beauty to see. It seems illegal that one woman should be allowed this much. Diana embodies the goddess whose name she shares – long lashes fluttering against flawless cheeks, a graceful neck arching like a swan, a body as lush and full as any sensual Renaissance painting.

No one could ever see her and want me.

No. Wait. Where did that thought come from? That's some next-level emo shit. You wouldn't want anyone who fell for Diana, anyway. She's an Orphean. She might not've been cruel like the others, but she still thinks she's better than everyone else because she's rich and clever and beautiful and studies art. Stop feeling sorry for yourself and focus on making it through this class.

Diana remains perfectly still for a full hour as Madame Ulrich circles the room and admires our work. Madame offers suggestions, correcting and discussing composition and lighting with each student, sometimes holding up her tablet to show them a particular painting or color she refers to.

I spy a bottle of black ink on William's easel and wonder if I can grab it and spill it on my paper before she gets to me. I want to crawl into a hole and die.

"Remarkable, William." Madame Ulrich walks behind him, admiring his work. She bends his head and the pair of them whisper together, as if what they have to say about art is so sanctified they can't risk mere amateurs like me overhearing.

"Let's see how our new student is getting on." Madame Ulrich steps toward me. I whip my head back to my own canvas, my cheeks flushing as I realize what a complete mess it is. It's a child's drawing. She stares down at my sketch, her lips pursed as she looks to my paper, then to me, then back again.

William isn't as subtle. He walks behind my canvas and starts laughing. That draws his friends. They all gather around my canvas and laugh and laugh. I shove my hands in my pockets, hoping to find a miniature trebuchet I can use to go medieval on William's ass, but all I find is lint and Cadburys wrappers.

Finally, Madame Ulrich puts an end to my torture. She snaps her fingers and the students head back to their own easels.

"Thank you, Diana. You've been an excellent model. I hope you'll enjoy at least *some* of the interpretations of your form. We'll take a five-minute break before we bring out our next sitter." Madame beckons me with her finger. "Miss Fisher, follow me."

Heat flares in my cheeks. It's bad enough the whole class is laughing at my drawing; does she have to scold me in private, too? I just want to leave and escape to my room so I can drown my sorrows in a pint of chocolate ice cream.

I follow Madame Ulrich into a side room, where a variety of canvases and art supplies are stacked in neat cubbies. In one corner is a French screen with a vanity table and several silk robes hanging from silver hooks.

"You may undress there." Madame Ulrich points to the screen. "Leave your clothes on the stool, although I appreciate it if you don't put those disgusting boots on the furniture."

"Excuse me, what?"

She shoves me behind the screen. "Hurry, please. No talking. My students pay good money for my classes and I won't keep them waiting."

"What are they waiting for?"

"You. They can't learn to paint the human form if the form is covered in these—" she pinches my Clash hoodie and wrinkles her nose like it smells bad "—*clothes*. Of course, someone like you couldn't paint the human form if I held a gun to your head, but perhaps what you can't do yourself you can inspire in others."

"There's been some mistake," I splutter. "I'm not going to model for you. No way am I'm getting naked in front of...*them*."

"I don't tolerate time wasters in my class, Miss Fisher. You agreed to model when you signed up for the class. You filled in the paperwork and signed the release form." She holds her tablet in my face so I can see my signature printed on the bottom of a form. "If you don't model, I write you up."

William.

That bastard.

This is his revenge. Someone in his group has access to my schedule on the app – that's how they were able to remove the Greek class so easily. He must've learned that I signed up for this class and forged my signature on the release forms.

I want to cry.

To a privileged wanker like William, this is a harmless prank. But if I get written up, my scholarship money is withdrawn. Not even Gabe would be able to save me. Either I go out in front of the class, in front of William Windsor-Forsyth, *naked*, or I don't get to stay at Blackfriars.

He's trying to ruin my life.

He's trying to show me that he's the one with all the power, that if he snaps his fingers I'll have to get in line like all of his other servants.

Not going to happen.

Tears well in my eyes, but I blink them back. I won't give him the satisfaction of breaking me. I won't let him win.

Madame Ulrich tosses me a silk robe and taps her gold watch.

Behind the screen, I peel off my clothing and lay it in a neat pile on the stool. To spite her, I stack my scuffed boots on top of the vanity, knocking a bunch of mascara tubes to the floor. Diana had her face heavily made up to accentuate her classical features, but I have something different in mind – an idea I borrow from my friend Claws.

If they want to paint me, they will have to paint me just the way I am.

Just the way they made me.

I find the perfect tube of lipstick in blood red, and when I'm ready, I shrug on the silk robe and belt it at the waist. I rub my freezing arms, but I can't stop the trembling.

I can't believe I'm doing this.

William didn't give me a choice, but there's one thing he doesn't realize – the person standing on that dais might be stripped bare, but they hold all the power in the room.

I walk out with my arms crossed and my head held high.

Twenty pairs of eyes follow me, raking over my skin like a knife scraping through butter.

My resolve lasts until I sit on the edge of the couch. I know they can see the trembling in my limbs. I can't take my eyes off the dark prince. William's eyes are perfectly calm and cold on the surface, but beneath a dangerous current simmers.

"Disrobe," Madame Ulrich snaps. "We don't have all day."

I shrug off the robe and toss it to the floor. My eyes never leave William's face as his gaze rakes down my body, across the cartoon tattoos that adorn my skin, over the sweep of my breasts...

...to the huge cock and balls I've scrawled on my stomach, beneath the words BIG GEORGE ENERGY.

To the insults and curses painted on my skin in blood-red lipstick.

Freak.

Queer.

Weirdo.

Slut.

All the words people like them have flung at me. All the insults that I try to let wash over me like water off a duck but that instead burn in deep, like scars that heal over but never disappear.

You want a piece of me, Your Highness?

You think this can break me? You know nothing about me.

Madame Ulrich takes a step back, pursing her lips. I expect her to yell at me, but instead, she actually looks *impressed.* I may not be able to draw for shit, but I've definitely demanded a reaction. "Don't stand there gawping," she snaps at her students. "This isn't a peep show. Get to work."

William bites his lip. He looks away, busying himself with his palette.

Pencils and brushes scrape on paper. I feel every one as I lean back on the sofa, deliberately placing my limbs in a sprawling, unflattering way. I'm not going to pretend to be Diana. William demanded my nakedness, my *truth.* I make sure he has it.

For the next fifty-five minutes, I control this room.

And it feels *good.*

I keep as still as I can, my gaze trained on William. He's mixed the first of his washes now. His eyes flick from his canvas, to me, then back again. Beneath the ice glade of his eyes, the currents stir and shift. He doesn't look at me the same way he looked at Diana. He doesn't see beauty. He sees *me.* He sees George with her short blue hair and her too-small tits and her round little stomach and all the scars I've carried with me across the seas.

And just like that, it became too much. I feel the ice crack beneath me and I'm falling, falling into William's eyes. I'm tossed about in the deep, fathomless ocean inside him, and the words I wear as armor wash away, leaving me bare and cold and *alone.*

"Make note of the different shapes," Madame Ulrich intones as she circles the room, her stilettos *clack-clack-clacking.* "The torso is short, and there's a softness around the stomach. Without the hair spilling over the shoulders, note where the bones and muscles stick out, like a sack of potatoes covered in skin—"

I go somewhere else. My friend Claws says that she stores all her horrible memories in a metal box inside her head. She wraps the box in chains and pushes it out to sea. So I ball my heart up in my fist and toss it in a box, and I lock the box tight and throw it into the ocean of William's eyes, and that's the only way I make it through as the minutes tick by and the brush-strokes cut my skin.

When the bells toll the hour, I leap from the couch, yanking the silk robe over my shoulders. Madame calls after me but I don't stop, don't turn. As I pass William's easel, I twist, trying to glimpse what he's drawn, but he yanks the canvas and tucks it under his arm. His eyes are wild, like a caged animal, as he beats me to the door.

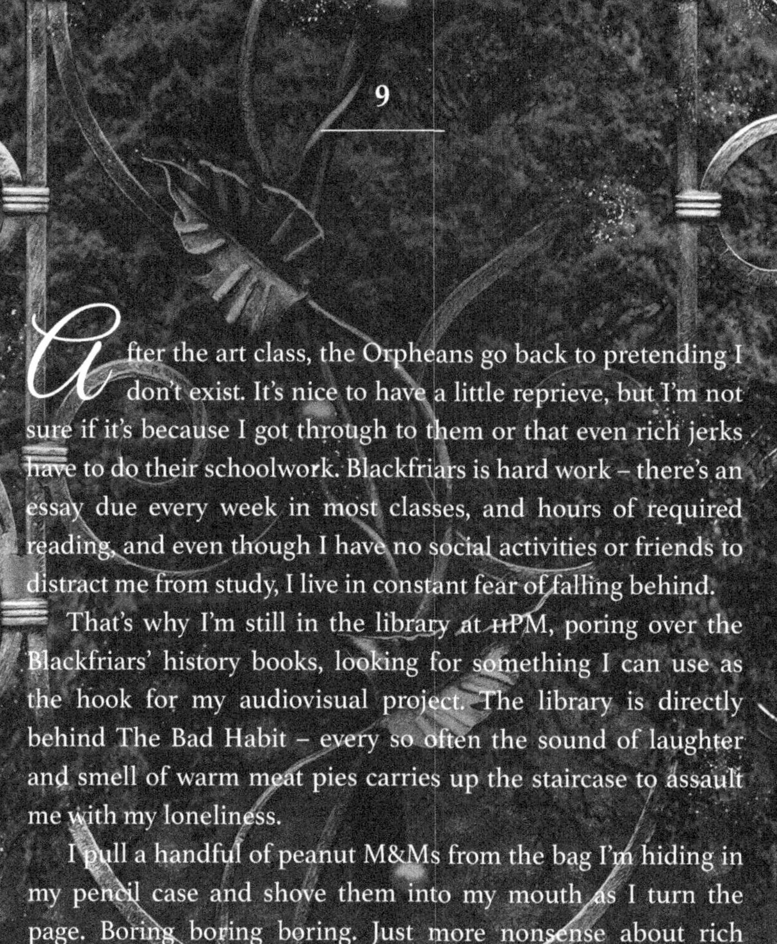

9

After the art class, the Orpheans go back to pretending I don't exist. It's nice to have a little reprieve, but I'm not sure if it's because I got through to them or that even rich jerks have to do their schoolwork. Blackfriars is hard work – there's an essay due every week in most classes, and hours of required reading, and even though I have no social activities or friends to distract me from study, I live in constant fear of falling behind.

That's why I'm still in the library at 11PM, poring over the Blackfriars' history books, looking for something I can use as the hook for my audiovisual project. The library is directly behind The Bad Habit – every so often the sound of laughter and smell of warm meat pies carries up the staircase to assault me with my loneliness.

I pull a handful of peanut M&Ms from the bag I'm hiding in my pencil case and shove them into my mouth as I turn the page. Boring boring boring. Just more nonsense about rich white men gifting money to the school and—

Hang on. What's this?

The word Devil's Night leaps off the page.

I remember the master's dire warning to students about

staying in their rooms the night before Halloween. So far I hadn't seen anything about it beyond a few passing mentions of Devil's Night pranks in the student newspaper. But this is different.

I turn the book on its side and angle my lamp so I can read the grainy image of an article from the student newspaper, dated twenty years ago. It's about a first-year student named Khloe May who disappeared on Devil's Night after partying with friends in the woods.

Khloe May...Khloe May...that name sounds familiar.

I slide my laptop across and type in her name and 'Blackfriars' into the search box. A moment later, a long list of articles comes up. As I scan them, I remember where I've seen her name before. Khloe came up on the missing person's list for the county, but I never paid attention because the records said she'd been suffering from depression and had most likely taken her own life. Police found the sweater she'd been wearing in Blackfriars Wood, and even though they have no body, the case is considered solved.

But not by Khloe's parents, it appears. They spoke to the press about their daughter's recent lust for life in the days leading up to her disappearance, about a new group of friends at college and a boy she liked. They said she'd been in treatment for depression for years but she was doing much better.

'If she killed herself, where is her body?' Khloe's mom asks, her sorrow reaching through the screen to wrap around my heart. 'I'll tell you why they can't find my baby girl. There's no body because Khloe didn't kill herself. Someone *hurt* her – someone with wealth and influence at that fancy school – and now they're using their power to cover it up.'

The Mays wanted the police and the university to keep searching, to keep asking questions. Their heartfelt pleas to draw attention to the case went on for three years after Khloe's disappearance before they fell silent.

And they weren't the only ones asking questions. The student who wrote the article, the one that piqued my interest, had gone back through the university's history and found five other students in the last hundred years who've either gone missing or died in strange accidents on Devil's Night.

Now I'm intrigued.

The article in the photograph cuts off after a paragraph, so it doesn't give the names of the students. The text in the book isn't much help, either. The book's author uses the article as an example of how students often sensationalize and mythologize events around the university. He points out numerous other urban legends about Blackfriars – a werewolf that roams the woods on the full moon, a rumor that if a student's roommate dies during term, they'll automatically be given a passing grade, and the gargoyles and grotesques of St. Benedict's Cathedral coming to life to terrorize students caught out after dark. The author even mentions the Orpheus Society alongside some other fantastical-sounding secret societies, clearly implying it's made up.

The back of my neck itches, and my heart pounds with excitement.

This is it. This is my story.

I'm going to get to the truth behind Khloe May's disappearance.

I'm blowing Devil's Night wide open.

10

I may have had a wobbly start, but I *love* Blackfriars. I love my classes, and all the silly old traditions, and the big, imposing gothic buildings. I've given all the gargoyles names, and I call out to them when I pass by. I even love the dreary English weather, and how the grey skies and old stones make me feel like the heroine of a gothic novel.

My favorite thing by far is my weekly Greek lesson with Sebastian. He's a brilliant teacher, patient and understanding, and he knows about so many things. He never minds that our conversations meander from irregular second aorists to Aristophanes' plays or the archaeological excavations at Troy or the nature of democracy. I always leave late in the night with an armload of books he wants me to read and a warm ache in my gut. He's lent me a valuable old Bible with gilded decorations, handwritten in Greek by one of the Blackfriars monks for me to translate.

I'm even starting to enjoy hot tea.

My second favorite thing is Criminology class. For one thing, Diana is the only one of William's friends taking it, and by herself she's lovely. But mostly I just find everything about it *fascinating*. Professor Melinda Hipkins teaches the course – she's a leading forensic researcher who's worked with law enforcement and the BBC on violent crime. I've heard her speak on true crime podcasts and I've read all her books. She's shorter than I imagined in real life and has a gallows humor about death that makes the other students uncomfortable, but I love it. Whenever I walk into class I feel like I'm in the presence of God, if God drove a motorcycle and kept a collection of skulls on her desk.

After I dropped Figurative Drawing like a hot potato, I picked up Professor Hipkins' optional lab component. Every week she brings in different experts to talk to us about forensic entomology, the history of autopsies, anthropology and antiquities crime, all sorts of interesting stuff. Today, she has a forensic pathologist, Dr. Lauren Grainger, talking us through the intricacies of an autopsy.

I've already had up-close-and-personal autopsy experience with Claws' friend Galen, but they weren't exactly performed in laboratory conditions, and Galen was looking at how to cover up a crime, not how to detect it. While the others fidget and groan at the gross images, I lean forward in my seat, glued to Lauren's slides as she describes how to tell if a strangulation is from autoerotic asphyxiation gone wrong (hint: it's the socks), and quotes the poet-undertaker Thomas Lynch. "Both sex and death are horizontal mysteries that possess similarly disconcerting effects."

How right you are, Mr. Lynch.

When she finishes, Professor Hipkins gives us our assignments for the term. "As well as your weekly papers, each of you will design a forensic experiment and you will submit a report on your results at the end of term."

I know exactly what I want to do, and I'm hoping I might be able to tie it into my audiovisual project and save myself some work.

After class, I head over to the biology lab, where I know a group of third-years are conducting nocturnal experiments on rabbits. A lovely and impossibly-tall Irish guy named Shawn explains the experiment – I don't understand a word – and shows me the cages of lab-bred white rabbits.

"Unfortunately, because we're testing in the field, the experiments have a high mortality rate," he says. "Rabbits have a lot of natural predators, and sometimes they just die in their cages and we don't know why."

"What do you do to them after they...expire?"

Shawn nods toward the incinerator.

"I don't suppose I'd be able to have a few?"

"A few...dead rabbits?" He looks confused. And a little frightened.

"Yeah. It's not for a satanic ritual or anything." Probably I shouldn't have worn my *Drink Tea. Worship Satan* t-shirt. "I'm doing a project for Professor Hipkins' Criminology paper."

As Shawn heads into an office to check with his supervisor, I make a mental note that I will *not* be telling Claws about this on our next phone call. Claws can't deal with the idea of any animal getting hurt, and when she gets angry, she gets stabby.

I LEAVE the biology lab with three plastic bags filled with rabbit carcasses. It's a little chilly, but I decide not to go back to my dorm for a sweater. If Keely sees me with my booty, she'll make a scene. And she already threw my deodorant out the window this morning after she found it on her side of the room.

Instead, I head straight down to Blackfriars Wood.

The university is surrounded on all sides by the dense wood. Apparently, Blackfriars Wood used to be much larger, but the land has been systematically cleared to make way for villages, monastic buildings, and now the university. Even so, it's an impressive spread of greenery dotted with hiking trails and hiding all kinds of secrets.

I take the student path behind the cricket pitch, stepping off near an ancient stone pilgrim's cross and following the tree line down toward the village of Blackfriars Close. Apart from my brief stop at the train station when I first arrived, I haven't been into the village. Everything I need is right on campus, and shopping and the village pub aren't fun by yourself.

I *am* pretty curious to see the old amphitheater, through. According to a conversation I overheard in the dining hall, there's a Roman amphitheater about a half-mile off the path. Every year in March, the university puts on a theatrical festival there, but the rest of the time it just sits out in the woods, looking all cool and Roman while being devoured by nature. And I want to see it.

The first clue I'm heading in the right direction is a broken piece of column lying between the trees. Lichen coats its fluted surface, painting it with lurid shades of green and pink and brown. I step over it and continue along the ridge, tripping over more broken bits of masonry, until I wander into a clearing and come to stand in the center of a circular orchestra. In front of me is the flat stone of an altar and rows of stone seating curving around the hill.

The stage area is mostly gone, although there is a newish-looking wooden platform where I presume the yearly performances are held. I'm surprised by how little trash or graffiti is around the place – you'd think students would come out here to party. But something about this place commands respect.

I suck in a breath of crisp, damp air. It rained last night, so the stones glisten in the pale light, and a faint mist clings to the edges so the earth behind the stage appears to slope away into nothingness. It's a beautiful spot, heavy with the magic of ancient gods. I have to show Claws. She'll love it.

I pull out my phone and set it on panoramic shot. I stand beside the altar and spin around in a slow circle to get a picture of the theatre seats around the *cavea*, the altar, the broken columns, and the trees sloping away into the mist. My neck cranes up to watch the light filter through the dense trees – no sun today, just low-hanging clouds that seem to draw the heavens closer. I open my mouth and sing lines from my favorite punk songs, marveling at the way my off-key voice bounces and echoes in the vast space.

As much as I want to sit down with a book or my Greek flashcards and enjoy the atmosphere all afternoon, I can't stop. I've got a trash bag full of rabbit corpses and an assignment I want an A on.

I head deeper into the forest, stopping every few trees to carve a symbol into the bark so I can remember my way back. More masonry pieces litter the woods. I wonder what other remains lie in the forest, hidden beneath layers of dirt and neglect.

When I think I've gone deep enough that my site won't be disturbed by carousing students, I stop in a small clearing with a gnarled, ancient oak on the edge and roll out the orange tape I borrowed from the janitorial closet. I hammer one end into the oak (so happy I brought along Dad's toolkit) and wrap it around three other trunks before bringing it back into a lopsided square. I add the laminated sign I made on the lab computer. "Science experiment. Do not disturb."

Then, I set out my animals. I use two as a control group, placing them on the ground without any other adjustments. One I bury a foot in the earth under the oak tree. One I hang from a branch with a noose made from a silk tie. Another I leave above ground in the plastic bag. The last carcass I set alight. It reeks as it burns, and I have to hold my sleeve over my nose and turn away. I already know from experience (don't ask) that human bodies need a long time and a high temperature to burn completely to ash, but I'm not after complete combustion – just enough to give me interesting results.

What I want to find out is what the search parties might've expected to find if they stumbled across Khloe May's body in the woods. One of the key questions raised by Khloe's parents in the press was that given such a thorough search, how come no one found her body? Unlike a murder, where the perpetrator hides the body (by, say, burying it or burning it), a suicide is usually easy to find. The university responded that the weather in November could cause a body to decompose quickly, so in the time before the searches began in earnest there might not have been much left to see.

My rabbits will put that theory to the test.

By the time I'm done, I'm covered in dirt. My hair sticks to the back of my head and a couple of impatient flies buzz around me, already anticipating their feast. I look like shit but I feel amazing. This is exactly what I came to Blackfriars to do – I'm excited to see what I can learn about decomposition and to maybe help shed some light on Khloe's disappearance.

I snap a few pictures of my makeshift 'body farm.' Thinking that it might make a good podcast episode, I decide to take a selfie for social media. I squat down under the oak, hold the camera up high, and flash a thumbs up and a broad smile.

When I angle the camera to get more of the tree in the frame, I notice something move behind me.

Not something.

Someone.

11

My chest tightens. I have ethics committee approval for this project, but Dr. Hipkins warned me I needed to keep it out of sight of students. I don't want anyone to stumble on my body farm and wreck it, or kick up a stink and get my project shut down. But it looks like that's exactly what's about to happen.

Oh, goody.

"Hello? Who's there?"

I stand, sliding my phone back into my pocket and grabbing the spade.

"I'm warning you, I'm armed. Who's out there?"

The figure steps out from behind a tree.

William.

He faces me with those ocean-blue eyes and one hand in his pocket, his trousers impeccable despite walking through the damp forest. He tilts his head to the side, quirking that aristocratic mouth of his into a smile.

It's a cruel smile, one that stretches the gap between us. He's so beautiful it's almost ethereal – the kind of beauty that's dangerous. He's a fae king upon his throne, surveying his quarry before the Wild Hunt.

The breeze whips my hair into my face. I reach up with one hand and slide the hairtie off my wrist in a vain attempt to tame it, but I know it won't help. I'm down here with the worms and insects, covered in dirt, playing with rabbit carcasses. And William Windsor-Forsyth believes that's exactly where I belong.

Great.

"Well, well, well." William jumps down from his perch, landing on the other side of my tape so softly I can almost believe he *is* a fae. "What do we have here, Georgie Pie?"

A different kind of fear seizes me. William didn't stumble upon me randomly. He *followed* me into the woods. And now he's leering down on me with his dangerous smile, like a dagger wrapped in silk. He can't have any good reason for being here.

I've seen William and his friends smashing plates in the dining hall, kicking sods of grass, treating the scouts and other university staff like their personal slaves. They're used to doing whatever they want without consequences.

What does he want to do to me?

I'm all alone in the woods, miles from school. If I yell for help, no one will hear. No one will come running. I haven't told anyone I'd be out here today. William can do anything to me... who the hell will believe my word over a prince?

And that's not even the worst thing he can do to me.

It would be days before they found my body.

If they even found it at all.

They never found Khloe May.

Panic jerks in my limbs. I bite my lip, trying to hold back the memories that surface like black fog. *This isn't like last time. You're awake. You've had all those self-defense lessons. It's not the same. He's not the same as—*

I jerk the spade at William's chest. "Don't come any closer."

William smirks as he ducks under the tape and takes another step toward me.

"What do you intend to do with that?" He glances at the spade with amusement.

Go away. Just please leave me alone. The darkness pushes in at the edges of my mind, and I gulp back the panic attack rising inside me. "I swear if you touch me, I will smash your skull in."

He laughs – a harsh, barking sound that's completely devoid of mirth. "Georgie Pie, you think so little of me. As if I'd want to touch you. I saw you by the theatre and I was curious what you were doing out here, so I followed you."

He was at the theatre? I didn't see anyone there. But I guess it would be easy to hide amongst the ruins, and I wasn't exactly quiet when I walked in.

He heard me singing? That's almost worse than being naked. Zeus, kill me now.

William's gaze turns to ice as he takes in the rabbit corpses scattered across the clearing. I remember the way he looked at me when I lay on that couch with my pain scrawled across my flesh. Blood rushes to my ears, and my heart clenches so hard I have to clasp a hand across my chest to keep my heart from leaping out of my ribcage.

Am I having a panic attack?

William doesn't seem to notice. He wanders between my experiments with his hands behind his back, peering at the rabbits like they're exhibits at a museum. "Madame Ulrich hasn't stopped talking about you. She's upset you dropped her class. She thinks you might be one of the greatest artistic minds ever to set foot in this school. Wait until I tell her you're a psychopath."

"It's a project for my Criminology class," I manage to say. I feel like invisible fingers press at my throat, choking the life out of me. "Please don't move anything or tell anyone this is here. I know you hate me, but if you could possibly not destroy my hopes for an A, I'd appreciate it."

"I don't hate you." William takes another step closer. His chest brushes against the spade. He's not afraid of me. "I don't think anything about you at all."

"Really? That's rich. You and your friends sure do spend an awful lot of energy thinking up ways to torment me."

His grin spreads wider. That sensual mouth could melt the panties off an ice sculpture. Too bad beneath that smile is an empty shell of a human. "Tormenting plebs is fun. It's a public service. You have to get used to being walked over by your betters."

"You made me strip naked in front of a whole class. Do you not understand how fucked up that is? Didn't your mother teach you about consent?"

Storms darken the edges of his eyes. "I didn't expect you to actually do it."

I want to scream. I jab the spade at his chest. "If I didn't do it, Madame Ulrich would have written me up and I'd have lost my scholarship. I'd have been on the first plane back to California, with community college in my future."

He turns away. "I wouldn't have let her do that."

I snort. "Right. Because you're a regular prince in shining armor. You prance around this school like you own it. You've never had to think about the consequences of your actions, so why should I expect anything more when it comes to my humiliation?"

"I don't prance."

"Whatever." I nudge his chest with the spade. "Go away, William. As much as I love listening to a posh wanker talk out of his ass, I need to take a shower. If you're going to ruin my life, just get on with it. I see no reason to continue this fruitless conversation."

I just called William Windsor-Forsyth a posh wanker. I wish I could call my friend Gabriel and tell him I used my two favorite British words on an actual prince. He'll never believe me.

William closes one hand around the shaft of the spade. He brings a finger to his lips. The gesture only draws attention to that sinful mouth and the plumpness of his lower lip. "What will you give me for my silence?"

"What do you mean?"

"Nothing in this world is free, Georgie Pie."

Is he *serious?* "I've got twenty-two pounds in my bank account. Do you take cash, or do I have to swipe my credit card between your ass-cheeks?"

I'm channeling Claws to mask the fact I'm terrified of William getting me kicked out of Blackfriars. But as usual, I ruin the awesomeness of my barb by blushing. I can feel my face and neck flushing with heat. William sees it too, because his eyes light up with a wild hunger that makes my heart thud with something that isn't entirely fear.

He's too close. He's too dangerous to be this close.

I want to run. I want to forget about my stupid project and get as far away from William Windsor-Forsyth as possible.

I want to fall into him. I want to crawl inside his skin.

One of these thoughts is sensible. The other is dark fae magic.

"Mmmm." William moves closer, twisting his grip to tilt the spade to the side. The handle crosses our chests – the only thing separating my skin from him. "I had something else in mind."

"What?"

"A kiss."

He reaches out a hand to my face. I don't stop him. I couldn't even if I wanted to, and I'm not sure I want to. His thumb grazes the edge of my chin, tracing my cheekbone with cruel, careful reverence. He tugs at the corner of my lip.

"Just a tiny kiss. One little peck and I'll keep your secret, Georgie Pie."

I swallow. I blink, and the moment where the world plunges into darkness gives me time to rally. "You have girls and guys literally falling at your feet. Why do you want to kiss me?"

He shrugs, his fingers wrapping around my neck, tilting my chin back so all I can see is the outline of his aristocratic face against the misty forest. "Maybe I only want things I shouldn't have."

That makes two of us.

His hand on my neck is soft but firm. He tips his wrist, and my head falls back even further, exposing my throat. I feel like a deer caught in a hunter's sight. William's finger slides over my exposed skin, reminding me that this could go so many different ways.

It's not fear that shakes my limbs and stutters my heart against my ribs.

It's *excitement.*

"What do you say, Georgie Pie?" William's breath caresses my earlobe.

I swallow. *Why is my mouth so dry?*

Why am I suddenly so aware *of him? Of the way his body takes up space so casually, of the broadness of his shoulders shifting the air around me, the throb of blood pulsing in his neck, the elegant arch of his eyebrow and the sweep of his sharp cheekbone.*

Of his scent. His goddamn oil paint and leather books and vanilla and dark chocolate scent filling my nostrils, breathing magic into the air itself.

"Just one kiss, and you will leave my experiment alone?" I try to sound incredulous, but I'm afraid I come across as eager as I feel.

This is insane. He's blackmailing you. This isn't hot or sexy. It's sick.

Tell that to my body, which hums under his touch. Tell that to my heart, which is ready to leap out of my chest and fly away. Tell that to the George who is sick to fucking *death* of following the rules.

I want to kiss William.

There. I admit it.

I wanted that pouty mouth on mine ever since the day I saw him standing on the lawn.

He's completely wrong for me on every level. He's everything I despise in a human and yet...

Screw it.

I want to taste posh boy on my tongue. And here he is, making me the offer. And maybe it's fucked up, but who cares? This isn't a marriage proposal – it's one kiss. I've done way more fucked-up shit than kiss the wrong boy.

William thinks he's in control. He thinks I don't want this, that he's stealing this kiss in exchange for something else he can lord over me. So fuck him. Maybe I want to steal something of his.

Besides, if he tries anything, I'll clonk him with the spade.

William nods. "One kiss and I'll keep your secret. I swear to you on my mother's grave."

His voice cracks a little. I remember reading in the articles that his mother was dead. It's weird to think I have something in common with William Windsor-Forsyth, that he might know something of the crushing grief I've lived with for the last three years.

"Fine." I hear the word come from my lips, in my voice. But it doesn't sound like me. Who is this George who wants things she can't have and makes deals with dangerous fae princes?

William's eyes shroud with grey, reflecting the mist that

obscures the forest. The grey sharpens his blue-blooded apathy into something feral, pagan.

Dangerous.

He makes this growly noise in his throat that undoes something inside me. His fingers stroke my neck, tipping my head back. The air between us stills.

William brushes his lips oh-so-softly against mine. His touch is so featherlight it can't technically be called a kiss at all, and yet an electric shock jolts through my body. I feel like I'm Frankenstein's monster and the good doctor has just plugged me in. I'm alive, and everything feels new and strange and wonderful.

I want to pull away, and I don't want it to ever end.

William looks surprised, too. His eyes are open, locked on mine, and the ice-blue peeks through the grey, so clear and fathomless and alert, as if he intends to remember every second of this kiss. His hand grips my neck, his fingers tightening a little as he draws me closer. He keeps his lips pressed against mine, soft but firm. The spade handle digs into my flesh as his body pins mine, setting little fires everyplace we touch. His tongue nudges, forcing me open to accept him.

My tongue tangles with William's, and I have never known hunger like this. He tastes the way he smells – full of magic and potential, of broken promises and crushing hurt. He gasps as his fingers cup my cheek to pull my face closer, his tongue diving deeper as if he wants to crawl inside my skin. The warmth of his body makes me feel drunk, disoriented.

I don't want to like kissing William. I don't want him to taste like sin and enchantment and to make me feel like I could float away, but *damn*. He's so soft and warm – the kind of warmth that goes right to your toes. His hand on my neck doesn't feel controlling – it feels like protection. I find myself reaching up to run my fingers through that tousled hair, and I'm breathless, drowning in the magic of him and—

No.

I can't.

I won't.

This isn't about the things I want a kiss to be. This isn't about how good it feels, because it feels *too* good. But I know these feelings are empty. This isn't me – kissing some guy I don't even like because I want to prove I'm a rebel. I may have wanted this, but it's still about William Windsor-Forsyth having power over me.

And I've been here before.

I've had my power taken away, my ability to consent. I've had my own body betray me, and I've lived with the horror of it for far too long.

How can I let this happen again?

The tremble starts in my hands. It's so bad I drop the spade. It lands on William's foot. He bites down on my lip in surprise, drawing blood.

"Ow." He jerks away and grabs his foot, hopping on one leg as he rubs it. He glares at me. "What did you do that for?"

I step back, gasping. I need air. All of a sudden this vast wood feels like a tiny closet. "We kissed. I paid your price. Now leave me alone."

He reaches for my cheek again. "George?"

My name on his lips is too much right now. I throw my hands out and shove William. Hard. His foot catches on a gnarled root and he stumbles over, scraping his arm on the tree as he scrambles for purchase.

"Stay away from me." I whirl around, grab my backpack, and take off at a sprint before he can see that my whole body is shaking and tears are streaming down my cheeks.

Trees whirl around me. Branches scrape my arms as I crash through the wood, barely even able to see the symbols I made through my tears. I need to be somewhere, anywhere he isn't.

William's dark laughter follows me, but I can't be certain I didn't imagine it. I can't be certain it's not someone else's laugh, from another time, that has escaped the lockbox of my memories.

I run all the way past the theatre and back to the main path, my chest heaving, my face streaked with tears, before it occurs to me that for the first time, William Windsor-Forsyth called me by my real name.

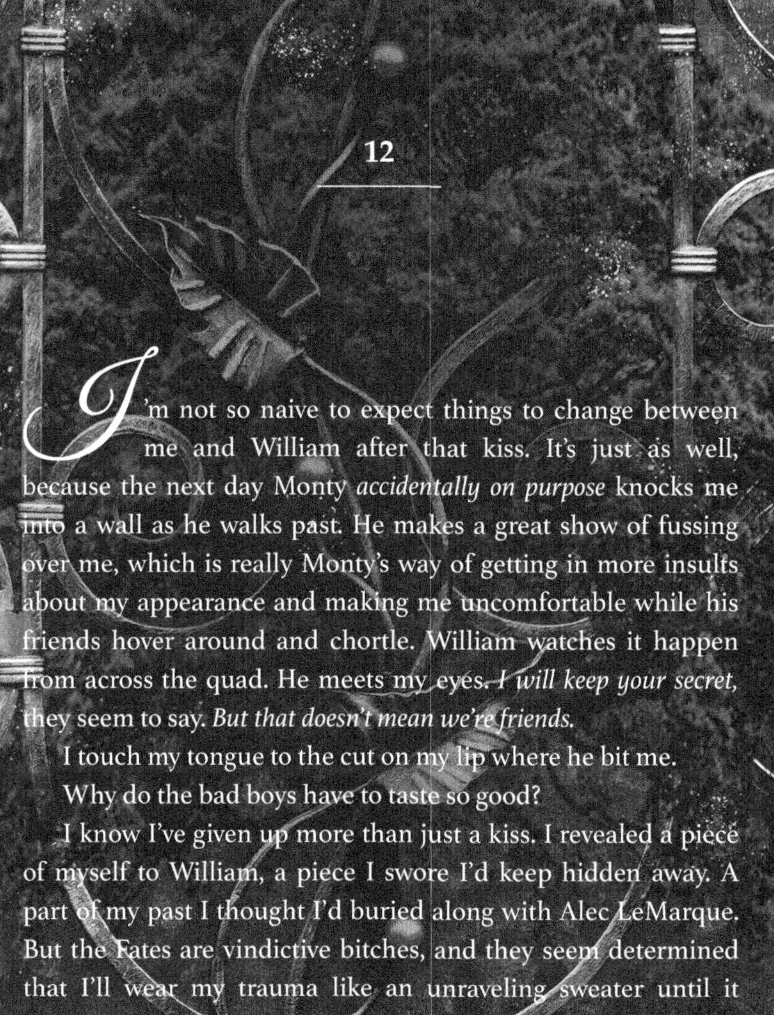

12

I'm not so naive to expect things to change between me and William after that kiss. It's just as well, because the next day Monty *accidentally on purpose* knocks me into a wall as he walks past. He makes a great show of fussing over me, which is really Monty's way of getting in more insults about my appearance and making me uncomfortable while his friends hover around and chortle. William watches it happen from across the quad. He meets my eyes. *I will keep your secret,* they seem to say. *But that doesn't mean we're friends.*

I touch my tongue to the cut on my lip where he bit me.

Why do the bad boys have to taste so good?

I know I've given up more than just a kiss. I revealed a piece of myself to William, a piece I swore I'd keep hidden away. A part of my past I thought I'd buried along with Alec LeMarque. But the Fates are vindictive bitches, and they seem determined that I'll wear my trauma like an unraveling sweater until it tangles up my life and undoes every bit of progress I've made.

My days at Blackfriars start to blend into each other. I get up early so I'm the first one to the dining hall, and I eat breakfast underneath the Black Monk's portrait at one of the long, empty tables. Sometimes I see the dark-haired girl across the hall. Sometimes our eyes meet over the buffet as we both reach for the bacon tongs at the same time, but we've never spoken a word to each other.

Keely is hardly ever in our room, but when she is she makes it so unpleasant I find myself avoiding going there during the day in case I have to face her. I do most of my coursework sitting in the empty amphitheater or under the trees in the Cloister Garden. I send Claws texts and snaps of my picturesque collegiate life, leaving out the parts about the crippling loneliness and how my stomach is all tied up in knots over two forbidden men.

I go to my classes, the library, the laboratories, and my Greek lessons with Sebastian. I almost tell him about William and the kiss, but I remember the weird way he acted when I brought up William before and I decide against it. Plus, I don't want him to ask about why I pushed William away – I can't talk about *that* with a priest.

Especially not a priest whose kind smile and deep voice fill my dreams.

It's amazing how much Father Pearce and I find to talk about, given all the things I can't tell him. I can't say that his History of Religion lectures and Greek classes are the only things that get me through the week, or that the way he smiles at me makes my knees feel weak and my heart grow bird's wings. I can't tell him that sometimes I sleep with his beautiful Greek Bible resting under my pillow because it smells like him.

The kiss plays on constant repeat in my mind. Every time I see William with his arm slung casually over Diana's shoulder, a knife digs into my chest. I wish the kiss meant something to him, and I hate myself for wishing.

Every day I have to weave my way through groups of friends to get to my classes, and my stomach aches from wanting to be a part of it. I wonder if this is what the anchoress felt like, listening to the world go by from inside her dark, cold cell. I message Claws most days, and Gabriel sends me audio tracks of his band's new songs, and I talk to my mom, but it's not the same as having a friend here to hang out with.

I don't want to admit the truth.

I'm lonely as fuck.

I'M at The Bad Habit for an early dinner, eating a steak and Guinness pie (extra fries, no mushy peas) and working on a gnarly Homeric translation Sebastian set me.

All around me, conversation buzzes about Devil's Night. Some students are organizing mini parties in their rooms. You're not really supposed to get together on Devil's Night, but I hear students whispering that if the groups are small enough no one will break them up. Even the staff must be locked away for the night.

I've been debating asking Sebastian if I can hang out at his place and sleep on his couch on Devil's Night, but I can never push the words out. It feels like crossing a line, and I've already stomped all over my personal boundaries with William.

I still don't attend Formal Hall, so I haven't heard another lecture about Devil's Night, but large posters all over the university remind us 'plebs' of the rules. Notifications pop up on the app whenever I open it, and this morning a note was shoved under our door that Keely pointedly left on my bed.

Do not go outside. Stay in your room. The gates will be locked and no one may enter or leave campus until morning.

No one comes out and says it, but I put together bits of information from the hushed and reverent conversations. On Devil's Night, the Orpheus Society has the campus to themselves. An entire university shuts down so some rich toffs can have a party. It's insane, but more and more I'm learning that there are different rules for William Windsor-Forsyth and his friends.

I hear the crash of crockery breaking. I ignore it, because I'm in a pub and things break all the time, especially when the Orpheans are around. But when I go to stab another piece of pie with my fork, I discover my plate has gone.

I look up, straight into Monty's mischievous eyes. Tabitha is behind him, not even trying to disguise her snigger. Monty peers down at me over the tops of his horn-rimmed glasses, his sticky-looking mouth turned up into a smirk. "Sorry, George, old chap. I'm awfully clumsy."

Behind him, I see my dinner in a pile on the floor. My stomach rumbles. I slept in this morning and didn't get to the dining hall early enough, so I skipped breakfast. Then I trekked out to my makeshift body farm to record my observations and forgot to pack something for lunch. I'm *famished* and now I have no dinner and no idea if Monty intends to fuck off so I can order more or kidnap me and flush my head down a toilet.

Don't engage with them, just walk away. I turn my back on them and start packing my books into my bag. Monty slides into the booth beside me, blocking my exit. Tabitha slumps into the other side, waving over another Orphean named Richard who takes the remaining seat. Panic rises in my throat as I realize I'm completely hemmed in.

Monty keeps talking in that pleasant voice of his, swiping his messy blond hair out of his face with one hand. "You shouldn't eat such rubbish anyway. The food here is terrible. And I don't believe in wasting time on terrible food, do I, Tabby?"

She shakes her head as she reaches into her purse for a compact, which she uses to reapply her lipstick. "Monty here is a regular gourmet. There's nothing he hasn't eaten."

She says it in such a way, with her golden years trained on him, that I understand she's not talking about food.

"That's nice." I glance around the room, wishing there was someone I could call out to who will save me. I reach for my phone. *Maybe I can get Claws to call me and I can excuse myself to take it—*

"Quite so, quite so." Monty reaches across the table and swipes my glass of Coke, sucking on the straw with a slurping noise. "Why, last summer I was in Sardinia with the other chaps, and we had this local delicacy called *casu martzu*. Have you tried it, George my lad? It's a traditional sheep's milk cheese that contains live maggots, and it is *unbelievable*." He smacks his lips together, making this horrible wet sound. "Highly illegal, of course. Very dangerous. The European Union says it's a no go, but the Sardinians believe it's an aphrodisiac, and you can't keep a good Sardinian down, if you catch my meaning. The cheese has a remarkable taste; the acid excreted by the larvae softens the cheese until it feels like silk on your tongue. You have to hold your hands over your sandwich so the little blighters don't leap off into your wine. Dicky Boy here couldn't keep his lunch down." Monty slaps Richard on the shoulder. "It was such a lark."

"That sounds—"

"Anyway, George, old chap. We're not just here to shoot the breeze. We want to buy you a beer, our way of saying thanks for being such a good sport about William's little art class prank. The family jewels are still intact, so everything's even now." Monty claps me on the shoulder so hard I nearly faceplant into the table. "And we'll get some nibbles while we're at it. I'm sure not everything here will be as ghastly as that pie I saved you from."

Something in the friendly tone of his voice warns me that this isn't an altruistic gesture, but I literally can't move so I have two options – yell for help and hope someone takes pity on me, or suffer through it. "Sure," I mutter.

Monty snaps his fingers and Kit, the pub's owner, rushes over. Normally, you have to go to the bar to order drinks, but I guess if you're an Orphean, you get special treatment. Monty orders a round of gin and tonics – "Top shelf only, there's a good girl, none of that 8-pound walrus piss you serve the plebs" – and every platter from the extensive sharing menu. "Don't bother cleaning that up," he tells Kit as she frowns at the broken plate. "We're hungry."

Kit throws me a sympathetic look as she steps over the congealing pie to take our order to the kitchen.

When the food arrives, the three of them pounce on the platters like they've been lost in the desert. Monty orders more drinks, which disappear in moments, but Kit seems to be used to serving Orpheans because she arrives with another tray. I watch Monty like a hawk as he hands me mine, making sure he doesn't have a chance to slip anything inside.

"Not drinking, old boy?" He elbows me. "You're behind."

I sink down in my chair and watch them, weirdly fascinated by whatever the fuck is happening. Monty says something in Greek as he bites into a chicken wing, licking the juice from his fingers before finishing his third drink and starting on mine. Tabitha tears pork belly with her teeth, while Richard makes a serious dent in an enormous pile of cheese and pickles. They talk with their mouths open, recounting parties and dinners and trips abroad to places I've never heard of, switching topics with deft enthusiasm to Proust or Russian poetry or the political issues in Burma. Monty keeps trying to include me in the conversation, and I might think it was sweet if I weren't certain he was trying to trap me into saying something dumb so he can use it against me.

I stare at the dwindling pile of food, my mouth watering. I

reach out and take a pork rib slathered in BBQ sauce and bite into it. I can't help it. I'm *starving*. And they did destroy my dinner, so it's the least they can do. Besides, if I'm chewing, I don't have to answer Monty's incessant questions about my podcast and my father's ashes or respond to the loaded barbs about my clothing choices from Tabitha.

Do they know about the kiss? Is this their way of telling me to keep away from William?

Or is Monty really trying to make good in his own despicable way?

Monty's carbon-grey eyes never leave my face as I pick at the food. He has this way of focusing his full body on people he's interested in – his attention can feel like a sledgehammer swinging over your head, but for the first time I feel myself coming alive under his scrutiny. He says something about me in Greek – *slowly the sour grapes become honey* – and I answer him. His lips curl back into a savage smile, his chin smudged with meat juice and sauce, like a hunter drinking the blood of his kill.

I've impressed him. Knowing this gives me a surge of power. I reach for my drink and down the last of it.

Monty orders shots, and soon I'm laughing and slapping his shoulder as we fight over the last of the pork belly and loudly debate the merits of various arthouse films. I sense through an increasing fog of alcohol that I'm actually having *fun*. I can't believe it. Maybe I'm really making friends. Maybe I actually impressed them with my art stunt, as William had implied. Maybe this is the start of something...

By the time all the platters are empty, I'm seeing double. Two Montys knock back their final drinks and shrug on their blazers.

"Well, George, old chap. It's been fun. But I must be to bed." The Montys slap me on the shoulder as they exit the booth. "This one's on you, right?"

"What?" My head swims. Suddenly I feel sick. We must have

drunk several bottles of top-shelf gin, not to mention the food, and the shots, and what was that Scotch Richard kept quaffing like water? I barely have enough money to cover textbooks. This will wipe me out. "No, I can't—"

"Thanks, George. You're a sport." The two Tabithas smirk as they prance out after the Richards, leaving me with a table piled high with discarded glasses and a gnawing sick feeling rising in my stomach.

Kit rushes over and starts picking up the broken bits of crockery. I realize with growing queasiness that the pie Monty smashed is still lying on the floor. He wouldn't let her clean it up, so she didn't. How could I ever think they were being friendly?

"You look a little green, lass," Kit says. "I take it they stuck you with the bill?"

I hand her some napkins. "Apparently, I'm a character in a Donna Tartt novel."

"This is nothing." She scrubs at the mince crusted on the carpet. "Last Devil's Night they broke in here and smashed every single glass in the place. At least I've got insurance to cover any damage they do. It's you I'm worried about, pet. They seem to have taken a shine to you, which is a dangerous place to be with the Orpheans. Don't worry about the bill, just don't let it happen again. You need me to find someone to walk you back to your room?"

"Thanks. I'll manage." I slide out of the booth. My legs wobble, and a fresh wave of nausea washes over me. The room spins, but I don't think it's the alcohol. The walls contort as the humiliation washes over me, and I half-run, half-stumble out the door. I can hear Monty's laughter crackling in my head, even though he's nowhere to be seen.

Outside, it's raining. Cold droplets pelt my face, washing away some of the alcoholic fog. *I wish I was back home in Emerald*

Beach, snuggled with Claws and Gabe and my other friends in the Malloy Manor theatre room watching some trashy horror film. I wish—

I can't believe I fell for their stupid prank. I can't believe I thought Monty Cavendish was interested in talking with *me*. He's probably telling the story to William right now, and the pair of them are laughing their stupid snooty laugh—

A tear tumbles down my cheek. I dab it angrily with my finger. I hate myself for being so desperate for a friend that I leaped on the first people to show me some kindness, and I couldn't even see they were mocking me the whole time. I wish I could talk to the dark-haired girl at breakfast, but I can't face the idea of her laughing at me. I can't deal with another rejection.

I'm such a mess.

No. Don't be this person. So what if they're horrible – it's no different from the kids at Stonehurst Prep. And I endured a decade of a lot worse shit than this before Claws came along. I helped run a criminal empire for a year. I'm a fucking badass. So why am I letting the Orpheans get to me?

Here I am at this prestigious university on a full scholarship, a place I've *dreamed* of attending for years, and I'm falling to pieces because of a couple of stupid dudes with dumb posh haircuts.

No. Not happening.

The bells clang.

Before I know what's happening, my feet are moving, shuffling me across St. Benedict's Quad toward the church. I'm transfixed by the raindrops pelting the towering glass window, splashing prisms of color over the wet pavement. Something tugs at my heart, like a cord pulling taut, reeling me into the church. Not God, exactly. Not Father Pearce, either. Not this time.

I need sanctuary.

I want to look up at that vast nave with the towering columns and stern-faced saints and Jesus writhing on the cross. I want to feel small. I want to drive out this sick twisting in my stomach and replace it with *awe*.

What I wouldn't give for just a taste of that serene calm that washes over Sebastian's features when he prays? How amazing must it feel to know with such certainty that you're on the side of divinity?

How wonderful to feel safe within walls of sacred stone.

Maybe Father Pearce is on to something with this god stuff.

It's well past midnight, so I expect the church to be locked, but when I push on the wooden door, it creaks open. I walk inside, my gaze drawn upward by the stone columns and gothic arches. I don't think I've ever been inside a building that felt so *vast* before.

They're all here – Jesus and the saints and the Virgin Mary holding her babe. Their eyes seem to follow me as I take a step inside. They're familiar to me now from the stories Sebastian tells me, and for the first time, I feel a sense of uncanny calm wash over me. To sit with their still, serene faces and the stories of their miracles and suffering seems like the most natural thing in the world.

They're the closest thing I have to real friends.

For the first time, I haven't come looking for Sebastian. I don't want to talk to him right now. I just want to sit alone and think—

"Out of my way." An elbow hits me in the gut. I throw myself to the side as a figure darts from inside the confessional booth and barrels past me, heading for the door.

It's William.

He doesn't look back at me. I'm pretty sure he hasn't registered who I am. I catch a glimpse of his face as he flies for the door. For once, he's not perfect. His hair is rumpled, his mouth is set in a firm, tight line. His eyes blaze with blue fire.

He looks...*rattled.*

The door slams behind him, the sound echoing through the nave like a gunshot.

Is this why he wasn't at The Bad Habit with Monty? He was here, at midnight, making a private confession?

I can still feel the spot where he elbowed me. It feels like a brand – a mark on my skin reminding me that to people like him, I am nothing. I hate the fresh tears that pool in the corners of my eyes. This is old George, high school George. I'm in college now. I don't care what assholes like William Windsor-Forsyth think of me.

Except that the tears rolling down my cheeks tell another story.

Suddenly, the church feels too big, too open. I'm exposed on all sides. I run into the south transept and collapse into a pew at the back of Benet's chapel, lying down with my knees curled up so no one can see me. The alcohol and five servings of pork belly churn in my stomach.

Get it together. Get it together. Get it—

I scream as a face looms over me.

"Jesus Christ, you gave me a fright." I bolt up, hugging my knees as if they might be able to calm my pounding heart. Sebastian smiles down at me. His dark hair is framed by the flickering candles behind him, making him shimmer with a golden halo.

"Sorry to disappoint. I'm not the son of god," he says. "But I am wondering if you're okay."

"I'm fine." I fold my hands behind my head and try to act as though it's totally normal to be lying on a church pew at midnight on a Friday with breath reeking of gin and BBQ ribs. "I was just having a nap. My roommate's got friends in our suite and I just needed some quiet..."

My words trail off as a lump wells in my throat. *Don't cry. Don't cry in front of him.*

But my stupid fucking tear ducts don't listen. The sadness leaks out of me. I close my eyes because I can't bear to look at him as I lose myself in my own pathetic misery.

"George?"

Sebastian slides into the pew beside me. His hands cradle my neck, pulling my head into his lap so that I'm resting on his thigh. It feels so incredible that it makes me cry harder.

He wipes a strand of hair plastered to my cheek. His touch is so caring it makes my heart hurt. I'm the sick one, the broken one, the one with heat pooling between my legs. The one who wants to do filthy things to a priest and a teacher. No wonder no one wants to be friends with me – I'm fucked up.

I bite my lip. I want to talk to him. I want to talk to someone.

"George." His voice is so gentle. "Look at me."

That deep voice *does things to me*. I have to obey.

I open my eyes.

I'm greeted with Sebastian's nostrils. He's bent over me, closer than I expected, so close I can smell a hint of red wine on his breath mingled with his usual seductive scent. I gaze up into his face framed by the frescoes on the ceiling above, and the concern in his eyes makes me feel even worse.

"There's my girl." He strokes my cheek with his finger, tracing the trail William laid with his hand only two weeks before. His touch lights fire against my skin. "You're safe here, George. No one can hurt you within these walls, and no matter what you choose to say to me, your secrets will remain your own. You don't have to talk to me if you don't want to. I'm happy to sit with you while you talk to God. Or maybe you'd rather be alone—"

"No." I grab his wrist. "Please, stay."

He folds his fingers in mine. "Do you want to talk?"

I turn to him. I want to talk to him. I know that getting the words off my chest will feel better. But I can't bring myself to say the words in front of him, to admit that I'm a loser with no friends who wants desperately to go home. That would be one humiliation too many.

And if I open my mouth, I don't know what other secrets might topple out, such as how much I loved the way William kisses, with his hand cupping my cheek and his tongue demanding more. Or the fact that all I'm thinking about right now is what would happen if I leaned up and kissed Father Pearce.

He's my teacher.

He's a priest.

I can't.

I shake my head.

"I understand." He strokes his thumb over my knuckles. "Would it be okay if I prayed for you?"

I nod. I don't trust myself to speak.

I feel like the slightest breeze will send my body hurtling over the edge into a forbidden oblivion.

Sebastian squeezes my fingers in his. With his other hand, he makes the sign of the cross and bows his head. Silence descends over us, but the silence feels heavy with meaning, with anticipation. My skin prickles, and I feel certain we're no longer alone. I tilt my chin to look around, but I don't see or hear anyone else.

Sebastian speaks.

His words are a mixture of Latin and English and some other ancient language I don't recognize. In English he asks his God to watch over me, to take away my tears and my pain. He asks his Jesus to walk beside me, to be my friend and guide, and to carry me when I fall. There's a bit about redemption and eternal life, about Jesus' blood washing away sin and sadness. Every beautiful word falls through my skin, soaking my insides with a fragile, gossamer peace.

I can't move. I can't speak. I'm awed by this gift he's given me. No one has ever done something so beautiful for me before. I don't believe in God, but I know Sebastian does. He invites me inside his spiritual world and deems me worthy of his God's attention. His prayers aren't hollow platitudes – they feel deeply personal. Each word drips with the reality of life, of human emotion and suffering. I think that's what attracts me about the Church – how gritty and *real* Catholicism is with their litany of imperfect saints and their harrowing god nailed to his cross and their endless rituals to create meaning from chaos.

I know. I know. I'm here because of the naked priest. But somehow I feel I wouldn't be so drawn to Sebastian if he was an Episcopalian.

"Okay, come on." Abruptly, Sebastian lowers his hands and slides his legs out from beneath me. I sit up and rub my arms. The prickly feeling has gone. The church is just a building again. The air is just air. The divine has left the building. Sebastian beckons to me.

"What?"

He raps the back of the pew with his fist. "Come on, move those legs. I want to show you something."

I get to my feet, shakily, half certain Monty's going to jump out from behind the altar and drop pigs' blood on my head. Sebastian collects two taper candles in iron holders from the rack beside the altar and lights them. I follow him out the same door we go through to get to his apartment, except that instead of continuing along the corridor to his apartment, he unlocks the first door, revealing a curving stone staircase.

"We don't allow students up here unless it's part of a designated tour," he says, handing me one of the candles. In the light, his face looks grave. "There was a tragic accident up here a couple of years ago. So don't tell anyone you were up here or they'll make me attend a boring health and safety lecture."

I follow him as he ascends the stairs, his feet sure-footed on the worn stone. I keep my hand plastered to the wall, feeling my way in the gloom. Sebastian stops to show me cuts in the stone, believed to be the marks of swords clashing against the walls as the priests fought off the king's soldiers in this narrow space.

We climb and climb until my breath comes out in ragged gasps and my candle is a puddle of sweet-scented wax. We reach a narrow wooden walkway through the bells, behind the large clock face that faces out into St. Benedict's Quad. Sebastian points out the ropes where the bell-pullers used to work to ring the heavy bells on their headstock, and the new equipment. "It's all automated now. A shame." He points to a Latin inscription on the largest bells. "This explains that ringing this bell will drive away tempests and demons and call the faithful to prayer. At the monastery, the bells were rung each day to signal the Liturgy of the Hours, as well as during certain feast days and at a funeral. When Blackfriars became a university, the turret clock was installed, and now the bells chime on the hour to help students get to class on time."

Sebastian shows me a narrow space beneath the lock-out mechanism that prevents the bells from swinging. He has to turn his broad shoulders at a practiced angle to fit through the gap. He shuffles through, his feet in their laced boots disappearing into the darkness. A moment later, he thrusts a hand out for me. I waver for a moment, but then I accept it.

Big mistake. Sparks shoot along my arm as his fingers wrap around mine. My heart is in my throat as he pulls me through the narrow trapdoor. *Where is he taking me?*

Sebastian drags me into a narrow, darkened stairwell. He has to move sideways to fit, and even with my small size, the rough stone walls scrape my arms. At the top, he shoves open a wooden door. I suck in a breath as a gust of wind nearly bowls me backward. Sebastian's grip tightens, and he touches my arm with his other hand as I steady myself. My skin burns where he holds me.

It takes a moment for my eyes to adjust. We're on the roof of the tower, on a narrow platform that runs around the edge of the spire. Above us, the stars spread out their shimmering blanket across a witching sky. Sebastian leads me to the very edge, where the wind screams up from below and all that protects us from falling is a high stone parapet decorated with gargoyles. I lean against the cold stone and suck in deep breaths, bracing my body against the cold, against the protective feel of him behind me, as solid and immovable as stone.

I look down, over the school. Directly below us is St. Benedict's Quad, shrouded in near darkness, the only sign of life a few lonely windows lit and two students standing beside the Cloister Garden gate looking at a phone screen. Beyond, voices and laughter rise of Martyrs' Square as people congregate around the pub – tiny fleas hopping around their circus. Beyond even that are the empty athletic fields. At the edges, the wood encroaches, trees hiding the low spires and shading the buildings, so it seems like nature is chewing at the edges of the university.

"It's beautiful," I say. The wind whips my words away.

Sebastian sweeps his arm wide. "This parapet is designed to be defensive. No one can see you from down there. It's the perfect place to come and be alone with your thoughts, especially if you don't want to feel small."

"Do you come here often?" I have to yell to be heard over the wind.

He swallows. "I come up here to be closer to God."

That's right. *God.* The big kahuna, Frank Sinatra of the clouds, the angry guy in the sky, the potter of human clay with the twisted sense of humor. The very reason why this warm, tingly feeling in my body is so very, very wrong. I shuffle away from Father Pearce so our arms aren't touching.

"Sometimes, sitting with God can make us feel small and insignificant, like our problems couldn't possibly matter. But up here, I feel like I can reach out and touch him. And sometimes, especially when things are hard, we need to feel like God has a powerful hand on our shoulder." Sebastian fumbles in his pocket. "Hold out your hand."

I obey, because how could anyone not do whatever Sebastian Pearce says? His mouth quirks up into a mischievous grin as he places a large, old key in my palm.

"This is the key to the staircase. Any time you need to feel God's hand on your shoulder or his breath in your ear, come up here. You don't have to tell me. This is just for you. Share this with anyone and I'll make you sit through the health and safety lecture, and trust me, you do not want that."

He faces me. He's standing so close, his words whisper against my skin.

I can't speak. If I open my mouth, I won't have control over what comes out.

Sebastian folds my fingers around the key. I clasp it tight. It hums with Sebastian's warmth. This is the closest I'll ever get to him, but it's enough. It has to be enough.

"Thank you," I whisper. "For everything. I—"

Before I can say another word, his lips are on mine.

I try to pull away. I think that maybe he slipped, that somehow this is an accident. But he pins my hand and deepens the kiss, devouring me with desperate reverence, and I can't deny him.

I think I must've toppled over the edge of the tower, because

I feel weightless, the stars spinning around me, and the ground reaching up with midnight fingers to pluck every last shred of virtue from me.

This kiss is nothing like the languid softness of William's pouty lips. It's hard and needy, wicked and wrong and oh so right. Sebastian's fingers tighten around my wrist as the wild hunger he's stamped down with prayer and ritual takes over. His body slams into mine and drives my back against the parapet. The wind rushes around me, tugging at me, begging me to fall and let the night take me. But Sebastian's arms come up around me, hemming me in, protecting me while his lips trace the most sacrilegious fire across my mouth.

His tongue grazes mine, and I see stars at the edges of my vision – a vast universe unfurling inside me, stoked into being by the magic of his kiss. The moment hangs in the air, immortal, until I don't remember ever not kissing him. Until his kiss washes over me and I'm baptized by him, remade anew as a believer because only a man of God can kiss with his soul as well as his lips.

I'm kissing Sebastian.

What is this? What does it mean?

I have so many questions. The world feels like it's rolling away beneath my feet, but if I stop to take a breath, this moment will be over. We'll go back to being the priest and the student, the pure and the broken, the lost and forbidden.

I don't ever, ever want this to be over.

Please, kiss me until I believe you can be mine.

Kiss me until your God blesses our betrayal.

Kiss me until sin has no meaning.

As if he hears my prayer, Sebastian tears his lips from mine. He scrambles for purchase as he darts away, putting as much room between us as he can on the narrow platform. His chest heaves, and his wretched face breaks something inside me.

"I'm sorry," he cries.

"Please, don't be sorry—"

"No, you can't say that. This is unforgivable. I broke your trust, George. You came here tonight, hurt and vulnerable, and I...I..."

Sebastian doesn't finish his sentence. His face crumples with agony, so broken by his sin I don't think he can ever be put back together again. He pushes past me and bolts for the door, leaving me alone to face the bitter night.

13

Devil's Night.

All day the air fizzes with nervous energy. No one can sit still. Everyone stares at William or Monty or Tabitha or Diana – any of the Orpheans who bother to show up for their classes. Whispers swirl around them, stories of past Devil's Night shenanigans and speculation about tonight.

What are they going to do? What pranks will they pull? Who will be their victims?

I make surreptitious notes about some of the more salacious stories, in case they might be useful for my Khloe May project. I'm convinced it's no coincidence that Khloe and those other students disappeared on Devil's Night. But why those years and not other years? What's the connection to the Orpheus Society? I know tonight is my chance to get answers, but I'll have to be careful. I can't risk being caught breaking any rules, or my scholarship will be on the line.

I finish up in the forensics lab around 5PM and race to the dining hall to catch dinner just before they close the buffet line. There will be no Formal Hall tonight, so the place is busier than usual as all the students rush to eat and head back to their rooms before curfew. I scarf down some pumpkin soup and roast chicken and head to my staircase.

I'm not looking forward to spending the whole night alone with Keely. It doubleplus sucks because Halloween is tomorrow and it's my favorite holiday. Back in Emerald Beach, Claws and Gabriel and Eli and all our friends will be having dinner at Malloy Manor before heading out to Colosseum in elaborate costumes for some kind of debaucherous party. But Halloween isn't really a thing in England, and I have a feeling people will think I'm lame if I put up skull decorations on my door.

I wish I could head over to Sebastian's. I'd happily spend the night asleep in the chair in front of his fire. But ever since the kiss he's been avoiding me. He's done it in a polite, British way, which is almost worse – he messaged me to cancel our next three weeks of Greek lessons because of some youth ministry course Father Duncan wanted him to attend. Sebastian handed off his History of Religion classes to a doctoral student for the same reason. I've been so desperate to see him I even went to church services twice, but both times I had to sit through an hour-long Mass with Father Duncan that convinced me organized religion will never be my jam.

I cannot get his kiss out of my head.

I touch my fingers to my lips. Even though I just polished off a bowl of ice cream and sticky date pudding, I can still taste Father Pearce on me. And William, too.

Sebastian is so different from William in every way that matters. He doesn't take his privilege for granted. He wants to help people, make the world a better place. He's kind.

He's also completely impossible. And I have to stop thinking about him, about that kiss, even if it means thinking about another kiss with an equally impossible boy.

Urgh.

I stomp up the stairs.

I've gone from having a non-existent love life to making out with two of the hottest men on campus.

And I can't date either of them.

I shove open the door of my room. I've only got ten minutes to have a shower before Sally forces us all back to our rooms and locks the staircase door. I fumble for the light switch and reach for my toilet bag that's hanging on a coat hook and—

What the fuck?

14

Someone trashed our room.

Nothing has been spared. My laptop and podcasting equipment are smashed to pieces all over the floor, and my whole desk is buckled down the middle, as if someone hit it with a cricket bat. There are holes punched in the walls, filth smeared across the window, and the closet lies in splinters at my feet.

Keely's clothes have been torn from their hangers and piled on her bed. An acrid smell assaults my nostrils, and as I step closer I realize someone pissed on them. My feet crunch on broken glass as I walk over her smashed cosmetics, grinding swirls of colorful makeup into the carpet.

The only thing that isn't touched is William's artwork. The girl under the water stares back at me. Today she looks pensive, contrite.

My boot scuffs a torn piece of paper. I pick it up. It's the corner of the photograph of me and Dad I keep on my nightstand. The frame has been broken in three places, the glass crunching beneath my feet.

I panic when I can't see Sebastian's Bible amongst the wreckage. I drop to my feet, picking my way carefully through the ruined objects, and to my relief, my hand closes around it. It had been shoved under the bed. Not by me. Probably one of them kicked it under there by accident. At least it's been spared.

I crawl under my covers and prop the Bible on my legs, opening it to a random page. Most of the Greek is still gibberish to me, but a few words leap off the page. *Disobey...word of God...destroy...*

They destroyed everything.

I know who did this to our room. William. Monty. All their friends. Did it matter who swung the cricket bat and who slashed the pillows and who needed to pee? They did this because he told them to.

But why destroy Keely's stuff?

Keely is one of them. She's been sitting with them in the dining hall since the beginning of term. Monty makes her carry his books between classes and rub his feet while he works in the library. She's in. She's been tapped, anointed by their society of shitbags. So it makes no sense that her side of the room has more destruction – but then, she does own more crap.

And where is she? Keely should be back in our room now. That's what the rules said.

Below, I hear a noise in the quad. I lean over and peer out the window. Five figures in white robes stand on the rim of the well where the monks used to draw their water. At the sound of some kind of weird horn, they raise their arms and dump cans of colored paint into the ancient well. The paint splashes over the ancient stones, mixing together in vibrant patterns and splashing their pristine robes.

More robed figures rush in, hooting and laughing as they dip their hands in the paint and smear it over each other. They carry flaming torches, like they're medieval witch hunters.

What is going on?

Keely's not here and they destroyed her things. Now they're celebrating beneath our window.

It can only mean one thing. For some reason, they've turned against her. Maybe they found out that her family doesn't have the money or connections they thought it did. Maybe she said the wrong thing or slept with the wrong person. But for whatever reason, she's out. And she's not locked up indoors like she's supposed to be.

Don't go outside on Devil's Night. The warning repeats over and over in my mind as I watch those robed figures dance in their colorful destruction. One of them guzzles from the Champagne bottle and tosses it into the well.

I glance at the time on my phone, then the door to our room. Where is Keely? I'm positive she's not down there with them. It's hard to tell with the robes on, but they look like men with broad shoulders, except for the smallest figure who is far too short to be Keely. I watch as more robed figures join the group. They open containers of chemicals and pour them onto the pristine lawn. I can see smoke curling from the grass as the chemicals burn away the plants. They're writing something, but I don't know what. When they're done, they pass around Champagne bottles and smash the empties on the cobbles. The shards of glass sparkle in the moonlight, mirroring the destruction in our room. I don't think any of the new arrivals are Keely, either. I've lived in close quarters with her long enough to know her posture, her stature. And she wouldn't be there if she saw what they did to her stuff.

If Keely's not causing mayhem with the society, then they must have her trapped somewhere. I think of all those stories I've heard, and the missing women whose stories have been hushed up over the years.

Tonight is Devil's Night. The Orpheus Society is doing something awful to Keely, and no one is going to lift a finger to help her.

I set down my Bible and glance over at Keely's ruined bed. I don't know what to do. We're supposed to stay in our rooms all night.

But if the Orpheus Society intends to hurt Keely, I can't just let it happen. Women should look out for each other, right?

I swallow hard. My jacket hangs over the back of my chair. It's a thrift-store denim jacket I've sewed band patches all over. Keely wrinkled her nose when she first saw it. The left sleeve has nearly been sliced off, but I can work with that. It looks kind of rad.

Trying to ignore my heart pounding in my chest, I throw the jacket over my shoulders, slide my phone into my pocket, shove my feet back into my New Rocks, and crack open the door.

15

I poke my head into the hallway. It's eerily quiet. I can hear movies and music blaring from the surrounding rooms, but no doors slamming or voices calling out like usual. Every student really is obeying the order to stay in their rooms.

Except me.

I pull the door wider and step outside. The floorboards creak under my foot and I freeze, my heart racing, certain a white-cloaked ghoul will leap out from the darkness to attack me or Sally will write me up for breaking the rules.

But all that happens is my heart pounds in my ears.

Keely's last class of the day was on Shakespeare's tragedies, which is in Martyrs' Quad. I'll just head over there, check if she got stranded, and if not then I'll go to Sebastian. Kiss be damned. I'll make him listen to me. He'll be able to get staff or teachers to stop the Orpheus Society from hurting her.

It's time William and his cronies learned they can't just do whatever they please.

Sucking in a breath, I inch the door closed behind me so it doesn't make a sound. I click the lock into place and freeze.

No one comes out to yell at me. I creep to the end of the hall, past the bathroom and rows of doors. No one stirs.

Why does everyone obey this rule?

What hold does the Orpheus Society have over this school?

My boots clap and squeak on the stairs. The sound is deafening in the silent stairwell, but I don't stop. My heart leaps in my throat as I make my way past the junior common room. It's eerily silent – the chairs in disarray, the usually-blaring television silent and still.

The main door to our staircase is locked from the inside – as if they're more concerned about keeping people out, rather than locking the students in. Unease settles in my gut as I push open the door and step out into the quad. It's empty. The Orpheus Society has moved into the St. Benedict's Quad, leaving behind a coating of twinkling glass shards and a chemical smell from whatever it was they poured on the lawn. I decide to cut through the Cloister Garden into the theatre department – it means ducking through the corner of St. Benedict's Quad and risking someone seeing me, but they're too busy partying to notice, and it'll be quicker and less risky than walking the long way around.

I keep close to the buildings, ducking low so no one will see my head if they're looking out of their windows. I dart between the lights, being careful to avoid the shattered glass. I make it to the other side of the quad without raising an alarm.

I hang in the shadows of the archway, watching the Orpheans gather in front of the church. A few of them stream in from Martyrs' Quad, and I can hear another group partying in the old refectory, the flames of their torches flickering in the burned-out windows. I can't see a figure I recognize as Keely, and they don't seem to be holding anyone against their will. They pour Champagne over each other's heads and chant words in Ancient Greek. I catch a few I know that chill my bones – *demon...evil...ecstasy...sacrifice...*

I think I can see the glow of Sebastian's fireplace through his window, but it could be the flickering torches reflecting on the glass.

I wish I was inside with him, talking about God and the universe or studying demonstrative adjectives.

When I'm certain no one is looking this way, I suck in a deep breath and dart into the quad, sticking to the shadows as I approach the gate to the Cloister Garden. It makes a loud screech as it swings inward, and I curse Sebastian for not oiling it. My head whips around, but no one turns. No one cares.

For once, I'm glad to be invisible.

I leave the gate open and charge through the orange trees and herb borders. The tall gardens lean in toward me with looming terror. Shadows swallow the lights from the torches, and the enclosed walls and tall gardens warp their laughter until it sounds otherworldly. I creep around the still fountain (they turn it off at night to save power) where I first saw Sebastian's naked ass, and I feel the blush in my cheeks as I touch a finger to the still surface of the water.

Ripples burst beneath my finger, capturing the moonlight on their edges to create brilliant prisms of light. It's strange how our brains tell us that water is blue, and so we ignore the true spectrum of its beauty. That's what makes William's paintings so arresting – he uses color to capture truth. I think of the woman peering at me from beneath the surface, and not for the first time, I wonder what his painting of me looked like. But I know it's best I never find out. He probably drew me as a Gorgon—

Stop it. I can't think about William right now. I need to stay alert.

On the other side of the cloister, the door leading into the theatre department is locked. Of course it is. I curse myself for my stupidity. They've locked all the doors so no fool goes out when they were explicitly told not to – only they didn't count on George Fisher, the biggest fool of them all.

Keely, you better appreciate this.

An idea occurs to me. I fumble in my pocket. My fingers close around the key Sebastian gave me for the church. It's old enough to be original, which would put it at the same period as the Cloister doors. *I wonder...*

I fit the key in the lock and turn it. It clicks. I let out a little squeak of triumph before remembering I have to stay dead quiet. I go to clamp my hand over my mouth, but someone else gets there first.

"Caught you," a voice rasps in my ear.

16

My breath rasps against the hand. The skin is rough and broken, the fingers hot and sticky with Champagne. I struggle against the grip, but I'm tiny and the body of my attacker closes around me.

I try to remember what I learned in Antony's self-defense class, but panic claws at my mind, and I can't think of a thing except waking up from a nightmare with blood smeared on my thighs. I kick and flail, but it's useless. My attacker – a man, judging by the size of him and the deep voice – starts to drag me backward, and all I can think of is another night, another dark place, another boy who took too much from me.

I find that dark, rotten place inside me, the place where I keep the George who slays monsters by becoming them. I bite down hard on the man's fingers. He yelps and drops me, clutching his hand. I scramble to my feet, swallowing the metallic taste as I run for the gardens. I glance over my shoulder as he plunges his hand into the fountain. Crimson blooms in the water, and the moonlight reflects the planes of his face through the fluttering white hood.

Monty.

"The bitch bit me," he yells over his shoulder. The leaves rustle to my left, and another robed figure runs to him – a woman, I think. She takes his hand from the water and inspects it.

"She *bit* you? Like an animal? That girl is messed in the head. You should see all the weird things she keeps in our room," she says in a chirpy Irish accent. *Keely.*

I guess that means she's not in danger. But then why did they destroy all her stuff?

"We have to find her," Monty whirls around, peering into the gloom.

"If you want to ditch the party, we can go back to your room and I'll help you forget all about her." Keely raises Monty's finger to her lips and sucks it, rolling her tongue over the tip suggestively.

"No, no. We're going to teach Georgie Pie a lesson." Monty pushes Keely away. "She needs to know what do we do to plebs who think the rules don't apply to them—"

The gate creaks. Monty's head jerks around. In a flash, he darts into the trees, Keely hot on his heels. I swear they must be able to hear my heart pounding. I wait for what seems like an eternity. The gate creaks. An owl hoots. The sounds of the party distort into an inhuman cacophony, an ancient rite of fertility and fucking. I think I might be safe to sneak back to my room.

I rise to my feet, squeezing my body into the shadows of the trees. I peer around the side of the garden. Nothing. There's no one here. Monty's given up. The water in the fountain has calmed into a sheet of glass.

Go. Now. Run.

I make it five steps toward the gate before the figure steps out of the shadows in front of me. The white cloak furls around me as I'm grabbed and dragged. I try to force out a scream, but an arm around my throat turns the sound into a wheeze.

"Don't fight," an arrogant voice hisses in my ear. "Be still, and they won't find us."

William.

He drags me into a narrow crevice between the old cloister wall and the newer construction of the theatre building (New by British standards, which means the 17th-century.)

William tugs me deeper into the gloom. Rough stone digs into my back, and my chest crushes against his in the narrow space. I suck in a breath, but I can't find any air that doesn't contain him. Oil paints and dark chocolate invade my pores. William's sharp chin rests on the top of my head. His heart races against mine, and I realize he's shirtless under that thin white robe.

I can't breathe.

My chest heaves as I strain to hear what's going on outside. Footsteps clatter on the cobbles, voices calling to each other. Monty's back, and he's brought reinforcements. More Champagne corks pop, and glass smashes into the garden beds.

"I think she went this way," Monty calls, his cheery voice edged with danger.

"She's not here, Monty." I recognize Tabitha. Someone shuffles past our hiding spot, smashing a bottle against the bricks. I stiffen, but they can't see us this far back in the gloom. William's fingers curl around my arm.

"She won't have gone far. Georgie Pie, come out, come out wherever you are." Monty's singsong voice shoots ice through my veins.

"Forget about her, Monty," Abigail simpers. "She's not worth it. She hasn't seen anything that she could report. I want to get to the party. You said you had a surprise for us."

"Fine, fine. I don't want any of you to miss the surprise. You'll be positively *delighted*." Monty says something in Greek I can't hear. Their footsteps retreat. The gate swings on its creaky hinge. I try to wriggle free, but William clamps his arm in front of me, blocking me in. The moonlight reflects the deep pools of his eyes.

Our kiss replays over and over in my head, a constant reel of torture.

We listen to an owl hooting and the sounds of a party retreating into the distance. William's skin burns against mine. I try not to think about what's under his robe, but we've already decided I'm going to hell, so what's a little masochistic fancy?

It's only when William's shoulders sag and he lets out a ragged breath that I realize he's been on edge, too.

But why? Monty is his friend. Why did he hide me from them?

William drags me out of the crevice. My elbow scrapes along the stone, tearing another hole in my jacket. "Ow. What—"

"Shhh," he barks. Once we're back in the Cloister, he leaves me shivering beside the fountain and runs to check the gate, the robe flapping around his feet. He returns with an unsettled look on his aristocratic face, biting that pouty lower lip. His robe is damp with our sweat and torn in ribbons from the rough stone, and I can see every plane of his body beneath – and he is *not* wearing any underwear.

Fuck me dead.

"What are you doing out here?" His fingers tighten around my shoulder. "No, don't answer that. Curious George, has to stick her nose in where she doesn't belong."

Even though his words are cruel, there's a softness in his voice that I might've mistaken for admiration if I didn't know exactly who I was talking to.

My skin sizzles beneath his fingers. I have to struggle to keep my eyes focused on his face instead of sinking below. *Don't think about the kiss. Don't think about—*

"Someone trashed our room, and Keely didn't come back. I thought..." I squeeze my eyes shut. It's too hard to look at him and not remember his lips on mine, the way his body fit so right... "I thought you were going to do something awful to her."

"Keely's being initiated tonight," William says. "The Orpheans trash the possessions of those they tap. It's part of initiation. We've all been through it."

"Then why ruin *my* stuff?" A lump rises in my throat as I think of my torn books, broken equipment, and smashed photograph.

Monty's laugh echoes through the cloister. My eyes fly open. William shoves me into the garden, covering his body with mine. If anyone were to walk past, they'd see an Orphean having their way with someone in the bushes, and they wouldn't ask questions because the Orpheans own this school. The backs of my legs press against the concrete garden bed, a tree tickles my back, and I'm shoved between William Windsor-Forsyth's toned thighs. I can feel *everything*. Every clench of his muscles, every ragged breath against my ear, every pain-filled growl as he shifts uncomfortably. *He's hard,* I realize with a start as he rubs against me. *He's hard as fucking stone right now.*

That's not for me. It can't be. And yet—

I'm terrified of what he might do, but there's a part of my heart that's racing with excitement instead of fear. I tell myself it's our bodies reacting to the tense situation, but I'm not sure that's true.

Why is he hiding me?

Devil's Night magic hums in my veins. Or maybe it's the magic of having a dark prince between my thighs, his fingers tightening around my hips, his breath hot on my ear.

We both strain to listen. When it's clear the sound is from far away, carried by the crisp breeze and Monty's impressive vocal cords, William relaxes his grip, staggering back and running a hand through his rumpled hair. He doesn't turn away and doesn't acknowledge the tent-pole sticking out from his robe.

"Monty got carried away in your room, and of course Richard and Percy follow his lead. I tried to stop him, but it's hard to talk reason to a man with a cricket bat."

I think of the Bible shoved under the bed, and hope blooms across my chest.

Hope for what, I don't know.

"I'm taking you back to your room, and you have to stay there, like a good girl. You were never outside and you never saw anything, you got it? Some of the members treat Devil's Night infractions with deadly seriousness."

Clearly.

I follow William through the garden beds. He pushes the gate open with an ominous *creak* and peers around the deserted quad. "We're safe." He grabs my hand, and I try to ignore the sizzle that rockets up my arm, straight into my poor demented heart.

We walk hand in hand through the eerie silence.

"Where have they all gone?" I ask. Even though I whisper the words, I cringe at how loud they sound.

"There's a party." William turns his face toward the moon. "In a secret place."

"You don't sound so excited about it."

He frowns. "What do you know?"

We reach my staircase. William grabs the door I left unlocked and jerks it with enough force to rattle the hinges.

"I don't know anything." I shrug as we walk up the steps, trying to look casual even though my heart is dancing bachata in my chest. "All I'm saying is, if you want to blow off your party, I've got a desk drawer filled with junk food and a pack of cards and magnetic board games your friends didn't piss on. Rich boys like you always know how to play poker, or are the Windsor-Forsyths more of a Connect 4 family?"

That earns me a genuine smile from William. I blink in

surprise. When he smiles – *really* smiles – his whole face relaxes. There's a dimple on the left side of his face. With his hair mussed up and leaves and twigs sticking out, he almost looks... goofy. Like someone who'd actually be fun to beat at poker.

I blink again, and the smile is gone. His wall of arrogance is back up, and those piercing eyes of ice strip me bare.

We stop at my door. William reaches around me to push it open. His chest brushes mine, and heat flushes my cheeks as I remember his hardness pressed against my thigh.

"You don't know how tempting that offer is." His face was in darkness. "I need you to forget everything you saw tonight. Don't pull a George and start sticking your nose in Orphean business."

"I don't understand. What did I see? Apart from Monty being his usual dickish self—"

William parts his lips, and I'm certain he wants to say more. Instead, he shoves me through the door. I cry out as I stumble against the end of my bed and topple over my desk. Books fly in all directions, their pages toppling out where their spines had been severed.

"Stay away from me," he hisses, his eyes cold, hard. The door slams shut behind him, echoing like a gunshot.

I lie back on my slashed pillow and draw my knees up to my chest, trying to calm my beating heart.

What did I see tonight? What did I see?

17

Keely doesn't come back to the dorm that night.

I lie awake until the early hours, listening to the sounds of raucous laughter and more crashes and bangs from the quad as the Orpheans emerge from their party, hoping to hear the telltale click of the lock as she returns.

It's fine. She's not in danger. She's out partying with the Orpheus Society.

Staying out all night at college isn't exactly a crime. But I can't help the unease churning in my stomach as I think about William's hissed warning. Sleep isn't happening, and the curfew officially lifts at 6AM, so I rise with the sun, collect my books, and head down for breakfast.

I'm surprised to see the staircase abuzz so early in the morning. Everyone looks extremely well-rested (the bastards), and there's an air of anticipation.

"Did you hear a door slam last night?" Sally asks as she jogs past me on the staircase. "I'll kill whoever it was who disobeyed the rules."

"I didn't hear a thing." I shake my head. I follow the other students streaming toward the dining hall, trying to convince myself I was looking at their faces out of anthropological interest and not because I was searching for William.

I peer into the dining hall, and stop dead in my tracks.

What the fuck?

All the furniture – the long wooden tables, the buffet serving stations, the carved chairs, even the glass lanterns – hangs from the gothic rafters, suspended midair by wire and steel pins. The tables are set for formal hall with gold-rimmed china and silver cutlery, but floating ghosts or capricious fae are the only diners who could possibly reach them.

"Get out of here." Sally chases a group of students filming on their phones beneath the tables. "We don't know if the old beams will support all that weight."

"Bloody Devil's Night," a groundskeeper named John snarls as he sets up a ladder. "Every year we have more of this nonsense. This ceiling was designed by Christopher Wren, and those poxy bastards poked a bunch of holes in it."

"How did they possibly have time to do all this?" I ask out loud. This must've taken *hours*. I was out last night – I watched them all congregate in St. Benedict's Quad then disappear to their party. When did they find the time to do this?

"Oh, they don't do it themselves. Lord Sonny Jim and his chums won't lift a finger to do any actual work." John picks cutlery and china off the first table to stack into a plastic bin Sally holds up. "They hire laborers from the village. Pay them more than I earn in a month to do the heavy lifting and keep their traps shut. There's no point even calling the police – they buy them off, too."

Holy smokes. That kind of corruption is usually reserved for organized crime empires like the one Claws runs, not upper-crust university supper clubs. My true-crime podcaster senses tingle. "Do you think—"

"Out." Sally shoves me toward the door before I can ask my

questions. "No students in the dining hall until this is sorted. I won't have a squashing on my staircase."

All day, I encounter signs of Devil's Night shenanigans. The symbols burned into the grass in Cavendish Quad turn out to be a Greek poem worshipping Dionysos. Colorful bubbles burst from the Martyrs' Quad fountain. The old well in the middle of Cavendish is streaked with paint and piled high with junk. There's talk that an original Gainsborough painting in the master's office was defaced with a giant penis.

My stomach churns every time I pass these monstrous art projects. Maybe it's because before she opened her health food store my mother spent half her life cleaning hotel rooms in Emerald Beach for rich assholes. But all I see are the hours and hours of work the university staff will have to do to clean up, and the ancient buildings and priceless painting that have been defaced.

I hang out in the library and audiovisual lab as long as possible. If I sit in my room and stare at my ruined stuff and think about William's face when I asked him to come to my room last night, I'll go crazy.

Around and around my mind swirls. William and Sebastian. Sebastian and William. Two men who are completely wrong for me. Two men who've made it abundantly clear they have no desire to pursue anything with me. And yet... And yet the ghost of William's erection still jabs at my thigh, and I taste Sebastian's hunger every time I swallow.

What the fuck am I doing?

Eventually, hunger drives me out of hibernation. I find a table in the corner of the pub and eat my pie and chips, listening to the buzz of conversation around me. Everyone is talking about the Devil's Night pranks. Barely any of the Orpheans have shown themselves in class today – I've only seen Diana, and even she looks wan, stretched – not her usual ethereal self. I'm guessing they're all nursing killer hangovers.

When I finally drag my tired body up the staircase (why, why no elevators? Medieval architects have a lot to answer for), I pass a couple of women with overalls from a local cleaning company carrying boxes of clothing. I don't think anything of it until I throw open the door, and my mouth drops open in shock.

My room is spotless.

The broken glass swept up, the walls plastered and repainted, the piles of destroyed clothing carried away. New doors on the closet, new desks, new bedding and pillows on both our beds. Keely's remaining shoes stacked neatly on her rack.

From her spot over Keely's bed, the woman under the water watches me with a knowing gaze.

I stand over my new desk, my knees trembling. On top is a stack of textbooks – not my ruined secondhand ones, but brand new copies for all my classes, and a couple of the recommended reading books I planned to check out of the library since I couldn't afford to purchase them. It's then that I notice a large, white box on my bed, tied up with a bow.

I tiptoe over to my bed, too frightened to touch the box in case it's a bomb or a trap. I lift the corners of the bow gingerly, but nothing happens.

I fumble in my pocket for my phone and scan my list for Claws' number. I hit VIDEO CALL. It's mid-morning in California, and she picks up on the second ring. Her face fills the screen, Ice Queen eyes glaring at me with interest while a black cat curls around her shoulder, and I feel a pang of homesickness.

"Someone broke into my room and cleaned it," I say. "And they left me a present. Should I open it, or is it a bomb?"

"If you're worried about a bomb, why the fuck are you calling me instead of running for cover?" She sounds exasperated as she untangles the cat from her golden hair. "Aren't you taking a bomb-defusing class at that fancy school of yours?"

"It clashed with my History of Religion tutorial." I turn the camera so she can see the present. "I don't think it's a bomb. But I'm afraid of what it could be."

I hear papers shuffling in the background. "Eli's at some zoo in Boston, rehoming the lions, so I'm stuck doing the accounts. Who knew running a criminal empire was so *boring*. Please distract me by rewinding and telling me the whole story. Someone broke into your room to *clean* it? And left you a not-bomb? Crooks sure are different in Jolly Old England."

In a breathless whisper, I explain everything that's happened – from the moment I met a naked priest to William's body pressed against mine in the garden. Claws listens intently, stopping me every now and then to ask questions, and I can practically hear her mind whirring over the shambles I've made of my life.

"You telling me you've made not one, but *two* hot, unavailable men fall at your feet to worship your awesomeness?" she laughs. "George, you're something else. Open the damn box."

I prop my phone up against my pillow so Claws can see. I tug the ribbon and lift off the lid. Inside is a brand new laptop and podcast setup – a professional-level microphone and headset, nestled on a bed of American candy. I'd never be able to afford this equipment in a million years. On top of the mic box is a beautiful glass photo frame, just the right size for the picture of my dad.

I lift out the laptop case and a stack of envelopes fall out.

"You're killing me here," Claws moans. "Open them."

I tear open the first one and pull out a £500 gift voucher for New Rock Boots, and £2000 for Vivienne Westwood.

Holy, shit – Vivienne Westwood.

I feel lightheaded. I sink onto the bed, my stomach churning. Claws is calling out to me but I can't hear what she says.

What is this?

Someone paid to tidy up the mess in my room. But more than that, they're trying to make amends for the things that were destroyed.

They took note of my style. They know the classes I'm taking. They considered what I might actually like.

Keely? But there are three more envelopes in here, for an online music shop and another couple of punk clothing labels. I know Keely's financial situation isn't as great as she wants people to believe – that's why she has to share a room with me. Besides, whoever did this actually thought about *me* and what I might like. And Keely doesn't give a shit about me.

My mind flashes to William, but I shake it off. I don't want to read into this. Because this is actually thoughtful, in a fucked-up, stalkerish way. And I can't entertain the idea that William Windsor-Forsyth might actually be a thoughtful person, that his erection in the garden and that haunted look in his eyes when I asked if he wanted to hang out were anything other than more efforts to fuck with me.

But if not William, who else can it be?

Sebastian.

He knows a lot about me from our conversations during our Greek tutorials. He would be thoughtful like this. But we haven't spoken since the kiss, so he had no way of knowing my room had been trashed.

William or Sebastian? Sebastian or William?

Why do they both have to be so...

Argh!

I throw myself down on the new bedspread. It feels like butter against my skin. My head spins. I need advice, and I don't have anyone to turn to at Blackfriars. I hold the phone on my chest as my friend cracks up laughing. "I'm in so much trouble."

Claws puts her hands on her hips and gives me this look like she'll reach through the phone and shake me. "George Fisher, you've never been in trouble a day in your life, and that's tough when you're best friends with a crime boss. It sounds to me like you have a thing for two guys, and if they both took their heads from up their asses they'd see they have a thing for you, too. That's not a big deal. I mean, yes, a priest and a prince – you sure can pick them. But it's not as if you used the wrong Latin noun declension, which I know is a hanging offense at that ridiculous school."

Despite myself, a laugh bubbles up inside me. I miss her so much. "Okay, so *maybe* I do kind of like them. *Maybe* Sebastian makes me feel safe and William makes me feel reckless. *Maybe* I'm thinking about my priest teacher and a posh wanker all the fucking time. But they don't feel the same way. Sebastian hasn't talked to me since the kiss, and William pulled that horrible stunt in art class and he blackmailed me with a kiss—"

"Like I said, heads up asses."

"—and it's all completely pointless. Sebastian has his vows and William has his millions and his secret society and neither of them will throw that away for me."

"I wouldn't be so sure." Claws smiles. "And here's the thing I learned from being with Noah, Eli, and Gabe. You don't have to choose. Not choosing is way more fun."

We chat a little longer and then I hang up and lie back on my bed. My fingers find one of the packages of candy, and I tear it open and pop a few in my mouth. They taste like home, like cool nights sitting in trashy movie theatres with my dad watching a new independent horror film, and my stomach twists with homesickness.

I find the picture of my dad, slide it into the new frame, and prop it on my nightstand. My gaze falls on Keely's bed. I haven't seen her all day. Even though her remaining things are tidy, it doesn't look like she's been here. Her bed is cold and undented, her few remaining clothes haven't been riffled through, and today's gross green smoothie sits unopened in the fridge.

She's not here because she's sleeping in someone else's bed.

I force myself to think of her and William, together. Kissing, touching, moaning, lying naked in his bed and laughing about me. I imagine them older – a wedding, children, a big castle in the country. I imagine him gripping her neck the way he did to me, stealing a kiss with such wild abandon I thought I might never breathe again.

I spit out the candy. I feel sick.

I touch the spot on my head where William's chin rested as he held me in that crevice. I can still feel the weight of him, the *warmth* of him, how safe he made me feel with his arm wrapped possessively around me. But I don't understand what he was protecting me from.

Forget everything you saw tonight, he said.

But what did I see?

18

Keely doesn't return to our room the next day.

Or the next.

Her fancy catalogs and magazines clog our mail cubby, so even though she's yelled at me before about collecting hers, I bring them in and stack them on her bedside table.

She's not in her classes, either. She's not in the back of History of Religion with the other Orpheans, and I don't see her at The Bad Habit or around the quad.

I'm worried.

One night of drunken revelry and a bit of crumpet I get (thanks to my friend Gabe for the excellent metaphor). Three days without a word or sighting – while her so-called friends are still roaming the campus as if they own it – seems off. Keely would want everyone to know she was in with William and his friends.

I don't *want* to be the dork snitching on her fun, but I can't help the niggling doubt creeping down my spine. It's the same feeling I got when I held my dad's ashes. I can't help but think of those other students who disappeared on Devil's Night, or Khloe May's body still missing.

When I return to my dorm after lunch to pick up my Criminology books, and there's still no sign of Keely, I make my decision.

I know exactly where William will be. His Greek class ends at the same time as my Criminology tutorial, and I always see the Orpheus Society congregate for drinks or a picnic while they work on Father Duncan's compositions. I sneak out of class five minutes early, cut across Martyrs' Quad, and duck through the narrow stone archway to wait for him. I hear his group approaching – it's impossible to miss Monty's loud voice and Abigail's throaty laugh. Diana's there too – she tugs on Monty's sleeve, and her voice rises in pitch as she grows agitated. "It's quite one thing for you to indulge your peculiar tastes, Monty, but you shouldn't drag the rest of us into it. This is Sardinia all over again, only this time—"

I step out in front of them. Diana stops in her tracks but Monty surges forward, his elbow driving into my shoulder, knocking my books to the ground and nearly sending me flying after them.

"Oops, sorry, George, old chap. I didn't see you there."

Monty doesn't look sorry. He looms over me with this expression that can only be described as *hunger*.

The air sizzles with tension, but not the kind that lights my body on fire whenever Sebastian or William touch me. This is the tension of a hunter savoring his kill, walking on a knife edge between mercy and brutality.

I don't stoop to pick up my books. That's how victims end up with their underwear pulled over their heads. I stare at William with what I hope is a completely neutral *I-didn't-feel-your-erection-jabbing-my-thigh* expression. "Can I talk to you a sec?"

Monty stares. "No no, little Georgie. We don't keep secrets. Whatever you have to say to our William, you can say to all of us."

"Monty, it's fine. George just wants to borrow a book. Isn't that right?" Before I can reply, William steps away from his friends and beckon me to follow. We walk slowly toward the entrance to Martyrs' Tower. I notice his shoulders are stiff, his walk a little stilted, like he's aware they're watching our every move.

"What do you want?" he hisses. "I told you to stay away from me."

I glance over my shoulder. Richard has joined Monty and Abigail, and he's delighting them both with an impression of me in their art class. "Keely hasn't come back to our room. It's been three days. I'm worried." I swallow. "Is she...with you?"

"Forget about Keely," he snaps.

"Look, your love life is your own business. I don't care." The words taste like soap in my mouth. "All I want to know is that my roommate's okay."

A storm brews on the edge of William's eyes. "She's not with me."

Why, why do those words make my heart feel like butterflies?

"Did you see her leave your Devil's Night party? Who was she with—"

William fumbles in his satchel. "Look, I put your room back together, so you don't have any reason to complain."

"You did that?" I can't hide the surprise in my voice. "You gave me all those vouchers? And that frame? But why—"

"You need to stop asking questions about Keely. Just forget about her."

I snort. "Saying that makes me more determined to find out. It's got something to do with Monty, right? That's why you hid me in the Cloister Garden. I know you and your friends think you have free rein to do whatever the fuck you like at this school, but a girl is missing and—"

"She's not missing. It's none of your business, so just drop it.

I'm late." He thrusts a book into my hands. "Take this, so Monty doesn't annoy me with a million questions. Consider this your last warning – don't talk to me again."

"But—"

William turns away without looking at me and hurries off toward the Tower, satchel flapping against his long legs as he marches across the grass in blatant violation of the STAY OFF THE LAWN signage. Monty and the girls chase after him, but William doesn't look back or wait.

I still don't have any idea where Keely is. But I did find out one useful fact.

Actually, two facts.

One. William had my room cleaned and repaired. He gave me that thoughtful gift. I can't reconcile the stack of vouchers and the new laptop with the cold way he just looked at me, but thinking about it makes a warm ache bloom in my stomach.

Two. His highness is *rattled.*

Just like he was back in the Cloister Gardens. Something that happened on Devil's Night frightened William Windsor-Forsyth, and I'm going to find out what it is.

"I'D LIKE to report a missing student."

The porter looks up from her computer, her mouth set in a firm line. She's the same woman I talked to about getting into Duncan's Greek class, and from the way she rolls her eyes, I know she recognizes me.

"I'm not a lost and found service for drunk students," she snaps.

"I understand that. My roommate, Keely O'Sullivan, hasn't been back to her room or to any of her classes since Devil's Night. Has no one else reported her missing?"

"On Devil's Night?" she narrows her eyes. "She's one of them lot, I presume."

"If you mean the Orpheans, I think she wanted to be. They trashed our room, which I suppose means she's in. But they won't tell me anything about that night. I think they're trying to hide—"

"We don't take attendance at this school." She scribbles something on a pad. "If Ms. O'Sullivan doesn't want to go to her classes, we can't make her."

"I know that, but—"

"Look, you American students are too used to being babysat. You're in Great Britain now, missy. We expect students to manage their own schedules and take care of their own affairs. Now, your friend will be back when the drugs run out or she's had enough of whatever lad she's shagging. Perhaps she got sick of having such a silly twit as a roommate." She turns away. "Get out of here. I'm busy."

I step out of the porter's office, reeling at her callousness. I'm more certain than ever that something is going on.

But what?

Where the fuck is Keely?

19

Father Pearce's History of Religion class is pure torture. He looks amazing as he strides around the lecture hall in his black trousers and perfectly-tailored shirt. But it's more than just the way he looks that stops my breath – it's his whole presence. He's so comfortable and confident in himself, in who he is and what he stands for, but not in the dickish way William and Monty are. I hang off his every word as he leaps between topics, going from fertility goddesses to the Roman calendar and the story of Maui fishing the country of New Zealand from the ocean. His voice is pure milk and honey.

He doesn't look my way the entire class. I think of nothing else but our kiss and that wild look in his eyes when he fled the roof. Is Claws right? Did something happen between us that wasn't just a mistake?

I linger after his lecture in the hope I can catch him. I desperately want to tell him about Keely and about William's gift. I want to ask his advice. I miss him – not just his lips, which I know I can't taste again. I miss his friendship. But he slips out a fire exit before I can push my way toward him.

My next tutorial is on the Social History of Cinema, and it's torture for completely different reasons. The topic could be interesting, but Professor Fletcher looks like he's just woken up from a nap and can't quite remember what he's doing here. His voice drones on as he fumbles his way through his slides. I navigate away from my notes file, where I've written the words 'where is Keely?' thirty-six times, and pull up an old episode of *Bones*. I slip my headphones in my ears as surreptitiously as I can, hiding the cord under my jacket, and before I know it I'm embroiled in a fascinating forensic mystery.

Behind me, I hear someone shift in their seat.

I didn't think there was anyone behind me. My heart hammers, thinking it's Monty ready to embarrass me in front of everyone again. But when I peer over my shoulder, I see the girl from the dining hall. She's leaned forward over her papers, her eyes flicking across my screen. She snaps back when she sees me looking at her. I might be imagining the faint flush on her cheeks.

I grin at her and turn back to my screen. A few keystrokes, and I've put on the subtitles. I angle the screen so my head's no longer in her way. For the rest of the lesson, we watch *Bones* together in companionable silence.

When Professor Fletcher finally finishes up, I'm almost sad to snap my laptop shut and pack up my things. "Hey," I wave to the dark-haired girl. "Do you want to maybe get a coffee?"

The girl shakes her head. My heart plummets to my knees, but she says in a thick British accent. "No coffee, but I'm dying for a bevvy."

"What's a bevvy?"

She looks horrified I had to ask. "A pint, o'course."

Ah, yes, I'd forgotten. In America, you ask a potential new friend out for coffee. In Britain, no matter the time of day, you go for a beer.

Beer tastes gross, but I'm willing to make that sacrifice.

I follow her out of the tutorial room and across the quad to The Bad Habit, where she marches up to the bar, her black ponytail swishing down her back, and orders a pint of cloudy apple cider. She turns to me. "What are you having?"

"The same, I guess." I've never drunk cider in my life, but it's got to taste better than beer, right?

The black-haired girl pays for our drinks and a basket of fries (sorry, *chips*), and we settle into a booth in the corner. I nervously twiddle the zipper on my leather jacket, a million nonsense questions swirling in my head. When I get nervous, I tend to babble, and I'm trying to hold it back so she doesn't think I'm a complete loser.

Turns out I don't need to worry, because she's either a nervous babbler too, or she's been so desperate to talk to someone all the unused words come out at once. "Thanks for sharing your screen with me. I'm regretting signing up for that class. I thought learning film stuff would be boss, but all the films are antwacky and shite." She has a different kind of accent than William and Sebastian – not posh and fancy-sounding, but brash and badass. She tips her chips toward me. "I'm Leigh, by the way. Leigh Cho."

I accept a chip. "I'm George. What's antwacky mean?"

"Old-fashioned, and not in a good way. Like everything else around here." Leigh holds up her glass. "Cheers. Nice to finally talk to you, George."

We clink. I take a sip. Okay, cider is delicious. I've only spent five minutes in Leigh's presence, and already the world is a brighter place.

Leigh tells me she's from Liverpool (where the Beatles come from!), where her family has lived for three generations, since her great grandparents immigrated from Korea. "I never dreamed of going to a toff school like this. I thought I'd drop out after GCSEs to help my dad at his job as groundskeeper on an estate, but then the old man went and won the lottery. Eleven-million pounds in the bank and no idea what to spend it on. Changed our lives, not all of it for the better. That's why I don't talk to no one here – I don't want them to start begging or expecting me to act like a toff. But you seem alright."

She's second year, majoring in sculpture. ("Not antwacky shite. I'm into, like, natural forms and historical tools.") She talks a mile a minute, and sometimes she uses words I can't understand – "Trabs" for her sneakers and "The Ozzy" for the hospital (where she had to go in the first week of term when she fell down her staircase after too many bevvies). Seeing her across the silent dining hall, I took her for a quiet, scholarly type. But now that I'm facing her across the table I see she's wearing a faded Rolling Stones t-shirt under her red blazer and she's got some great tattoos winding down her forearms. I think we've both been starved of people to talk to, because we spend our whole conversation exclaiming loudly over everything we have in common.

We have the same taste in music, and she's a huge fan of my friend Gabe's band Octavia's Ruin. I tell her a story about one of Gabe's last concerts where a guy showed up in the crowd wearing a white robe and carrying an enormous wooden crucifix, so Gabe invites him up on stage where the two of them sing a cover of Iron Maiden's *Number of the Beast*. Leigh's so delighted she slaps the table and knocks her cider over. Sticky liquid splashes off the end of the table just as a jock walks past with an armload of drinks.

"Watch it, bitch," the guy snaps at her. "If you can't drink properly, go back where you came from."

"You mean back up your mother's arsecrack?" Leigh flashes him the finger, then flips her hair over her shoulder. "You'd think this place would be all liberal and woke, but it's full of fucking meffs."

And I see that however hard it's been for me fitting in here, it's been a hundred times worse for Leigh, who might be from this country but is still made to feel like she doesn't belong. But she orders another round of drinks, allowing his stupidity to roll off her back like water off a duck. I want to change the subject, so when she mentions she's into true crime, I tell her about my podcast, and she squeals because she's listened to it. ("You're proper famous. That's so boss.")

So I tell her about the problem I'm having finding a topic for my AV project. "I found out that this girl disappeared on Devil's Night ten years ago. They think she committed suicide but no body was ever found, and there have been others over the years who've gone missing on Devil's Night. I'm investigating her case for the next season of the podcast, but something about it isn't clicking."

"'Course it ain't. That story's not personal. Your listeners heard you tell the story of your father's death. They might've come out of morbid curiosity, but they stayed because of *you*. You made them care, and the only way you'll make them do that again is if you choose another personal story. So come on, George. Cough up. What skeletons have you got in your closet?"

I shove my hands under the table so Leigh can't see the tremble in my fingers as I think about Claws and Alec and everything that happened last year. I see a flash of Brutus' face twisting as he burned on his funeral pyre. Flash again, and I'm listening to Alec's screams as he's boiled alive inside the brass bull. Another flash, and I'm on the roof of the church tower, kissing Father Pearce.

Some skeletons need to stay buried deep.

"You're right." I wring my hands. "I need to find the personal angle."

Leigh jerks her finger at the door, where Monty and William and Richard are entering. A bunch of first-year girls scramble out of the way to give them their usual table, where they sit like royalty presiding over a feast. "Maybe you do a story about being tortured by a bunch of rich wankers."

"So you know—"

"—that the Orpheans have it out for you?" Leigh glares at William's back, and I know then we're going to be friends for real. "Everyone knows. Can you believe their bollocks? The whole school shuts down for a night so they can have a shitty party. They're a bunch of tosspots— well, not Diana. She's in my fine art tutorials and she's proper lovely. I can't believe she hangs out with those twats."

"Do you study under Madame Ulrich?" Heat creeps into my cheeks at the thought that Leigh might've been in figure-drawing class that day. I don't remember seeing her but I did get distracted by William, and being stark fucking naked...

"Aye. She's a proper old bag." Leigh waves her hand. If she was in that class, she's not telling me to save my dignity, which I appreciate. "But don't change the subject. We're talking about those toffs in the Orpheus Society. Did you hear they poisoned the seven-hundred-year-old oak tree down the end of the cricket pitch? That's criminal. I wish someone would bring them down. But that little club of theirs will close ranks to protect them and their secrets."

I wished that, too. I wished someone would show them that their actions had consequences, that people aren't ants to be crushed underfoot but living, breathing parasites that can worm into your skin and chew your soul to pieces from the inside out, the way William has done to me. But the only way to do that would be to actually be on the inside, and I will never achieve that.

I can never beat the Orpheus Society. The only thing to do is to don my armor – my punk band t-shirts, my tattoos of things that make me smile, my multi-colored hair, the knowledge that I pull myself out of bed in the morning when my whole heart screams 'no,' all the things that make me remember who I am – and raise another pint of cider with my comrade-at-arms before we go out there to have our heads knocked off.

IT'S late by the time Leigh and I leave the pub. The place has started to get loud as students congregate after cricket practice and debating society. The Orpheus table is the loudest of them all, as hangers-on crowd around Monty and William and the others, shouting them drinks and doing stupid stunts to try and catch the attention of the anointed.

I walk Leigh back to her staircase in St. Benedict's Quad. She throws her arms around me in a hug so fierce it drives the wind from my lungs. "I'll see you at breakfast?"

"You got it," I wheeze.

She waves and jogs up to her room, leaving me alone, surrounded by the touch of her scent. Cigarette smoke and wild herbs, earthy and breathy and a little bit pagan. My new friend.

My smile fades from my lips as I realize I'm staring up at the church, pausing on the light shimmering in the stained glass windows – Jesus and the Virgin Mary surrounded by violent vignettes of saints. Michael the archangel battling a horned devil, St. George slaying his dragon, Thomas à Becket with a sword through his head, St. Benedict wearing his black habit and carrying a poisoned chalice, And there's St. Sebastian, his body pierced with arrows…

Before I know it, my shoulder leans against the heavy wooden door, pushing it inward and stumbling inside. Through my cider haze, I register rows of candles flickering at the altar and in the chapels on either side of the transept, the source of the light I'd seen.

Tonight the church feels too large and exposed. My skin tingles, flayed open by the rawness of the secret loneliness I revealed to Leigh, and all the secrets I still hold close. My stomach churns with the memory of the tower, and the key in my pocket weighs as heavy as the stones that killed St. Stephen.

I can't go up there tonight, not when so many things hang unsaid between me and Sebastian.

At the idea of confronting him, I taste bile in my mouth. *What am I doing here?*

The church feels too holy, too *good* for the evil in my heart. I duck into the confessional booth, wrapping myself in the cloistered darkness and sucking in breath after breath until my vision swims with red lights.

A moment later, I hear a bolt slide, and the rustle of clothing as someone settles themselves into the other side of the booth.

The air scents with frankincense and cinnamon.

A match strikes. A candle flickers to life, haloing a silhouette on the other side of the screen.

My skin feels like tissue paper, thin and combustible, like the heat emanating from his body is enough to burn me to ash.

My mouth goes dry. I've spent the last few weeks thinking of nothing but him, but now I'm here, I have no idea what to say. The words stall on my tongue, weighed down by his God and his vows and the surety that I cannot, *will not*, sit in his sanctuary and ask him to break his promises.

Silence stretches between us, wide and empty, devoid of holy intervention.

I can't take it any longer. I settle for the movie cliche. "Forgive me, Father, for I have sinned."

"Not you, George," a deep voice says. "You're not the sinner here."

His voice cracks on the last syllable. I hate hearing him so tormented. That's what he sounds like – a lost soul, beyond the reach of his God. All he did was kiss me, and it was the most amazing kiss. Nothing about him could ever be so wrong, so irredeemable, that he could lose his holiness. If that's true, then his God doesn't deserve him.

"It's my fault," I say. "I kissed you back. I wanted to kiss you back."

A moan tears from his throat. The confessional booth no longer feels cloistered and safe. There's no air in here that isn't filled with him.

"I took advantage of you, George. You were upset and vulnerable. You came to me for comfort and I..." He can't say the words. His head bows, and I hear the click of rosary beads in his fingers. "Never mind what the university will say when they find out I was fraternizing with a student, but I made my vows and I believe in them. I betrayed God and my faith and the students I came here to serve."

"You speak like you're going to tell them what happened."

"I'm going to confess to Father Duncan tomorrow. I've prayed long and hard over this, and it's the right thing to do. I sinned and I must accept my penance, even if that means being sent far away from here, from what I came here to do."

He breathes hard, and I can taste his fear in the hot, sticky air.

"And what about my penance?" I ask. "Seeing you has been one of the only bright spots in my time here. You're my only friend, and the last couple of weeks without you have been torture. I came here tonight because something wonderful happened. I think I made a new friend – a girl named Leigh. And my first thought was how much I wanted to tell you. I feel safe with you, and I don't want to lose you."

He laughs – a bitter, cold laugh that makes me think too much of William. "You think I'm safe, George? You think that because I wear the cloth I'm not a man underneath, a man who right this moment is dreaming about smashing the screen between us, dragging you onto my lap, and plunging my hard cock inside you until you scream my name?"

His words are so un-Sebastian-like that it takes a moment before they register. When they do they pool heat in my belly, between my legs. I press my thighs together. And maybe it's where we are, but I'm so so tempted to confess all the things I wish he'd do to me.

"I never doubted my path before," Sebastian continues, the rosary clinking in his hands. "But then you walk into that garden and I'm made dizzy by you, by the divine you carry inside you. By your quiet strength and your curiosity and your kind heart. Being near you is an ecstasy that feels blessed by God's kiss, like wanting you is the most holy, most perfect thing I can do."

"No one's ever felt that way about me," I whisper.

His voice sounds strained. "I find that very hard to believe."

"It's true. I had one boyfriend last year, for a little while. But we broke up before it got serious." Isaac was a metalhead stoner I had a crush on for the longest time. He was such a sweetheart, but we never got past a couple of heavy make-out sessions before I broke up with him. I told Claws it was because I wanted to keep him safe from becoming collateral damage in her gang-war, which is true, but only half the story. I was scared of the way I felt about him, of the giddy, lighthearted sensation when I was around him that had nothing to do with the weed. I worried I'd fall so hard for him that I'd lose myself, and I end up stuck in Emerald Beach forever.

But now, with Sebastian (and with William, God save me), I *want* to run headfirst into heartache and damn the consequences. I survived Dad's death, the bullying at school, even cleaning the blood off Mom's kitchen cabinets after that guy tried to kill me. Maybe losing myself would be kind of fun.

"You're a virgin." His fingers rake the metal screen like he's trying to make good his fantasy of tearing it away. "Fuck. This is...fuck."

"You do so much good here. The students adore you. They trust you so much more than Father Duncan. And..." I'm grasping at straws, but something tells me I've read the situation correctly. "William needs you. I need you."

The only sound for a long time is Sebastian's husky voice murmuring Latin prayers, and the *clack-clack-clack* of his rosary beads as he battles with his immortal soul.

"Are you asking me to lie to my confessor?" Sebastian asks, a hint of dark humor in his voice.

"I'm asking you not to ruin the good you're doing because of one mistake." My shoulders shake, and I'm dangerously close to breaking into tears. "I won't kiss you again. I promise. I don't want to lose you as a friend."

"I don't want that, either."

"So we agree? We go back to the way things were. We have our Greek lessons like usual, and no more being alone together on the roof, and you don't have to run away every time you see me."

Hope flutters in my chest. Sebastian clicks his beads again. Finally, he sighs.

"Come outside."

I'm almost relieved to step out of the heavy air into the lofty nave. My eyes fall on the stained glass of St. Sebastian. Moonlight haloes his serene face and the arrows that stick from his body like porcupine quills. *Sebastian the martyr.*

A moment later, the curtain flutters and Father Sebastian Pearce towers over me. He's clothed in darkness, and his eyes twinkle in the flickering candlelight.

In that moment, I'd sell my soul to the devil to kiss him again.

"Friend," he smiles, offering a hand. "I"m glad you came

tonight. Will you stay awhile? I'll make some tea, and you can tell me all about this new friend you made."

Friends.

I accept his hand. I try to ignore the heat sizzling down my arm and the heavy ache between my legs as he leads me around the church to lock the door and snuff the candles.

There's nothing wrong with a teacher being friendly with a student, or a priest passing the time with one of his flock.

As long as we don't kiss again, everything will be fine.

Right?

20

Another week passes and Keely still hasn't shown up. I start kicking my boots off on her side of the room and laying out my toiletries across the full width of the vanity, half hoping my blatant disregard for her rules will somehow bring her back from the unknown to kick my ass.

I don't particularly want to talk to the snotty lady at the office again, and William was no help, and I need to do *something*. Never mess with the roommate of a true-crime podcaster with criminal underworld connections. I make one call to a guy I know, and It takes him all of twenty minutes to hack into the university server and get me the names and numbers of Keely's family in Dublin. I call her parents, but no one picks up, so I leave a message and tell them to call me back. It's not much, but it's something.

I can't take the silence of our room any longer, or the way the woman under the water glares up at me. Today, her brow looks furrowed in disappointment, as if she can't believe I'm giving up on Keely already.

I'm not giving up, I promise.

I head to the library, to continue my research into Khloe May and the Orpheus Society. I know Leigh's right – I'm not connected enough to the case to make it work for the podcast, which means I'm basically wasting research time I should be spending on coursework. But it's too similar to Keely's disappearance for me to be able to let it go.

When I get to my usual corral in the St. George Reading Room, I discover someone has already set up right next to me, in blatant defiance of library etiquette, which says not to encroach upon another user's unofficially-claimed territory.

This isn't an accident. William Windsor-Forsyth knows exactly where he's sitting and why. He wants to get a rise out of me, and I don't want to give him the satisfaction; but also, I can't read about the Orpheus Society with him spying over my shoulder.

I hover in the doorway and watch him work while I decide what to do. His lip curls with concentration as he taps his pen against his paper. He's translating Greek, and he's crossed out the same sentence four times. I creep across the room as quietly as I can and peer over his shoulder.

"It's a past participle," I say.

He jumps. "What are you talking about?"

"There. A past participle." I tap the paper. "You're trying to use the perfect, *has sacrificed*, but it would be more correct to use pluperfect, *had sacrificed*."

"The pluperfect?" He flicks a messy strand of russet hair behind his ear and stares at me as if I'm a complete stranger.

"You mean you haven't studied the pluperfect yet?" I arch my eyebrow. "Don't tell me Father Duncan's super exclusive class is more about drinking port and mocking the poor than getting any actual work done?"

William doesn't dignify my question with an answer. Instead, he tugs my Liddell and Scott from the stack of books in my arms, running his finger along my colored tabs with a sensuality that makes my knees weak. "You know Greek?"

Instead of answering him, I change the subject. *Two can play this game.* "Keely still hasn't come back to my dorm. Do you know anything about that?"

His jaw tightens. "I told you to drop it."

"Too late. I've already reported it to the office. I called her family. And I'm going into the village today to talk to the police myself. In fact, I think I'll head there now. Oh, and here's your book back."

It takes all my self-control to drop the book he gave me on his papers and turn away from him, to pretend I'm done with this conversation. Apparently, William Windsor-Forsyth isn't used to being dismissed. He thrusts his arm across my chest, pulling me off balance until I'm sitting on his lap. My books slide from my hands and topple to the floor. I'm very aware that my pleated tartan skirt has risen up my hips.

Every part of my body hums with raw, vulnerable lust. His hand brushes the small of my back and his pouty lips part ever-so-slightly. I can feel his body stirring, and I don't fucking know what this is, but I don't want it to stop. I *know* I'm getting my heart all twisted up by this dangerous boy. And I don't even fucking care.

"Listen," he whispers, darting a look over my shoulder before fixing those cold eyes on me. "You shouldn't have done any of that. You'll make things so much worse."

"Why not?" I whisper back. "You haven't given me any good reason not to. I'm worried about Keely."

"Why do you care about her? She hated you."

I shrug. The movement grinds my thigh against William, and he bites his lip and I don't know what to think about that, but some brattish part of me wants to do it again. "So what if she hated me? If she's lying in a ditch with her head smashed in, her rotting corpse deserves justice."

William leans forward a little, his finger brushing the top of my skirt where my Buzzcocks tee has come untucked and left a little sliver of skin exposed. He runs the tip of his finger over my skin and a tiny moan escapes my lips.

He smirks at me and my cheeks redden. "And is that what your little experiment is all about? Getting justice for rabbits?"

Shit. Is that a threat? "I kept up my end of the bargain. You said you wouldn't tell."

"If you go to the police about Keely, I won't have a choice."

"Fine. Do it. I don't care." I tear myself from his lap and storm out of there, leaving my poor, defenseless books scattered all over the place.

Damn him. Damn him to hell. My body sizzles from his touch as I march across Martyrs' Quad. I can't drop it. I feel that same way I did when I held that tiny container of ashes that was supposed to be my father – all raw and tingly all over, and not from the way he touched my skin.

Fuck William Windsor-Forsyth.

I'm going to get to the bottom of this.

I march back to the office. Just my luck, the same lady is on duty again. I almost turn and leave, but I'm determined this time. She's talking on the phone, her head bent away and her back a rigid line of annoyance.

"Hi, I came in here a few days ago about my roommate, Keely O'Sullivan—"

"I remember you." She made an exasperated wave of her hand. "Come back later. I'm busy."

"—Keely's still not back, and I'm just letting you know that I'm making an official report to the police today, and probably contacting the local paper, and if word gets out that a student is missing and the university ignored my pleas for help—" I shrug. "I'm guessing that won't look good."

She slams the phone onto the cradle and pulls a face like she's sucking on a lemon. "Look, Miss Marple, I'm not supposed to give out this information, but it's worth the risk of losing my job if you'll leave me alone. Your roommate isn't missing. She dropped out."

"What?"

She nods. "That was her on the phone just now, confirming her withdrawal. Family reasons, she says. Not that it's any of your business, but Keely O'Sullivan is no longer a student at Blackfriars."

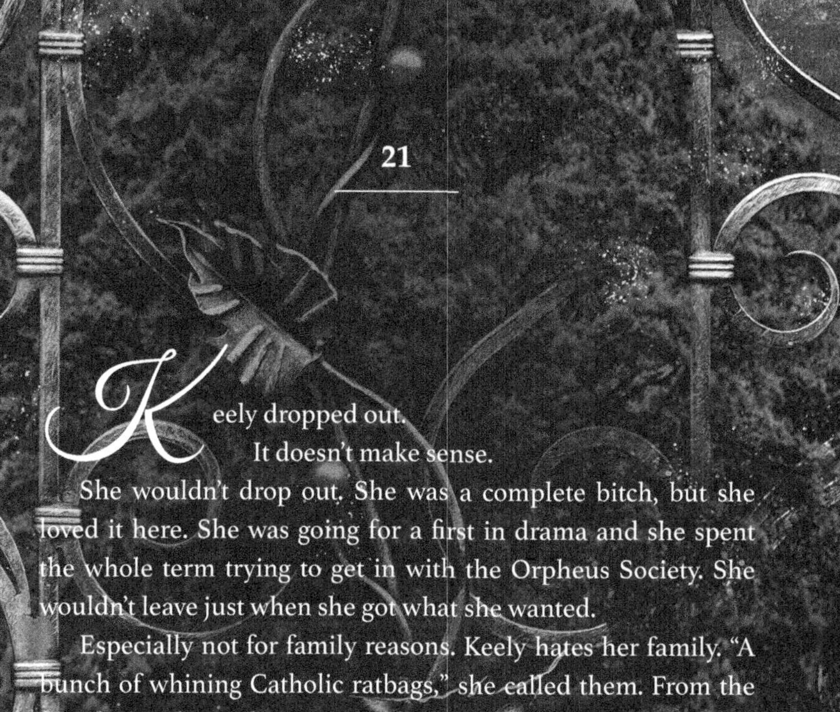

21

Keely dropped out.

It doesn't make sense.

She wouldn't drop out. She was a complete bitch, but she loved it here. She was going for a first in drama and she spent the whole term trying to get in with the Orpheus Society. She wouldn't leave just when she got what she wanted.

Especially not for family reasons. Keely hates her family. "A bunch of whining Catholic ratbags," she called them. From the few things she said to me, I gathered they didn't have as much money as she wanted people to believe, and she seemed to view becoming an Orphean as a way of distancing herself from them. Why, I didn't know.

Besides, she left all her things behind. I throw open her drawers. Even with the boxes of ruined things the cleaners took away, they're bursting with designer clothes. Her shoes are lined up in the rack beside the door, taking up all the space so my New Rocks have to live under my bed. Her piles of cosmetics and creams crowd into hanging containers draped over the mirror.

Why would she drop out and leave all her stuff here?

What other explanation is there? If she was kidnapped, where's the ransom note? Where's the nationwide media coverage? Why wasn't the university all over it?

If she snuck off to party, why hasn't she emerged by now? Why isn't the campus buzzing with tales of her debaucherous exploits? It's as if everyone at Blackfriars suddenly forgot she existed.

If she ended up like Khloe May…

I shudder. I don't want to think about it. I can't.

Why does William keep telling me to forget about her? He was supposed to be her friend. Why did he look so frightened on Devil's Night?

Something happened to Keely on Devil's Night, I'm certain of it.

I slide into my desk and open my laptop. It takes me a few minutes to set up my mic and adjust the settings. The drafty dorm room doesn't have the best acoustics, but my new setup can do amazing things.

I hit Record.

"A lot has happened to me since the last season of the podcast, where I exposed the truth behind the illegal body brokering at Everlasting Hart Funerals. Lots of good things have happened since then. The podcast won a ton of awards. I graduated high school in one piece. And I enrolled in a Bachelors' degree program at Blackfriars University. It's crazy being an American in Britain. Everyone sounds like they belong at Hogwarts, and the food is strange, and the weather is terrible. What else is terrible? Oh, yeah – my roommate, Keely O'Sullivan, has disappeared. One day she was here and then *poof*, she's gone, and everyone is pretending she dropped out of school, but she's left all her stuff behind. And it's all connected to a secret society here on campus called the Orpheus Society and their

Devil's Night ritual. No one will talk about them, but that's never stopped me before." I pause for a breath. *Am I really doing this? Hell yes I am*. "My name is George Fisher, and for season two of my podcast, I'm going to get to the bottom of the Orpheus Society."

22

Now that I'm thinking about the search for Keely as a podcast season, I can be more structured in my approach. Previously, I focused my efforts on Khloe May and the other stories of missing persons, but I need to widen my knowledge. I need to get inside the Orpheus Society without actually getting inside it, because I was never going to be one of them.

An online search reveals a number of entries, none of them useful. People know the Orpheans exist, and that many important politicians, business leaders, and entertainers were members. But they aren't as notorious as Skull and Bones at Yale or the Bullingdon Club at Oxford, so they don't get as much media attention. Listicles about famous secret societies are peppered between historical essays about the mystery cults of the Classical World.

Hmmm. My mind flashes to the Roman amphitheater in the woods. There's a long history of Roman occupation in this area – according to the history brochure I memorized, Blackfriars is built over the site of an old Roman villa.

I wonder if there's a connection between the Roman history of Blackfriars and the Orpheus Society. It certainly explains their propensity to say random things in ancient languages. Learning more about the old rituals might give some clues as to what the Orpheans actually *do* beyond the stupid pranks.

Good thing I know someone who's a Classics freak.

I glance at my watch. It's late in Emerald Beach, but I know Claudia is a night owl. I video call her.

As I suspected, when she picks up the call she's in a dojo, her forehead sheened with sweat. Noah – one of her three boyfriends – is in the background wearing nothing but a pair of boxer shorts, running through a complex series of moves. Claws waves at me as she takes a sip of water. "Are you praying knees-up with the hot priest yet?"

I shake my head vigorously. "We talked, and we've agreed to be just friends."

She snorts. "Let me know how that works out. What about the brutal prince? Did he butter your crumpet?"

"*Claws,*" I moan.

"What? You're giving me nothing, so I'm going to fill in the gaps with my depraved imagination."

"I'm giving you nothing because there's nothing to report. I'm blissfully boy-free. Remember that secret society I told you about? My roommate has gone missing, and I think they're connected. I've been doing some reading about the university's history, and the Roman settlement that was here before the monastery. I think they might've borrowed some of their rituals. I keep coming up against this term – 'mystery cults,' relating to Classical Greek and Roman religions, and I thought you might know something about that."

"A little. The Greeks and Romans had these 'state' religions for their official gods – big-ass temples and feast days for Zeus, Athena, Aphrodite, etc. You know the deal – big statues, say your prayers, sacrifice a goat, read the bird entrails, pay an obol to the priests on the way out. But for some people, Big Religion didn't really fill their spiritual and intellectual well, so they took part in these underground mystery cults...sometimes they were *literally* underground, in temples beneath the earth to be closer to the underworld. The cults were usually localized and often focused around a specific god or myth, and they were more individual – you chose to be in a mystery cult, and they were open to women and slaves. Only members knew the rituals, and they didn't keep written records. The authorities tolerated mystery cults alongside the state religions as long as they didn't try to buck the status quo. If they worried the cults were getting too big for their boots, they'd get stabby and start separating heads from bodies."

"So we don't have any idea what these cults actually did in their rituals? The one here is called the Orpheus Society, if that means anything."

"You mean Orphism? Orpheus is a mythical poet. Orphists were all about being vegetarians and living a simple life, but then some bored rich dudes came along and decided the myths should be celebrated with dancing and drugs and orgies, and they became the cult of Dionysos, who as we all know is the god of partying and excess and chaos and generally good times."

"Sure. Of course." We don't all know that, but Claws grew up with her dad talking about this stuff all the time. She just assumes everyone has a working knowledge of Classical mythology alongside the proper ratios for cutting cocaine and how to load and clean an assault rifle. I like that about her.

I tell her about their motto, *kakodaimonistai,* and what Sebastian told me about the ancient Greek supper club where the members ate. "It sounds like a bunch of posh rich boy wank, as Gabe would say. They want to run around in silly robes, fuck like rabbits, eat and smash and say and do whatever they want with no consequences. Which honestly is what rich boys can do anyway, so why they need a special club to do it is beyond me. But people like to feel as though the things they do have a bigger meaning, to avoid the inevitable conclusion that we live in a world of chaos, and we're all just trying to hold on so we don't get sucked into the black abyss."

I think of Sebastian in his church, surrounded by his dead saints and chalices of Christ's blood, and the Orpheans in their robes destroying the school. And then I glance down at my podcast notes, and wonder if I'm trying to do the same thing – ascribe a bigger meaning to Keely's disappearance, to my father's murder, because that gives me something to fight for, something to distract me from the grief of losing him.

Maybe. But that doesn't change the fact that something happened on Devil's Night. William knew it – that was why he kept telling me to drop it. But I don't take orders from wicked princes.

IN THE LIBRARY, I get lost in the Classical Studies section, piling up every book that talks about mystery cults, Orphism, and Dionysos. I take them back to my usual corral (William isn't there, thank the gods) and start making notes.

These mystery cults are *wild*. One scholar describes revelers dancing to the beat of a drum that stirred their blood to a state of *ekstasis* (ecstasy) so profound that they lost themselves. They climbed mountains and fornicated in caves, bathed in goats' blood and tore the flesh from each other's limbs, drunk hallucinogenic potions and invited animal spirits to possess them. And in the moments of their rapture they became one with the god himself...they took on his spirit, his divine power.

An Orphic poem describes an initiate inviting Dionysos inside himself:

> *"I call upon loud-roaring and reveling Dionysos,*

primeval, double-natured, thrice-born, Bacchic lord,
wild, ineffable, secretive, two-horned and two-shaped.
Ivy-covered, bull-faced, warlike, howling, pure,
You take raw flesh, you have feasts, wrapt in foliage,
decked with grape clusters...

I learn that the Orphic poems depict Dionysos as the son of Zeus and his daughter Persephone. Claws taught me that all Greek mythology can be summed up in five words – *unfortunately, Zeus is horny again*. And Dionysos' story is no different.

Zeus' wife Hera gets jealous and orders a race of magical giants called Titans to tear Dionysos to pieces, cook him, and eat him. But the goddess Athena saves his heart, and Zeus uses it to resurrect him.

(Zeus also strikes the Titans with lightning, they burn to cinders, and from the ashes arise the first humans. So that's...a thing.)

It all sounds so insane, especially when I remember the Orpheus Society was started by a devout monk. But it makes a mad kind of sense. After all, Catholics drink the blood and eat the flesh of the son of God to wash away their sins. They believe in Jesus' death and resurrection.

According to Euripides, for the Greeks, drinking wine – which is the blood of the god Dionysos himself – lightens the burden of mortal misery. Initiates to the mystery cults must embody the god by going through a ritual dismemberment, death, and descent to the underworld, before they can be resurrected anew. I can see how Benet of Blackfriars might've drawn parallels between them, especially after his religion was suddenly deemed satanic and dangerous, forcing him underground.

I need to know more.

I pick up my books and head to the Medieval Studies

section, but after hunting for the book I wanted for twenty minutes, I come up empty-handed. I ask the librarian, "Excuse me, the catalog says you have this collection of the Black Monk's writings, but I can't find anything on the shelves."

"That's because it's part of our special collection. Follow me." She pulls an archaic set of keys from her desk drawer and marches toward a narrow staircase blocked off with velvet rope.

She pushes the rope aside and leads me through a dimly lit basement and down two more flights of stairs. Her swipe-card dings as we pass through security doors and temperature-controlled stacks.

I had no idea the library was so vast. It must stretch right beneath Martyrs' Quad. "How deep does this go?"

"There are another three levels below this," she says, pointing to the gothic stone arches holding up the ceiling. "These are the old cellars where the monks stored their beer, but these lower levels are even older than that. You're studying Greek, aren't you? You might enjoy this." She shifts a couple of archive boxes from the end of the shelf and points her phone's flashlight at the stone wall. At first, I don't understand what's so exciting about a few smudges, but then the shapes resolve into a faint drawing.

It's a Roman fresco – Dionysos as a youth with his head wreathed in laurel leaves, surrounded by satyrs and maenads waving *thyrsus* (sticks wrapped in ivy with pinecones stuck on the end for...reasons) and flinging about comically large phalluses. The god carries a drinking cup in one hand and a double-edged ax used for animal sacrifices in the other. My heart pounds in my chest. Somehow, I have a feeling this isn't a coincidence.

"Do you know why this was painted here?"

She shrugs. "I organize books. Father Pearce might know. He

was involved in an archaeological study a couple of years back. There was a whole team down here."

I have to ask Sebastian.

The librarian leads me through a thick door into another, much smaller room. Metal shelves on rollers line one wall. On the other are several desks containing velvet-lined cradles. "This is where we keep the codices that survived from the original Blackfriars library. These manuscripts were all written by hand by the monks who lived here. They need temperature-controlled storage so the paper and parchment don't break down."

She cranks the handle to reveal the third shelf and pulls out a small volume. "This book does not leave this room, do you understand? For some books, we advise students to wear gloves, as the oil in their fingers can damage the pages. But for this one, it's not necessary." She sets the book into one of the cradles. "I'll leave you to your work. When you're finished, leave the book in the cradle and come upstairs and let me know. Will you become a regular?"

"Huh?" I'm so transfixed by the crackled leather cover of the small volume, I miss what she says.

The librarian looks at me like I'm crazy. "Most students studying these books require frequent visits to the collection. Some of the books are digitally scanned, but not this one, I'm sorry. No translations, either, except for a few short passages in Father Duncan's latest book. When you return the key, I'll book you into our calendar and give you a swipe card."

I wait until she leaves, pulling the heavy door shut behind her. The light overhead buzzes angrily. My temple already aches from the dry air.

Gingerly, I reach for the corner of the book. The cover feels surprisingly supple, almost like new. I flip it open to reveal a page crowded with sloping, florid handwriting.

I can't read a word.

It's written in Greek.

Of course it bloody is.

I don't know what I was expecting. No, that's a lie. I know exactly what I was expecting – I was expecting it to be in English because I'm a heathen.

I don't have my Liddell and Scott with me, and even if I did, I can tell from the first page that I don't understand enough grammar to make sense of this. I'll need to take it away to work on a translation, and the only way to do that is...

With a sigh of frustration, I pull a fresh notebook and pad from my bookbag, and set about copying down every indecipherable word.

23

I work on my translation every chance I get. I return to the library three times to copy out the remainder of Benet's writing, and even then I still have several pages to go. I pin my copied pages to the walls of my room as I work on them. His account begins with the horrific battle at the monastery, and every word is a battle of my own against archaic syntax and complex grammar. I wish I could tell Sebastian about it so he can help me, but I know he'll just try to convince me to stay away from the Orpheans. Instead, in our next Greek session, I try to surreptitiously ask questions that give me the answers I need. By the end of the week, I have half a page translated.

This is going to take forever.

I scribble notes as I walk across the quad toward Criminology class. My bladder is bursting, and I veer off toward the bathrooms. It's only when I look up from my translation and see Monty in front of the urinals that I realize I've walked into the men's bathroom by mistake.

Monty smirks as I back toward the door. "Oops. My mistake. Go about your business."

"No, no." Monty grabs my wrist. I yelp a little – his grip is like iron, his smooth skin surprisingly strong. "This is a lucky happenstance, George, old chum. I've been meaning for the two of us to have a little chat."

"Oh?" I play it light, even though my heart pounds in my chest. A quick scan of the stall doors reveals the place is empty. It's just Monty and me, and I'm not liking the callous disinterest in his eyes.

"Yes, indeed." Monty's fingers tighten around my wrist. "You see, I have friends all over this campus, and I've heard that you're digging that little nose of yours into my affairs. Now, I'm a believer in basic, inalienable rights, as I'm sure you are, too. A man's got the right to his privacy, you see. And my friends and I, we go to great lengths to keep our business private. So consider this my most cordial suggestion that you find another hobby. The women's cricket team is short a member, or that pimply fellow in the biology lab could do with more test subjects..."

I tilt my head to the side and try to look like I'm sizing him up, like I'm not at all terrified of him. "Are you threatening me?"

"No, no, not at all. How *gauche*. I just wanted to let you know that I was aware of your clandestine investigations. I'd like to suggest that if you have any questions about me or my friends, you come to me directly instead of skulking around in library stacks."

Ah. The librarian. I bet she told Monty I'd requested Benet's book. That confirms there are clues in the old monk's writing that might lead me to the truth. "Fine. Where's Keely? I know she didn't quit school."

Monty wipes his floppy blond hair from his eyes, which bear down on me with callous glee. "I don't know what you're talking about. Keely is back with her family in Ireland. We miss her dearly, of course, but she had a family emergency, can't be helped, such a shame. You're a good girl, a very *good girl*, to be so worried about her. Admirable quality, although I assure you

Keely is in perfect health so you needn't worry any longer. I know you heard about what happened to dear old Khloe May all those years ago, but you can't allow your imagination to run away with you. That can only lead to dangerous places, as Khloe learned."

I swallow my gasp. Monty's implication is crystal clear – I stop looking into Khloe, or I end up like her. He laughs. "Don't look so scandalized, George old boy. This is just a friendly chat." He beckons me with a finger. "Come here. I want to show you something."

As if I have any choice with him gripping my wrist? Every muscle in my body screams at me to run, but I see out of the corner of my eye that Richard has entered the bathroom and is closing in behind me. He has his hands in his pockets, whistling a tune. Anyone watching the scene might think we *were* having a friendly chat. But they couldn't feel the tension in the air or see the menace brewing in Monty's eyes.

"Another time." I bend my head, try to tug my wrist free. "I have to get to class—"

He moves like lightning. He bends my wrist back over my head, slamming it into the cold tile. Monty's breath caresses my cheek, hot and alcoholic and panting with excitement. "Dicky, your tie."

Richard smirks as he unties the thin tie from his neck and hands it to Monty. I swing out with my foot and manage to clip Monty's leg, but all I get for my trouble is a sore foot. Monty is incredibly strong. He clamps my hands over my head and wraps the tie around them, securing it to the Victorian pipes that run along the top of the wall. He yanks the knot so tight my eyes water.

"Cheer up, Georgie Pie. We're just trying to help you figure out where you belong." Monty moves to stand in front of the urinal. He yanks down his fly, grabbing his cock. He doesn't even aim for the urinal, but pisses right on me. Warm urine soaks my legs, sticking my jeans to my skin.

I turn away. It doesn't make the humiliation burn any less. I close my eyes, but Monty's shit-eating grin burns inside my eyelids.

Monty washes his hands and flicks the water in my face.

Richard steps up to take his turn. He pees into the urinal in front of me, sloshing his cock around with a huge grin on his face so some of his piss splashes me. Monty tells him in Greek to 'get the others' and a moment later I hear the door swing shut. I'm alone with Monty again. I still can't bring myself to open my eyes.

Monty leans in close. I feel his breath on my cheek again. "You don't belong here, Curious George," he whispers. The casual callousness in his voice is so much more terrifying than if he yelled. "Go back to California. Leave with your dignity...or what's left of it. Leave with your life, while you still have it. This is your last warning."

A whimper escapes my throat. Monty leans back, tapping his foot and humming a tune. A moment later, the door swings open and I hear voices, laughter, smatterings of Greek amongst posh British joviality. One by one, the Orphean men take their turn to piss on me, then they leave in peals of laughter.

I bite down on my lip until I taste blood. I take myself far away, back to a safe manor house in Emerald Beach filled with laughter and friendship and crazy kittens, back to a dark theatre and the smell of buttery popcorn and the warmth of my dad's shoulder as I lean against him while we watch another horror movie together. I hope with all the hope left inside me that Dad isn't a ghost haunting my ass, because if he saw me now it would be like him dying all over again.

Another bunch of guys come in – not Orpheans this time. They're laughing and snapping pictures of me. "What'd you do to piss Monty off?" one of them whispers as he relieves himself beside me. "You choke on his cock or something?"

"I'm sorry," another guy whispers. "I'd get you out of here, but I can't cross Monty."

I float above myself, watching with a detected, almost academic interest as my clothes stiffen with drying urine, as a dark puddle expands around my feet, as my socks fill with vile liquids and men with cold eyes and sneering lips do nothing to save me.

My arms are numb, my shoulders screaming, my heart shattered glass, when the door swings open again. As the figure strides toward me, I'm drawn back into my body for Monty's final, horrible punishment.

Please, no. Please, anyone but him.

William's eyes flick over me as he steps up to the urinal right next to me.

"William, *please.*"

The words are out of my mouth before I can stop them.

Monty's head snaps up. He's not watching me – his steel gaze fixes on William, who nods once, then unzips his trousers.

His hands don't tremble.

Everything about him is cool, detached, unfeeling.

This isn't the William on Devil's Night.

He won't save me.

William's eyes bore into mine as he pulls out his cock. I don't want to look, but I can't help it. Even flaccid it's *insane* – long and thick and veined around the tip. Even after everything that's happened, a hot flush creeps along my cheeks.

This moment is too raw, too intimate, and yet, behind William's shoulder, Monty leers over us both – the puppet-master pulling the strings. We can't go back from this.

"Untie me," I beg.

William doesn't acknowledge me with words. He keeps his

eyes locked on me as he pees into the urinal. Piss splatters on me, every droplet like acid burrowing into my skin.

He takes forever. He must've drunk a ton of coffee. Or maybe it was just my mortification.

William zips himself up, washes and dries his hands and – with a final pointed look to Monty over his shoulder – flees the bathroom like he's running from a ghost.

I LOSE track of how long I hang there while guys move in and out, carrying on their conversations and going about their business like I don't exist. I know they're afraid of Monty and that's why they won't help me, but a little piece of me dies each time they leave without freeing me.

Eventually, a guy from my Criminology class has the balls to untie my hands. I want to thank him, but I'm cold and my arms hurt and I'm covered in piss and I have no words for the horror or the humiliation.

Laughter and whispers scorch me as I bolt for my dorm.

The videos and pictures are all over Blackfriars the next day. They're pulled from the school's official social media pretty quick, but from the way people look at their phones and then at me, shooting me furtive, sympathetic looks, I *know*.

I spent two hours in the shower scrubbing my skin raw, but I'll never wash away the memory of it.

I'm marked. I'm officially an enemy of the Orpheans.

Monty's message is loud and clear.

If I don't stop looking into Keely's disappearance and the connection to Khloe May, I won't just be humiliated. I'll be six feet under.

24

Every day after that, an official Blackfriars document is stapled to my door – withdrawal papers, already filled out for me in William's loopy handwriting with only the space for my signature. Every day, I tear them down and toss them away.

Is this what they did to Keely?

Is this how they got her to leave?

I'm not giving up.

They're only doing this because they're afraid. Because for the first time, someone isn't bending over to kiss their boots. Because they know I'm close to whatever secret they're desperate to protect.

I'm afraid. Of course I'm afraid. The memory of the men's bathroom scratches at my eyeballs every time I try to fall asleep. But it's not the worst thing that's ever happened to me. Not by a mile. They may own this school, but I have resources of my own. Claws and her soldiers are on standby if I need her. Leigh's been sleeping in Keely's bed every night since it happened, a curved hunting knife under the pillow. I have an audience of millions waiting to hear this podcast.

All Monty did was prove that I'm doing the right thing by exposing them.

Sally watches as I tear down today's paper. "I don't know how you got on their bad side, kid. But you should take this seriously. Two years ago, a girl called the police after an incident with Montague Cavendish at a party. Three months later, she was wheeled out on a stretcher after throwing herself off the roof of the church."

I remember Sebastian's face when he told me the roof isn't open to students. Fear churns in my gut. But it's tampered down by righteous anger. When I swing open my door, I stifle a scream.

Someone's hung a noose from the eaves outside my window. The wind whips the rope against the glass.

I set down my takeout container of roast beef and vegetables, and prop the window open. Freezing rain slams into me. I peer down at the quad, where Monty, William, Richard, and Abigail peer up at me, their faces stony, deadly serious. Only Monty smiles – a smile that chills my blood.

How did they get this noose up here?

They can't have scaled the smooth stone walls. Either they climbed out from a room next to mine or... I glance around. If they'd been in my room, surely they would have destroyed my notes on Benet's manuscript. And yet... did I leave that sweater over the chair like that? Was my glass always on the edge of my desk? Is that the faint aroma of fresh oil paint and dark chocolate scenting the air?

I text Leigh and a few minutes later she bursts through the door, shaking off her soaking-wet hair as she wraps me in a damp hug. "I came straight from sculpture masterclass. Passed those posh wankers in the quad, staring up at you with their designer umbrellas like they're waiting for you to slip your neck in. What are you gonna do?"

"I have an idea." I pull out an expensive teddy bear from under Keely's bed that somehow escaped the destruction. I find a heavy black felt tip pen amongst my stationary supplies. I can't quite fit the words 'Orpheus Society' or '*kakodaimonistai*' on its chest, so I draw a lyre and a wine cup. We slip the bear's neck into the noose and swing it back outside.

"Now this is what I call 'poking the bear.'" Leigh laughs as she jabs the bear with a broom handle so it swings wildly. By now a few other students have gathered in the quad to watch. "You're crazy, George. You're not scared of anything."

"Not true. I'm fucking *terrified*. I'm just not going to let them see it."

"You gonna tell me why they got a target on your back?"

I shake my head. "I can't. Not yet. I don't want to put you in danger, any more than you already are by hanging out with me."

She waves her hand. "If you aren't afraid then I ain't afraid, neither."

We eat our roast beef, then I empty my bank account and send Leigh into Blackfriars Close to buy a fancy lock for my room while I keep working on the translation. Somewhere within Benet's words is the secret to unlocking the Orpheans, I'm certain of it.

For three days, rain pelts the campus – a Noah's flood that sends waterfalls over the creaking gutters and turns the cobbled quads into slippery death traps. Mostly Leigh and I stay in my room, huddling under the blankets and studying. The school hasn't assigned me a new roommate – and although I'm determined to find the truth about Keely, I definitely don't miss her. Leigh and I check each other's essays, curl up together and watch horror films or make playlists, and venture out only for classes and pies.

My trash can overflows with crumpled withdrawal forms. There's been no other threat from the Orpheans, but that doesn't mean they're not plotting something. Even though I know they can't get inside my room now, I struggle to fall asleep. I stare at the ceiling and smell the piss and soap of the bathroom. I feel the ghost of a hand on my thigh. Monty's sneer dances in the corners of my vision, sometimes melding with Alec LeMarque's features to become a monstrous hybrid of the two men I fear most in the world.

Sebastian texts me a few times to make sure I'm surviving the dreary weather okay. I try not to think about how much I love hearing from him.

When the rain finally eases and Blackfriars emerges glittering in the glaring haze of crystalline grey, I know it's time to do the final assessment of my 'body farm.' The last time I checked on it was the day before Devil's Night, which means that now is perfect timing for when Khloe May's sweater was discovered. The three days of non-stop rain will give some interesting observations.

Leigh's in class all day, and although I don't want to walk anywhere alone, I also don't want to scare away my only friend with my macabre science experiment. I wait for a gap in the weather when I know the Orpheans are in Greek class, then I tug on a red bobbly hat I found at the thrift store in the village, hoist my bag onto my shoulders, pick up the scary-looking hunting knife Leigh gave me for 'protection,' and set off down the path toward the amphitheater.

I walk quickly, my boots sloshing in puddles. Every few feet I glance back over my shoulder and touch my fingers to Leigh's knife in my pocket, just in case one of the Orpheans is following me. But no one's there, and I don't meet anyone else on the forest path. The rain may have eased, but it's still freezing out, so I guess the rich students take their cars to the village on days like today. My breath puffs in angry clouds in front of my face.

I veer off into the trees, following the now-familiar path into the amphitheater. My boots splash in deep puddles between the stones. I can see students have been here recently – there are broken bottles and the remains of a small fire. Under a corner of the stage, where the rain hadn't washed it off, someone has drawn a crude image of a bull – a symbol of Dionysos.

A chill runs down my spine that has nothing to do with the cold.

The wind whips through the trees, and I'm starting to regret coming out. I'm cold to the bone, and there's a tension in the air that wasn't here before. One of the college ravens crosses the path in front of me. It stops and stares up at me, yellow eyes unblinking. If I were an ancient Greek, I'd see that as a bad omen.

As I follow my marked trees deeper into the wood, I think about Claws' promise to lend me the soldiers I need to keep safe. There's comfort in knowing she's got my back, that there's nothing the rich assholes in the Orpheus Society can do to me without bringing the wrath of the notorious August family down on their heads. But I also know if posh nobs start disappearing like flies, it could cause trouble for her, and she's had enough trouble to last a lifetime. I can't run to my best friend every time someone treats me like—

Shit.

I stop in my tracks.

My orange tape flaps loose in the breeze, torn away from the trees. Footprints smear the earth, filled with water now, and the piles of leaves are kicked and disturbed where several people have stomped over the site.

Someone's been here.

I use the branches of the oak as a staircase down the slope and race to my first carcass. The plastic bag has been kicked ten feet from where I placed it, and a pile of cigarette stubs litter the ground. Loose dirt covers the second carcass – one of my control animals. It looks like someone's made a half-ass job of burying it. Now it's useless as part of the experiment.

Tears prick the corners of my eyes.

My experiment has been compromised. My final results will be contaminated.

This is deliberate.

Apart from Professor Hipkins and the ethics committee, only one person knows about my experiment. And I never told Hipkins the exact location. Only one wanker (great word, perfect for him) would come all the way out here in *this* weather with the explicit purpose of ruining my project. Only one person would break the bargain we struck and get his friends in on the Devil's Night prank.

William.

I wipe the tears away, my hands shaking with anger. I won't give him the satisfaction of crying. I walk the perimeter of my ruined body farm, taking in the damage and hoping against hope there's something I can salvage.

The hanged carcass is still in the noose, although the ground beneath is so disturbed I won't get any good data. The one I buried is still intact, too – although there are cigarette butts and broken glass around the grave. There's a bootprint in the middle of my burned specimen, and the second control body has been kicked into a bush a good ten feet from where I placed it.

And that's not all. Someone dug a hole in the middle of the farm and stuck a fake human hand out of the dirt, like some film prop. My dad wouldn't have been caught dead using something so obvious – it looks all weird and mottled and completely unrealistic...

Real funny, guys. You're comedians...

The hairs on the back of my neck stand up with bad mojo. I look down at the hand again, at the blotches of rot blooming across the surface. Gingerly, I kneel down in front of the hand. I pull one of the brushes from my bag and brush aside the dirt, revealing a slender wrist wrapped in a delicate silver chain.

My mouth dries as I keep brushing, revealing an arm, bent at the elbow, the edge of an emerald evening dress. A collarbone and jaw, the skin rotting away to reveal the bones beneath. A mouth hangs open in a silent scream, maggots crawling between the lips.

Staring up at me from the shallow grave is Keely.

25

"She's been dismembered," Lauren says.

I nod as if I'm totally cool with this horrific statement delivered in Lauren's deadpan voice.

Inside, I scream.

Dismembered.

I'm not supposed to be here listening to this. The school wants to keep the details of Keely's body as quiet as possible. But after I discovered Keely I went straight to Professor Hipkins, and she was so impressed with my body farm experiment that she offered me a hands-on internship. So I'm helping the Scene-Of-Crime Officers (that's what they call CSI in Britain) examine the scene. The pathologist, Lauren Grainger, is removing the body for study, and I'm assisting by fetching things and tripping over my own feet. She keeps asking if I'm okay, if I need to leave, and I'm not going to give her the satisfaction of seeing me throw up.

Corpses are practically a constant in my life.

"We're missing both legs and her left arm." Lauren stands back, giving the SOCO's room to roll Keely's torso into a heavy-duty black bag. Most corpses are transported in white bags, unless there's a lot of 'wet' material and decomposition, and then we need the black bags. I learn something new every day, especially on the day of my ex-roommate's autopsy. "I'll know more when we get the remains back to the lab, but her limbs look to have been removed with a large, sharp blade. She sustained these injuries before death."

This time even I can't help the gag that escapes my throat. Someone cut Keely's arms off *before* they murdered her?

They didn't just kill her. They *tortured* her.

Very few people will have the stomach for that. For the first time, I waver in my conviction that the Orpheus Society is to blame. This is bloody, barbarous, *messy*. I can't see even Monty going in for this, not if he gets his designer trousers dirty.

Maybe there's another reason someone wanted Keely out of the way. I have enough experience of gang killings to know that a murder like this is designed to send a message. But who is the message for? I remember Keely's disdain for her family, and their indifference when I finally managed to get through to them on the phone. Is there something there? It's as good a place as any to start.

But why dump her body all the way out here? In a place where I would obviously find it?

I've already been interviewed by the investigating officer, Inspector Jones. He's a grizzled old man with whisky breath and humor so dry it will disintegrate in the breeze – the cliche of a British copper you see on TV. If he has an opera collection and a drinking problem, I won't be at all surprised.

I tell him everything I know about Keely and how she acted before her death, including the names of everyone she was hanging out with. I leave out the fact I was out on Devil's Night and my suspicions about the Orpheans – I remember what John told me about them buying the police. It turns out, Inspector Jones knows all about the Orpheus Society already – they're infamous for smashing up restaurants and leaving without paying – and he assures me he'll be talking to them next, although I know they won't give him much. I also tell him about Keely's problems with her family, in case they really are responsible.

It's on the tip of my tongue to tell Inspector Jones about the threats Monty's made against me, but I remember how dark and afraid William seemed. Against my better judgment, I keep quiet. For now.

I help the team photograph and bag up every cigarette butt and broken piece of glass. Lauren finds a couple of shoeprints she might be able to use and has the team make casts of them. She finishes up in Keely's grave and staggers to her feet, her white SOCO suit streaked with mud. "That's me out. You'll get my report once I've processed the remains."

"I'll help," I say immediately. "If you'll have me."

"Very well." She peels off her gloves with a defiant snap. "I'll see you at the morgue in an hour."

IT'S FREEZING cold in the morgue. And that's just the beginning of my discomfort.

Cutting up dead bodies ain't no thing for me anymore, not after last year. But something about the rooting around and the horrific smell brings back memories of the night I helped Galen do exactly the same thing to Claws' uncle. Only Brutus' body wasn't dismembered and he hadn't been buried in dirt and rained on for weeks. Some parts of Keely's body were little more than a black sludge crawling with insects, which Lauren carefully counted and extracted with fine-tipped tongs to send to a forensic entomologist for closer examination.

"These cuts are remarkably clean," Lauren explains, pointing to the severed stump of shoulder. "Usually with dismemberments we see ragged wounds, but these are fine, precise. Surgical, almost. They were done with a very large, very sharp knife by someone who knows a bit about anatomy. And this wasn't done in the wood, or we'd see a lot more contamination. She was killed somewhere else and brought to the wood."

"This would have been bloody, right?"

She nods as she extracts another sample. "Yes. Buckets of the stuff. Which means whoever did this would have spent hours cleaning up the murder site. Unless they're very, very careful, they'd have left us with a trail of physical evidence to hang them with."

Looking at the sorry collection of body parts on the table, I can't see the girl who'd made my dorm life hell. Except when Lauren turns Keely's skull around and I see the matted hair still streaming down her back. And I remember Keely hogging the mirror as she brushed and fussed with her hair, and I need to sit down.

"You did well." Lauren hands me a bottle of water when she's finished hosing down the morgue.

"I nearly fainted." I can still see Keely's lips open in that maggot-filled scream.

"That's surprisingly stoic for someone your age. Most people take one sniff of this place and they're heaving into the sink." She looks up at me then, and there's admiration in her tight features. "I did, my first time."

She hoses the remainder of the…juices…into the drain, and I help her clean down every surface with bleach. When we're done, I'm ready to sleep for days, but I feel a weird kind of calmness. Keely has been buried in that shallow grave for weeks and no one gave a shit. The school ignored my concerns. Her family didn't want to hear from me. No one cares.

Well, *I* care. Keely might not be able to tell us who hurt her, but through the clues left behind on her body, we may bring her killer to justice.

I think of another girl who disappeared on Devil's Night ten years ago. Another girl who might still be buried in the same wood. And I think about holding that tiny container of Dad's remains, and helping Eli throw open the cages beneath Nero's club to let dozens of wild animals free.

I think about the fire blazing beneath a brazen bull.

I brought the funeral home that fucked with my father and their clandestine body brokerage to justice. And I made a podcast so that no one else would ever have to go through what I did again.

Now it's time for season two, and I found my cause, my personal connection. My roommate has been tortured and killed, and I'm going to make sure she has the justice she deserves.

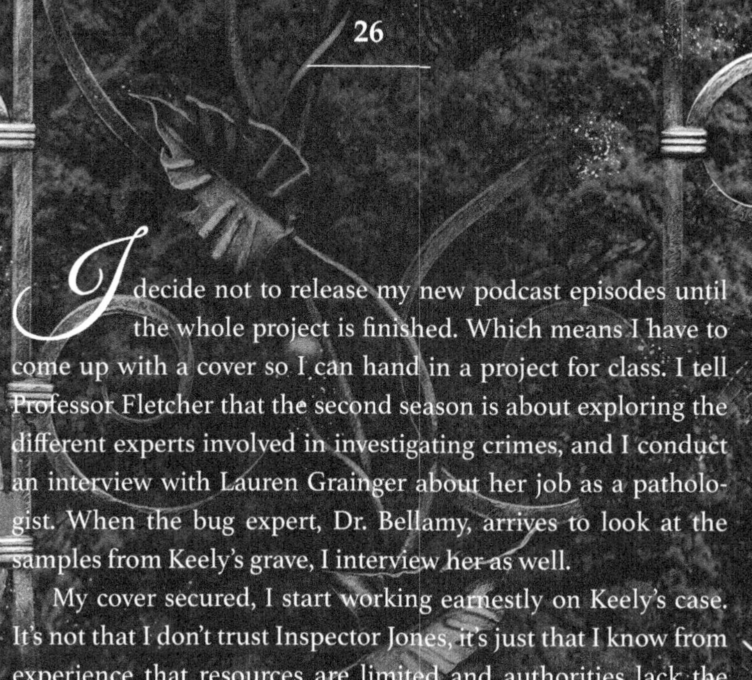

26

I decide not to release my new podcast episodes until the whole project is finished. Which means I have to come up with a cover so I can hand in a project for class. I tell Professor Fletcher that the second season is about exploring the different experts involved in investigating crimes, and I conduct an interview with Lauren Grainger about her job as a pathologist. When the bug expert, Dr. Bellamy, arrives to look at the samples from Keely's grave, I interview her as well.

My cover secured, I start working earnestly on Keely's case. It's not that I don't trust Inspector Jones, it's just that I know from experience that resources are limited and authorities lack the imagination to see things like illegal body brokering and sadistic secret societies unless the evidence is presented to them. That, and he could have pockets lined with Orphean money.

I also know that no matter what my gut tells me, I can't fixate on the Orpheans – I need to explore every possible angle. So I ask Claws to follow up with her contacts in Ireland and find out if Keely's death was a hit.

While I wait for Claws to get back to me, I pour myself a cup of tea from the JCR kitchen, crank up the Sex Pistols, and hack

Keely's social media accounts. It's not hard – the girl has no imagination, and her passwords are unbelievably easy to guess. KEELYWINDSORFORSYTH gets me into her Facebook and Instagram, where I can see her private photographs and read through her old messenger logs.

What I learn is that Keely has been after William for at least two years, ever since she met him at a private party in Dublin when she was sixteen. She spent two weeks of last summer partying at the Windsor-Forsyth estate with the rest of the Orpheans, and she's got a group chat going with some of her girlfriends where she goes into nauseating detail about her every interaction with William, and plots revenge on every girl who gives him a second look.

Good thing she never found out about our kiss, or I'd be dead meat.

I save copies of everything to the secure server I set up for Claws. I also learn through Keely and William's messages that the Orpheus Society has a private Instagram account where members share photographs from their various debaucherous events. Abigail granted Keely access at 11:59PM on Devil's Night, and the silly wench saved the password in an email, so now I have it, too.

My heart constricts as I type in the password and a grid of photographs fills the screen. The very last one shows Keely with her arms thrown around Abigail and Diana, who both wear the white robes I saw on Devil's Night. Their hoods are thrown back and they smile broadly, drinks in hand. Keely wears an emerald gown – the same one her limbs were wrapped in – with a wreath of ivy encircling her head. Her wide smile and sparkling eyes made something hard twist in my gut.

How long after this photo was taken was Keely chopped to pieces?

I scan the rest of the photographs as I upload them to the server, looking for clues. There are a couple others taken at what

I presumed was the same party – members of the Orpheus Society I recognize holding drinks and kissing and grinning, Monty smiling foppishly as he flips something in a frying pan. There are some images of the Devil's Night pranks being set up, but none of those show faces. They're careful about that, even on this account they believe is private.

The further I scroll back, the more elaborate parties I see – videos scan twenty-foot tables groaning beneath the weight of feasts. Expensive bottles of alcohol, naked men and women gyrating together in a kaleidoscope of colored lights. Swords. Drugs. Darkened, candlelit rooms that look to be inside caves. Bare skin tangled in silk sheets. Captions quoting Epicurus and Nietzsche and the Orphic poems and other sources I don't recognize. Every second photograph is of Monty eating something strange and amazing, or bouncing a girl on his knee while he feeds her with his thick, sticky fingers. And in the background...

I stop at once.

Is that...it almost looks like...

I zoom in on the image and lean closer. The face is blurry, half-obscured in shadow. The figure holds a tray of something and waves a fork at Diana. It's dated six months ago.

Why is Father Duncan at an Orpheus Society party?

27

I arrive early for my Greek lesson as Sebastian is finishing his Compline prayers. I slip into a pew and watch him, his head bent in supplication, the curve of his shoulders as he kneels at the altar, the way his lower lip trembles a little as he speaks the words.

He's so certain his God is listening. But would his God be here, wallowing in daily devotions, and not saving innocent girls from being dismembered in the forest?

Sebastian rises and sees me. He comes rushing over with none of his usual graceful ease. He kneels on the carpet beside me and takes my hands, looking up at me with those huge, cavernous anthracite eyes. It's such a strange way to see him, as if I'm the god he worships.

"Are you okay?" Sebastian wraps his fingers in mine. "I heard about your roommate. That you were the one who found her body."

"I—" My words die away as he envelops me in a warm hug.

I never ever want him to stop hugging me.

But as the hug deepens, as his hand strokes my hair and his thumb fingers the edge of my jaw and rubs light circles in the skin, it stops feeling like a hug between friends. My body is on fire, aware of every inch where I touch him, of my tits jammed up against him and his thigh over mine and the hard planes of his muscles like a castle of protection around me.

I pull away. "I'm fine. Really. I mean, I'm shaken up, but it's not the first dead body I've seen."

Sebastian quirks an eyebrow at me, but he doesn't ask me to elaborate. And suddenly, I want desperately to spill every sordid detail of my past to him. But I can't. As much as I see Brutus' burned face and hear Alec's tortured screams in my nightmares, it's not my story to tell.

"Do you think this means I get an automatic pass now?" I say, to change the subject before I say something I'll regret.

"Pardon?" He looks confused.

"There's that urban legend around campus that if your roommate dies, you automatically get a pass. Which, to be honest, I could use because there's this tough course called History of Religion with a slave-driver of a don, and it's really kicking my ass."

Sebastian laughs. "I'm glad to see your sense of humor has survived this ordeal."

"It has. And Professor Hipkins is letting me work with Dr. Grainger, the pathologist, for course credit. I helped her perform the autopsy. It actually made me feel better in a way, like I was able to help Keely in death the way I couldn't in life." I take a deep breath. I know what I have to ask, but I also know exactly how he's going to answer. "Lauren's been working on time-of-death. It's hard to be exact, but Lauren thinks Keely's been in the ground since Devil's Night."

Sebastian stiffens.

I hurry on. "I think the Orpheus Society is involved and I wondered, since you and William are so close and he's a member—"

"Not here," Sebastian hisses. With a glance over his shoulder around the deserted cathedral, he pulls me down the narrow passage into his quarters, where he sits me down in my usual chair and goes about preparing the fire and boiling the kettle for tea.

"What gave you the idea William and I are close?" Sebastian hands me a glass and settles into the chair beside me. The blaze hasn't quite had the chance to warm the room, and the chill gives it this kind of solid, lived-in feeling I like – as if it knows I need reassurance that I didn't invent Sebastian.

"Just...things you've both said. He's your biggest fan. He keeps warning me that you're a monster."

Father Pearce smiles wanly at that. He touches his finger to the collar at his throat. "To him, I probably am."

I shudder, thinking of the men's bathroom. "He should look in the mirror."

"William wasn't always a cruel-hearted prince. There was a time when he was the sweetest boy you'd ever meet." Sebastian sips his tea. "Losing his mother changed him. And Monty Cavendish sensed his vulnerability and snapped shut the jaws of his trap. It will take all of William's strength and goodness to untangle himself from that particular snare. I hope one day he will have the strength to do it."

I notice Sebastian doesn't tell me how he knew William as a boy, and I can't quite bring myself to ask. Not after I see the shadows creeping into his eyes. Instead, I hit him with my real question.

"Is Father Duncan an Orphean? That's the real reason he only allows Orpheus Society members into his class."

"Lying is a sin of pride." Sebastian's mouth quirks at the side, but there's no mirth in his eyes.

"I'm not accusing you of anything. I'm asking a question."

"I suppose he might have been once. He did study at Blackfriars before he went to the seminary." Sebastian flips through the books on the table, his face turned away from me. "But he won't have anything to do with the society as it exists today. Only current students can be active members, as far as I'm aware. Why do you ask?"

Because I know he attended one of their parties a month before Keely died. "No reason. I was just curious. Was he on campus on Devil's Night?"

"He had dinner with a visiting cardinal in York," Sebastian says. "He took the train and stayed overnight. You're not trying to link Father Duncan to Keely's death, are you?"

"I'm just asking—"

"I know her murder affected you greatly, but you must let the police do their jobs." He reaches out a hand for me. "If you need it, there is grief counseling available from the campus Health Center. You might also find comfort in prayer, if you'd like me to help you—"

For the first time, I shove his hand away. "The Orpheus Society has bought off the staff at this school. What's to say they don't own the police, too? Keely was *dismembered*. While she was *still alive*. I'm not going to let that go unpunished, no matter what they—"

I stop myself before I reveal too much. But Father Pearce's face hardens as he parses the meaning of my silence.

"George, if the Orpheus Society is threatening or hurting you in any way, you have to tell me." He leans across the arm of the chair, his face earnest, his mouth set in a firm line. For the first time, I see a sternness in him that he's never displayed before – the teacher, the disciplinarian. I half expect him to bend me over his knee.

I'm surprised at how much I enjoy the thought.

I snort. "They don't scare me."

"They should. I know you love a mystery, but there are

powerful forces within their ranks that will do anything to ensure their secrets remain hidden. You have no proof they're connected to Keely's death, and all you'll succeed in doing by investigating them is bringing yourself into their line of sight. This is not your battle, and I won't allow you to make it yours. Stay away from them."

His eyes flick across the room in the direction of the tower, and I know he's thinking about the girl who flung herself from the roof, and the illicit kiss we shared in the very spot where she drew her last breath.

So many secrets. Sebastian knows more than he's saying. I sense it in the shifting air, in the stilted way he changes the subject to my classes and Leigh. But who is he protecting with his silence? Me, or William, or himself?

28

"That's it." Leigh slams her book shut. "If I have to stare at this page any longer, my brain's gonna ooze out my ears. Want to come foraging?"

"Is that what you call thrifting in Britain?" I peer at Leigh's gorgeous red boiler suit she found at a junk shop. "Because I could use a new winter jacket—"

"No, you meff. *Foraging* – as in, finding dinner on the side of the road. C'mon, it'll be boss. I want to get a decent haul before the end of the season."

I assume Leigh means dumpster diving, which is not exactly my idea of a 'boss' time. But I haven't left my room in three days except to shower, so I agree. If nothing else, it seems unlikely the Orpheus Society will want to follow us if we're getting up close and personal with the Asda dumpster.

Leigh tugs a black puffer jacket over her suit, and tugs her boots on over her woolen socks. I pull on every warm item of clothing I own, which I realize after months living in Britain is not nearly enough. Weather isn't your enemy in California the way it is here. Leigh tugs a bright red wool beanie over my head, tucking my hair underneath.

"This is cute." The hat has a huge pompom on top, which makes me look taller. It's also very, very warm.

"Thanks. I made it." No surprise there. Leigh's sculptural work is all based around traditional crafts and skills. She does a lot of knitting, crocheting, wood and stone carving, and can even make her own paint pigments. Leigh dumps her books out of her satchel and grabs the door handle. "Let's go."

We head off toward the forest path, looking over our shoulder every few minutes in case we're followed. I'm still getting the withdrawal notices pinned to my door every day, and they've been joined by other threats – letters about my unsatisfactory conduct sent to my scholarship committee (luckily my friend Gabe has influence with the committee, and convinced them it was a prank before they rescinded my scholarship), a request to revoke my mother's food truck license, even one revoking Leigh's contract with a local art gallery. A quick call to Claws – who has people in City Hall – stops their plans for my mom, and Leigh didn't want to do the gallery show, anyway. But what will the Orpheans do when they realize their plan didn't work?

To my surprise, we veer off the path into the forest, heading in the general direction of the amphitheater. "We're not going to the village?" I ask. Fat raindrops roll off the leaves and splatter on my shoulders. I tug my sleeves over my hands, wishing I had a pair of gloves.

"Nope." Leigh kneels in front of a scraggly weed and pulls out her knife. "Everything we need is right here. Look, this is hairy bittercress. The leaves in the center are nice and tender, and it has a peppery taste. Great in salads or add it to soup."

Leigh chops off a bunch of leaves and stuffs them in her bag, before moving to a clump of bushes further up the ridge.

"This is bullace – it's a kind of wild plum." She holds out her hand so I can look at the tiny purple fruits. "Look for the ripe ones, or they taste arse. If we get enough I can make wine. Otherwise, they'll do for dessert."

We move along the bushes, filling Leigh's satchel with the ripe fruit and tasting the best specimens. It's not long until my fingers are icicles stained red with juices, but the tiny fruits are so delicious I don't even care.

"Where did you learn all of this?" I ask as we move deeper into the woods, Leigh's satchel bulging with fruit.

"From my pops. He used to be the groundskeeper at a posh estate. He'd spend all day in the woods, chasing away poachers and bringing in edible mushrooms for the toffs' dinner. He'd bring me along sometimes when I didn't want to be in school. There was this old stone circle there, really ancient, with these worn carvings in the rocks. No one knows who raised the stones, or why, or what the carvings mean, but it's got this kind of electric, magical feeling, right? It's why I started sculpting – I wanted to get inside the heads of the people who built it. So, anyway, I keep telling Pops he should write a book about all the things he knows, but now he's rich all he wants to do is sit at home and yell at the telly. Ah," Leigh jumps over a log and crouches down. "Here's a treasure trove."

She pulls back the log, revealing a patch of white-capped mushrooms.

"Are those safe to eat?"

"'Course. You have to be careful, though. This one," she holds up one of the little fungi, "is the wood mushroom. It's edible and delicious, especially like this, when it's young. But this one—" she hops over to a nearby birch and wiggles a mushroom growing in the roots that looks completely identical to me, "—is one of the most deadly mushrooms around. This little blighter is the destroying angel, and it's responsible for half the mushroom poisonings in the UK. Eating a stew cooked with just a slice of destroying angel will lead to a horrible, excruciating death. And it's crazy, because you'll feel arse for a day or so, but then you'll get better, and you'll think you're perfectly fine, but then—" she makes a slitting motion across her throat. I swallow.

"How do you tell the difference between the two?"

"Easy." Leigh rattles off a list of differences – the off-white color of the wood mushroom's cap, the grey gills, the aniseed smell versus the pleasant, mushroomy scent of the destroying angel. She picks a bunch before beckoning me deeper, telling me to keep an eye out for sweet chestnuts, as if I have any idea what they look like.

I don't realize we're close to the amphitheater until I hear voices. I creep along the ridge, trying to see who's nearby. I've never seen anyone else at the amphitheater before. Leigh calls out to me, but I hold up my hand for silence, and she meanders off in the opposite direction.

I'm nearly on the other side of the *cavea* before the figures come into view. It's William and Monty. From the way they face each other and the storm brewing in William's eyes, they're having a disagreement.

I stifle a gasp and back behind the stones, but they don't seem to have noticed us. Leigh's wandering up the ridge, almost out of sight, her head bent toward the ground. She won't see them, and they won't notice her.

"—relax, will you, old boy?" Monty pats William's arm. "I have everything under control."

"Like fuck you do," William jerks away from his friend. The curse word sounds so foreign on his lips. "You underestimate her. She's not going to quit school, and it's pointless now anyway. The police are investigating Keely's death, and we're harassing the person who found her body. All you're going to do is make us look guilty."

They're talking about me.

And did William just all but admit they had something to do with Keely's death?

I press my back hard into the stones and strain to hear every word.

"I'm not concerned about the police," Monty says. "But she's a problem."

"She can't know anything—"

"She has Benet's diary." Monty says the Black Monk's name like they're close, personal friends.

"Yeah, and how do you think she's getting on with that?" William's voice is sharp. "You've had five years of Greek lessons at public school and you'd struggle to translate that rambling monk. She'll get bored and distracted and give up, but not if you keep after her – that just tells her she's onto something."

William knows I read some Ancient Greek. He saw me in the library. So why is he lying to Monty?

"And you know her so well?" Monty sneers. "Prince William fancies the sad weirdo with the true-crime fetish? Maybe it's not me tarnishing the reputation of our distinguished society, but you and your little girlfriend—"

"I know her type, and I know your way of containing this is going to drive her straight to our secrets. Now it's time to try things *my* way." William folds his arms, and from the way he looks at Monty, I know he believes he's won. "Diana and Tabitha agree, and the others. You've gone too far, and you need to be careful or you'll turn them all against you."

Monty narrows his eyes. "Are you threatening me, old chum?"

William's voice rises. "I didn't ask for this, Monty. None of us did. You've made us complicit—"

"I made you a *god*." Monty's eyes blaze. "Did you not *feel* him inside you? Was not the surrender the most glorious experience in your life? It is, after all, the point of the thing. I rather think our friends are too distracted by earthly concerns – it's all become an excuse for banal partying. So gauche. So ordinary. Well, I never wanted to be ordinary. For centuries we've been tasked with unlocking the key to the frenzy, to Plato's telestic madness. And here I present that key to you, and you spit it back in my face?"

"You're sick." William glares at his friend. "Stay away from her. Or I'll break this wide open."

Monty smiles. It's a cold smile, without mirth. "I fall and you fall, my friend."

William turns away. "Maybe I don't care anymore."

Monty watches him leave, his hands in his pockets, whistling a tune as if he doesn't have a care in the world. When William's back has been swallowed by the trees, Monty turns in the direction Leigh wandered off.

"George, old chum," he calls out. "I know you're out there. I saw your little head over the hill."

Shit.

"No need to be afraid," Monty says in a voice that makes me very, very afraid. "We just need to have another chat. Come out, come out, little rabbit. I don't bite...much."

As Monty moves casually toward the trees on the opposite edge of the *cavea*, I dart back down the slope as silently as I can, scanning the trees for Leigh. Behind me, Monty laughs maniacally. I glance over my shoulder, but he doesn't seem to be following. My phone buzzes in my pocket. It's Leigh, telling me she'll meet me at the top of the path.

My chest heaves and my thighs ache as I sprint toward Blackfriars, vaulting over fallen Roman columns and dodging low-hanging branches. I don't stop until I see Leigh swinging her bag and laughing at my gawky running.

"You look like a right-silly chicken! I found some chestnuts, which means we have everything we need for a feast—" she stops talking when she sees my face. "What's wrong? You look like Jason Voorhees just asked to bum a ciggie."

"We have to get out of the forest." I shove her toward the school. "Go. Now."

"All right, don't lose your hat—"

"Monty's back there."

Even though she doesn't know the full story, Leigh can see I'm terrified. She leads me straight back to her room. She's got a single with her own bathroom – one of the perks of being a lottery winner, of which there weren't many according to Leigh. We usually hang out in my room, even though it's smaller, because hers is stuffed to the brim with half-finished sculptures, weird bits of driftwood or tree stumps she's 'rescued,' junk store finds, and a dozen unfinished craft projects. I go into her bathroom to splash some water on my face and am surprised to see two glass containers filled with dark liquid sitting on the vanity.

"What are these?"

"That one's blackberry wine. I foraged the berries myself." Leigh taps the darker of the two. "The other is mead. I've been helping John look after the college hives. We extracted the honey in May, then I make the mead and age it. It's a sweet fortified wine, will get you well maggoted. This one won't be worth drinking for another few months, but I have a bottle I did last year we can share."

She pulls a box from under her bed, clattering around in dusty bottles until she pulls out the right one. She pops the cork and pours out two glasses of amber-colored, sweet-smelling liquid.

"To outsmarting the Orpheus Society for another day." Leigh holds out her glass.

I touch my glass to hers. "Cheers. I'll drink to that."

I take a sip. The drink is sweet – it tastes like a dessert wine, only with a heavy, warming, honey flavor. I settle into Leigh's desk chair, absentmindedly plucking the strings of her bass guitar, and turn over that wild and weird conversation between Monty and William I overheard.

"Sooo..." Leigh starts chopping mushrooms. "You ready to tell me about why Monty Cavendish has a vendetta against you?"

It comes out in a rush. Keely's disappearance, finding her body, all the weird things that have happened since I arrived at school, even about kissing Father Pearce on the roof. Leigh listens as she chops the hairy bittercress and hunts out other ingredients from a collection of mason jars on her bookshelf. She has a hot plate, which we're not technically allowed in our rooms, but I'm not gonna complain. I'm still talking when she places a bullace-filled dough ball into a pot of steam and hands me a bowl of warm mushroom soup. We crawl out through her window onto the sloping roof and rest our feet against the crenelations, and eat overlooking the athletic fields and the edge of the wood where the path leads down to the village. Silence stretches between us as Leigh considers what I told her. She refills our mead glasses.

"You really think they might've killed Keely?"

I shrug. "I don't know another explanation that fits what I just overheard. But Monty's right – if they've bought the faculty at Blackfriars, then they can buy the police, too. They won't be brought to justice. That's why I want to do the podcast – once I go live with my evidence, they can't shove those skeletons back in the closet. Only problem is, I currently have *no* evidence."

"I'll help if you want," Leigh says. "Monty came to a lecture I gave last year about the diet of Neolithic people in Britain. He's always bugging me to supply their parties. Maybe I can bargain some kind of access, get in on the inside."

"Supply them with what?"

"Alcohol and hallucinogenic mushrooms, mainly. Anything

rare. The guy is *obsessed*. If there's something no one else has tried, he wants to try it. Last year, for one of their events, he flew in a chef from Japan specifically to prepare fugu – you know, the insanely poisonous pufferfish that has to be cooked and cut in exactly the right way or you'll die a terrifying, paralytic death? Apparently, no one would touch their food, so Monty ate the whole lot right off their plates."

"That's insane."

"That's Monty. I've always said no because I don't want to hang around those wankers, but I can make an exception."

"That would be amazing, but I don't want to put you in danger." An image of Keely's glassy eyes and gaping mouth filled with dirt presses itself into my eyelids.

"You heard your boyfriend, Prince William. We're not in danger. They can't touch us while the police are investigating Keely's death, not if they want to keep their secrets. Do you really think they killed her? I can't believe William *dismembered* a girl." Leigh slurps up the last of her soup. "I work in the same studio as him all the time. When he paints, he doesn't get a speck of color on his clothes. He wouldn't do anything so messy."

"You're right," I laugh, too, but I can't stop the unease swirling inside me. I kept going over what Monty said. *If I fall, you fall.* What had he meant by that?

How deep is William in all this?

A rugby game winds down on the far field, and as the mud-caked students head back toward the dorms for dinner, a lone figure bursts from behind the monks' cemetery, jogging toward the path. Running shorts hug toned thighs, dark hair is swept back in a low ponytail, and the look of utter concentration on his face draws something dark and primal and needy from deep inside me.

Sebastian.

Leigh sees me looking, and cracks a smile. "I'm no Catholic, but I'd pray at the temple of that fine arse."

I punch her in the arm. Father Sebastian Pearce rounds the corner of the path and disappears. I watch that spot long after he's gone.

Has William got him mixed up in this thing? Is that what he meant when he called Sebastian a monster?

Can I trust my priest?

29

"You know, being a priest is a lot like being a Christmas tree," Sebastian says as he sets down two steaming cups of hot chocolate – the final touch on our Christmas feast of beef and cheddar sandwiches, boiled new potatoes, minted peas, and fruit mince pies and custard (courtesy of Mrs. Birtwhistle).

I pick up my plate and dig in. "How so?"

"The balls are just for decoration. I got you something."

I settle back into my usual chair, trying not to salivate over his ass (arse) as he bends over in front of his tiny Christmas tree (it's a real tree, in a plant pot, with a few baubles and a red star on top). The first term – called Michaelmas term because everything here is so bloody *British* – is over. My final assignments are handed in, and I have no exams until next term. Tomorrow, I get on a train to head to Manchester so I can catch a flight home for Christmas. I can't really afford the trip, but Mom surprised me with the ticket as an early Christmas gift, and I'm so desperate to check on her and Claws that I didn't argue. When I told Sebastian I'd be gone over the break, he insisted we have this early celebration.

And it's wonderful – we started with midnight Mass where those left at school gathered to sing carols in St. Benedict's. Then we holed up in his cozy rooms with the fire roaring while snow dots the cobbles outside. For a few hours, I can forget about Keely and the Orpheus Society and lose myself in our easy conversation and that electric spark that shoots through my body whenever we accidentally touch.

Truthfully, it's driving me crazy.

Being in the same room as Sebastian has become this exquisite torture, where every innocent word is loaded with meaning, and the kiss hangs between us like a pendulum, the cord tangled around us, drawing us closer together.

And it doesn't help that he changes the subject every time I ask about the Orpheans, William, and his life before seminary.

He straightens, and I try to flush my mind of any inappropriate thoughts as he hands me a rectangular package wrapped in red and silver paper.

"Open it now for me," he says.

I rest the present on my knee, touching the edges and trying to guess what's inside. My fingers spark on the edges, my whole body on high alert. I didn't get him anything, partly because nothing seemed perfect enough, but mostly because I know the reasons I want to gift him something aren't pure. But this...

Will whatever's inside this wrapping change things between us?

Sebastian settles down into his chair and sips his drink. I don't look at him, but I can feel his eyes boring into me as I tear off the paper. There's a saintly weight in the room with us, the weight of the sins we both long to commit.

Inside are two books, heavy and bound in leather, with gold stamping on the covers. The first is a copy of the *New Testament*. The second is a beautiful edition of Homer's *Iliad*, illustrated with Victorian lithographs. Both are in Greek.

"You're getting so good at the language now," he says. "Far better than I'd expect from someone learning for so short a time. And every Greek student deserves their own copies of the two finest works in that language."

I don't tell him it's because I've spent so many hours puzzling out the Black Monk's diary, which is still mostly a mystery. "Thank you, they're beautiful."

"When you get back, we can try some passages from the *Iliad*. Homeric Greek has its own idiosyncrasies, but I think you'll enjoy it." A frown passes over his features. "You do still want to continue our lessons? Exams are coming up. If it takes too much time away from your studies—"

"I have time," I say quickly. The last thing I want is to lose our weekly lessons.

"Good." He smiles, but the corners are tinged with sadness. "We haven't talked about your actual classes for some time. What did you choose for your AV project in the end?"

I think about the half-recorded episodes of my new podcast season stored on my laptop, and dash off my cover story about the interview series with Lauren Grainger. I hate lying to Sebastian, especially in the house of his God, but it's necessary. No one but Leigh and Claws can know about the podcast series until I release it. I can't risk tipping my hand to the Orpheus Society.

Sebastian interrupts my description of Dr. Grainger's morgue to ask, "May I say a prayer for your travels?"

"Of course."

He kneels in front of my chair and takes both my hands in his. He leans forward, and I lean also, so that our foreheads touch. Heat rushes to my head, and I feel a little woozy from the nearness of him. The innocence of this gesture somehow makes it even more taboo, sexier. *He doesn't know how he makes my heart race and my panties wet.*

Or maybe he does. Maybe he knows exactly what his chaste prayer is doing to me.

The rosary he wears around his neck swings forward and brushes my breasts. My lips part in a tiny gasp. The touch of the beads feels like an extension of him, like I'm being blessed by his fingers, his lips.

Sebastian draws my hand across my body in the sign of the cross. His eyes flutter closed as he speaks in Latin, a low, sexy murmur that forces me to press my thighs together, to try and keep my sacrilegious thoughts bottled up inside.

"St. Christopher is also called 'Christ-bearer,' because he carried the baby Jesus across a dangerous river." Sebastian lifts the rosary from around his neck and places it over mine. The black beads fall between my breasts, and my finger brushes the St. Christopher's medal threaded on the end. "I've asked him to protect you as you travel, and that the Holy Spirit be with you always. Amen."

"Amen."

He knits his fingers in mine, his breath blowing on my knuckles. And even though his head bends dangerously close to my thighs, and his whole body hums with need, this moment feels so right, so holy.

And yet also like foreplay.

When Sebastian finally rises from the floor, he turns away sharply. I can't be sure in the dim light, but I think there's a bulge between his legs. "You should go." He pokes the already-blazing fire, refusing to look at me. "I don't want to keep you too late. You'll still have to pack before your trip."

And even though I've already packed, I leave without a word, the rosary hanging heavy around my neck.

Christmas in Emerald Beach is a welcome break from the chaos that is Blackfriars. I bring pages of Benet's diary and my Liddell and Scott and don't look at them once. Between my mother wanting to spend every moment taste-testing new buckwheat recipes and Claws dragging me out for wild nights at Colosseum, I barely have a spare moment to think about William and Sebastian and poor Keely's bones.

While we watch horror films with Queen Boudica and Gizmo curled in our laps, Claws reveals to me the results of her search for Keely's family. "They're definitely in the business. Mid-level criminals, mainly involved in money laundering for larger outfits. You said she didn't seem to get along with them? If I had to guess, I'd say they feared she'd reveal their secrets to her powerful new friends and bumped her off."

"What about the Orpheans? Anything on them?"

Claws strokes Queen Boudica's sleek fur. The cat nuzzles her hand. "All the names you gave me are clean as a whistle, with the exception of Montague Cavendish. Would you believe he was one of Daddy's clients?"

"Wow." Claws' father ran the shipping arm of the Emerald Beach Triumvirate – drugs, antiquities, guns, art, anything illicit you wanted moving across borders, he could do it. That was the empire she inherited. If Monty was one of Julian's clients, that meant he was buying *whatever* when he was thirteen or so.

"He only purchased small things – some Greek artifacts, some illegal cheese, a few lesser-known narcotics. His name was on Daddy's list for the potential sale of some of the documents before all the shit went down. I don't have records for Brutus' years, but I assume the instability of our family made Cavendish nervous and he found other sources."

Interesting. I accept a file of documents from Claws – a paper trail that would condemn Monty while keeping Claws' business safe. I'm not sure how young Monty's taste in stolen artifacts and illicit cheese fits into the whole picture, but it points to a pattern of criminal behavior. It'll be the focus of one podcast episode.

Too soon, the holiday is over. It's a new year, and I have to board a plane back 'across the pond' to finish out my first term. Claws drives me to the airport, her golden hair streaming behind her as she speeds down the highway with the top down on Noah's Porsche.

"Just remember, if those bastards give you any more trouble, you let me know." Her eyes blaze with fire as she touches her fingers to the rosary I'm still wearing. She won't hesitate to make good her words. I picture William impaled on St. Benedict's spire, Sebastian crucified above his own altar. Monty Cavendish with his body cut to pieces, shoved in a shallow grave. The last image makes me smile.

"Thanks, but I want to handle this myself." I hug her back as she pulls over so I can get out. "You've got enough on your plate with those men and your cats. But I'll call you if I need you."

The flight is long and uncomfortable. I'm crammed in a middle seat between a mother with a screaming infant and a guy with terrible BO. I order the beef and Guinness pie for dinner, and it's soggy and cold. At Heathrow, I shuffle bleary-eyed to the luggage claim, pick up my suitcase, and make my way to the underground station. I nearly fall asleep as I wait for the tube to rumble into King's Cross Station, where I manage to haul my ass out before the doors close and make my connecting train in time.

Lent term, here I come.

I don't know what waits for me on the other end. Are the Orpheans still after me? They haven't sent me withdrawal papers since Monty and William argued in the forest, but that doesn't mean they don't have something sinister up their sleeves. And what about the investigation into Keely's death? Have the police turned up anything? Or has Monty bought their silence—

Wait, no.

I sink down into my chair as a familiar voice booms through the train car. *Of all the gin joints...it can't be them.*

But it is.

William and Diana and Monty and Richard and a couple of other girls whose names I don't recognize are crowded around two tables at the front of the car, making a racket as they put in drink orders and shuffle their luggage around.

I sink down even further in my seat, hoping they won't see me.

But, of course, the gods aren't that nice.

"Hey, George, old chum," Monty waves to me. Annoyed passengers turn their heads toward me. "Sit with us."

I bury my face in my book, my heart pounding. *Please, let him take the hint and lose interest—*

No such luck. Five minutes later I feel a presence looming over me. My lungs fill with the familiar scent of oil paint and leather books and dark chocolate. I peer over the top of my book and jerk with shock as my eyes meet William's.

I swallow hard. He leans against the back of the chair in front of me, looking completely bored and utterly gorgeous in a tweed blazer with the sleeves rolled up to reveal his toned forearms. I'm guessing he's been somewhere warm over the break, because his pale skin bears the faintest sun-kissed glow. He smirks down at me. "Monty sent me to make you sit with us."

"If Monty told you to jump off a bridge, would you do that, too?"

His gaze falls to the rosary hanging between my tits. He sighs. "Probably. Come. I guarantee it won't be as boring as that book you're reading."

I flip the cover over. Anna Karenina peers back at me, her pensive expression reminding me a little of the woman beneath the water in William's painting. I'd been trying to puzzle my way through the confusing Russian names since I boarded my plane, and had only managed to get fifty pages in. "You're not wrong about that."

I gather my things and follow William down the aisle. He walks with long, purposeful strides. I stare at a spot between his shoulder blades and try to remember the horrible thing in the bathroom and not to imagine what he looks like naked and undone, that blazer and crisp white shirt in a messy pile on my floor.

Not that I have to imagine much, not after his thin robe on Devil's Night and his cock jabbing into my thigh…

Stop it, George.

I'm walking toward trouble. I know it, but I can't stop.

William slides in beside Diana. The six of them are jammed tight in the seats. There's no room for me. I hover awkwardly in the aisle while they stare at me with curious incredulity until William places his hands on my thighs and draws me into his lap.

Sweet baby Jesus. His thighs are warm, the muscles hard, his stomach pressing against my back in a way that makes my skin stand on end. He clasps his wrists around my middle in a casually-possessive move that makes my heart flip.

What the fuck am I doing?

This guy is dangerous. He's done horrible things to me. And yet…every place where his body touches mine feels like it's made of boiling glass. Like I might burst into flames or shatter to pieces at any moment.

My foot dangles in the aisle, and my left butt cheek screams from the cramped angle, but I don't dare move. I don't want him to stop.

I'm fucking doomed.

"Hi, George." Diana pushes a can of soda ('fizzy' in Britain) across the table to me. Her smile is genuine, friendly. "Did you have a nice holiday?"

"I went to see my family in California. What about you?"

"Oh, we've been on Gran Canaria. Monty's parents have a house there." She bats her eyelashes at Monty, who sits across the table, leaning against the window and flicking an e-cigarette between his fingers even though they're not allowed. "It's marvelous. Have you been?"

"Um...no."

"Oh, you must come with us next time. Pristine beaches, the magnificent dunes of Maspalomas, cocktails at sunrise. We had such a laugh. Monty practically made himself sick scoffing some local potato dish smothered in *mojo picón* sauce. And Paris, have you been to Paris?"

"Er, no. My friend Leigh and I were talking about backpacking in Europe after exams—"

"Backpacking?" One of the other girls wrinkles her nose. She shuffles closer to Monty and lays a possessive hand on his bicep. Whatever. She's welcome to him.

A cramp shoots up the side of my leg. I can't take it anymore. I have to move. I wriggle a little to get my foot under the table. William leans forward, his fingers lightly brushing my hair away from my air. His lips graze my earlobe.

My whole body stiffens.

"Wriggle like that again," he warns in a husky whisper, "and I won't be held responsible for what I do."

Fuck.

Okay.

I'm pretty new at this sort of thing, but I didn't misunderstand. William Windsor-Forsyth is *flirting* with me.

Heat flares in my cheeks. I'm dancing with fire. And for the first time in my life, the prospect of getting burned excites me.

"...the Louvre, the best pastries you'll ever taste in your life.

You really *must* come with us." Diana's still talking about Paris. "We go every year during the summer holidays. Monty has a property along the Rue des Martyrs. It's where Benet of Blackfriars fled when he escaped Britain."

My ears perk up at that. Every year they go to a house in Paris connected with the Black Monk? It has to be for another one of their parties. Is it a ritual, like Devil's Night?

Benet must write about this place in his diary. I wonder if that's what they don't want me to figure out.

One of the girls looks to Monty in concern. He waves his hand in the air, trailing curls of vanilla-scented smoke. "Relax, Brenda. George knows all about our little supper club. Don't you?"

I refuse to come to pieces under the intensity of his gaze. I nod. No sense denying it. "Only what I've read in some dusty old history books."

"Listen, George, old chum." Monty takes a deep drag. "I just want to apologize about certain incidents I've had a hand in over the past few months. I've had my wires crossed, got the wrong message, but my good friend William here has straightened me out. No offense meant, all in good fun, eh?"

"Um..."

Is he serious? Is he actually apologizing?

Everyone at the table looks uncomfortable. Diana stares at her hands. Richard glares at Monty, his jaw practically hitting the table. Genevieve and her friend look ready to murder me. *What fresh hell is this?*

Under the table, William slips his fingers in mine and squeezes. I know better not to look over at him with Monty's gaze fixed on mine. *He's asking me to play along.*

I sense I've stumbled into a chess game playing out between William and Monty. But am I the queen, the most valuable piece on the board, or a pawn to be sacrificed at will?

I can't find out from the outside. And if accepting Monty's apology is going to get me on the inside, then I'll fucking take it.

"Sure," I say. The word tastes like urine. "No hard feelings."

"Excellent, excellent." Monty claps his hands. "Now, we've three hours until we reach school. That's enough time for me to trounce William at whist. Genevieve, be a dear and fetch us more booze. George, you in?"

William gives my hand a final squeeze before dropping it. Genevieve and her friend head to the dining car to procure more booze while Monty deals a pack of cards and starts explaining the rules. Under different circumstances, hanging out with this boozy group might be fun, especially when I got to spend the evening sitting on the lap of the hottest guy at school, a guy whose erection jabs into my thigh every time I adjust myself.

But nothing about this train ride is normal. Something very odd is going on with the Orpheus Society, and whether I like it or not, I'm being dragged into it.

30

My second term at Blackfriars flies by. Exams loom on the horizon, which means I'm so busy with study I hardly see anything of William or the Orpheus Society. Monty starts sitting with me in AV class, which is fucking weird and awkward, especially when he offers to help with my project. But he also happens to be brilliant, so I let him show me some ways to improve the quality of my podcast recordings and in the end, when I hand in my interview series for marking, I receive an A.

I still spend every Thursday night studying Greek with Sebastian, and every Friday night hanging out with Leigh. Sometimes we take the train down to York to see punk or metal bands, but mostly we just sit on the roof outside her window and drink mead and talk shit.

Every time William smirks at me across the dining hall or one of the Orpheans waves to me, I'm reminded that Keely's murder remains unsolved. The police released a report saying they have no leads, but they believe her death is related to organized crime, which tracks with what Claws told me. It all feels a little convenient to me. We'll see what the public thinks when I release my podcast.

Although I have precious little time for translating Benet's diary, I keep at it. I'm convinced that it holds the clue I'm missing, the piece of the puzzle that will blow this story wide open.

Now that I know about this house in Paris, I look for it in Benet's diary. I find no mention of it but I do find a strange word, Lutetia. A quick online search tells me that's the old Roman word for Paris, named for the swamps along the river Seine. I skip ahead to the entries that use this word and start there.

But it's slow going. William's right, Benet's archaic Greek and old-fashioned syntax – not to mention his propensity to wander off into undecipherable pigeon Latin and other languages I can't decipher – means progress is agonizingly slow.

The Friday before my History of Religion exam, I'm in Leigh's room, drinking mead and poring over the diary while she circles the cheapest hotels in her European backpacking guide. And there it is...the answer I've been looking for.

It's underground. Of course.

"I think I found it," I cry.

"Argh!" Leigh drops her books and flies across the room. She flops down beside me on the bed and tears my papers from my hands. "What is it? What am I looking at?"

"Benet's description of the underground chamber where the very first Orpheus Society meetings took place. And we're going to find it."

We take the train down to London and cross under the channel on the Eurostar. It's crazy to sit on a train eating a ham and cheese baguette and think that I'm thousands of miles underwater, but that's exactly what we do. We disembark at the Gare du

Nord station and make our way to the hostel Leigh booked for the next few nights.

Most of the Orpheans are spending their vacation in the Greek islands, so we don't expect to run into any of them in cold, miserable Paris. We skip most of the major tourist sites and opt for a tour of Père Lachaise, the largest cemetery in Paris. I lay flowers on Jim Morrison's grave while Leigh places her garland around the angel adorning the tomb of Oscar Wilde. We rent bicycles and cycle out into the countryside so we can visit Versailles, and Leigh can harass vintners for brewing tips in her terrible broken French. We line up in the pissing rain for a tour of the Catacombs, partly to see the bones of seven million Parisians artfully arranged in old quarry tunnels, and partly so I can slip a message to one of the guides, who moonlights as an anarchist urban explorer and has a reputation online for knowing the deep, hidden spaces beneath the city.

On the eve of our final night in Paris, I receive the email I've been waiting for – a map and instructions to find the spot of an Ancient Roman temple built underground when this land was still called Lutetia and occupied by a Romanized Gallic tribe called the *Parisii*.

Because of course Monty's house isn't important to the Orpheans. It's this temple they come to Paris for. And if I want to understand their rituals, I need to find out why.

We bundle up in our warmest clothes, pull on the waders our anarchist friend says we'll need, and follow the instructions to a manhole cover behind a row of dumpsters at the back of a restaurant two blocks from where Keely's Facebook messages said she went to visit Monty last summer. Leigh wrinkles her nose as I lift off the cover.

"What if there are alligators?"

"If I start screaming, you'll know there are alligators. Hold this." I hand her my phone. She aims the flashlight into the hole while I clamber down. Darkness closes around me as Leigh's silhouetted face retreats into a thin circle of light. I swallow against the encroaching panic, pushing back against the memories of monsters in the darkness that hover on the edges of my mind.

Alec isn't here. He can't hurt you.

My feet splash on damp stone. Leigh passes my phone down and I shine it around. I'm in a long tunnel, the ceiling arched with sturdy reassurance. A thin trickle of water runs along the center, and the graffiti adorning the walls writhes beneath my light – anarchist symbols, tags, names, strange animals leaping through a concrete jungle. I call up to Leigh. "No alligators."

I hold the flashlight as Leigh climbs down. We turn left along the tunnel and follow the instructions I memorized. We move quickly. The anarchist warned us that *cataflics* – police who patrol the tunnels – are active in this area. We count the junctions we pass – many of them have tunnels blocked off by concrete or cave-ins. My map is dotted with skull and crossbones marking unsafe spaces, and little cat faces indicating 'cat-flaps' – or small holes where we can pass laterally from one tunnel or chamber to another.

Luckily, we don't need to descend far into the dangerous lower levels. But as the tunnels grow smaller, the roof so low even I have to stoop my head, Leigh and I grip each other, our hearts pounding so loud mine is deafening in the gloomy silence.

My flashlight bounces along the wall, finding a black void – a jagged opening into a vaulted chamber. We clutch each other as we enter, holding our flashlights aloft to take in the impressive space.

"There it is," I whisper. A perfectly preserved Roman temple built underground. Six elegant Corinthian columns holding up an intact portico, surprisingly free of graffiti and rubbish. The anarchist said in his email that people hardly ever came here, that the place had bad juju.

You can say that again. I rub my arms where the cool air has raised goosebumps on my skin. The vaulted chamber rises five stories above our heads, carefully and symmetrically carved with fluted columns bearing the weight. This is different from the other spaces we've passed through – not the remnants of a limestone quarry, but something more deliberate, more *sacred.* And the temple, standing so proud, so untouched, her blackened entrance gaping open to invite supplicants inside. I sweep my light over the pedimental sculptures, noting the maenads and satyrs frolicking around the frieze. A temple to Dionysos. On the columns flanking the entrance, someone had carved two crucifixes.

We step inside.

Immediately, the air shifts. There's something dry and hot and sweet about it, the remnants of a ritual fire burning the back of my throat. There's a low stone altar in the center of the room, with stone benches around all sides. No statues, no color save for a few flecks of glittering gold that once adorned the ceiling. Not a typical Roman setup but then, what about this place is typical?

"The cult of Dionysos used to meet in underground temples," I say to Leigh. "They believed they were ritually re-enacting the descent of the god into the underworld and his triumphant resurrection. I can see how Benet might've drawn parallels between them and his outlawed religion, especially if he met his followers in this place."

"He wasn't the last person to worship here." Leigh shifts through a pile of objects on the altar. A pewter crucifix, several saint medallions, two impressive-looking and very dusty knives, a clay chalice stained with red wine residue. She holds up a large, flat bowl with a stand and two handles, the sides painted with cartoonish eyes. “What is it?”

“It’s an ancient Greek drinking vessel called a *kylix*. Well, it’s a replica.” I show her how when you lift the drink to your lips, the bowl blocks your view of the room. “That’s why they paint eyes on them. So Dionysos can watch out for you while you get shit-faced. Someone has been feasting down here. Diana said the Orpheus Society comes to Paris in the summer. This might be the remains of their last visit.”

I move deeper into the temple. Behind the altar, there’s a pile of rubbish. Food wrappers, more broken crockery, wine bottles, discarded clothing, all buried under soot from a fire.

Something about the shape of that pile, about the way it’s deliberately placed and the dark stains dotting the stone floor around it, makes my stomach drop. I know I’m making a terrible mistake, but I have to see. I have to know. The anarchist’s warning buzzes in my ears. I lift the corner of the jacket with my boot.

I stagger back.

A haunted whimper escapes my throat.

I don’t have to look again to know what I saw.

Bones.

Human bones.

31

"We should have gone to the police," Leigh shudders.

I nod at her from across my dorm room. In hindsight, that's exactly what we should have done – gone straight to the *Police Nationale* and told them we found body parts in an ancient temple beneath the city. But when we were there and I found those bones all neglected and chewed by rats, and Leigh went as pale as a ghost, we agreed to get out as fast as we could and try to forget it ever happened.

I know what Leigh was thinking – that her skin is a different color, that going to the police in a foreign country to report a dead body when we were trespassing in a place we weren't supposed to be is a massive risk. I was thinking the same thing, and also about word getting back to the Orpheus Society that we invaded their temple and found their little secret – the very secret Monty was trying to hide from me.

We were thinking about ourselves, not the person whose bones are hidden in that quiet temple, blood spilled in offering to Dionysos. From what I knew about decomposition, the remains had been there for a few months, maybe from the summer, and had been picked clean by rats. Not old enough to be Khloe May. Which wasn't good news. It meant there was another victim, another family out there who deserved answers.

Back on campus for term three – Benedict term – the guilt gnaws at us. We make an anonymous report to the *Police Nationale,* but we both feel certain it won't be investigated. I set up my microphone, and Leigh and I record the story of how we found the temple and what we saw. When I'm ready to release the podcast, the truth – and our own shameful part in it – will come out. Hopefully, we'll have got justice for this victim, too.

The only thing to do is keep going with my own investigation.

The first week of classes is chaos, but now that I know about the Paris temple I have another avenue of research. I'm careful on my next visit not to let the nosy librarian see the books I remove, and I settle into my favorite corral to see if I can figure out why Orpheus Society meetings keep turning up corpses.

Finally, in a book about underground political movements is a single passage that chills the blood in my veins:

> *...Benet of Blackfriars, a monk fleeing persecution in Britain for his subversive Catholic beliefs. Most of his writings are now lost; his early work was burned by Henry VIII, his later teachings destroyed by French authorities for their radical contents. Secondary sources are rife with elaborate and gruesome details – Benet of Blackfriars incorporating the Eucharist into pagan rituals of frenzied dancing, violent orgies, wild drinking and drug-taking, and Bacchanalian surrender. He enticed youth – men and women, radical in the medieval period – to join him in underground temples and chambers to recreate mythological stories. Some say the group practiced human sacrifice, although these kinds of claims made by authorities wishing to quash anarchist cells must be taken with a grain of salt. After they were forced out of Paris, records of the group show up in*

different places – Prague, Istanbul, Odessa – before finally disappearing from the historical record by the late 17th century. An urban legend states that descendants of the group returned to the Black Monk's original monastery in Britain, now a school—

A throat clears.

I slam the book shut and whirl around. William leans against the reading room doorway, hands in the pockets of a tailored black trench coat. A thin crimson scarf is wrapped around his neck and an expression of curious detachment plays across his features.

"What do you want?" I snap. That easy slope of his shoulders, that casual smirk, the itchy feeling down my spine that he's been watching me for a long time... it *infuriates* me.

I'm just so *confused*. William has done horrible things to me, and then, on Devil's Night, I think he might've saved my life. He's indifferent one moment, awful another, flirtatious the next. He hides behind this air of too-rich-to-give-a-fuck, and yet every time I walk into my room and see the woman under the water, I wonder if inside he's just as broken and messed up as I am.

William steps forward. The room seems to shrink in size until it's just him and me pressed together in a narrow tunnel beneath a Parisian street. From his pocket, he pulls an envelope, sealed with gold wax. He drops it on top of my book.

"Father Duncan asked me to deliver it to you. It's your new coursework schedule." William smiles, and it feels almost genuine, almost as if those pearly teeth and that haughty mirth are for me. "You're in our Greek class."

"I...what?"

He might as well be speaking Elvish.

"We start promptly at 2PM, Tuesdays, Thursdays, and Fridays. I think you remember the room. Come tomorrow with a one-page essay on Sophocles, written in Greek."

I stare at the letter, then back to William again. "What's this about?"

"Does it matter? You wanted to learn Greek. Well, now you'll get course credit for it." William slides the envelope toward me. I pick it up in shaking fingers. The paper is heavy and fancy, exactly the kind of paper I imagine Father Duncan taking great pride in. I slit it open and pull out a personal note from Father Duncan, and a list of texts written in his sloping hand.

I still can't believe it. "But...the class is full."

William nods. "It is."

"It's already the third term. I'll be hopelessly behind."

"Modesty doesn't become you. I know you've been studying on your own time. That's the only way a girl from *California* knew about pluperfect construction before I did." William says the word 'California' like it's a contagious disease. His shoulders stiffen.

Interesting. I may just be a true-crime podcaster, but I'm guessing this sudden invitation has something to do with me spending every Thursday evening in Father Pearce's rooms. As much as it annoys me that William can't own that he's being a possessive caveman, I kind of like it, too.

Besides, William is *welcome* to believe earning a place in Father Duncan's class will mean I give up working with Sebastian. He'd be wrong, but he can believe it.

I wave the letter at William. "Monty's in this class. Won't this tip him off that I can read Benet's diary?"

He stiffens. "You know about that?"

"I know that you conveniently got your friend to stop trying to torment me into quitting school by convincing him I'd never translate that diary. So won't this put Monty on my case again? Because I don't enjoy Greek enough to die for it."

At the word *die*, William shrinks away. Instead of answering me, he tugs on the lapels of his trench and tosses the end of his scarf over his shoulder. "Are you coming?"

"To Greek class? You said I start tomorrow—"

William turns away, his hand gripping the doorframe. I can see he's agitated, nervous. He wants us to leave the library. "No. To the beach."

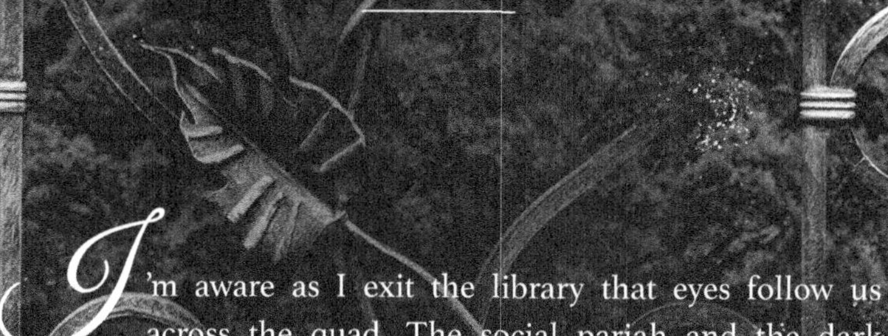

32

I'm aware as I exit the library that eyes follow us across the quad. The social pariah and the dark prince in public together, in broad daylight. The horror! The scandal!

If William notices, he doesn't care. He takes his time, setting a meandering pace as he talks about the medieval architecture and a new series of paintings he's working on inspired by the grotesques and gargoyles decorating the cathedral.

I shove my hands deep into my pockets, fingering the edges of Father Duncan's letter.

In the student parking lot, William unlocks a Bentley. If he expects me to be impressed, he's in for a shock. My friends back in Emerald Beach drive stupid fancy cars, and they're all the same to me. I slide into the passenger seat, trying to ignore my heart slamming against my ribs. "Take me to London, Jeeves."

William snorts, but doesn't dignify my silliness with an answer. We drive through the village – a surreal experience where people look up from their conversations as we careen past or whip their phones out to snap pictures of the car. On campus, people are so wary of the Orpheans and there are such strict harassment rules that I forget William is tabloid fodder. William drives without stopping, his jaw clenched. We speed through the small village and hit a bumpy, unsealed road.

Ten minutes later, we're at the coast.

Take a second to get this picture in your head. I've grown up a few minutes' drive from one of the most iconic beaches in the world. Emerald Beach is named for the crystalline color of its waters, the snowy white sand, and the glittering jewelry of the wealthy people who make it their own. I'm used to ice cream trucks 365 days a year, bikinis and flip flops as party attire, and humid salt air pervading *everything*.

I thought beaches couldn't impress me, but I've never seen a beach like this.

This beach is *wild*. Grey skies hang so low the sheer cliffs seem to extend directly into the clouds. Waves batter the shore, kicking up great plumes of white foam that churn like the fictive tears of a vengeful god. It's the kind of beach where it feels wrong to do anything except run into the waves wearing my best silk nightgown, holding a battered leather journal and screaming my lover's name.

There's no sand, only jagged rocks that jut from the earth like teeth, their faces worn smooth by the relentless onslaught of the ocean – as if we stand in the mouth of some ancient, Eldritch creature rising up to drink life from the Earth itself.

"Wow."

The wind tears the word from my mouth. I press against William while nature howls, unrestrained, around us. My heart patters for an impossibly long moment before he wraps his arm around my shoulders and pulls me closer.

Not even the ocean's pull can mask the scent of him – cracked leather, oil paints, turpentine, dark chocolate, vanilla, and something sweet and sinister and undeniably William floods my nostrils. I'm adrift in the wine-dark waters of

Dionysian revelry. Just give me a silk nightgown and I'll make a total ass (arse) of myself, that's how much I want to lose myself in him right now.

"I've spent my whole life overthinking everything, trying to find some deeper meaning," William says, his eyes fixed on the horizon. "In my house, everything came easy – even love, even sacrifice. I never felt like we earned our happiness. I always felt this mounting dread that an ancient and capricious God had laid his hands upon us and bargained our present joy for future sorrow. And then, when my mother drowned, I had the audacity to feel vindicated. That's the emotion I remember – more than the numbness, more than the soul-splitting grief. It was the high-handed imperiousness that I'd been right all along."

"How very dramatic."

"But of course," he says sardonically, a hint of humor in his voice. "What did you expect? I read Classical literature for fun."

"I didn't know your mother drowned."

William snorts. "If you expect me to believe the creator of one of the most popular true-crime podcasts on earth didn't do a Google search on the guy who stole her kiss in a forest of the dead, then you must think me a fool."

I smile. "Okay, so I did know. And if you've heard about my podcast then you know I lost my dad, too."

"*My Dad is a Gerbil* is such a profoundly silly name. I listened to the whole thing," he says casually. "Five times. Come with me."

He takes my hand, dragging me over the rocks as my mind reels from that shocker. I know I should pull away, but...he listened to my podcast? *Five* times? I haven't even listened to it five times.

I try to picture William Windsor-Forsyth lying in some princely bed, my voice entering his ears through expensive headphones. But I can't see it. Nothing about this is right.

Why did he listen to my podcast?

Why did he bring me here today?

I'm starting to wonder if I'm in danger. My mind flashes back to the bathroom, to all the awful threats the Orpheus Society has made. Does William intend these jagged rocks to be my tomb? I should have messaged Leigh and let her know where I am, but William's tugging my hand and it's too late, too late. Whatever path he's leading me down, I'm ready to follow him right to the murky depths.

Water sprays us as we clamber over the slippery rocks. At one point, the wind roars through a tunnel created by the formations, threatening to bowl me over. I crouch low and crab walk on my hands, with my ass waving in the air. So dignified. My cheeks flush when I stand upright, but William's mouth quirks. He takes my hand again and leads me along a narrow rock shelf. I flatten my ass against the cliff face, certain at any moment I'll fall, or he'll push me, and the wild ocean will swallow me.

"Turn around. Look at these." William cages my body in his arms as I cling to him and shuffle my feet around. Facing away from the ocean is even more terrifying. Hooray. Adrenaline courses through my veins and suffocates any protest I try to voice. William points to the worn cliff face, and I can't see anything, and the grim certainty that I'm about to become the victim of the ultimate Orphean prank freezes my blood. But he tugs and points, his face lit up with a feral excitement I'd never seen before. William Windsor-Forsyth almost has an *emotion*.

So I look. And I see dark shapes embedded in the rocks. Skeletons of long-dead creatures.

"Fossils." William points to each in turn. "These are ammonite, with the swirly shells. This is a belemnite, and I think this is some kind of plant remains. These all date from the Jurassic, over a hundred and forty-five million years ago. Last year I found bones from a pterosaur, which are now sitting in the back room at the Blackfriars Close museum."

"They're beautiful." I bend to peer closer at the intricate shapes. "Do you come here to look for them?"

"All the time. It feels like the gods are close enough to touch. And maybe that's my problem – I've always looked for God in fallible people – first Sebastian, then Monty. But as soon as I stepped foot on this beach last year, I knew God isn't in lofty churches or at the bottom of a bottle of Scotch. God doesn't save you from the storm. God *is* the storm. God is surrender, and art, and long-dead creatures trapped in rock. I think they're the most beautiful sight in the world." William flicks a loose strand of hair from his forehead. "Present company excepted."

Um...

Yes.

Right.

Even with the frigid ocean reaching her icy fingers toward me, I feel the flush of his words hit my cheeks. I have to turn William's statement over in my mind, testing it for all the ways I can misunderstand, all the plausible meanings that don't mean *this*, because *this* is impossible...

I swallow. "Let me get this straight, you brought me here to say..."

"That I fancy you?" He looks at the fossils, raking his fingers through his hair. His brow furrows, as if I've asked him a particularly gnarly grammar question. "I did. Although 'fancy' feels like too capricious a word for what you are to me. You are the protagonist of my daydreams, a poem I long to know by heart but whose perfect words trip on my tongue. There is not a single moment when I'm not irretrievably possessed by you."

Wow. Okay. Wow.

I think my heart's trying to commit suicide, the way it batters against my chest for freedom. Or maybe it's because I've never dreamed someone like him would say those words about *me*. "But why did…"

"Why did I set about to destroy you? A fair question." A dark cloud forms at the edges of his eyes. "In the beginning, I was afraid. The only way I can keep going, keep functioning, is by turning my heart into one of these." He taps the beautiful ammonite. "Encased in rock, frozen in time. And then you came along and made me *want* to feel things again. So I was afraid, and my fear made me callous. I wanted you to hate me so you'd go far away from me and the Orpheus Society and live your amazing life somewhere else, with someone who deserves you. Then, when you started sniffing around the Society, the others got nervous. Hence, the bathroom."

I fold my arms. "Finally, we get to the heart of the thing."

We glare at each other, neither wanting to reveal the secrets that dance on our tongues. I break William's gaze to glance toward the top of the cliffs. "Is Monty up there, ready to shout 'what ho, George, old chum,' before you push me over the edge?"

William grabs my shoulders. I cry out as his fingers dig into my flesh. "You have to listen to me. You're too clever for your own good. Trust me when I say whatever you think you know about the Orpheus Society, it's so much worse. And I'm caught in the middle of it."

"And now you're dragging me into it."

He spins away, tearing at his hair. "You dragged yourself into it when you went out on Devil's Night, when you started digging around in old books and translating Benet's diary, when you started fraternizing with Sebastian fucking Pearce."

My mind reels. "Who even says 'fraternizing'? And what's Sebastian got to do with any of this?"

"Don't." William grabs my shoulders again. His eyes reflect the storm of the ocean. "I can't stand that monster's name on your lips. He can't protect you, George. You were there in the bathroom – you know the power Monty has over this school, over all of us. People will do whatever he tells them, including me. All Sebastian's prayers and angels won't make a difference if Monty decides you're a threat again."

"And why doesn't he believe I'm a threat now?"

"Because I'm a selfish bastard." William's hands tremble. "It's too late for me. I'm already a dead man walking, George. But I can save you. You have two options. You leave Blackfriars. Or you stay. As my girlfriend."

As my girlfriend.

The words sound so *impossible.*

So perfect.

I swallow. "I don't understand."

"I want us to be together," he says. "And that's allowed, so long as Monty believes you're under my spell. I have him convinced that your interest in Benet's diary isn't about Keely, but about *me*. He thinks you're obsessed with me and that I'm in need of a new plaything, and I know that offends the very core of who you are, but it also keeps you safe as long as you ask no questions and demand no answers. It's too much, I know it's too much to ask of you, but I don't want to send you away where I can't be near you."

This is all so *insane*. William took me to these cliffs to declare his feelings for me, and he hasn't told me *anything*.

"I can't be your girlfriend," I say. "You were in that bathroom. You helped Monty do that to me. How can we go back from that?"

He hung his head. "I did it because I knew you were strong enough, because going against Monty would make things even worse for you. I'm not saying it's easy, or fair. I'm asking that if you care for me even an ounce as much as I care for you, can you find a way to make this work?"

Tears prick my eyes as I shake my head. "I can't."

"Then you have to leave Blackfriars," he says, his mouth turning down at the edge. "Either of your own choice or in a body bag. Don't think I'm being dramatic. It'll come to that in the end."

But I've seen that dead look in Monty's eyes enough to know that the threat of him is real. I've uncovered the bones of two people who crossed him. And they deserve justice. If I want to find the truth, I have to stay.

I've no intention of stopping my investigation.

And William...poor little prince, so utterly lost, so perfectly tragic. He stands upright but unravels at the edges, his shadow bending toward the wild surf. I haven't realized how much I want him until I see him like this, and I think I've never wanted anything more.

"Yes," I whisper.

"Pardon?"

"Yes. I'll stop, if it will keep you safe. I want—" I swallow. "I want you—"

My words cut off as William presses his mouth to mine.

I'm so shocked that I stagger backward, my feet slipping on the narrow ledge. The world reels as my body goes floppy like boiled spaghetti. Ocean and rock fly up to meet me. And then I'm spinning and crying and I'm being swallowed by salt and any moment now I'll dash my brains on the rocks and—

Warm, solid arms collect me, jerking me from the ocean's jaws. William drags me back from the brink. My back hits the rock face, scraping my skin raw through my soaked shirt. William cages me in his arms so I can't move. He quirks his mouth again, and the raw vulnerability in his eyes makes me cling to him, digging my fingers into the flesh of his forearms.

"I'm such a menace," I moan, my chest heaving as I look over his shoulder at the unforgiving water.

"I'm sorry," he says. "I shouldn't have done that."

"Um."

"Last time I stole your kiss. It was wrong, but I've thought of nothing else since. I wanted this time to be different." He plants his hand beside my face, and I can't move even if I wanted to. "May I?"

My stomach drops into my knees. "Well, you did ask very politely."

He kisses me again, and even though I know it's coming, it still sends a shudder through my whole body. He crushes my soul beneath his tongue, and it's so hard and raw and perfect. A kiss made of poetry. Because of course we have our first real kiss on a precarious ledge in the company of million-year-old fossils while the ocean demands her sacrifice with a bellicose roar.

I was cold a minute ago.

But as William Windsor devours me, I don't know if I'll ever feel cold again.

33

"You kissed William *again?*" Leigh spears a piece of sausage with her fork. "*The* William Windsor-Forsyth? You filthy hussy."

"Technically, he kissed me." The blush makes my ears hot. "And last time didn't count."

It started bucketing down with rain while William and I were at the beach, so instead of our usual hang-out spot on the roof, Leigh and I are lazing in front of the fire in The Bad Habit with our favorite British comfort foods spread out before us – beef and Guinness pie, bangers and mash, and two tall pints of cold cider. I've just spilled the whole sordid story and she's taking the news like any true friend would – by teasing me mercilessly and making gagging noises when I told her he considered me *a poem he longed to know by heart*.

Okay, that is pretty corny.

But also, wow.

Leigh licks gravy from her fingers. "Like fuck it didn't. You're so boss. William only dates like, duchesses. Are you a secret duchess?"

"We don't have duchesses in America." I flip through the

dessert menu, wondering if 'spotted dick' tastes more appetizing than it sounds. "I *am* friends with a mafia queen, if that counts?"

"That totally counts. You're the *most* boss. I can't believe it. Are you two dating now?"

"I think so? He was too busy with his tongue down my throat to define the parameters of this...whatever it is. And then the sky opened up and we ran back to the car and he dropped me off and I came to find you and holy crapballs he's behind you *right now,* so maybe keep your voice down. Don't look. No, *don't look.*"

Of course, Leigh looks. She's not subtle either, turning around in her chair to gape at the Orpheus Society table, where William settles in with Monty, Richard, Diana, and Abigail.

"He's looking this way," Leigh squeals.

"That's because you're making a scene," I mutter into my pie, wishing I could burrow beneath the pastry crust and disappear forever.

"George," William calls out. "Come sit with us."

The pub is so quiet you can hear my heart thud on the floor.

"What are you waiting for?" Leigh nudges me. "Go recite tragic poetry to each other and make Monty throw up."

I grip her arm. "You have to come with me."

"I'm not invited."

"Yes. You are." I drag her to her feet. Every eye in the place watches as I drag Leigh over to their table, which is suddenly a million miles away. Even Kit watches from behind the bar with a wary gaze. I guess she doesn't want to get stuck with my unpaid bill again.

William slides over in the booth to make room for both of us. As I drop down beside him, he slides an arm casually around my shoulders and extends his right hand to Leigh. "I don't believe we've met. I'm William Windsor-Forsyth."

"Leigh Cho." They shake vigorously.

I think my shoulders are going to spontaneously combust.

"William, you know her." Abigail sneers at Leigh. "She's the *lottery winner.*"

She says that the way someone might say, 'she's on Jerry Springer.'

"Actually, Pops drew the winning ticket." Leigh reaches across the table and whips Abigail's drink from in front of her. "I just mooch off his good fortune, which is something you can relate to, eh?"

Abigail glares at Leigh, who slurps happily on her drink. Monty cracks up laughing.

"I like you, Leigh Cho. Telling it like it is. I'm positively *desperate* to have you cater one of our private shindigs. We'll talk, yes? Can I buy you ladies a drink? No, no, don't you panic, Georgie," Monty shakes his head at me. "It won't be like last time, I swear. William will make sure I behave. Kit, what about another round for the table?"

As Kit comes to take orders, William leans over me, brushing his lips over mine. "Are you okay?" he whispers against me, so quiet I almost can't hear over the thundering of my heart.

I nod. I can't formulate words with his tongue dancing sin in my mouth.

He traces his thumb along my jawline, his kiss deep, possessive. It's a kiss that tells everyone in the room that I'm his. It's a total caveman play, and I love it so fucking much. "And you won't say anything about Keely or—"

"I'm just here for a good time." I fist his collar, bringing his face closer for another kiss that takes my breath away. I hear Monty and Leigh wolf-whistle. I admit, part of me knows I need to play my role perfectly if I'm to get on the inside of the Orpheus Society.

And the other part of me is ready to lose myself utterly to the dark prince.

When we pull away, William's ice eyes shimmer with a

whole universe of hidden secrets. I rub my raw lips, disarmed by the sense that I'd stepped through a shadowed doorway into a world from which I can't escape. Kissing at the beach felt like falling inside one of his paintings, but this kiss is almost *too* real.

Kit returns with drinks and a couple of baskets of fries. I'm full from my pie, but I take a few just to have something to do with my hand. Monty sips his drink and watches Leigh with an intense gaze I don't like at all. "What are you ladies up to this weekend?"

"My band is playing on Friday night at the Undercroft," Leigh says. "George was going to come along and get maggoted in the mosh pit, right, George?"

"That's the plan."

"Perfect." Monty slaps the table. "A band. What fun. We'll all be there, won't we, chaps? William here loves music. He played piano with the London Philharmonic, did you know? Loves his Shostakovich, does William. Will you play any Shostakovich, Leigh?"

I RACE from Criminology across the campus and scramble up the stairs of Martyrs' Tower, determined not to be late. I arrive at Father Duncan's office sweating and disheveled. I try to smooth my hair with one hand as I juggle my Liddell and Scott and rap on the door with the other.

Monty opens the door. "George, old chap. Welcome, welcome."

He sweeps his arm around, indicating the room, which looks exactly the same as last time I saw it but for one exception – an extra chair at the table.

For me.

I swallow. *This is it.*

I may not be part of the Orpheus Society proper, but they let me into their exclusive little Greek club. They trust that I'm not listening to their secret conversations or trying to dig up dirt on Devil's Night. I don't know how William convinced Monty I'm nothing more than his latest plaything, overwhelmed and besotted by the attention of such powerful people. But Monty is so full of his own shit and so bored with his easy existence that the idea of having a new toy around is worth letting his guard down.

I'm going to make him regret it.

I take my seat. William reaches under the table and squeezes my hand. Diana and Abigail compare their compositions while Father Duncan bustles around a little side room, which contains a simple kitchen. He emerges a moment later carrying a tray of tea and a selection of tiny berry tarts. I see Sebastian isn't the only one who's in Mrs. Birtwhistle's good books.

"George Fisher, what an absolute delight." Father Duncan pours my tea with his own hand, but makes the others fix their own. "We're all excited to hear your composition."

William and I stayed up until the library closed last night perfecting my Sophocles essay. The actual composition didn't take that long, but we kept getting distracted with – as Leigh so eloquently puts it – *snogging*.

I felt a little guilty canceling my Thursday night with Sebastian, since he would have loved to discuss Sophocles with me. But William wanted to help and I'm learning just how difficult it is to say no to my dark prince. Besides, things are still weird between me and Father Pearce, and I don't quite know how to tell him about William.

When the tea is poured, Father Duncan begins the lesson. He starts by having each of us read our compositions aloud, stopping us when we say something he disagrees with or wants to explore further. "What provoked Sophocles to use *Oedipus* to examine a human being's responsibility for their own moral sanctity?" he asks William. To Diana, "Does tragedy hold a spiritual significance for Sophocles?" For me, he wonders, "Is the justice in Sophocles' plays of a divine or a human origin?"

Father Duncan jumps around topics like a child in a toy store, moving from Sophocles to Shakespeare to the modern age of media, with a brief but memorable stint mired in Nietzsche's *Thus Spoke Zarathustra*. He speaks of capricious gods and pagan spirits like they're his close, personal friends, and he hangs on every word his students speak like they contain droplets of the elixir of life.

I can see why they adore him so, and why they closely guard this special world against outsiders. I see too, what Sebastian means when he says Father Duncan is attracted to the power of the Orpheus Society. Interspersed within our discourse are his allusions to summertime visits to their family estates, invitations to holiday with them in Paris, and offhand references to famous people he knows. Father Duncan doesn't see his students as *people*, but as interesting window-dressing on his life. His indifference has none of the callousness of Monty's personality, and yet the two could be brothers.

The conversation leaves me giddy and disoriented. Apart from reading my essay, I barely say a word the entire class. Father Duncan doesn't seem to notice, so enamored is he of his own voice.

Their gentle intellectualism hides their incestuous nature. There are no outsider opinions, no impassioned speeches that rock the boat of Father Duncan's personal divinity. They've all read the same books, attended the same posh schools, and danced at the same parties since they were in diapers. They're brilliant, beautiful, and bound for glory – and it's clear that until I worship at the altar of Duncan, I'll never be one of them.

But I have to remind myself that I'm not here to become one

of them. I'm not even here for William's hot mouth on mine, as much as my body believes that's my sole purpose.

I'm here because Duncan's face was in that picture.

He's more to the Orpheus Society than a favorite teacher, and I am going to get to the bottom of it all.

34

I never intended to go anywhere near the Undercroft, which is the Blackfriars student club. It's literally in an undercroft beneath Martyrs' Quad where the monks used to store their wine, and every weekend night it's packed with the kind of people I normally wouldn't touch with a ten-foot monk pole.

I certainly never expected to be showing up on the arm of William Windsor-Forsyth, seventeenth in line to the throne. But ever since that day on the beach, my life has gone from terrifying to surreal. William is with me every moment, so much so that I haven't even been able to see Sebastian. He's messaged me a couple of times today, asking if I'm okay, and I dashed off a quick answer because I needed to get back to kissing William. I swear, he's become like oxygen or horror films – utterly essential for existence.

Tonight, he looks fucking dangerous in a black wool coat, dress slacks, and crimson scarf, his hair artfully tousled, his hands smelling of oil paint and India ink. I'm wearing a white dress covered in a print of anatomical drawings of bats, with a wide black belt, black torn stockings, and my red New Rocks.

Our picture belongs in the encyclopedia next to the entry for 'least likely to fuck,' but when William rests his hand in the small of my back and smiles at me like I'm Aphrodite in the flesh, I wonder if I've wandered into a fairy tale. *How is this my life?*

Because it's not real, I remind myself as we descend the narrow staircase into the packed club. *Because he's trying to save you from yourself, and you're trying to hang him by his own noose.*

William hooks his arm behind me, squeezing us through the crowd toward the bar. Everyone is much taller, cooler, and drunker than me. I accept the pint of cider William offers me and gaze around nervously, wondering what this crowd will do when Leigh's punk band takes the stage. I spy Monty in the corner, his arm around Diana's shoulders as he talks to two girls from our AV class. He doesn't see us, thank fuck – he's utterly absorbed in the conversation, staring at the girls with the same rapt attention he gives everyone he talks to. Monty has this way of making you feel like the complete center of his world, like no one is more interesting or beautiful or witty than you. And all the while he's churning over some manipulative question or nasty retort.

He reminds me too much of Walter Hart, the man behind the crematorium that gave me a gerbil's ashes instead of my father. Only Monty is more cunning, more intelligent, and more dangerous. *And I'm going to take him down—*

"George, you came!"

Leigh bounces over to us. Her hair is wrapped in twin buns with red ribbons streaming down her back. She wears a red corset and black tutu skirt and knee-high Fluevog boots and doesn't give a shit that a bunch of guys further down bar are talking shit about her. I love her so hard right now. She shoves a glass into my hand. "Drink this. My drummer Hank got it for me but if I have another bevvy I'm going to pee myself on stage. Hi, William."

"Hello." He refuses to yell over the music, so his greeting is more of a lip-reading exercise. Leigh chatters excitedly until word reaches her that the vocalist has locked himself in the bathroom, so she leaves us to wrangle her fellow musicians.

"You sure you're going to enjoy this?" I ask as we push toward the front of the stage. The bar security has set up metal barriers – they expect a rowdy pit tonight. Much more my style. "It's not exactly the scene you're used to with the London Philharmonic."

"Don't underestimate us classical musicians. We've had some wild nights," William whispers against my ear, his hands wandering possessively over my hips.

"Oh yeah? I find that very hard to believe."

"It's true. I partied with Broken Muse on their last UK tour. I woke up the next morning in the middle of Hyde Park wearing nothing but a giant diaper with a jelly mould for a hat." He nibbles my earlobe until I gasp, "Did I mention you look like a goddess tonight?"

"Sure. I'm Medusa." I fix him with a stony glare and make a snake puppet with my hand. I expect him to laugh, but he frowns.

"Don't put yourself down, George. Every guy in this room is jealous of me tonight."

I doubt it very much, but the earnestness and conviction with which William spoke makes my head spin. I find myself unable to look at him, so I fold my hands on the barrier and wait for the music to start and the stupid red flush to dissipate from my ears.

Leigh's band takes the stage. They're terrible. They're out of tune and out of time and their singer cannot pull off their Iggy Pop cover.

They're terrible and I don't care. As soon as the first ragged guitar riff sounds, I go to a happy place. I'm sixteen-year-old George again, flinging myself around my bedroom to angry music – the only ritual that drives out the demons.

I *need* this. I need soul music. And I'm not the only one. Someone slams into me from the side as the crowd gets going. Bodies crash and churn around each other, carrying me away on an ocean of flailing limbs and wild abandon.

I shove my way to the front of the surging mosh pit, jumping with the crowd, enjoying the way elbows slam into me and the crowd presses in on all sides. I've lost William, but I'm not bothered. This is not for him. This is not music for people who have everything. These are the anthems of the lost and the lonely, the small and the broken.

I'm right at home.

The band launches into a cover of the Sex Pistols' 'God Save the Queen,' and the whole place goes *crazy*. Leigh leans over her bass to tug me on stage. I climb up and peer out at the surging crowd, their friendly jostling now tinged with violence. Leigh gives me a shove and I dive into the drunken sea, arms flailing, trusting the music to catch me.

It does. They do. Hands hold me above the fray, passing me from person to person as I swim toward the back of the room. My veins hum with liquid fire. The music roars in my ears. This is the most fun—

And, suddenly, I'm dropping. There aren't enough people back here to hold me up, and they're too drunk, too wrapped up in the song to see I land properly. Panic seizes me as my shoulders dip. My head hurdles toward the ground. I throw my hands out in a vain attempt to catch myself and—

Warm arms slide around my waist, halting my fall, leaving me dangling ass-up with my dress around my thighs and my Snoopy panties on display for the whole bar to see. My savior flips me over, setting my feet back on the floor.

Sebastian.

He looks amazing in a red shirt and black jeans and midnight hair loose over his shoulders. He's not wearing his collar, and the absence of it combined with his hand lingering on my arm feels dangerous. In his rooms, we have the safety of our Greek studies and that white binding at his throat to create our boundaries. But here, things aren't defined. We aren't student and teacher, supplicant and priest. Here it's raw music and sticky alcohol and *he's not wearing his collar*.

"Are you okay?" He grips my shoulders so hard I feel bones crack. "I saw you start to dip and I just reacted—"

"Thank you." I busy myself smoothing my dress so I don't have to look at him. *Father Pearce just got a nose full of my Snoopy panties. Can I please die now?* "What are you doing here?"

"You don't think a priest can enjoy punk music?" He makes a mock-hurt expression. "How little you know me."

"I know you have great taste. I just meant—" I gesture to the surge of bodies and the sticky floor and the terrible band on stage. (I love Leigh, but seriously? They just fucked up 'Blitzkrieg Bop' and that song has, like, three chords.) "This isn't too juvenile for you?"

"Christ almighty, how old do you think I am? I'm not shipping out with Charon just yet." Sebastian smiles. "The truth is, I came to look for you. It's not like you to cancel your Greek lesson, and I missed talking to you."

"You...you did?" My stomach does a flip.

He nods. "And I saw the posters Leigh put up and figured you'd be here. So you're doing okay? Are you here with anyone—"

Someone slams into us, shoving Sebastian into a bar leaner. I look up to see William, his face wild with fury, hands curled into fists at his sides.

"Don't you touch her," William growls. His mouth quirks at

the edge in that way that might to an outsider look like a smile, but I can sense violence rising inside him. Unspilled blood tangs the air.

Sebastian rights himself, apologizing to the girl whose drink he knocked over. He arranges his face in a pleasant expression as he faces William. "George was about to have a nasty fall. I caught her—"

"I bet you did. I bet you're poised in the wings to catch her in your arms, to be the kind shoulder she cries on after I tear her heart out and leave her broken and desolate. Isn't that right? Isn't that your plan?"

"William, I—"

"You have to ruin *everything* good in my life. What do I have to do to be free of you?" William smooths down the labels of his jacket and fixes Sebastian with such a look of loathing I know whatever happened between them cannot be repaired. "We're leaving."

"I'm not." I fold my arms. "You don't speak for me. I want to finish watching the band."

"You're actually enjoying this cacophony?" He looks from me to Sebastian with disgust. "Or is it *him* you don't want to leave? Are the two of you going behind my back? Are you laughing at me while you fuck in the sacristy?" He snatches a glass of red wine from a girl and throws it in Sebastian's face. "Does her cunt taste as good as communion wine? Does it taste as good as my mother's?"

Oof.

Yikes.

Did he just say that Sebastian...

I'm aware that people are staring. William's eyes dart wildly around the room. He looks like a fox cowering from the hunt. *Any second he's going to bolt.* "William, please. Talk to me. What's this about?"

"I'll go." Sebastian's eyes bore into mine. "I don't want to cause a scene. Have a lovely night, George, William. I hope the two of you commit some sins worthy of the confessional booth."

Sebastian turns his back and starts to move through the crowd. William lunges for him, but I grab his arm. "What are you doing?" I hiss. "Everyone's watching."

William shakes my arm off. "I'm going home."

I follow William out of the club. I know Leigh will forgive me.

We don't say a word as we step into the bitter cold night. The awkwardness hangs between us. On the other side of the quad, Sebastian leans against the wall of the old refectory, watching us with those intense anthracite eyes.

I grip William's arm so he can't wriggle free. We step in front of Sebastian, and he meets my eyes. The pain in those midnight depths almost sends me reeling. Whatever happened tonight sprung from seeds planted long ago and has been haunting both of them ever since. William's body trembles with rage. I fold my arm over his. "William and I are taking a walk through the old refectory," I call pleasantly to Sebastian. "Would you like to join us?"

The air sizzles with tension. I expect William to turn away in disgust, but he clings to me like I'm the only thing keeping him upright. Sebastian shrugs. "Of course."

He falls in step on the other side of me. I long to take his hand, too, but I don't dare. As we walk, William pulls a packet of cigarettes from his pocket and withdraws one. He flips a silver lighter, but Sebastian plucks the cigarette from his lips before he can light it and tosses it in a trash can.

"Those things will give you cancer," he says.

William stiffens. It's such a weird exchange. I don't say anything. I want to watch the two of them, try to figure out this secret that poisons them.

At the entrance to the refectory, Sebastian hangs back, allowing me and William to enter first. I poked around in here on my first day, but I haven't had any reason to come back. It's different at night with the moon shining through the jagged lines of the missing roof – a beam of cold light hitting the fresco on the far end *just so* to highlight the lines of Jesus' face. He always looks so serene. How can he be so calm in the face of what awaits him?

I can't stand it anymore. I fold my arms and frown at both of them. "Okay, time to tell me the whole story. How do you know each other? What's this stupid fight all about?"

"We're brothers," Sebastian says.

Of all answers I anticipate, that isn't one of them.

"We're nothing of the sort," William huffs. "And you don't have to explain. George will have already figured it out."

Sebastian sighs. "Even our George can't read minds, William. We owe it to her, especially since you insist on placing her in such danger. Isn't it time we both unburdened ourselves of our sins?"

Sebastian's hand falls on William's shoulder. That simple gesture tells me *everything* about their relationship. Sebastian feels a responsibility to William, and even through his hatred, William believes Sebastian is his salvation.

I remember all those weeks ago when William crashed into me as he fled the confessional booth. I recall how white Sebastian's face was when he emerged to talk to me. What sin exists between them? What evil did William confess that could flap unflappable Sebastian?

Is Keely's murder on his conscience?

"I have no sin to confess." William shrugs Sebastian's hand away with an ugly scowl, and storms into the night.

He doesn't look back.

35

I'm at a party. I don't remember how I got there or who I came with, but I'm alone now, trapped by a sea of sweaty bodies writhing to shit music.

And then, in a moment, the party is snuffed out. The lights go out and the press of people becomes the fetid claustrophobia of being pressed in a polyester sleeping bag with someone's body on top of me. Alec LeMarque with his hand over my mouth, the reek of his alcohol breath panting against my neck as he shoves his hand down my pants. Me, trying to scream, even as I buck my hips, trying to force him deeper, to show him *exactly how I like it...*

I wake with a start, throwing myself upright in bed. I rub my arms. I'm drenched in sweat and trembling. My duvet and sheets are in a ball on the floor, and there's a tear across the breast of my snoopy camisole where I raked myself trying to get Alec to let go of me.

No.

I squeeze my eyes shut, but he's right there behind my eyelids, whispering *show me how you like it...*

No.

I thought I was over this. I haven't had a nightmare about Alec for a long time, not since Claws took care of Alec for me.

So why now?

I know what the nightmares are about – it doesn't take a genius to figure out that I get them when I feel as though my life is spinning out of control. I had them all through the podcast release. I had them when Dad died, and they made me feel so fucking guilty because I wanted to dream about his smile and all my brain would give me is that stupid fucking night when I was fourteen...

And now, with Sebastian and William, I'm not in control. I'm a ball of feelings and lust, which is so completely foreign to me I don't know what to do, and I—

No.

That's not it.

The realization slams into me as I see the shadow move in the doorway.

The *open* doorway.

Someone's in my room.

I open my mouth to cry out, but another shadow lunges across the bed and shoves a bag over my head. What little I could see in the gloom becomes a terrifying blackness.

No. Please, no.

I lash out, kicking and scratching the way Claws taught me. *Don't give them a chance to get the upper hand.* My foot connects with something I hope is dangly and sensitive.

"Oof," someone grunts. More hands grab my arms, wrenching them behind my back. My attackers whisper to each other in a language I don't understand. There are too many of them and *I can't see, I can't see—*

The panic overwhelms me as everything goes dark.

36

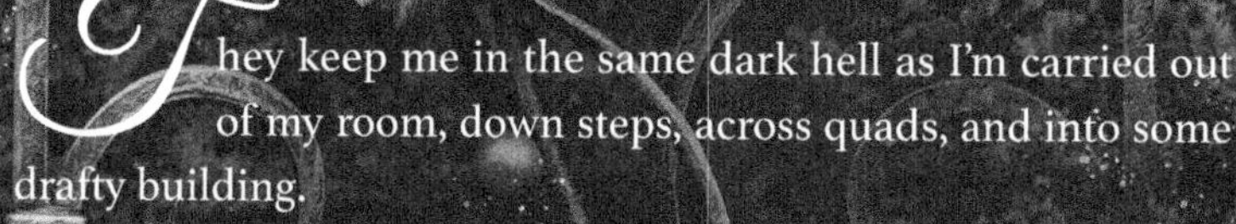

They keep me in the same dark hell as I'm carried out of my room, down steps, across quads, and into some drafty building.

Hands grip me under my shoulders, dragging me across cold stone. The air feels slightly damp, with the hint of a draft rising from somewhere near the floor.

Where the fuck am I?

I assume the people who've taken me are doing it to get to Claws, or because they think I have information about her. Which means they're not going to kill me. Yet. *But that doesn't mean they won't torture me—*

The bag is torn away. I blink as bright orange lights dance in my eyes. I stare up at one of my captors, who wears a monstrous horned mask that covers the top half of his face. The eyes that glare at me through the mask are blackened orbs edged with orange, and they're impossibly cruel.

They're also...familiar.

Monty?

Is it Monty? It's impossible to tell.

Fuck fuck fuck. That's even worse than trained assassins. The Orpheus Society has nothing to lose if I disappear off the face of the earth.

Did they search my room? Did they find my podcast episodes on my hard drive?

Am I about to join Keely in a shallow grave?

One of them holds my arm, and I can't tell through the satyr mask, but the slope of the shoulders and the warmth of the hand on my skin makes me think it's William. I haven't talked to him since he stormed off on Friday. He hasn't answered my texts, and I banged on the door of his rooms, but if he was inside, he didn't open up. Is he so pissed at me and Sebastian that he'd turn me over to Monty?

"Prepare her," a male voice barks from behind maybe-Monty, muffled by his horned goat mask. I see others standing around in their white robes, their faces obscured by grotesque animals heads, their shoulders wrapped in fawn-skins.

Definitely Orpheus Society.

Fuck.

I whimper as hands shove me forward. I try to turn to charge my attacker, but someone else grabs me, yanking my arms above my head. I think they're tying me up, and I scream and kick. But then they wrangle a white robe down over me, covering my Snoopy sleep shorts and camisole. A mask is pulled over my eyes – it's scratchy and limits my peripheral vision.

I'm so fucking scared.

I can see now that we're standing in the antechamber near Sebastian's room. The door to the roof is on my left, closed and locked. But the next door is open, revealing narrow steps curving down into the darkness. The only light comes from flaming torches held by Orpheans, the kind of torches you use to burn witches.

"What do you want with me?" I ask, trying to keep my voice

steady. But I'm a fucking panicked mess. My legs don't work. They collapse beneath me, and the Orpheans holding my arms have to bear my full weight.

No one answers. Maybe-Monty waves a long staff wrapped in ivy and topped with a pinecone – the *thyrsus* from Dionysian myths. He points it at the gaping chasm of darkness. "Get downstairs."

"Please, no—"

Someone shoves me. I stumble, but manage to pull myself upright. It's no good. There are too many of them. They drive me into the stairwell and force me to descend. I'm sobbing and stumbling, nearly blind in the gloom.

I keep my hands on the walls, sliding my feet forward to find the edge of each step. I notice a faint glow coming from the bottom of the tunnel, and voices rising up to meet us. The sound of water rushes in my ears.

Where are they taking me?

I think of Keely's bones spread out on Dr. Grainger's slab, of all the other missing girls whose disappearances have been covered up by the school, of the anonymous bones left in the underground temple.

They're taking me underground.

Cold fear clamps around my heart as it dawns on me that I'm the next girl who needs a grave.

I poked the bear. I asked too many questions and trusted the wrong people. I dug too deep and now I'm a walking corpse. These people are going to make sure I stay quiet permanently.

My feet are lead. The people behind me practically push me down the stairs. The person I think might be William has his fingers clamped over my arm like a vise. Sweet-smelling vapors curl through the air around us, making me feel nauseous. Or maybe that's the fear of my impending death.

The tunnel spreads out. My eyes water from the sudden

onslaught of light and noise and sensation. As the vapors swirl and clear, I get my first look at my doom.

"What is this place?"

37

I stand in a vast underground chamber.

But this isn't the rough-hewn bedrock of the staircase. The walls are dressed stone supported by elegant fluted columns, rising up to create a vaulted ceiling painted with cavorting Greek figures. Steps lead down to a large octagonal pool, steam rising from the water as groups of masked people wearing white robes or – in the case of some of them – strings of beads around their waists and *nothing else*. There are two other pools beyond this, one small and deep and circular, the other larger and rectangular, with many people sitting on stone benches built into its sides. Beside the pools are couches piled with cushions and tables bowing under the weight of food and drinks. I count maybe fifty people in total in attendance.

The man next to me throws off his mask. It's William, and he looks both proud and a little afraid. "Welcome to the Orpheus Society."

I want to punch him. "You mean you're not going to murder me?"

"Wouldn't dream of it, George, old boy." Monty's finger tugs at the corner of my lip. "Why ever would you think that?"

"I don't know, maybe the fact that you kidnapped me from my bed in the middle of the night and brought me to this...what is this place?"

William threads his arm through mine and leads me around the steaming pool. One of the naked girls glides into the water, her back arching with ecstasy. Two of the guys swim over to her, lean her back against the tiled edge, and start fucking her.

"This is a *thermae* – an old Roman baths. The Roman settlers built this underground chamber to perform the mysteries of Bacchus – that's Dionysos—"

"I know Bacchus is Dionysos," I say. "I know about mystery cults. A lot of sex and drugs and running around naked in the forest with bull horns on your head."

"Right." William's mouth tugs into that alluring half-smile as he fingers the curling tip of his horned mask. "Mysteries recreating the poet Orpheus' journey into the underworld were performed underground, too. That's what we're doing tonight – keeping the Orphean traditions alive. Usually, Roman baths are segregated for men and women, but in the mysteries everyone bathes together."

The girl is moaning now, her mask falling down over one eye. While his friend pounds away at her, the second guy leans down to claim her nipple with his mouth. The vapors curling around me are heavy with the scent of sweet herbs and sex. My head feels light, like it might float away in the steam, while a heavy ache settles between my legs.

"Why am I here?"

William turns me to face him. He plants his hands on my shoulders. Despite the debauchery going on around us, his deep eyes are deadly serious. "You're here because I want you to be here."

I swallow.

"You're a guest. I convinced the Elders to let you join us for our *Bacchanal*. I know you read too much Dan Brown and you think the Society is a sinister organization bent on world domination. I know you believe we had something to do with Keely's murder. But Keely left us alive on Devil's Night – alive and happy."

"You're trying to show me I have nothing to fear." I search his eyes, but I see nothing but ice and amusement. Monty stands right behind him. Is this for his benefit, or does William truly believe inviting me to a party will make me forget what I see, what I *know*?

"You fear the wrong things. No one is going to cut your arms off and dump your body in the woods. But this room is filled with the sons and daughters of some of the most powerful families in Europe, and they won't take kindly to an American poking her nose in their affairs and telling wild stories about dark rites and ritual murder. The Orpheus Society is an elitist drinking club, nothing more. But I knew you wouldn't leave us alone until you saw it for yourself. So what do you think?"

I take another look around me. The masked students circle the tables, picking at the food and feeding it to each other. In the corner, two of the naked girls anoint Percy with scented oils. A pulsing, slow music pounds through invisible speakers. In the corner, a guy throws up down the front of his white robe, then wipes his mouth and continues drinking from a kylix cup, the painted eyes of Dionysos glaring back at me. Unlike the replica we saw in Paris, this looks like a real ancient artifact.

William's right. This is a college party, albeit with the trappings of an ancient Greek mystery cult. It's elitist wankery, but it's not sinister.

I can't help but feel a little disappointed.

But then I remember they're showing me what they want me to see. This is exactly what I wanted – a way inside the Orpheus Society. So what if it turns into a dead end? For tonight, I get to be one of these elitist wankers, and I may as well enjoy it before I go back to being a nobody.

For my listeners. Of course.

"Is this really happening?" I knit my fingers in William's and let him lead me away from Monty.

He studies my face as he replaces his mask. In the flickering light, the grotesque features seem to move, to become one with his own skin. The vicious horns curl back into sharp points, and his goatskin slides down, revealing the shape of his toned shoulders and...and *more*...beneath the flimsy robe. I can almost believe I'm gazing upon a god. "We don't usually allow visitors, so this is a big fucking deal. You have to follow our rules."

"You haven't given me any rules."

His finger traces the line of my chin, the edge of my nose, the corner of my lip – the only parts of my face visible beneath my mask. "And you do so love rules, don't you?"

I swallow. "Out with it, *Your Highness*. What are the rules?"

"No identifying members outside of this room. Officially, there are only ten of us in the Society, but past members often return for our *Bacchanals,* and many of them will not be happy for their affiliation to be revealed."

Does that mean Father Duncan might be here tonight?

"—Anything you hear or see tonight is for your ears only. And no giving away our location – only our members and a handful of staff know of the existence of the baths, and we'd like to keep it that way."

"Does Sebastian know? Doesn't the steam cause damp issues in the church? What about subsidence—"

"No questions." William presses his finger to my lips. His touch burns hot. I'm giddy with the sensory overload of this place, and the adrenaline of believing I was going to die still churns in my veins. Mostly, I'm enchanted by his presence. Tonight, he truly is a dark prince, a creature not of earth but some underground fae realm. And tonight, I don't have to be Sensible George, either. "Are you hungry? Thirsty?"

I nod. He leads me over to the tables and picks up a ceramic bowl. I have to give them points for the aesthetic – this place looks like it was designed by a dark academia Instagrammer. William fills the bowl with exotic fruits, slices of meat and cheese, stuffed olives, little savory-ball things.

"You lie like this." He reclines on the cushions, propping his body up on one elbow. The white robe falls completely off his shoulder, revealing the curve of his bicep. I wet my tongue. *Fuck, he's dangerous.*

I sit gingerly on the edge of the couch. William's fingers circle my wrist and he drags me backward, pressing my back into his chest as he arranges the cushions around me. His skin burns like fire, every touch searing straight to the pit of hell in my belly.

The guy on the couch next to us rolls over to face us. It's Richard, his eyes are wide, swimming with drugs and other vices. "George, old chap. Pleased to see you. Whereabouts are you from again?"

"Emerald Beach."

"Emerald Beach." He lolls his head to the side. "Jolly good. The best coke in the world comes out of Emerald Beach."

"Not anymore," the guy next to him pipes up – he looks to be in his mid-twenties, with a mustache curled at the ends like the Monopoly Man. "The gangs there had a massive turf war, and now you can't get shit out of there unless you're willing to pay double. Bloody greedy Triumvirate, want to keep it all for themselves."

I don't tell him that it's my best friend who caused the turf war and raised the prices to pay for her animal shelter. She may be a crime lord, but she tries to at least be halfway moral.

"Open," William commands, his breath warm on my ear.

And I don't normally respond to being told what to do but tonight...tonight I'm not George. I'm someone different, something whose body responds to commands with flutters and heat.

I part my lips and William slides the grape inside. The taste explodes on my tongue – cold and sweet and refreshing, with the tiniest hint of William from his fingers. It's the best grape I've ever tasted.

He picks food off the plate at random and feeds me, his fingers sliding between my lips as I savor each bite. I suck and nibble on the tips of his fingers, and from the way his breath hitches I can tell he's enjoying this as much as me.

On the other side of the table, Monty lies on his own sofa with one of the naked, beaded girls. He rolls her over onto her back and lines up a trail of delicacies along her torso – tiny cakes on her shoulders, dabs of pate on her nipples, little cuts of meat lined up over her abdomen. He cuts a line of cocaine across her collarbone and splashes wine from his kylix into her navel and between her legs. She giggles and squirms as he bends over her and one by one eats each morsel from her skin. Except for the coke, which he sniffs through a tiny straw. When he reaches her navel, he licks and sucks and bites, trailing down, down, down until his mouth is between her legs, and he devours her hungrily.

I want to look away, but I can't. I'm frozen by Monty's flicking tongue and the girl's complete surrender. We've in the middle of a throng of people and she's able to completely abandon any sense of shame. She owns her body and her pleasure, and even though I have zero desire to have sex with anyone in front of these people, I respect her for giving it a go. William is having an argument in Latin with Richard. I don't think he's even noticed what Monty is doing, or that a second girl has a large carrot in her hand and is trying to tug Monty's robes over his naked ass.

I can see where this is going, and I'm not sure I want to see Monty like that—

"Would you like a swim?" William asks.

I nod. *Get me away from here.*

It's only as William drags me *away* from the water and *toward* the girls with the oil jugs that I realize he intends to perform his bath just as the Romans did, naked and oiled.

Goody.

William strips off his robe and my eyes pop out of my skull. He's completely naked underneath, and completely *perfect*. Every inch of him is toned and taut, and not from busting his ass in the gym, either. His spry physique is borne of rugged hills and hunting trips – the epitome of a vigorous country squire. I try not to look, but that only makes it more obvious that I'm looking, that my eyes are drawn over the smooth planes of his chest down to that delicious V of muscle to his cock, which even semi-hard is fucking enormous.

Somehow, stripped of everything, he's even more remote and powerful and untouchable. An alabaster god. It's never more clear to me that no matter how many kisses William steals from me, no matter the poetry that spills from his pouty lips, we exist in two different worlds.

I'm surprised to see he has a tattoo. I thought posh boys see ink as uncouth. But swirling around his thigh is a beautiful abstract piece in blue and turquoise. It reminds me a little of one of his paintings, but I know it's not. I've seen that style before – in an article I found about his family. It's his mother's artwork.

It can't be true that Sebastian slept with his mother, can it? He's supposed to be celibate, and he'd never—

"You coming?" William's mouth quirks into that adorable, infuriating smirk.

My hands tremble as I slide my fingers down the front of my white robe. I've still got my Snoopy pajamas on underneath, but

I know the challenge in William's eyes. He wants me to match him, to show him I'm made of strong stuff.

And I think of the person I was before I met Claws, and the person I believe I am now. I think of my father, who never gave a shit what the elite in Emerald Beach thought of his movies – or anything he did. He didn't just bear his freak status, but embraced it.

It's time to embrace myself.

The robe falls at my feet.

38

The humid air kisses my bare shoulders as I stand in my pajamas. And even though I'm wearing a tank top and sleep shorts and William already saw me bare all in art class, I feel worse than naked. From the way his eyes rake over my body, I feel as though he sees through my skin into the marrow of my bones.

I close my eyes, but I can still see him in the darkness – the sharp intake of his breath, his eyes like the deepest parts of the cosmos. My heart thuds. I slide the strings of my tank over my shoulders and tug it free.

My nipples pebble instantly, not from cold or from fear, but from the chilling exhilaration of freedom. I open my eyes and see William staring at me – not at my tits, but deep into my soul.

He nods to my boxer shorts. I shake my head. It's too much like...like things I don't want to think about right now. I need the imaginary shield of a thin buttress of fabric, a chastity belt that exists only in my mind.

He takes my hand. It's such a genteel gesture in a room pulsing with hedonism. We walk to the first pool. It's perfect – warm but not overwhelmingly so. Flower petals dust the surface, and purple lights around the bottom give it an ethereal glow. My tits rise up as I sink into it.

William traces his fingers through the surface of the water, his face transfixed by the light playing across the surface. I wriggle my fingers beneath his. "It reminds me of one of your paintings."

"I paint water a lot." His features soften as he knits his fingers in mine. "Everything about it captivates me – the movement and shade, the way it reflects and imprisons and refracts light, the way it's held sacred for its life-giving powers, but also feared for its ability to destroy without mercy. The way it both obscures and makes known everything beneath the surface. Even the sound it makes – utterly silent and inert in a glass, but with movement, it becomes a babbling stream or a great roaring waterfall. It's impossible to capture water in a moment because it's always rippling away from you. Not even Monet in all his brilliance could depict the true beauty of water."

He looks away suddenly, and I might guess he's embarrassed if I was talking to anyone else. "I don't usually talk like this," he says. "I don't talk about my art to other people. Only to you."

I can feel heat creeping along my cheeks. "I like hearing about it. I still have your painting on the wall in my room. The one you gave Keely? There's a woman hiding under the surface of the water, and sometimes I think I see other things, too. Sometimes her expression seems to change..."

William's fingers tighten around mine, and he pulls me closer so I can feel his cock, hard as a rod now, rubbing against my thigh. And I'm suddenly very, very aware that my sodden Snoopy shorts are the only thing between us right now...

"I like the way you look with the water lapping against your skin." William traces the line of my chin. "So, is this what you expected from the secret, underground, evil Orpheus Society?"

I think of the bloody underground fights I've seen back in

Emerald Beach – I once watched my friend Noah beat a man until his face was pulp. Another man was torn apart by a lion while the crowd roared for blood. "Honestly, it's a little tame."

"Is that what you think?" He closes the gap between us, laughing his quick, dark laugh. "Everything about you surprises me. What mischief *did* you get up to back in California, Georgina Fisher?"

William leans in close, skimming my bare arms and making small circles with his fingers on my back. He touches everywhere *but* my breasts, chuckling darkly as I lean forward to close the inch that separates us. My hard nipples graze the skin of his chest and the water sizzles with impossible heat—

A splash soaks us with water, startling us out of our trance. I turn just in time to see Diana barrel toward us like a sea-witch.

"George!" Diana throws her arms around me. She's naked – her body slick with scented oils so that she slips off me and falls beneath the water, her nipples dark in the purple light. She emerges again, running her fingers through her slick hair. "I'm so happy you're here. A few of the others didn't think it was a good idea to invite you, but William won them over. I must say, it's nice to have a new face around here."

"Thanks—"

"Come, you must meet some of the others." She grabs my hand and tugs me away.

I look over my shoulder at William, who tosses his head back and laughs. This is nothing like the cruel way he laughed at me during the figure drawing class, or the barking rasp when I suggested he come to my room on Devil's Night. This was pure, unadulterated joy. This is William, unencumbered by his demons. And if a little anointing oil and some naked swimming could lighten him so, is the Orpheus Society really a bad thing?

Yes. Keely's silent, maggot-filled mouth cries to me. The skull in the Paris temples grins inside my head. *Yes, it is.*

Diana leads me into the corner of the pool, where a group of girls recline on the stone benches. I recognize them all from my first day at Blackfriars, standing around the fountain – so they're current members of the society. They're all naked, their necks and ears and foreheads and arms adorned with gold jewelry that glitters in the flickering light. Even when they all have more skin showing than I do, they manage to make me feel underdressed.

Diana does introductions. "This is Matilde Wittelsbach, of the Hamburg Wittelsbachs, and Fatima is the daughter of a Saudi sheik, and I think you've already met Tabitha." They take turns to grab my shoulders and air-kiss my cheeks.

"Hi," I give a wave. "I'm George Fisher, daughter of Grant Fisher, the horror movie producer."

Tabitha – who's in my AV class with Monty and Abigail – looks visibly sick at the sight of me, but Fatima takes my hand. "It's wonderful to meet you, George. William has told us so much about you. You came from California, yes? I'm just so *fascinated* by America. And your father makes movies? Tell me everything."

I don't tell her my father's dead. Instead, I give them some of my dad's best stories – like when they were filming an alien landing scene in the Tunisian desert and the government had to ask him to move because the Libyans thought they were testing some new kind of military vehicle, or the time their haunted house movie set was *actually* haunted. Or the night he brought Bruce Campbell home for dinner and my mom burned the lentil lasagne. By the time I get to the bit where my dad tells her to 'hide it with garnish' and Mom serves this famous cult actor a brick of charcoal buried in a mountain of rosemary sprigs, they're all in hysterics.

"What did he do?" Fatima asks, tears of laughter rolling down her cheeks.

"He was a real gentleman about it," I say. "He ate every bite. He even had seconds."

They howl with laughter, falling against each other. Behind them, one of the girls wearing the beads fills their empty cups with wine. Watching the Orpheans brings to mind an image of the furies hanging on the wall in Father Duncan's office—

Wait, what's that?

A flash of skin and beads and blood. A girl storms through the room. At first, I assume she's drunk and looking for someone, but she's not singing, she's yelling at the top of her lungs, grabbing cups and plates from people and smashing them on the tiled floor. She looks familiar, but I can't think from where.

"You're sick," she yells. "You're all depraved. And he's the worst of all of you."

Conversations slip away as she whirls around, her trembling, bloody finger pointing to Monty. He leans against a pillar, that dark smile playing on his lips. And I remember her face now – she was the girl he was using as a plate before, although mingled with the sticky residue of food on her skin is blood trickling from cuts above her breasts.

Monty's stark naked, and his cock is still erect, coated in oil and blood.

"He should be in fucking jail," she yells as she scrambles for the stairs, leaving a heartbeat of silence in her wake. A pair of bloody handprints adorn her shoulders like broken wings. Monty grins and snaps his fingers, and the party continues like nothing happened.

Except it did.

Except that her bloody footprints still dot the tiles.

Matilde sighs. "We should go after her. We don't want her to get the police."

She slips out of the pool, and Tabitha and Fatima follow. The beaded girls are on them in a moment, holding out fluffy towels and fresh white robes. Fatima blows kisses as they rush off.

"What was that about?" I ask Diana.

"Monty." She leans back into the bench and rolls her eyes, like he's an annoying younger brother pulling pranks and not a dangerous predator. "I swear that boy is always breaking his playthings." She pats my thigh. "Don't you fret. They'll calm her down, make sure she doesn't do anything silly. She needs Monty's cooperation to get her dream job. She knew the price to pay when she offered herself tonight. They all do. That's what the beads symbolize."

I can't get the image of the bloody handprints on her back, the slice across the top of her breast, the blood smeared on Monty's skin. I know exactly what the three girls are doing.

They're silencing her.

Just like this party is supposed to silence me.

William thinks I can be brought with secrets – the same way the Orpheus Society has bought others off with money, with favors, with threats. What did he say to me? *I want us to be together, and that's allowed so long as Monty believes you're under my spell.*

He knows I can bring him down, bring them all down.

He thinks he can throw me with this one night where I'm part of the inner circle, and I'll leave Keely's bones in peace.

If William thinks that, he doesn't know me at all.

Pretty girls make graves, Jack Kerouac said and The Smiths sang. But I'm so much more than William's pretty girl. I'm not digging my own grave, but *theirs*.

Monty is an abuser. And his friends are allowing his crimes to go unseen. I've been a victim of another Monty, another guy who thought he owned the world. Never again.

I search for William. He's in the opposite corner of the pool, locked in a heated discussion with a very drunk Percy. My fingers have pruned to the max. I tell Diana I'll catch up with her later and haul myself out of the water. One of the beaded guys (I notice now several guys are wearing the beads, too) hands me a towel. It's the fluffiest, most amazing towel I've ever felt, and a sweet scent wafts from the fabric. I dry off, and my beaded friend helps me into a new, dry robe, adjusts my mask so it's straight, and offers me a platter of desserts. I look around the room with this weird sense of detachment, like I'm sitting behind my shoulder observing myself at this crazy party with these people who would never normally give me the time of day. It's dazzling.

But that's exactly what they want. They want to dazzle me with their charms and their secret underground pools and their amazing chocolate mousse. But I have a job to do. Keely's face flashes in my memory, mashed onto that bloody, fleeing girl.

Behind me, William calls my name, but I pretend I don't hear him as I disappear into the crowd.

You're wrong, William Windsor-Forsyth. This room is alive with secrets.

And this time, I'm the hunter.

I move toward the wall, turning my back to the room as I pretend to study the frescoes. I strain to listen to the conversations around me, but with the splashing and the music and the way the vaulted ceiling bounces sound, all I can hear are snatches of words like "...stock overvalued... Majorca for the summer... not Monty's fault she didn't read the contract..."

At the back of the room, I push my way through a crowd of people to discover another doorway. I shove my way through and find myself in a slightly smaller room. The ceiling here is even more elaborately decorated, with maenads beating off overeager satyrs by hitting them over the head with their *thyrsus*. In the center of the room is a small raised dais topped with a flat slab of stone about the size of a coffin. Off to the side are small open doorways, from which emanate the sounds of carnal shenanigans.

I make my way to the dais, running my hands over the cold marble. The top surface is worn smooth, the edges rounded and chipped and uneven. Dark stains mar the swirling veins of the stone. Something about touching it makes my skin crawl. Bad juju, as my French anarchist friend says.

I bend down to study the Greek words scrawled around the base. I wish I had my Liddell and Scott so I could at least look up some of the words, or my camera so I could take a photograph to translate later. But even though I can't read what it says, it's clear that this is some kind of ritual space. But what rituals take place here?

Is this where Keely drew her last breath? Did they chant these mysterious Greek words while they chopped her up—

A deep voice rasps against my ear, "It is an Orphic hymn to the god. 'I call upon loud-roaring and reveling Dionysos—"

The voice thrums in my veins, and my body stirs with recognition. He crept up so quietly, and I'd been so wrapped up in my thoughts that I hadn't felt his arms slide around me. I duck from his embrace and whirl around. His face is covered in a grotesque mask, the features twisted in agonized revelry. But I recognize the ink on his naked torso – the Celtic cross tattoo I'd seen the day I found him swimming naked in the Cloister fountain.

What the fuck is he doing here?

He points to the words as he translates:

"—primeval, double-natured, thrice-born, Bacchic lord,
wild, ineffable, secretive, two-horned and two-shaped.
Ivy-covered, bull-faced, warlike, howling, pure,
You take raw flesh, you have feasts, wrapt in foliage, decked with grape clusters..."

The lewd, licentious words spin in my head, and I feel drunk even though I haven't touched a drop. "S-S-Sebastian?"

"Shhhh," he whispers, holding a finger to his lips. "No one can know I'm here."

"Why are you here—"

He grabs my hand and drags me across the room as a gaggle of Orpheans enter, passing a wineskin between them. I yelp in protest, but Sebastian holds me fast. He ducks into one of the smaller rooms. Two guys and three girls writhe on a mattress that's draped in silks. One of the guys is Clement, who's in William's figure drawing class and looks like a Victorian pugilist. He beckons with a curled finger. "Join us, friends."

"Thanks. We prefer to watch." Sebastian pins my body to the wall.

"Suit yourself." Clement shrugs and returns to his orgy.

I'm frozen. My back rests against cool stone. Sebastian's chest presses against mine, his forearms hard against the wall, boxing me in so I can't escape. His grotesque mask leers at me as his warm breath caresses my lips.

"Pretend we're making love," he whispers.

"Wha—"

He licks my earlobe, and the shudder that runs through me isn't faked. Sebastian kisses along my neck, his hand sliding up to cup my face, tilting my neck to brush his lips against mine.

What is he doing?

His lips press and part, breathing fire but nothing more. It might not be called a kiss, but it makes my knees weak and my heart burn with wanting.

"I'm here for the same reason you are," he whispers against me, shifting his body so his chest rocks hard against mine. "I think the Orpheus Society is involved in something dark. I came to watch out for William. And for you."

"I'm fine. I know what I'm doing," I whisper back. "I wondered how they hid this elaborate party under your nose—"

"I've known about this place for a long time. A few times a year, the school pays for me to attend an overseas pilgrimage. A chance to visit a sacred place, access famous libraries, lose myself in prayer. It's pitched as a perk of the job, but I know it's so the Society can get me away from campus on the nights of these parties." He chuckles against me, the rumble of his body dropping deep into my core. He breaks the kiss to nip at my earlobe, and the sharp jolt of pain is almost more intense than a kiss. I jerk against him, and a tight moan escapes his throat.

"Hey, mate?" Clement's voice wheedles behind us. "You a eunuch or what? Just fuck her already."

"Don't stop," I whisper, my heart clenching. "Make them believe it."

I'm going to hell for this.

I'm tempting a priest away from his God.

But I'm too far gone – too possessed by Bacchanalian magic – to care about his immortal soul. Not when his very sinful body is pressed against me. Not when my veins are alive with carnal need.

"I'm so sorry." On the other side of the mask, Sebastian's eyes are lust and darkness. He looks anything but sorry. His hands drop to my hips, pulling one of my legs up to bend it around him. Pressed up tight like this, I can feel his hardness rubbing against me. I'm wearing only the thin robe and my sodden boxer shorts and he...I think he's naked under his robe. He *feels* naked – and hard.

And I should be afraid of him. Because he's my teacher. Because we're in the middle of a party filled with people who might kill us. Because of a million little things William has said.

But I'm the opposite. My body is made of starlight. I feel as though I've been sleeping and have only just woken up to what pleasure can be. I tilt my hips, and he bites my lip as he grinds harder, the shaft of his cock rubbing my clit through the fabric. *And it's so wrong and filthy and I can't...*

And the heady, vapor-filled air and the moans and skin slapping and harsh instructions to 'fuck fuck fuck her' from the bed behind us only make things more insane and hot and dreamlike. And his mask...only his eyes and his chin were exposed behind the grotesque, so I had to search for every reaction, clinging to the hitch of his breath and the storms smudging the edges of his black orbs for the man I'd come to think of as my Sebastian.

How can any of this be wrong when it's not even real?

Sebastian's hand palms my breast, his fingers rolling and pinching my nipple until a sweet lick of fire kisses my veins. I reach up to hold his shoulders, to touch every inch of his exposed skin.

He pinches my nipple a little harder as he cups his other hand between my legs. His head rolls back, a frustrated groan tearing from his lips.

"Forgive me, Father," he gasps out. And before I can react, he throws me over his shoulder and bolts from the room.

I catch my robe as it flies up around my face, and Sebastian's hand grips my thigh, so close to where I desperately ache for him it drives me to the point of insanity. Clement yells after us. "That's it, take her like an animal. Hail Dionysos!"

The party spins around me in a blur of monstrous faces as Sebastian runs runs runs. Around a corner, down some steps, into a darkened corridor where he finally sets me down. He flings himself away from me, covering his face like he can't bear for me to see him.

"George, I'm so sorry. I can't—" his voice breaks.

"It's fine." My body thrums with heat. I can still feel the ghost of him fitted against me, the sting of his fingers pinching my nipple until it hurt just right.

"Fuck. Fuck. Fuck." Sebastian rips off the mask and tears at his hair, so distraught with the horror of it that his pain crawls up my spine. "I tried to be good. I tried so hard. I prayed. I fasted. I stayed away. But it's impossible. We're impossible."

I slip off my own mask and step toward him, wanting to comfort him. "Please, don't—"

"Stay away from me." He holds out a hand, his eyes wild. "I want the length of a giant crucifix between us. I can't control myself when I'm around you. You make me forget who I am. I'm supposed to lay down my life at God's feet, but all I want to do is serve you."

Well, fuck.

I step back until I hit the wall, my hands raised in supplication. "Okay. I'm all the way over there. I'm picturing a row of frowning nuns separating us." *And it's not making me any less wet for you.* "Now, can you tell me what the fuck is going on?"

"What's going on is that I broke my vow and I broke your trust." He paces across the narrow space. "I told myself I was going there tonight to protect you. To protect him. But I knew I was walking into a den of sin. And I did it anyway because all I fucking want to do is sin with you."

I press my palms together. "I don't think this was a sin."

"I'm your teacher. I'm a priest. I'm in a position of power, and it's taking advantage—"

"I don't feel evil. I don't feel sinful." I close my eyes. I can't bear to watch his face as I say the words. "There's this symmetry between what they're doing down there and what you do up here. They spill the blood of their god – the wine of Dionysos – to offer thanks for their blessings. You drink the blood of Christ in the Eucharist. Through our gods, we are all blessed, and being with you is a fucking blessing. When you kiss me, when you touch me, that's the only time I ever felt like gods could be real."

He lets out a wild sound – half scream, half groan, all wild animal desperate to be free. I squeeze my eyes shut. I can't bear witness to his spiritual undoing, knowing that I'm the cause of this pain. But something slams into me, and it's warm and hard and needy, and I'm kissing him before I realize what I'm doing.

"Tonight, I'm not a priest," he whispers, his hands in my hair. "I'm not a teacher. And you're not a student. Tell me, what do you want?"

His fingers close around my hand as he pulls me deeper into the tunnel. I nearly trip on the narrow staircase. We rise, up and up, and the gods follow us. Sebastian pushes on a dark panel in the wall, and it slides away to reveal a small opening. Beyond, the church is in darkness save for the row of candles beneath Benet's chapel.

"I light them for Keely," Sebastian says. "So her spirit can find her way to the Lord."

He pulls me toward the chapel's altar, leaning me back against the cool stone. His hands open the front of my robe and slide around my hips, pulling me against him. His body shudders as his hands glide over my skin.

He takes a breath and steps closer. Our chests press together, our bodies fitting perfectly. This time, his heart beats with the frenzy of a sacred drum. He presses his lips to my collarbone, sliding his hands up my back, taking his time as he pushes the robe away.

I don't want to take my time. I don't want either of us to stop and think and realize this is a huge fucking mistake. A bridge that explodes as soon as we cross it. We can't go back.

I don't want to stop. I don't want to go back.

But the altar... Sebastian holds my neck with one hand and bends me backward. I grip the edge of the altar. "We shouldn't. Not here. Not where—"

His vows. Sebastian's job means everything to him. He lives

for the rituals, the service, the devotion of it all. He loves to be needed, to help those who need it most. He loves his God. And right now, with each sizzling touch, we set fire to everything he's worked for.

We can't do this.

It's wrong. It's going to end in heartache. He'll lose everything – his vocation, his reputation, his God. But I can't tear my lips from his.

"It must be here. Because here is where I perform my sacred duties. And you're right, George. This cannot be a sin," he whispers against my lips. "How can God say the way I feel about you is wrong?"

And I have no answer for that except to kiss him until my lips are raw and bleeding, until he's pushed me back onto the altar, knocking silver candlesticks and an ornate chalice to the floor. I try to pull him on top of me but he holds me at arm's length, gazing down at me with rapturous intensity.

"You're too innocent for all the things I want to do to you," he murmurs, his fingers tracing a line from my nipples to the heat between my legs.

"What do you want to do to me?" I whisper.

"Everything."

Everything.

My heart stutters. I've seen so much tonight that should have filled me with dread, but somewhere along the way, I've taken the spirit of Dionysos inside me. The god, loud-roared and reveling, bellows for worship.

"You're a priest. How do you..." *how do you make my body feel like it's on fire?* He kisses with a confidence borne of experience. And I wonder how many other women he's broken his vows for.

Like William's mother.

If there are other, I don't care. It doesn't make this thing between us any less real, any less sacred.

He draws a ragged breath. "I've been a man a lot longer than I've been a priest, George."

True. He said he went to seminary when he was twenty-two. He came from the same world as William, the world of wealth and avarice, where every possible pleasure fell open at his feet. Of course he wasn't a virgin before he purified himself for God.

And maybe that's good and right and perfect, because letting go of my own virginity on a sacred altar feels like just the trick to wash away the terrible thing that happened, to lay down my own sins and seek absolution from my priest.

My priest.

He arranges my hands into a praying position, and brings my fingers to his lips to kiss. "Let us pray," he whispers.

"Sebastian..."

"This is how I want it to be. Blessed by both our gods." He leans over me, his fingers sliding between my legs. He teases my entrance until I writhe beneath him. With his lips pressed against mine, he murmurs, "Breathe in me, O Holy Spirit, that my thoughts may all be holy."

It's the Prayer of St. Augustine. I've heard him say it a hundred times, but never, never with his body pressed against mine and his finger circling my clit. Never as a great holiness surges in my belly.

"Act in me, O Holy Spirit, that my work, too, may be holy."

His mouth circles my nipple as he dips one finger inside me. I cry out, my back arching over the altar. His hands are everywhere.

"Draw my heart, O Holy Spirit," he cries out, "That I love but what is holy."

He plunges his head between my legs, his tongue thrusting inside me, tasting me. He cries out like he's lost in the desert and he drinks me like I'm a guardian angel made of water. And I'm aglow with his adulation. My body is made of fire and I'm floating somewhere away and apart, where all that matters is him and I and…

I wait for God's wrath to rain fire from the heavens, to collapse the ceiling and bury us beneath the weight of our sins, but instead, I'm lit up from the inside out by a glow that feels like so much more than sex. A miracle made flesh. He is my miracle.

"George."

My name pierces the church, rising through the lofty space to echo over our heads.

My name, spoken by a god fallen.

My name, cursed by a broken prince.

Sebastian jerks back. I freeze, my body numb with fear as I turn my head.

William stands in the aisle, his face a picture of agony as he glares at his once-brother bent between my legs.

39

I've never heard such silence in the lofty church. It's the kind of weighty, all-consuming silence I imagine the anchoress felt in the dark of the night, when it was just her and God left and He wasn't in the mood to talk.

A million coded messages pass between Sebastian and William. Sebastian rocks back on his heels, kneeling beside the altar, his hands flapping at his sides, his eyes desolate.

William's mask dangles from one hand, but he arranges his features into another mask – an alabaster statue that doesn't feel or hope or long for anything. He snaps his fingers. The sound is like a gunshot.

"George, we should go."

My whole face burns. I don't want to leave just because he snaps his fingers, like I'm some kind of puppet to do his bidding. But I'm aware of the voices and music wafting from downstairs – that at any moment someone who is not William could wander up from the party and see us and ruin Sebastian.

I'm aware that ever since the beach I've been with William, and yet I have my legs spread for another man.

I slide off the end of the altar and gather my clothes from the floor. Sebastian holds the robe while I shove my hands inside. I'm shaking all over. Sebastian touches my cheek. "Please," he whispers, tears pooling in his eyes. "Don't leave like this."

William spins on his heel and strides toward the doors. I run after him. I run until I catch him at the door of the church, until the panic of what just happened bubbles up inside me.

"George, wait," Sebastian calls out.

But I can't look back. I run across the quad, my bare feet sinking into the forbidden grass. William is striding ahead of me, his steps long, purposeful. If I turn around, I'll see Sebastian's beautiful tears and I'll lose my fucking mind, and I'll run back to him, and I'll ruin his life. If I haven't already.

Because I know William loves Sebastian. But I also know he hates him, too. And for the first time in his life, William has something he can hold over the Saintly Sebastian. His own personal sword of Damocles.

And I know William enough to know how much he'll enjoy twisting that sword deeper.

So I keep facing forward, focusing on the tension in William's shoulders as he strides toward Cavendish Quad.

"William, wait."

He does, and I jog up to him, staggering as I twist my ankle on the uneven cobbles. "You can't tell anyone what you saw in there."

William says nothing, his face a wall of stone. He keeps walking.

I duck around in front of him and thrust both hands into his chest. His body collides against mine. It's like plugging myself into an electrical socket, the way his warmth shoots through me even when his eyes are icicles piercing my skin.

"Why should I?" he growls. "Why should I keep his secrets? Once again, he gets everything, and all I have left are ashes and bones."

And suddenly, I want to slap the petulance from those beautiful cheekbones. I have to ball my fists to keep from doing it. "Have you listened to yourself? Poor little rich boy, lashing out because mommy died. Here's a newsflash for you – people *die*. It fucking sucks, but it's no one's fault. It's not Sebastian's fault, and blaming him doesn't hurt him half as much as it hurts you. I mean, look at you! The rest of us fucking get on with our lives. We bear the pain and the hurt and the grief because that's what you have to do to keep going. We don't use it as a license to become a miserable shitbag and push away everyone who cares about us—"

"No one cares," William cries, his hands tearing at his hair. "My mother was the only one who ever cared about me and she's gone and I'm just supposed to—"

"I care," I whisper. "I wish I didn't, because caring for you is like taking a bullet for a suicide bomber. It's painful and pointless. But there you go."

"What did you just say?" he demands, stepping closer, boxing me in with his body.

"I'm not repeating it." I glare back. "But I care about him, too. He's been my only friend at this school for a long time, the only one I could talk to when you and your friends were horrible to me."

"Do you fuck all your friends on altars?" he sneers.

"Do you?" I shoot back. "I never made a promise to you. We never discussed it, because we never discuss anything that really matters. And maybe what I did with Sebastian makes me a horrible person. So go ahead, make my life hell. Spread it all around this school that I'm a whore, that I'm a no-good ugly freak who doesn't deserve to be treated with any kind of respect. Do whatever you want to me. I don't care. Just don't hurt Sebastian, because he doesn't deserve it—"

I can't speak. I try to force out my rage but my mouth is

blocked. For a moment I don't understand, but then I taste the tongue that devours me.

William.

William is kissing me.

He's kissing me like he needs me to breathe.

He gasps into my mouth as his fingers circle my wrists, his grip tight, punishing. A whimper escapes my throat, but it's not a whimper of pain. It's something more, something I want to ask but I don't have the words.

His lips burn against mine. And then he's not kissing my lips anymore – he's tilting my head, trailing kisses along my jawline, his finger skimming the edge of my breast. My nipple, naked beneath the thin fabric, pebbles under his touch.

"Come with me." William's lips brush my earlobe, send a shudder through my body. "Come back to my room."

And maybe I really am filled with the god, maybe Dionysos' blood runs in my veins, because without hesitation, I say, "Yes."

40

William stalks across the lawn toward his room. His chin high, his hands in his pockets, as if he's taking a casual stroll about the grounds. I jog behind him, my heart racing.

Did I really just agree to this?

William's staircase is in one of the earlier medieval towers, accessed through a short vaulted passage on the far side of the quad. I worry that we'll walk for so long that he'll change his mind, that he'll remember he's a prince and I'm the American freak he's been tormenting for the last year, the one trying to bring down him and his friends.

I can't have Sebastian. What we did tonight can never happen again. But William breaks no vow by being with me, except probably one he made to the Orpheus Society. And I don't give a crap what they think.

Right now, I just want to feel good. I want to chase the heat in my veins, or I'm going to burn the whole fucking school down.

William leads me up his staircase, past open rooms where students yell and laugh and fuck over blaring music. I can see these dorm rooms are larger and fancier than mine. They also look like mostly singles, which I thought were reserved only for fourth-year and masters students. I should have known William and the other Orpheans wouldn't be content to rough it with the rest of us plebs.

I've been here before, looking for him, but never inside his room. Rumor around campus is that apart from Monty, William never lets another soul inside his room. His scout isn't even permitted to clean it – William does that himself. It's hard to imagine my dark prince pushing a vacuum around.

At the top of the staircase is a single room in the turret itself. William swings open the door. He doesn't flick on a light, but instead draws a lighter from his pocket and lights a line of candles, casting the room in a spectral glow.

I gasp as the flickering light reveals his room to me, a little at a time, as if the darkness knows I can't take in all of William at once. It's nothing like I expected and yet, it's *everything*.

It's enormous – larger than I expected. It could be divided into several rooms like an apartment, but it's one single, nearly circular space. The walls are bare stone, not that you can see much of them as they're littered with rickety wooden shelves filled to bursting with books and rocks and crystals. The spaces that aren't filled with shelves are crammed with his art. I gasp at the onslaught of light and color. Some are distinctly his – water studies, mostly – but I suspect many are painted by his mother. Large canvases are stacked against the wall, and one rests on the foot of the bed – bold slashes of violet and cobalt blue crashing against red cyclopean towers. I recognize the spot at the beach where William took me. He's even painted the fossils embedded in the cliff, and a dip in the rocks where I slipped and he caught me. A large desk made of dark wood is piled so high with books I can only see the top of the computer monitor buried beneath them, and in the corner is an easel and stacks of art supplies.

The easel is turned away from me, facing the window, so I can't see the canvas.

William locks the door behind him. He presses his back against it, his eyes boring into mine. There's a shift in the air – it's subtle, but we both feel it. I tilt my head to the side. "Are you okay with me being here?"

"I don't know," he answers. "I'm still deciding. I don't bring anyone here."

I remember Keely telling me that the Orpheus Society keeps an apartment above the pub in the village, which William uses for his conquests. I want to ask if he ever took her there, but it's soooo not the time.

So why am I here? What's different about me?

Is it that he doesn't want anyone to see us together? He doesn't want his friends to know he's slumming it?

Or is it that he wants me to see...all this? To see him.

I sit gingerly on the edge of the bed, kicking out my feet. I look ridiculous in this room of excess and art. "What am I doing here?"

He moves in a fluid motion, like a vampire stalking its prey. One moment he's on the door, looking like he's ready to bolt. The next he stands over me, kicking the inside of my foot with his so I part my legs around his thighs. He touches a finger to my chin, tilting my head back.

"You're here because I've thought of nothing else but taking you to bed since the day I saw you."

Taking you to bed. Such an old-fashioned way of saying it. A perfectly William expression that makes my chest flutter. "But why? I'm nothing special. I'm not—"

"Is that what you think?" His finger traces my chin.

I shut my eyes. I'd better get this out of the way. "You know I'm not."

"Open your eyes," William commands. "I want to show you

something."

He moves away from me. I think for a moment that he's rejecting me, but he stalks to the corner of the room and picks up the easel, turning it around so I can see the canvas he's working on.

I gasp.

It's me.

I've never seen myself like this before. I'm draped over the chair in the art studio, staring straight at the viewer. My arms hang out at my sides, elbows akimbo, knees wide, lipstick penis smudged across my belly, one leg dangling off the edge. Not the pleasant reclining Renaissance lady pose Diana chose but a complete fuck-you to the artist and the viewer. And yet my body has been rendered with tender strokes and my features arrest the viewer with a look of radiant defiance.

I don't look short, or afraid, or weird. I look triumphant. Powerful.

Beautiful.

I'm also underwater.

The lightest wash of ice-blue – the color of William's eyes – obscures the image, distorting my limbs with ripples. My hair floats around my head like a purple halo, tendrils of dye leaking into the water. The silk sheet unfurls to float in shimmering patterns around me. One chair leg is off the ground, making it appear as if the current is dragging me away from the viewer – a siren queen returning to her watery kingdom.

"I…" I can't tear my eyes away from the image. "I can't believe…this is…"

"How can you believe you're nothing special?" William's arms go around my waist again, pulling me against him, grinding his cock against me until I see stars. "You're *enchanting*. You're like a siren calling to me – I can't break the spell even if I wanted to. For years I've been existing in this numb haze of grief.

Nothing's captured my interest. Nothing has made me *feel*. Until you."

I cling to him, letting the emotions bubble up inside me as William's words unlock the chains around my secrets. I know why I was dreaming about Alec – I've been living in my own numb haze, merrily helping Claws build her empire and throwing myself into all these mysteries to avoid dealing with my own bullshit.

But now my bullshit was in the room with us – the monster under the bed.

I swallow. William tucks a strand of purple hair behind my ear. Back in the church with Sebastian, I wasn't thinking. I was high on the sacrilegious thrill, on the Dionysian *abandon* of it all. But in the silence of this room, beneath the weight of William's feelings, the old fear creeps back. The old stories I've told myself scream from the shadows. My limbs tremble. William strokes my hair, pressing my head against his chest.

"I want to do this," I swallow again. "But I feel there's something I should tell you."

"It's okay. I know you're a virgin. I'll make sure you feel so good."

"Not..." I swallow. "Not exactly."

William's fingers grip my hair, crushing my head into his chest. His heart thunders in my ears. "You don't have to tell me if you don't want to."

I fight against the chains that keep me silent. I need to get this out or it will live in the space between us forever. I've never told anyone this before, not even Claws. I take a shaking breath.

"When I was fourteen, I went on a California state science camp. It was out in the desert – we did all these fascinating studies about the unique ecosystem, and at night we took turns to camp under the stars and observe the skies with telescopes. Anyway, there's this guy who's been in my class since the first grade, Alec LeMarque. He's pretty much your typical arrogant jock, the kind you see in teen movies—"

"I've never watched a teen movie."

I laugh, even as tears prick the corners of my eyes. "No, of course you haven't. Well, picture the American stereotype – blond hair, blue eyes, square jaw, so perfect he looks kind of fake. I suppose he wanted to be a famous actor. I live in California, lots of kids think they're going to be famous. And they all knew that my dad was a big-name producer. He did horror movies, which most people find dumb because they're elitist fools. But that summer he was running auditions for a big-budget thriller – the kind of film that could make the career of a young teen actor. So I think Alec figured he'd try to get in good with me, in the hopes it would give him an advantage in the audition. Or maybe he just came up with a different way to mess with me, I don't know. All I *do* know is that at camp, he was actually *nice* to me. He'd choose me as a partner, ask me to sit at his table, gang up with me to try to beat the other schools. I thought maybe he was a different guy away from his jock friends. He could even be kind of funny sometimes. And yeah, I couldn't believe a popular guy like him was hanging out with the school freak. So I rolled with it. Big mistake.

"It was our night to stay up with the telescope. We had to make observations every hour, and for the first couple of hours we talked and shit. He snuck out a flask of alcohol and some chocolate and he kept pouring me drinks. And then it got late and I was having so much fun and it was three in the morning and I...I got sleepy. I fell asleep in my chair. And when I woke up..."

"George, what?" William's grip tightens.

"He was on top of me, telling me to *show him how I liked it.* And my top is pulled up and my panties were around my knees and his hands are..." I squeeze my eyes shut. My hands ball into fists. Talking about it sucks. It doesn't help. It brings everything back – that wild panic when I woke up and didn't remember where I was and felt his weight on top of me, and that terrible nagging doubt that's crushed me ever since. "I don't know what happened. I don't know how far he went or what signals I gave him. That's the worst thing. I remember dreaming about him that night. Or maybe it was some musician I was crushing on at the time. But someone was touching me in my dream, and I liked it. I *wanted* it, was writhing and begging for it like an idiot – and I don't know if the wanting was from the dream, or from what Alec was doing to me. Maybe...maybe after so many years of being the nobody freak everyone hated, I felt good being wanted. On some level, I felt like it was him validating me. I kicked him and ran away, but he kept saying he'd never normally go for a freak like me but I'd begged him for it and he felt sorry for me and I...I never told anyone."

"That's fucked up." William rasps. He clamps his arms around me, as if he can somehow squeeze the tremble from my limbs.

"I know. I'm sorry." I try to rise. "I don't expect you to be okay with it when I don't even understand myself. That's why I wanted to tell you. I'll go now—"

He circles my wrist. "That's not what I meant. It's fucked up that this guy took advantage of you. You were *asleep*. And you can't keep telling yourself it's your fault, that you asked for it. Because he's not a fucking idiot who can't tell when a person is sleeping. That's not fucking consent. That's barbaric. Of course I'm not okay with it. I want to kill this prick."

Already done.

"Maybe that's just what I like," I sniff. "I'm messed up, even more now that my dad's gone. I was about to fuck Sebastian on that altar, and anyone could have seen us. Back in the forest, you *blackmailed* me into kissing you and I liked it. I *wanted* it."

Something hard and dark crosses William's face. "I'm sorry for that, too. I never should have done it. I would never have told a soul about your project. I wanted to kiss you but I…I didn't know how to be a gentleman. Instead, I became a savage. You're the only girl who's ever had the power to make me completely lose my mind, and that's dangerous. It's no excuse for how I behaved."

"But you *did* tell," I insist. "You told your friends, didn't you? And then someone buried Keely's body in my experiment."

He runs a hand through his head. "It's complicated. I…I can't tell you any more than that. But I'm so, so sorry. I'm fucked up too, and I made a mess of us right from the start. You have me so turned about, but I want to try to be better. You deserve the world from a man who will treat you like the goddess you are, and I'd like the chance to be that man if you'll have me. You don't have to make any promises to me, but for tonight, I want to be the one to make you feel good. Will you forgive me?"

He looks so…un-William-like, with his hair all rumpled and his lip wobbling, that I do something very un-George-like. I reach up and curl my fingers around his neck, lowering his head so I can press my lips to his.

I thought my confession might cool the fire between us, but it's only kindled the flames. This time when he holds me, it's with a possessive madness. The kiss burns right down to my toes.

"You're a fool with a heart and no brains, George Fisher," he murmurs, stroking my hair. "And I'm a fool with brains but no heart. And we're both unhappy, and we both suffer."

"Dostoyevsky, right? I think it was the other way around—"

He cuts off my protest with his lips. This kiss is everything William is – controlled but desperate, guarded yet raw, sweet but deliciously, impossibly filthy. His mouth is a hot, demanding brand even as he strokes my hair with tender reverence. I keep my eyes open – I can't close my eyes when I kiss someone because I'm still so afraid of what might happen if I fall asleep – and I watch him and he watches me and it's so fucking intimate it makes my heart hurt. The blue of his eyes is the exact shade of the water he painted in my portrait.

"Stay with me," William begs, kissing with such ferociousness I don't have a moment to protest even if I wanted to. He leans me back on the bed. I sink into the plush duvet, and his arms cage me in at the sides as he presses on top of me. I expect to feel trapped, but I don't. I feel cocooned, protected. Nothing can hurt me in his arms.

Not unless I want it to.

There's a mirror attached to the ceiling – a heavy-looking antique thing with a gilded frame. *Is he not afraid it'll come crashing down on him in the middle of the night?* I stare up at myself as William moves on top of me, trying to see the George he painted – that dazzling siren who beguiled him to his doom. His hand finds mine, fingers knitting together, pressing my wrist into the sheets. His other hand cups my head. My legs are splayed wide, skin exposed to my thighs where my robe has ridden up. William grinds his hard cock against me, and some remote corner of my brain registers that I've got only sodden Snoopy shorts to protect my virtue and I should probably be terrified right now. But I tip my hips up to grind back on him, desperate for something I can't name.

"Is this what you want?" William growls against my lips. "George, if you stay in this bed looking at me like that, I can't be held responsible for what happens. If you want to go back to *him*—"

He means Sebastian. And the offer almost brings me up short. But Sebastian is an impossible dream. Dionysos made me believe it could be real, but it was just the god's delusion.

William is here, and he's wonderful and he *is* real. And I don't want to ever leave his arms.

In response, I grin and cheekily tug William's robe to expose his glorious, naked ass.

Sorry, his glorious naked *arse*.

"Dirty girl." William laughs against my lips as I slap his arse. He keeps my other arm pinned as he leans back to kiss a trail over my chest. His cock rubs against me and I feel a little flicker of fear because he's so fucking *huge* and I don't want to be torn in half, but then he sucks my nipple into his mouth and nothing else matters except what his lips and hands are doing to me.

He circles my nipple with his tongue, then sucks the tip until I gasp. His eyes never leave mine, and he seems to come alive every time I gasp or squirm. I can't believe I ever said William's eyes were cold and empty – right now there's a fathomless ocean staring back at me, and if I'm not careful I'll drown in those depths.

Just when I think I can't take any more, he dives between my legs, and I can't help but note that his tongue touches the same places Sebastian has already touched tonight. As William laps at my clit while I lose myself, in a fucked-up way it's as if he's also kissing Sebastian. And I wish for something so impossible, so completely beyond comprehension that I know I'll make myself sick with it.

I wish I could have them both.

I know that technically it's possible. Claws has her three men – her reverse harem – so I have a real-life example that polyamory can work. But Gabe, Noah, and Eli are friends. Equals. They think nothing of sharing someone precious to them. But William's a jealous, possessive dick and there's too much between William and Sebastian that I don't understand and I...I can't ask them to overcome it for me.

Even if they were both available, which they're not. Even if they were both willing, which they are not.

I have to forget Sebastian. I have to forget the flickering candlelight on his tortured features, the way he held me against that wall and kissed me like his life depended on it.

And what better way to erase him than with William Windsor-Forsyth between my legs.

His touch is so different from Sebastian's. He's more raw, more primal, his muscles tight with tension as he writes his poetry on my clit. I flick my gaze between watching him lick and lap and suck, and watching myself in the mirror – his goddess in rapture, back arched, features soft and glowing beneath his worship.

William digs his fingers beneath me, dragging my hips off the bed as his mouth works me, his tongue painting landscapes across my skin. Despite myself, my eyes flutter shut, and I can't imagine how I ever thought I could sleep through this...this *ekstasis*. It feels like the molecules of my body are falling apart, but in the best possible way.

For a moment, I truly believe that I'm filled with the god's spirit.

When I am no longer a god but George again, I hear the crinkle of a condom packet. William kisses my eyelids as he leans on top of me again. "No, eyes open. I want you to remember every moment. I want you to know what you look like when you fall apart for me."

I open my eyes. There he is, my dark prince, stripped bare of his crown of arrogance. Beautiful and remote and raw, with his cheekbones that can cut glass and the special smile that's only for me.

I don't trust myself to speak. So I nod.

William rolls the condom on. He positions himself on top of me, propping himself up on one elbow as he guides the tip of his cock to my entrance. He presses the tip inside me, and I gasp.

"Are you okay?" His lashes flutter as he looks at me in concern.

I nod. "It's...intense. Good, but..."

"Kiss me," he whispers. "It might hurt, but I'll swallow the pain for you."

I can't argue with that.

I tilt my head back, and he captures my lips. This kiss is so different from the ones we shared before. William lets me control the pace, the depth, the intensity, holding back so that I come to him, chasing the god around his mouth with my tongue. He tilts his hips and slides deeper inside me, and it *does* start to hurt – a bright, tearing pain that makes my eyes water. But I cling to William and feed him the pain, and even as my body trembles, I let go of all the fear I've carried about this moment.

Inch by inch, William pushes all the way inside me. Every time I think he must be all the way in, he gives me more. I gasp against his lips because he's *so fucking huge* and I'm so tiny and I can't understand how this is ever supposed to work and I'm such a failure I can't do this and aaaaaah...

William rocks his hips gently, and at first it hurts, it hurts so much and I'm so afraid, but then the pain becomes something more – a stirring, an awakening, a *rapture*. And before I know it I'm bucking my hips to meet his and biting his lip and William has wrapped my legs over his shoulders, his hand sliding down between us to stroke my clit until I can see the god behind my eyelids again.

"Let go," he whispers. "Fall into me."

I fall.

I fall into this sad boy whose heart is made of poetry and broken shards. And he holds me and whispers ancient words in my ear, and we topple over the edge together. And I know that whatever happens now, nothing will ever be the same again.

41

I wake up.

It takes a moment for my eyes to adjust to the strange tendrils of grey light across the unfamiliar room, the glint of saturated color from the paintings stacked everywhere, the weight of the heavy, expensive covers over my naked body, and the sleeping prince beside me.

Last night slams into me. The memories bombard me in a relentless march. I close my eyes but I can't make them slow down.

The dream about Alec.

Being kidnapped from my room.

The *bacchanal*.

Swimming topless with Diana and her friends.

The girl running from Monty, bloody handprints smeared across her back.

Sebastian pinning me against the wall, in front of all those people...

The altar.

The painting.

William.

I rub my eyes. "Fuck."

I roll my head to the side and there he is, eyes closed, lips parted, hair flopping over his eye – looking every bit like the insouciant prince he is. It's too much. I jerk my head back, but then I'm looking into that goddamn mirror – at his body angled toward me, his arm draped with casual possession across my stomach.

The need to run starts in my feet. My toes curl and my legs itch to move. It rises through my body until it stabs at my chest, until it becomes a pounding between my ears. *I have to get out of here.*

I crawl out from beneath William's sleeping form and hunt around in the dark for some clothes. The fire he lit after the first time we had sex (first of three! Woo, go me) burned out some time in the night, and the room is freezing cold. I debate having a shower to warm up, but I don't want to wake William.

I need to get some distance. I need to *think*.

All I have are my ruined sleep boxers and that white robe. In William's closet, I find a black shirt and a leather belt. I pull the shirt over my torso – the hem drops nearly to my knees. I loop the belt around my waist – voila! Instant shirt dress. I bend down to pick up my boxers from under the bed. A hand closes around my arm.

"Stay," William murmurs, his voice husky from sleep. "I cherish you more than my solitude."

I shake my head.

"Are you doing a dine and dash?"

"I just...I have to go."

He bolts upright, his eyes wide with terror. "Did I do something wrong? Did I hurt you?"

"No. Last night was...it was amazing. But I just need some space to process it all, okay?"

"Okay. But once you process, will you meet me for a late brunch? Say, The Bad Habit at 11AM?"

I smile as I head to the door and twist the handle. William's sleep voice calls after me. "George?"

I turn. My heart beats an erratic rhythm against my ribs.

"I hope you got the answers you were seeking."

I close the door behind me. It slams, the sound reverberating on the empty landing. I jump out of my skin, certain some student will hear it and come out to see who's leaving William's room. But there's no one else up here. William has the entire floor to himself. Of course he does.

And besides, why do I care if they see me? I had sex with William Windsor-Forsyth. Three times. He made my eyes roll back in my head. That's nothing to be ashamed of.

So why do I feel so weird?

I think about what William asked me. *Did I get answers?*

I already know what the Orpheus Society is all about. I know they're trying to recreate the old mysteries of the god Dionysos. I know they have a long history, stretching right back to Benet the Black Monk, the patron saint of Blackfriars University.

I know they indulge in every sordid behavior, every privileged delicacy and rich wanker cliche ever conceived, and probably a few that haven't been invented yet.

I know that Monty Cavendish is a bastard.

But do I know if they're responsible for Keely's death?

No.

In fact, I'm now even more confused, and even deeper in this than I was before. Because I care about William, and William is one of them. And I think he wants me to be one of them, too.

As I walk down the stairs, footsteps rise to meet me. I turn back in panic, but I'm too far from William's door to step back inside and remain unseen.

Monty pauses as he sees me, and his eyes burn into me like

coals. I fold my arms tight across my chest, aware that I'm wearing nothing beneath William's shirt.

"Good morning, George, old chum," he says jovially. I wonder, as I sometimes do, if he's thinking about tearing my guts out and frying them with his kippers. "Jolly good fun last night, eh?"

"Yes. It was very enlightening." I try to smile, but I can't quite make it work. I can't stop seeing that girl running for the stairs with bloody handprints smeared across her back. "Thanks for having me as a guest. William said that doesn't happen very often, but I appreciate it. It was fun. Not the kidnapping bit, but the rest of it."

"Looks like it," he nods at my shirt. "Any friend of William's and all that. Maybe we'll see you at the next event, and your delightful friend Leigh."

I watch as he shuffles up the stairs and lets himself into William's room with a key, an ominous feeling settling in my gut.

I'D ONLY BEEN BACK in my room ten minutes and was gathering my things for a much-needed shower when Leigh barges in, two steaming cups of coffee in her hands.

"Talk. Now."

"Morning, Leigh—" But I can't even get the words out before she shoves the cup into my hand and pushes me back onto the bed.

"It's all anyone can talk about in the dining hall. You entering William's bedroom in the early hours of this morning. And is this one of his *shirts?*" She squeals and flops down on the bed beside me. "Tell me everything."

The blush in my cheeks deepens. I think my whole body is red as a lobster. "The whole campus is talking about it? Great."

"Don't lie, you love it. So tell me what happened."

So I do. I sip the coffee and tell her every sordid detail. When I get to the part about Sebastian leaning me over the altar, Leigh clinks coffee cups. "George Fisher, you are my hero."

"I'm not." My cheeks are on fire now. "I'm a terrible person. I knew I was letting a priest break his vow, a priest I care about very very much. But I didn't stop it. I'm going to hell."

"Eh, Heaven sounds overrated anyway." Leigh points to my Nirvana poster. "Hell's got all the good music."

"True. But you can't tell a single soul about Sebastian. If anyone finds out, he'll lose his job—"

"Of course I won't tell." Leigh mimes zipping her lips. "Now, let's forget about sexy priest for a hot minute. I want to hear all about your night with his Royal Highness."

I don't know how long Leigh and I talk. I don't remember falling asleep. All I remember is Leigh asking me a million questions and then the next moment, I open my eyes and I'm under the covers with the curtains drawn and Leigh's sitting at my desk scribbling notes for her art history essay.

"Wakey, wakey, sleepyhead." Leigh nods to the nightstand. "I got your favorites."

I roll over and see a steaming beef and Guinness pie and a half-pint of Leigh's mead next to my stack of true-crime books. My stomach growls, reminding me that the last thing I ate was that bowl of random tidbits hand-fed to me by William...

William... My head swims as the details of last night and this morning flood back to me. *I'm supposed to meet him for breakfast. What time is it...*

I grab my phone. "Shit. It's nearly 2PM. I was supposed to meet William three hours ago." I scroll through my chat and check messages, but there's nothing from him. That seems weird, but I'm too fried to question it now. I whip off a quick text to him as I scramble out of bed. My legs tremble as I run a brush through my hair and knock my books off my desk searching for my Liddell and Scott.

"Relax, would you?" Leigh shoves my Greek dictionary into my arms. "You had a wild night. You know it's okay to miss class occasionally, right?"

"Not Father Duncan's Greek class, I can't. Why didn't you wake me?" I grumble to Leigh as I try to pick up the steaming pie with my fingers. It's a Sisyphean task, but I can't bear to leave it behind.

Leigh wraps it in a paper towel and hands it to me. "I did. You kicked me and called me a very unladylike name."

"Oh, sorry." I shove my feet into my boots, grab my books, and kiss Leigh on the cheek. "Meet you after? We can grab a drink at the pub and you can help me figure out what the fuck I'm doing with my life."

"Deal. If you're not back in Prince William's room, shagging his brains out." Leigh's cackling laugh follows me down the staircase.

I'm halfway across Cavendish Quad before I realize I'm still wearing William's black shirt as a dress. Students crowd around me as they shuffle toward the Tower. Their whispers caress my skin, their surreptitious glances making me glow from the inside out.

For the first time ever, I kind of like people talking about me. I take a tiny bit of pleasure in the filthy look Abigail shoots me as she swings around the staircase ahead of me.

Okay, I lie. I take a metric *fuckton* of pleasure.

Despite my smugness, my legs are jelly as I walk up the Tower steps to Greek class. I'm about to see William again, and I want to take careful note of how I feel about it. I'm pretty sure I'm making a huge mistake getting involved with this guy, especially since he's trying to pretend he's not hiding secrets from me and I'm trying to pretend I'm not still hunting Keely's killer on the sly. But I feel like it's a mistake I'm supposed to make.

Abigail slams the door in my face so hard it rattles the hinges. I grin. Nothing she does can get to me today. I throw open the door and immediately stop short.

William isn't here. His chair next time mine is inexplicably, conspicuously empty. Monty, who sits on the other side of William, pats the chair with conspiratorial glee. "Sit with me, George, old chum. I need a little help with these irregular second aorists."

"Where's William?" I ask.

"Oh, he has a little chore to do," Monty shrugs. "For the society. I'm sure you'll see him around."

After that, I don't hear a word of the discussion, even though Father Duncan is talking about the criminal justice system in Ancient Athens, and the philosophical notion of justice, and all these other interesting things. My mind whirls through a million possibilities for what urgent 'chore' William needs to complete after a debaucherous bacchanal. I keep coming back to the girl with the bloody handprints on her back.

He says he's trying to protect me, but is he really trying to protect himself? Is he giving me just enough to keep me satisfied, to make me his, while continuing the society's clandestine crimes in the background?

No. This is ridiculous. I trust William. I've seen the fear in his eyes when we talk about Monty. He won't do anything evil. He's not capable.

I hate the way my stomach churns.

I'll feel better once I can talk to him.

After what seems like seven centuries, class ends. Everyone stands up to leave. I pull out my phone and check for messages from William. Still nothing. *Where are you? What is Monty making you do?*

"It's not too cold out. We're going to the amphitheater for a picnic, do you want to come?" Diana tosses her long hair over her shoulder.

"Um...another time. I have a mountain of work to do. Have you seen William?"

"Dear me, no. I thought he was holed up with you." She laughs her tinkling laugh. "Are you okay? You look kind of...manic—"

I sprint down the staircase and head in the direction of William's room. Diana calls after me but I keep walking. I'm focused so hard on finding William that I'm halfway across Cavendish before I realize it's not Diana calling me, but a deeper, richer, more panicked voice.

"George?"

I dare a look over my shoulder. Sebastian runs across the forbidden grass toward me, his black peacoat flapping around his legs. My stomach twists with guilt, with pain. I turn away. I can't face him, not after what happened in the church.

Not after the altar.

But I can't move. My feet are rooted in place. *Move,* I scream inside my head, but my body refuses to obey – it's always a stubborn bitch when it comes to Sebastian. A group of girls watch from the well as he races toward me, and I'm certain they can read everything that happened between us on his stricken face.

"George." He puffs as he catches up to me. "Please. Talk to me."

I shake my head, hugging my books to my chest. "There's nothing to talk about. We tried to be friends, but it didn't work. So I can't see you anymore. I'm not going to be the reason you get kicked out of the priesthood."

He clutches my shoulders and shakes me roughly. His dark eyes swim with pain, with desperation. "I don't care anymore. I'll give it all up – the job, the Church, being close to William. If they can't accept me as I am then I want nothing more to do with them. I don't need to be a priest to serve God. I'll teach, I'll start a charity. I'll hop around the world on one foot...I don't fucking care. All that matters is that I'm with you."

I shake my head, trying to hold back the tears threatening to flow down my cheeks. "This isn't you talking. Don't do this for me, because I'm not worth it. The church is your *life*, Sebastian. Your calling. I watch you when you pray, how close you are to your God. The students love you. You do so much good here. I won't let you destroy that because I've tempted you into sin."

"But we talked about this," he argues. "I still believe what I said, George. What we did, what we have...it *cannot* be a sin. I can do so much good with you at my side, if only the Church would let go of this messed-up belief that chastity creates a pure heart. But we can convince them together. We can go to the bishop—"

"You're not talking sense. We're not going to take on the entire Catholic Church." Nosy eyes burn into my back. "Please, we can't do this here. Not with everyone looking."

"I'm not leaving until you're mine."

I shake my head. "Please, go back to your sanctuary. I promise, you're safe from me now."

"Maybe I don't want to be safe," he cries. "Maybe I'm finally ready to fall over the deep end so that God will land me in your arms."

I can't do it. I can't be the reason you leave your calling.

I hadn't intended to say it, but I know it's the only thing that will make him stop this insanity. He needs to understand that it's over between us. I want to close my eyes to the pain I'm about to cause, but I know if I do that he won't accept it. So I stare up at him, cold and defiant. "I slept with William."

Sebastian's eyes squeeze close, but not before I see the pain stab him. The instant the news reaches his heart, it snuffs out the light that burned there for me. He straightens, his shoulders rigid. "I see."

His words are flat. Hard. The passion of a moment ago has disappeared, leaving behind an empty shell.

A sob escapes my throat. I want to explain, to beg, to lay out my dark and impossible wishes. But I did this for him. I'm breaking the bond between us so there is no way he'll throw his life away for me.

I'm not fucking worth it.

It takes every ounce of courage I possess, but I turn from Sebastian's broken, beautiful face, and I walk away.

42

It's easy to avoid Sebastian for the last few weeks of term. Exams loom large across the campus – every schedule is thrown into disarray. Leigh and I spend hours in silent study beside the glowing fire in the Junior Common Room, or quizzing each other with flashcards across pints of cider at The Bad Habit. I keep my head down and eventually, I stop hearing the whispers.

Exams at Blackfriars are, like everything else, a dramatic affair, shrouded with centuries-old traditions that must be followed. We don our subfusc and recite Latin pledges upon entry. Luckily, we have no exam for Ancient Greek. Father Duncan asks us to turn in an essay composed in Greek, accompanied by a work of translation. I write mine on one of my early translations of Benet of Blackfriars' diary and submit it via email. My heart pangs as I stare at the neat rows of perfectly formed Greek letters. I wish I could talk it over with Sebastian, but I can't see him. Not after everything.

We'll never again sit by the fire with hot cups of tea, talking about philosophy and capricious gods.

The last thing I want to do is study, but I need top exam

results or my scholarship won't renew. I close my curtains so I can't see the spire of the church every time I get up to make shitty instant coffee. I eat the rest of my study snacks and drink a bottle of Leigh's mead and collapse into a sugar-induced coma of sadness.

I did the right thing. I know it. Sebastian was born to be a priest. I've seen that serenity, that certainty, on his face when he prays. I've seen him with the students, how he calms people. This is his *calling.*

I'm...a distraction. I'm nothing more than a temptation his God has placed in his path to test his faith. But I'm not going to sit around and blindly fulfill his God's will if that will is to fuck Sebastian over.

Not even if the memory of his tongue between my legs still makes my toes curl.

I barely sleep. Every time I close my eyes I see Sebastian's cold face, or Keely's grave exposed in the light, her maggot-filled mouth screaming. Sometimes, instead of her, it's William staring back at me with glassy, accusing eyes.

Where is he? I send text after text followed by sobbing voice messages that get more and more desperate and pathetic. Every one goes unanswered. I check the gossip sites in case he's been spotted around the country, but there's nothing. He doesn't show up for his exams, and banging on his door elicits nothing but nosy stares from fellow students on his staircase.

I'm so nauseous with worry I duck into their first floor bathroom and throw up all my study snacks.

Before my History of Religion exam, I drag myself to the porter's lodge to make another fruitless missing person's report. Every question on my exam paper reminds me of Sebastian. I don't know how I get through it without screaming, but somehow I do.

When I emerge, blinking, three hours later, I spy a group

across the quad, walking in the direction of the parking lot. They're laughing and passing a bottle of Champagne between them. It's the Orpheans. I see Monty with his arm around Abigail's shoulders, and Richard and Percy having an intense argument about Nietzsche with lots of hand gestures. And behind them...

William.

I don't even care that I look like a complete fool and probably smell like I haven't showered in two days (I haven't). I sprint toward them and practically bowl William over as I crash into him. "You're alive?" I touch his face, his shoulders, his beautiful pouty lips. "I was so worried. I thought—"

"What are you doing?" He sounds annoyed as he shoves me off. "Get away from me."

What?

Monty breaks out into a smile. "George, old chum, we're heading out to dinner. Will you join us?"

Diana holds out the bottle. "Yes, do come. I want to hear how your exams are going. Which essay will you choose for Greek? I did Plato's *Republic*, but I think—"

"George isn't coming with us," William snaps. The bite in his voice hits my body like a physical blow. I recoil, and he takes the opportunity to grab my wrist.

"William, what are you doing?"

William's fingers dig into my arm. His eyes hood with shadow. I'm nervous, and I'm suddenly afraid of what's going to come out of his mouth, so my own words tumble out in a flurry as if I'm hoping to drown him in syllables so he won't have space for his own.

"I've been looking for you everywhere. I wanted to say thank you for...for *everything*. It meant the world to me. You were so kind and patient and lovely, and...well, it was really special. You're really special. And I hope it doesn't cause any trouble for you, but I had to tell Sebastian. I'm sorry, but I figure he'd find out anyway from some student and he and I—"

"You shouldn't have done that," William barks. Behind him, Monty's lip curls with interest. William drags me a little away so that Monty can't hear.

"Done what? Told Sebastian? I had to. He was saying all this crazy stuff, like I was the only thing that mattered to him and he was going to leave the church and I couldn't let him do that—"

"You're wrong. He'll never give up the cloth for a nobody freak like you."

His words hang in the air, cold and bitter like English winter. And I have no scarf or mittens to protect me from this sudden chill. I'm wide open, heart laid bare for him to flay to ribbons with those frozen eyes.

I lift my chin, trying to hold myself tall against his cruelty. "William?"

"Poor little Georgie Pie, you honestly believed Sebastian Pearce could possibly love you? You think you're the kind of girl men leave the priesthood over?" He scoffs. "You're nothing more than a poor lost little lamb he thinks he can save, and it's *pathetic* that you're throwing yourself at him. But even a man of the cloth can be weak, and Sebastian is weaker than most."

"That's not true, and you know it." I manage to find my voice, but my words come out choked, reedy. I try to jerk my hand from his grip, but he holds firm. "If this is about him and you, then deal with it. Talk to him, but don't lash out at me because you can't handle your feelings—"

"Feelings? *Please.* What did you think this was? You think I'm, what, your boyfriend now?" The icicles in his eyes stab at my chest. The old William is back – his eyes are hard, empty glaciers, his mouth quirking into a cruel smirk. "You think that with all the beautiful women who throw themselves at me, I'd actually choose *you?*"

"But—"

"It was a dare, Georgie Pie. An Orpheus Society challenge. Monty bet I couldn't make you fall in love with me by the end of Benedict term. But it was even easier than I thought. A little poetry and a stolen kiss and you practically begged me to take you to bed." He waves a hand, like he's dismissing a servant. "And now you're embarrassing yourself in front of my friends."

A dare? I'm shaking all over. His words have punched a hole in my chest and the air is leaking out like a torn balloon. "But you said to me…and the kiss at the beach…"

William laughs – a harsh, barking sound that held no mirth. "I had to wash my mouth out with soap when I got home that day. You're disgusting. Going to bed with you was like fucking a wet fish. We should have given you a pig mask to wear at the party."

And I know it's a cheap shot – that he's attacking my body because he knows I'm sensitive about it, that he's digging for the places where I'm most vulnerable. But that doesn't make it hurt any less. He's opened me up, cut me to pieces and buried me alive.

William throws my arm down like it's contaminating him.

"Stay away from me and my friends," he hisses. "Stay away from Sebastian. I don't want you. No one wants you. You shouldn't even be at this school."

He turns on his heel and stalks away.

No.

I want to run after him, to beg him to tell me what's *really* going on, why he felt he had to hurt me like this. I want to drag him back to his bed, where he let down his walls so I could see, where he treated me so softly and so kindly, and make him tell me what has him so broken inside.

But I'm rooted on the spot, beneath the terrible gaze of the

Orpheus Society. It's pointless. We have nothing more to talk about. William's already explained everything.

The painting. The beach. His bed... it's all so elaborate, such a beautifully executed cruelty. But then I think back to Devil's Night, where the Orpheans hung the entire dining hall from the ceiling. They do love an elaborate prank.

That's all I am to him...a prank. A game. And humiliating me in public like this is his final move.

Checkmate.

Everything he made me feel is a lie. This shattering in my chest as my heart breaks into pieces...it's not real.

It sure feels real.

The Orpheans accept him back into their circle, clapping him on the back, laughing. Diana looks over her shoulder at me and makes a sympathetic face, but her features twist and distort until she becomes grotesque – a laughing monster reveling in the spectacle of my pain.

They're like Roman citizens at the Colosseum, fists in the air, crying for their gladiator to finish me off, to drive his sword into my heart and twist until the light goes out of my eyes.

Too fucking bad.

I wipe a tear from the corner of my eye.

I should have seen this coming. Of course William Windsor-Forsyth doesn't want me. I'm insane for believing that someone like him could ever be interested in me.

The humiliation burns under my skin, but something else burns too. Something darker and hotter and much more dangerous.

My fingers close around the key to the church roof. I promised myself I wouldn't go near the church again, but I know Sebastian has already left for a summer of missionary work and if I can't talk to him, I can talk to his God. I run through the church and turn the lock, my shoulders trembling as I look at the other door, the one I know leads down to the baths. The heavy wooden door swings open. I pound up the stairs. I stagger across the roof, drunk with wretchedness. My fingers scrape on the stone parapet. I look down, and I gasp in breath after breath until I don't feel like I'm going to throw up anymore.

There's William in the parking lot, leaning against Monty's car. He throws his head back and laughs. They're all laughing. They're laughing at *me.* The icicle twists its way deeper into my heart – only it's not hurt that tears my body in half. It's not heartache.

It's anger.

I *hate* them.

And they know nothing about what I'm capable of.

If William Windsor-Forsyth wants a war, he's got it.

43

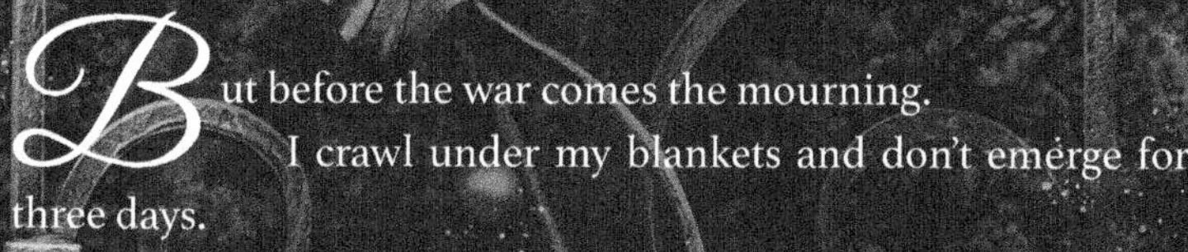

But before the war comes the mourning.

I crawl under my blankets and don't emerge for three days.

I miss the final formal hall and all the end-of-exam parties. I miss Leigh's band's last gig at Undercroft, and Father Duncan's farewell luncheon where he announces our grades (I came top of class – a small victory I long to rub in William's face). Leigh comes to check up on me, but I block the door with a chair so she can't get in.

I lost both of them. The two men who'd been there for me this wild, crazy year, and now they're gone.

You're disgusting.

William's cruel words run over and over in my head – a song on repeat, a mantra that will fuel my revenge. On my cloud drive sits five incomplete episodes of my new podcast, filled with all the evidence I've gathered about the goings' on of the Orpheus Society. I haven't got them for Keely yet, but maybe it's time the world knew just what they were up to.

Maybe it's time the prince lost his crown.

Leigh comes to see me before she leaves for Liverpool for the summer break, and this time I let her in.

"Look at you, you mad wench. You're a right mess." Leigh holds up a box stacked high with plastic food containers and candy bars. "I brought you supplies for your heartache-induced lockdown."

"You're my heroine. I'll see you in London in ten days?"

Leigh shakes her head as she starts unpacking containers of her foraged food and bottles of mead and bullace wine. "I decided I'm going to stay. I can't leave you like this. I've already given up my room, but I'll kip in yours and we'll plot revenge on those wankers. You need someone to get you maggoted and hold your hair while you puke your guts out."

"Leigh, *no*. Go see your family. I'll be fine. I'm looking forward to having this place to myself for a bit. I think I need the time to think. I'll see you in London as agreed." Leigh and I were going to spend the summer backpacking around Europe. Mom's disappointed. I can tell she wants me to come home over the summer. I haven't told her about William or Sebastian, but I think she suspects I'm not as chipper as I was last term. But I so rarely assert myself that she must know it's important to me. Dad talked about visiting Europe so often. He had his favorite cities and wild stories from his college days, and it feels like a rite of passage to create my own. And it'll be nice to hang out with Leigh – she reminds me of Claws in some ways, and she's a little kooky, like me. Plus, it's nice not to have to worry about being shot in the back, which is always a danger back in Emerald Beach.

Leigh folds her arms. "You sure?"

"I'm sure." I shrug. "Sometimes I just need to be off-grid of a bit, get my head straightened out. But I promise I'll meet you in London. I'm excited about our trip. I think it's exactly what I need."

"Okay." Leigh doesn't look convinced. "But if you want to talk..."

"You're a phone call and a short train ride away, I got it." I wrap my arms around her. "Thanks for everything, Leigh."

"Look after yourself, you mad wench."

When Leigh leaves, I peer around my room at the clothes strewn everywhere and the half-packed suitcase open on my bed. I'll be one of only a handful of students staying at Blackfriars now that exams are finished, but the board is cheap and I really am looking forward to being alone. They won't even be serving food in the dining hall and the pub will be closed, but between Leigh's supply of foraged stews and the pub in the village, I won't starve. I think I'll use my free time to explore the village and maybe go on some of the woodland walks or look for other Roman ruins in the area.

And work more on solving Keely's murder, obviously. Starting with getting Lauren to dig up Khloe May's old autopsy report. I've been too distracted with...with certain dark princes and hot priests, and it's time to get serious, especially if I'm going to release the podcast.

The only annoying thing is that they want me to vacate my room so it can be rented out to summer school students or tourists wanting to experience a slice of collegiate life. I have to move to a room the size of a closet near Martyrs' Tower. I've already carried my books and recording equipment over – now all I need to do is finish packing my clothes.

As I roll up my band tees and stuff them inside my bag, my eyes fall on the painting above Keely's bed. The woman stares back at me from the watery depths. She looks afraid.

After a moment of cruel indecision, I tear the painting from the wall and slide it into the zipped compartment in the lid of my suitcase.

Keep your enemies close.

I flop down on top of my overstuffed suitcase, jiggling to get the zipper shut. Dad's toolkit won't fit, so I pull it out and jam it into the deep pocket on my cargo pants. I won't miss this room. Keely's ghost peers out at me from behind the closet door and every darkened corner, reminding me that I haven't brought her killer to justice. When I return after the summer, I'll have a completely different room and – unless I can scrape together the funds to afford a room to myself – a new roommate. I'd like to say at least they couldn't be worse than Keely, but that would be tempting fate.

One thing Blackfriars taught me is that the Fates are fickle bitches.

I lock my door for the last time and bump my suitcase down the staircase and out into the quad. A lonely raven hobbles across the lawn. The quad is eerily silent – no laughter or music blaring from the rooms. It's so strange being here alone. Most of the students left a week ago. The place feels different – I get a sense of what it might have been to live here as a monk.

I approach the archway leading into St. Benedict's Quad, and I pause. I should go straight to my room and finish unpacking, but something tugs me.

It's silly. Sentimental. But I want to see the Cloister Garden again.

One last visit. Just to remind me how I felt when Sebastian kissed me.

To remember why I'm coming back next year. Why I'm going to spend every waking moment bringing William Windsor-Forsyth and the Orpheus Society to their knees.

I turn into St. Benedict's Quad and reach for the gate. That's when I see movement out of the corner of my eye.

The shadow darts so fast I don't have time to scream. A hand goes around my mouth and another yanks my suitcase from my grip and tosses it across the cobbles. The zipper breaks and my clothes go flying.

Panic rises inside me as my attacker leans backward, catching me off-balance. I kick and jab with my elbows, but a second person comes out of nowhere and presses a cloth over my nose and mouth. I try to claw it away, try not to breathe in the sweet vapors rising from the fabric, but the attacker wraps it tight around my lips and nose. My head spins. The corners of my vision cloud. Then the clouds reach inward, into my brain.

"*Vacate et scire,*" someone hisses in my ear.

Everything goes black.

I WAKE on a cold stone floor.

I lift my head and immediately regret it.

My brain feels like it's oozing out of my eyeballs. My entire head is ringed with fire, and a bunch of recalcitrant monkeys are twerking on the top of my spine. Whatever those bastards did to me, it's fucked me up.

I rub my eyes and blink, but I can't see a thing. It's pitch black wherever I am. Or so I think at first. As my eyes adjust I see a small sliver of light, and the faintest edges of shadows.

I drag myself to my feet and feel my way to a stone wall. The stones are dressed and even. I keep one hand on the wall and move around, measuring the boundary of my prison. It's small, approximately ten by twelve feet. There's a small window in one wall that points outside, but it's been covered with a piece of wood so only a thin ring of light penetrates the gloom.

I can't tell what time of day it is or how long I've been here.

All I know is that my stomach growls with hunger.

A sound penetrates my terror. The scrape of a metal tool

against stone. I slam my hands against the wall and cry out, "Help me. If you're out there, you have to help me!"

The words bounce back at me, hollow and weak. The tool scrapes again.

"What are you doing?" I slam my fist into the wall. "Let me out."

Nothing.

I think I hear a door slam in the distance, but I can't be sure.

I press my ear to the wall, but all I hear in reply is the haunting scrape of stone. I pound the wall with my fists and scream until my throat aches and my ears ring. But now even the scraping noise has stopped.

I sink to my feet, sweeping my hands around me to check the floor for objects. Weapons. Food. My suitcase. I had a knife in there. Maybe there's a way to remove the window panels and—

A scream boils in my throat, and I long to spill it, to give my terror free rein.

But there's no point.

I know exactly where I am.

I've been walled up in the anchoress' room.

And I'm the last person left on campus for the summer.

No one is looking for me.

No one can hear me scream.

TO BE CONTINUED

Devour the chilling conclusion to George's story in book 2 of Dark Academia, *Brutal Boys Cry Blood* – http://books2read.com/brutalboyscryblood

---

Want to get inside the heads of Sebastian and William? Sign up to Steffanie Holmes' newsletter and get two alternative POV scenes from George's men, along with a collection of other bonus material from Steffanie's worlds. Sign up here: http://steffanieholmes.com/newsletter

---

"I was baptized in bloodshed. To the bloodshed, I return."

Discover how George's friend Claws became who she is in the complete Stonehurst Prep dark contemporary reverse harem series. Start with book 1, *My Stolen Life*: http://books2read.com/mystolenlife

Turn the page for a sizzling excerpt.

FROM THE AUTHOR

University was one of the happiest times of my life. I'm a lot like George in that I'm a big nerd for learning and weird old stuff. I spent far too much time during my degree sitting in the back of lectures I wasn't enrolled in and reading random books that caught my eye in the vast library.

I studied Ancient Greek (and Egyptian heiroglyphs, and a few other useless dead languages to boot) in a sunny room in the Classical Studies department filled with overstuffed chairs and shelves of haphazardly-stacked books. The department itself was an old Victorian house covered in vines in the furthermost corner of the university. To get to my classes there, I would take this shortcut through crumbling stone archways and back alleys that always made me feel like I was a character in a dark academia novel.

Greek is a difficult language – lots of cases and tenses and irregular verbs – but it's also graceful and beautiful. I never quite got to the point of fluency, but I loved the satisfaction of staring at a page of complete nonsense and, with time and my handy Liddell & Scott, puzzling out a line of poetry or wisdom. It felt like uncovering a delightful secret. (And we all know how much I love secrets and mysteries :)).

At the end of my studies, I was one of 20 students selected for a field school in Greece and Crete. We spent six weeks visiting the archaeological sites we'd spent four years studying, drinking raki, and cracking obscure jokes only Classical scholars would get. I made friends on this trip I still have to this day.

When I sat down to write *Pretty Girls Make Graves,* I had all these ideas about Bacchanals and hidden rites and ritual murders bobbing around in my skull, but I *also* wanted to tap in to all of these things I loved about university. George struggles to fit in, but she experiences a lot of joy, too. My love of knowledge and learning and hidden things permeates these pages. Of all the characters I've written, George is probably the most like me, and many of her experiences are mine (I've never met a hot priest, though), so I really hope you enjoy her story.

I've taken some liberties with my Greek mythology. While some parallels can be drawn between Dionysos (Bacchus) and Christ, and these parallels would have been understood by contemporaries of Jesus when they heard the stories of the apostles, the symbology of wine as Dionysos' blood that can purify and cleanse is entirely my own invention – inspired by a common mistranslation of *Euripides*. I hope you'll forgive me this narrative indiscretion.

Writing *Pretty Girls Make Graves* has been a joy and a pleasure, but as always, it takes a village to bring a book to life. I'd like to thank my cantankerous drummer husband, for reading this manuscript and giving me so many ideas to make it better. And for being my lighthouse. And for making me so many bacon butties and keeping the house stocked with chocolate during lockdown.

To Meg and Eveis for the epically helpful editing job, and to

Stefanie Saw for the stunning covers. To Bea Paige, EM Moore, Laura Lee, Rachel Leigh, Caitlyn Dare, Becca Steele and especially my main girl Daniela Romero for killing it with the *Brutal Boys on Devil's Night* anthology, where this story first appeared.

To Sam and Iris and Amy and all my bogans for the FB and Zoom shenanigans that kept me sane while I spent my writing days stuck at home covered in cats.

To you, the reader, for going on this journey with me, even though it's led to some dark places. Warning: if you thought book 1 was tough, book 2 is going to knock your socks off. Grab Brutal Boys Cry Blood here: http://books2read.com/brutalboyscryblood.

If you're curious about George's friend Claws and how she became who she is, then you need the complete Stonehurst Prep dark contemporary reverse harem series. Start with book 1, *My Stolen Life*: http://books2read.com/mystolenlife

If you want to read more from me, check out my dark reverse harem bully romance series, *Kings of Miskatonic Prep.* HP Lovecraft meets *Cruel Intentions* in this dark paranormal reverse harem bully romance that's definitely not for the faint of heart. Hazel is the most badass FMC I've ever written, and I think you'll love meeting her. *Read Shunned now.*

If you want to keep up with my bookish news and get weekly stories about the real life true crimes and ghost stories that inspire my books, you can join my newsletter at https://www.steffanieholmes.com/newsletter. When you join you'll get a free copy of Cabinet of Curiosities, a compendium of bonus and deleted scenes and stories. It includes two chapters of *Pretty Girls Make Graves* rewritten from Sebastian's and William's POV.

I'm so happy you enjoyed George story! I'd love it if you wanted to leave a review on Amazon or Goodreads. It will help other readers to find their next read.

Ἐὰν ᾖς φιλομαθής, ἔσει πολυμαθής. Thank you, thank you! I love you heaps! Until next time.

Steff

ENJOY THIS EXCERPT FROM MY STOLEN LIFE

PROLOGUE: MACKENZIE

I roll over in bed and slam against a wall.

Huh? Odd.

My bed isn't pushed against a wall. I must've twisted around in my sleep and hit the headboard. I do thrash around a lot, especially when I have bad dreams, and tonights was particularly gruesome. My mind stretches into the silence, searching for the tendrils of my nightmare. *I'm lying in bed and some dark shadow comes and lifts me up, pinning my arms so they hurt. He drags me downstairs to my mother, slumped in her favorite chair. At first, I think she passed out drunk after a night at the club, but then I see the dark pool expanding around her feet, staining the designer rug.*

I see the knife handle sticking out of her neck.

I see her glassy eyes rolled toward the ceiling.

I see the window behind her head, and my own reflection in the glass, my face streaked with blood, my eyes dark voids of pain and hatred.

But it's okay now. It was just a dream. It's—

OW.

I hit the headboard again. I reach down to rub my elbow, and my hand grazes a solid wall of satin. On my other side.

What the hell?

I open my eyes into a darkness that is oppressive and complete, the kind of darkness I'd never see inside my princess bedroom with its flimsy purple curtains letting in the glittering skyline of the city. The kind of darkness that folds in on me, pressing me against the hard, un-bedlike surface I lie on.

Now the panic hits.

I throw out my arms, kick with my legs. I hit walls. Walls all around me, lined with satin, dense with an immense weight pressing from all sides. Walls so close I can't sit up or bend my knees. I scream, and my scream bounces back at me, hollow and weak.

I'm in a coffin. I'm in a motherfucking coffin, and I'm *still alive.*

I scream and scream and scream. The sound fills my head and stabs at my brain. I know all I'm doing is using up my precious oxygen, but I can't make myself stop. In that scream I lose myself, and every memory of who I am dissolves into a puddle of terror.

When I do stop, finally, I gasp and pant, and I taste blood and stale air on my tongue. A cold fear seeps into my bones. Am I dying? My throat crawls with invisible bugs. Is this what it feels like to die?

I hunt around in my pockets, but I'm wearing purple pajamas, and the only thing inside is a bookmark Daddy gave me. I can't see it of course, but I know it has a quote from Julius Caesar on it. *Alea iacta est. The die is cast.*

Like fuck it is.

I think of Daddy, of everything he taught me – memories too dark to be obliterated by fear. Bile rises in my throat. I swallow, choke it back. Daddy always told me our world is forged in blood. I might be only thirteen, but I know who he is, what he's capable of. I've heard the whispers. I've seen the way people hurry to appease him whenever he enters a room. I've had the lessons from Antony in what to do if I find myself alone with one of Daddy's enemies.

Of course, they never taught me what to do if one of those enemies *buries me alive*.

I can't give up.

I claw at the satin on the lid. It tears under my fingers, and I pull out puffs of stuffing to reach the wood beneath. I claw at the surface, digging splinters under my nails. Cramps arc along my arm from the awkward angle. I know it's hopeless; I know I'll never be able to scratch my way through the wood. Even if I can, I *feel* the weight of several feet of dirt above me. I'd be crushed in moments. But I have to try.

I'm my father's daughter, and this is not how I die.

I claw and scratch and tear. I lose track of how much time passes in the tiny space. My ears buzz. My skin weeps with cold sweat.

A noise reaches my ears. A faint shifting. A scuffle. A scrape and thud above my head. Muffled and far away.

Someone piling the dirt in my grave.

Or maybe...

...maybe someone digging it out again.

Fuck, fuck, please.

"Help." My throat is hoarse from screaming. I bang the lid with my fists, not even feeling the splinters piercing my skin. "Help me!"

THUD. Something hits the lid. The coffin groans. My veins burn with fear and hope and terror.

The wood cracks. The lid is flung away. Dirt rains down on me, but I don't care. I suck in lungfuls of fresh, crisp air. A circle of light blinds me. I fling my body up, up into the unknown. Warm arms catch me, hold me close.

"I found you, Claws." Only Antony calls me by that nickname. Of course, it would be my cousin who saves me. Antony drags me over the lip of the grave, *my* grave, and we fall into crackling leaves and damp grass.

I sob into his shoulder. Antony rolls me over, his fingers pressing all over my body, checking if I'm hurt. He rests my back against cold stone. "I have to take care of this," he says. I watch through tear-filled eyes as he pushes the dirt back into the hole – into what was supposed to be my grave – and brushes dead leaves on top. When he's done, it's impossible to tell the ground's been disturbed at all.

I tremble all over. I can't make myself stop shaking. Antony comes back to me and wraps me in his arms. He staggers to his feet, holding me like I'm weightless. He's only just turned eighteen, but already he's built like a tank.

I let out a terrified sob. Antony glances over his shoulder, and there's panic in his eyes. "You've got to be quiet, Claws," he whispers. "They might be nearby. I'm going to get you out of here."

I can't speak. My voice is gone, left in the coffin with my screams. Antony hoists me up and darts into the shadows. He runs with ease, ducking between rows of crumbling gravestones and beneath bent and gnarled trees. Dimly, I recognize this place – the old Emerald Beach cemetery, on the edge of Beaumont Hills overlooking the bay, where the original families of Emerald Beach buried their dead.

Where someone tried to bury me.

Antony bursts from the trees onto a narrow road. His car is parked in the shadows. He opens the passenger door and settles me inside before diving behind the wheel and gunning the engine.

We tear off down the road. Antony rips around the deadly corners like he's on a racetrack. Steep cliffs and crumbling old mansions pass by in a blur.

"My parents..." I gasp out. "Where are my parents?"

"I'm sorry, Claws. I didn't get to them in time. I only found you."

I wait for this to sink in, for the fact I'm now an orphan to hit me in a rush of grief. But I'm numb. My body won't stop shaking, and I left my brain and my heart buried in the silence of that coffin.

"Who?" I ask, and I fancy I catch a hint of my dad's cold savagery in my voice. "Who did this?"

"I don't know yet, but if I had to guess, it was Brutus. I warned your dad that he was making alliances and building up to a challenge. I think he's just made his move."

I try to digest this information. Brutus – who was once my father's trusted friend, who'd eaten dinner at our house and played Chutes and Ladders with me – killed my parents and buried me alive. But it bounces off the edge of my skull and doesn't stick. The life I had before, my old life, it's gone, and as I twist and grasp for memories, all I grab is stale coffin air.

"What now?" I ask.

Antony tosses his phone into my lap. "Look at the headlines."

I read the news app he's got open, but the words and images blur together. "This... this doesn't make any sense..."

"They think you're dead, Claws," Antony says. "That means you have to *stay* dead until we're strong enough to move against him. Until then, you have to be a ghost. But don't worry, I'll protect you. I've got a plan. We'll hide you where they'll never think to look."

Start reading:

http://books2read.com/mystolenlife

MORE FROM THE AUTHOR

From the author of *Pretty Girls Makes Graves* and *Shunned* comes this dark contemporary high school reverse harem romance.

Psst. I have a secret.

Are you ready?

I'm Mackenzie Malloy, and everyone thinks they know who I am.

Five years ago, I disappeared.

No one has seen me or my family outside the walls of Malloy Manor since.
But now I'm coming to reclaim my throne:
The Ice Queen of Stonehurst Prep is back.

Standing between me and my everything?
Three things can bring me down:
The sweet guy who wants answers from his former friend.
The rock god who wants to f*ck me.
The king who'll crush me before giving up his crown.

They think they can ruin me, wreck it all, but I won't let them.
I'm not the Mackenzie Eli used to know.
Hot boys and rock gods like Gabriel won't win me over.
And just like Noah, I'll kill to keep my crown.

I'm just a poor little rich girl with the stolen life.
I'm here to tear down three princes,
before they destroy me.

Read now:
http://books2read.com/mystolenlife

OTHER BOOKS BY STEFFANIE HOLMES

Nevermore Bookshop Mysteries

A Dead and Stormy Night

Of Mice and Murder

Pride and Premeditation

How Heathcliff Stole Christmas

Memoirs of a Garroter

Prose and Cons

A Novel Way to Die

Much Ado About Murder

Kings of Miskatonic Prep

Shunned

Initiated

Possessed

Ignited

Stonehurst Prep

My Stolen Life

My Secret Heart

My Broken Crown

My Savage Kingdom

Dark Academia

Pretty Girls Make Graves

Brutal Boys Cry Blood

Manderley Academy

Ghosted

Haunted

Spirited

Briarwood Witches

Earth and Embers

Fire and Fable

Water and Woe

Wind and Whispers

Spirit and Sorrow

Crookshollow Gothic Romance

Art of Cunning (Alex & Ryan)

Art of the Hunt (Alex & Ryan)

Art of Temptation (Alex & Ryan)

The Man in Black (Elinor & Eric)

Watcher (Belinda & Cole)

Reaper (Belinda & Cole)

Wolves of Crookshollow

Digging the Wolf (Anna & Luke)

Writing the Wolf (Rosa & Caleb)

Inking the Wolf (Bianca & Robbie)

Wedding the Wolf (Willow & Irvine)

Want to be informed when the next Steffanie Holmes paranormal romance story goes live? Sign up for the newsletter at www.steffanieholmes.com/newsletter to get the scoop, and score a free collection of bonus scenes and stories to enjoy!

ABOUT THE AUTHOR

Steffanie Holmes is the *USA Today* bestselling author of the paranormal, gothic, dark, and fantastical. Her books feature clever, witty heroines, secret societies, creepy old mansions and alpha males who *always* get what they want.

Legally-blind since birth, Steffanie received the 2017 Attitude Award for Artistic Achievement. She was also a finalist for a 2018 Women of Influence award.

Steff is the creator of *Rage Against the Manuscript* – a resource of free content, books, and courses to help writers tell their story, find their readers, and build a badass writing career.

Steffanie lives in New Zealand with her husband, a horde of cantankerous cats, and their medieval sword collection.

Steffanie Holmes newsletter

Grab a free copy *Cabinet of Curiosities* – a Steffanie Holmes compendium of short stories and bonus scenes, including alternative POV chapters from William and Sebastian – when you sign up for updates with the Steffanie Holmes newsletter.

http://www.steffanieholmes.com/newsletter

Come hang with Steffanie
www.steffanieholmes.com
hello@steffanieholmes.com

Printed in Great Britain
by Amazon

25574269R00209